A WHISPER OF SORROWS

A DCI JACK LOGAN THRILLER

J.D. KIRK

CRIME

A WHISPER OF SORROWS
ISBN: 978-1-912767-22-9

Published worldwide by Zertex Media Ltd.
This edition published in 2020.

3

www.jdkirk.com
www.zertexmedia.com

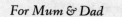
For Mum & Dad

BOOKS BY J.D. KIRK

A Litter of Bones

Thicker Than Water

The Killing Code

Blood & Treachery

The Last Bloody Straw

A Whisper of Sorrows

The Big Man Upstairs

A Death Most Monumental

A Snowball's Chance in Hell

Ahead of the Game

An Isolated Incident

Colder Than the Grave

Come Hell or High Water

Northwind: A Robert Hoon Thriller

CHAPTER ONE

THE ROOM WAS MOST NOTABLE FOR ITS MISSING BASTARD.

At least, to DCI Jack Logan it was. To anyone else, the most comment-worthy aspect of the room would likely be the tape outline across the threshold of the door, marking the shape of a person.

Or, perhaps it would be the stain on the floor, once red, now dried to a shade of rusty brown, or the similarly coloured spattering across the walls on either side.

If someone was looking very closely, the thing they passed remark on might be the missing leg of the chair, the rigid plastic sheared off at an angle to create a long sliver of a point.

Logan had noticed all of that. Of course, he had.

But it was the missing bastard that disturbed him most.

"You alright, Jack?"

Detective Superintendent Hoon's voice was uncharacteristically soft. It was also the longest sentence Logan had heard the man say without swearing, which spoke volumes about the gravity of the situation.

"No. No, I am not," Logan muttered. His eyes went from the tape, to the bloodstains, to the broken chair. Finally, it swung a right and stopped on the unmade bed that the room's former occupant had slept in for most of the last decade. A gush of blood had stained the clinical white sheets down near the foot of the bed, but it was the man-sized indent in the mattress that Jack focused on.

He glared at that imprint. Glowered at it, like he could summon the bastard back through sheer bloody force of will. He couldn't, of course. Not like that. But he would get him back.

One way, or another.

"Talk me through it again," Logan said, turning away from the bed and addressing the man standing out in the corridor.

DCI Samuel Grant—*Snecky* to pretty much everyone who knew him—had been stationed in Inverness until Logan had requested a transfer earlier in the year. Snecky had been quick to jump on it, believing he was destined for the Central Belt Big Time, despite having predominantly attained his rank by showing up often enough, as opposed to through any sort of actual aptitude.

He looked thinner than he had when Logan had last crossed paths with him. It had been nine or ten months since then, but Snecky had lost some of the excess weight he was carrying, and his already-receding hairline had started to beat an even hastier retreat.

The weight-loss didn't suit him. It made him look ill and gaunt. There was a haunted look to him, too, like he was screaming behind the eyes, and Logan felt a pang of guilt for throwing the poor bugger into the lion's den of his old stomping ground.

A flash of irritation flitted over Snecky's face that immediately eradicated Logan's guilt. The other DCI glanced briefly down at a stack of notes he carried, but it was done through habit, and he recited the information from memory.

It wasn't hard. There wasn't a lot of it.

"Orderly turns up to give him his medication on Friday

afternoon. Checks through the slot, Petrie's in his bed. Opens the door, steps in, crosses to the bed, and Petrie stabs him with the sheared off chair leg," Snecky recited. He sounded bored of the details now. Resentful of having to go over them all again. The Invernesian accent that had earned him his nickname was less pronounced now, hidden by the Glasgow accent he was trying very hard to affect. "Blood, blood, blood, scream, scream, scream, he staggers back, falls in the doorway. Voila."

Snecky stepped back out of the tape outline he'd been standing in and gestured down at it.

"Dies a couple of minutes later, but Petrie's already well on the move by then," Snecky continued. "Grabs a nurse, threatens to kill her, too, unless they buzz him out. So, they buzz him out."

"And the twisted fucker kills her, anyway," Detective Superintendent Hoon concluded.

Logan nodded, recalling the other person-sized outline of tape down in the hospital foyer.

"Why was the door open?" Logan asked. "Why didn't the orderly shut it behind him?"

DCI Grant glanced down at his notes again. "I don't know. Should it have been?"

"Yes. I want to know why it was left open," Logan told him.

Snecky nodded and started to turn, then stopped himself. He faced front again, pushing back his shoulders like a soldier on parade. "Aye, well, it's not your case, Jack," he said.

Hoon answered before Logan could open his mouth. "Less of your fucking lip, you jumped-up wee fuck, and do as you're fucking telt," he barked, stabbing a finger out the door and along the corridor.

Snecky literally sprang into the air in fright, almost dropping his notebook. "Aye. I mean, aye. Right. Aye, I was going to say I'd... Aye," he babbled, then he turned and scurried away, his tail tucked so far between his legs he was almost choking on it.

"Thanks," Logan grunted.

Hoon shook his head. "Tell you, Jack, swapping you for that clueless sack of shite was the best thing I've ever done," he remarked. It was, Logan thought, far and away the nicest thing the Detective Superintendent had ever said to him. "I mean, don't get me wrong, you're a useless bastard, but you're no' *Snecky* useless. And that's something."

"Aye. I suppose it is," Logan agreed.

Hoon had been waiting for Logan when the DCI returned from a case out on one of the Small Isles, and had broken the news then about Owen Petrie's escape.

They'd made the trip south to Carstairs State Hospital in Hoon's car. Most of the journey had been spent in silence, aside from a few dozen foul-mouthed outbursts from the Detective Superintendent whenever they came across another driver who had the audacity to be travelling at any speed not exactly matching his own.

It wasn't until they'd pulled screeching into the car park that Hoon had asked the question that had clearly been preying on his mind.

"Well?" he'd demanded. "Aren't you going to fucking say it?"

"Say what?" Logan had asked.

"You know full fucking well what I mean. 'I fucking told you so.'"

Logan had shaken his head and said that no, he wasn't.

What would be the point?

He *had* told them so, of course. Scores of times. Hundreds.

Owen Petrie might have fooled the doctors. He might have convinced everyone else that the head injury he'd sustained during his arrest had left him irreparably damaged, but not Logan. Logan had seen through it. Logan had known the truth, that the bastard was just waiting. Biding his time until he was ready.

Until now.

"Who was he?" Logan asked, looking down at the outline on the floor.

"Hm? Oh," Hoon said, following the DCI's gaze. "New guy. Another Jack, as it happens. Wright, I want to say. Twenty-fuck-ing-six. Poor bastard. Got a wee one at home."

Logan met the DSup's eye, an unspoken concern passing between them. "Aye. We've got Uniform keeping watch, but I doubt the bastard'll head there. To paraphrase that Australian bint, *you should be so fucking lucky.*"

"Never pegged you as a Kylie fan, sir."

"Aye, well I'm a man of many fucking mysteries, Detective Chief Inspector," Hoon replied. He dragged a hand down his face, and Logan got the impression it had been a few days since the DSup had slept. "You know the sick bastard's going to come after you, don't you?"

Logan looked around the room, nodding slowly. "Aye. Probably."

"No fucking *probably* about it," Hoon said.

He turned, leaned out of the door, and roared, "SNECKY!" at the top of his voice.

There was a bustling from out in the corridor, then the hurried clatter of footsteps as DCI Grant came rushing back to the cell.

"Sir?"

"The fuck've you been?" Hoon demanded.

Snecky blinked. "You said—"

"Jesus fucking Christ. Do you no' recognise a rhetorical question when you hear one?" Hoon indicated the stack of notes in DCI Grant's arms. "Show him."

Snecky looked down at the bundle, winced, then raised his head again. "Show him what, exactly, sir?"

"Fuck's sake. The photo. The fucking picture. It's no' diffi-cult. It's no' a big leap of fucking logic. Show him the photo."

"Right. Aye. Sorry," Snecky replied, fumbling through the

stack of paperwork.

Hoon shot Logan a sideways look, rolled his eyes, then sighed. "Just you fucking take your time, son. No rush," the DSup said, in a tone that made it very clear he meant the exact opposite of everything he'd just said.

"Sorry. Just... Aha."

Snecky tugged a glossy A4 photo from the pile and presented it to Hoon with a flourish and a hopeful smile.

"The fuck you giving it to me for? I don't want it. Him," Hoon said, pointing to Logan with a jerk of his head.

Snecky's smile lost some of its shine as he shuffled a half-step in Logan's direction and handed him the photo, instead. Logan took it and studied it in silence for a few moments.

The picture showed the very spot where they were standing, albeit with a body filling most of the frame.

As corpses went, it wasn't the worst one Logan had seen. Not by a long shot. The eyes were open, rolled back in the head, the face frozen forever in a rictus of horror and shock.

There were multiple stab wounds in the stomach, although the amount of blood staining the lower half of the orderly's white tabard made it impossible to tell how many just from the photograph alone. Going by the ravaged state of the material, though, 'a lot' would be a reasonable guess.

The sight of the blood on the lower half of the dead man's uniform didn't really disturb Logan, though. He'd seen it all before, too many times to count.

The blood on the top half was another story.

There was much less of it, and what there was had been daubed onto the otherwise unblemished material. Smeared into the fabric.

Six letters, crudely finger-painted across the man's upper chest.

HIJACK.

"This cretinous jizz stain reckons it means the bastard

escaped to carry out a fucking terrorist attack," Hoon said, indicating Snecky with a look that didn't so much border on contempt as fully muscle in on its territory.

"Well, I mean, it does say, 'Hijack!'" DCI Grant protested.

Logan shook his head. "It doesn't," he muttered.

Snecky leaned in and pointed to the letters. "I think you'll find—"

"It says, "Hi Jack,'" Logan said, cutting him short.

Snecky hesitated, his brow lightly furrowing. "Aye. So..."

"For fuck's sake. Were you dropped on your coupon as a wean, son? Is that the issue here?" Hoon snapped. "It's hi-fuck-ing-space-fucking-Jack. No' *hijack*. He's no' going to bring down the twin towers."

There was a moment of silence, during which Snecky's lips moved, like he was testing out his next question before voicing it.

"Who's...?" he began, then his gaze flitted across to Logan. "Oh. Shite. Aye."

Hoon pointed at one of his ears. "Fuck me. You hear that? The clang of that penny dropping?" he asked, then he gave DCI Grant an appraising up-and-down look that found very little worth praising.

"Where's his badge?" Logan asked, still looking at the photo.

"Badge?" asked Hoon.

Logan tapped the left of the man's chest, just above the letter 'K'. "They've got badges, haven't they? Where's his?"

Hoon ripped the photo from Logan's hand, considered it, then practically threw it at Snecky. "His badge. Why has no one else mentioned his fucking badge?"

"I, uh, I don't—" Snecky stammered, before Hoon silenced him with a glare.

"Then how about you fucking find out?" the DSup suggested. "And speaking of which, you find out why the door was open yet?"

"Uh, not yet, sir," Snecky admitted.

"Then why are you standing here with that glaikit look on your face? Away you fuck! Get out of my sight."

Logan almost felt sorry for the other DCI as he went scuttling off along the corridor again. Although, on the other hand, it was nice not to be the direct focus of the Detective Superintendent's temper for once.

"Looks like the shitestain's got a stauner for you, Jack," Hoon said.

Logan frowned. "Snecky?"

"No. No' fucking Snecky. Jesus Christ." Hoon stabbed a fingertip against the photo, almost knocking it out of Logan's hands. "Petrie."

"Oh. Aye. Well, hardly surprising," Logan said. His eyes widened a fraction. "Shite. I should—"

"Uniform's already watching them," Hoon said. "Your daughter's at work. Your wife's at home."

"Ex-wife," Logan corrected.

Hoon scowled at him. "Do I look like your fucking marriage counsellor? Do you want to piss about discussing your marital problems, and your *cock*-handed attempts to fire it up that Irish Pathologist bird—aye, don't think I don't know about that, by the way—or do you want to go out and catch this prick?"

Logan felt a prickly heat creeping up his neck and across his cheeks. He looked down at the photograph in his hand. "I want to go out and catch this prick."

"Aye. That's more fucking like it," Hoon said, then he spun around and roared out into the corridor again. "Snecky! Get your finger out your arse and get back here!"

The Detective Superintendent turned back to Logan, tutted loudly, then let out a long, weary sigh. "Seriously, that bawbag manages to make *you* look good," he said. "And believe me, that is some fucking achievement."

CHAPTER TWO

LOGAN, HOON, AND SNECKY STOOD IN SILENCE, WATCHING the fuzzy black and white security camera footage of Petrie's escape on four different screens. Each screen showed a different part of his route through the hospital, and their attention switched from monitor to monitor as Petrie dragged his prisoner through the corridors and down the stairs.

She hadn't cried. The victim. She'd stayed calm. Complied. Did everything you were supposed to do. No sudden movements. No heroics. Nothing that might increase the danger she was in.

And then, he'd killed her anyway.

There was no big finale for her. No moment of high drama. The security camera that showed her death was fixed in the foyer, and the low resolution meant the detectives could barely make out what was happening once Petrie had hauled her outside into the drop-off zone.

"Watch this bit," Snecky urged. He said it in a hushed whisper, like they were all watching a film together at the cinema. All that was missing was the rustle and crunch of his popcorn.

Still, had he not said it, Logan might not have noticed the

knife going in. Upper chest, he thought. Base of the throat. Two stabs, or maybe a stab and a twist.

Petrie dragged her out of frame then, her hands grasping at her throat. Right at the edge of the image, there was a bigger movement. A sliver of something—a suggestion—appeared at the bottom left corner of the screen, and Logan realised that's where she'd been dropped. That was where Petrie had dumped her, if not already dead, then dying.

"That's it," Snecky said. He jabbed a button on the control deck and all four images paused.

"Where did he go from there?" Logan asked.

Snecky winced like he'd been bracing himself for that question. "We, uh, we don't know."

The pressure in the security room altered a fraction, as if the walls themselves were holding their breath.

"You don't know?" Logan said, his voice taking on an eerie echo in the confined space. "What do you mean, you don't know?"

"There was a car waiting for him," Snecky said. The heat from the equipment had been making him sweat, and there was an anxious sheen across his brow as Logan loomed over him. "Blue Renault Megane. Five-seven plate. He, eh, he jumped in the back and it drove off."

"So... what are you saying, Snecky?" Logan demanded. "This was all planned? He had an accomplice?"

"Well, unless he's yer man from *Knight Rider* and the fucking car drove itself, then aye, I think it's safe to say he had an accomplice," barked Hoon.

"But don't worry. We're one step ahead," Snecky said. He looked all puffed up and proud, like this was his big moment. "We think we know who it was."

"The doctor," Logan said. "Dr... Ramesh, was it?"

Hoon snorted and pointed to DCI Grant. "Aw, look at his wee face there. He was pure fucking buzzing to tell you that."

Snecky smiled. It was supposed to be a relaxed, nonchalant sort of smile, but his disappointment was written there, plain for all to see.

"Aye. Dr Manan Ramesh. He's been in charge of Petrie's case for... well, nearly a year," Snecky said. "He was off sick the day Petrie escaped. Didn't report back afterwards, and there's no sign of him at any known address."

"I knew there was something about him," Logan muttered.

"You'd met him?" Snecky asked.

"Once or twice, aye," Logan said. "Wasn't a fan. Seemed very protective of Petrie."

"Aye, well, you hit the fucking nail on the head there," Hoon said. "Turns out your man was tugging it over Mister Whisper even more than you were, Jack."

"Ramesh did his PhD—aye, his second one, like—on Petrie," Snecky explained. "Or, on... I don't know, the primal urges that drive a man to torture and murder kiddies, or some shite. He interviewed him dozens of times, starting seven or eight years back and continuing up to about six months before he got the job here."

"This was planned," Logan said. "They've been working on this for a while."

Snecky nodded. "Aye. We checked out Ramesh's house. Nice place. He's no' short of a bob or two. He wasn't there, but he knew we'd be coming. He'd burned a load of old notebooks out back."

"Anything survive?" Logan asked.

"We had Forensics go over it. Got a couple of scraps, but nothing of interest. I can get photos over to you, if you like?"

Logan shook his head. "No. It's fine. I'll take their word for it."

He glanced around at the pokey wee room, then at the bank of security monitors showing the clinical but slightly decaying insides of the hospital. "You found Ramesh's body yet?" he asked.

The other DCI blinked in confusion. "Body? Why would he...? We don't think he's dead. We think they're working together to—"

"He's dead," Logan said, cutting him short.

"How the fuck d'you know that?" Hoon asked.

"Because I know Petrie. Ramesh is dead. And, if we're right, and Petrie is going to make this about me, then I think I might know where we'll find him." He held a hand out to Hoon. "Can I borrow your car, sir?"

Hoon's pock-marked features contorted in horror. "Give you my car? I'd sooner be gangbanged by the fucking *A-Team*. No, you cannot borrow my car." He fished the keys from his pocket and spun them around a pudgy finger. "I'm driving."

LOGAN REMEMBERED the smell of the place like it was yesterday.

The multi-storey car park on Cambridge Street was not particularly noteworthy in its design. It was an ugly bugger of a thing, all cracked concrete and metal mesh, and would've slotted right into any other part of Glasgow—or any industrial area anywhere in the world, in fact—without anyone batting an eyelid.

And aye, to pretty much anyone else, the smell would be equally as unremarkable. Diesel fumes and jakeys' pish for the most part. Maybe a wee whiff of Dettol garnishing the top of it, depending on what day of the week it was.

To Logan, though, the smell of the place was like a fingerprint. Once smelled, never forgotten. And, just like a fingerprint on a phone screen, the stench of the place unlocked everything as he stepped into the stairwell. The memories. The anger.

The fear.

He'd asked Hoon to hang off down in the car. The DSup, to his surprise, had agreed with only a moderate outburst of personal abuse.

Snecky had been sent back to base and told to wait on the call. It was a call Logan still hoped he might not have to make, but one he knew, deep down, that he would.

As he made his way up the stairs—two-at-a-time at first, then one-at-a-time, then with a moment's rest after each fourth or fifth step—he desperately wanted to believe that he was wrong. He wanted to believe that Owen Petrie wasn't targeting him. Wasn't about to single him out, and turn his life into a living nightmare.

He wanted to believe that. He really did.

But Jack Logan was no fool.

He emerged onto the uppermost level of the car park and gulped down a few gallons of fresh air, cleaning the smell of the stairwell from his airways and his memories. Behind him, the door closed with a *clack*. Ahead of him, twenty or more cars sat parked in bays, noses pointing out at all four corners of the city.

Logan took another breath, enjoying this moment of not knowing. Not for sure, anyway. This calm before the storm. This one moment, after which everything would change.

He exhaled.

He stepped forward.

It took him six seconds to spot it.

Renault Megane. Five-seven plate. Blue.

It was parked directly across from where he was standing, like it had been deliberately placed to be as visible as possible. Which, of course, it had been.

He fished a pair of gloves from the depths of his coat pocket. Pulled them on. *Snap-snap.*

The car was neatly positioned between the lines of the bay. Unlike most of the others, it had been reversed in. Textbook parking. Meticulous. Nothing that would make anyone look too closely.

His feet felt heavy as he approached it, as if the closer he got to it, the more of his bones were turning to lead.

By the time he was standing in front of the car, he had doubled in weight, each onward step requiring all his strength and effort.

The doors were locked. This was unexpected. The car had clearly been left here for him to find, so why lock it?

Cupping his gloved hands against the tinted back windows, Logan peered into the vehicle. There was a small bundle of blood-stained clothing bunched up on the back seat—Petrie's hospital gear, presumably—but nothing else of note.

The front seats were empty, too. That left the boot.

He ran his fingers along the underside of the metal ridge at the back of the car until he found the release button, then pressed it.

Locked, like the rest of the car.

The parcel shelf was down, meaning he couldn't see what was inside by peering through the glass. Bending, he tried a sniff test. If there had been a body in there for a day or two, he should be able to get a whiff.

Nothing.

Squatting, Logan checked behind the car's tyres, then ran his hands up under the wheel trims, searching for keys but finding none.

He stood up, plodded his leaden legs around to the front of the car again, and then stood there considering it, the honking and revving of the city rising from the streets on all sides.

The car was a message. That was why, of all the places in the country it could be, it was here. Now. On top of this car park.

Or... no. Not on top. Not quite. Not yet.

Logan turned, following the direction the Megane's nose

was pointing. Following it all the way over to the door that led to the stairwell.

His eyes went to the roof above it. Something that had been coiled up in his gut for a decade slithered as it drew itself tighter together.

"Aye," he muttered, and there was a waver in his voice that he didn't think he'd ever heard before. "Of course."

CHAPTER THREE

HE REMEMBERED THIS, TOO. EVERY RUNG. EVERY PITTED indent in the metal. He could feel them through the rubber of gloves, and through all the years that had passed since he'd last climbed this ladder.

He hadn't been alone then, of course. He'd known who was waiting for him—*what* was waiting for him—at the top. He'd known his duty. Known his job. And he'd known, in those moments, that he wanted to ignore them both. That he wanted to make the bastard suffer, like those kids had suffered. Their parents, too.

He'd wanted to end it, once and for all.

And now, here he was. Climbing that ladder, ten years later. Older, certainly. Wiser?

Time would tell.

There were nine rungs. His feet were on the fifth when he was high enough to see over the edge and onto the roof.

There was a sheet of blue tarp there, weighed down with bits of broken brick. The sniff test wasn't necessary—the smell presented itself almost as soon as Logan's head had drawn level with the rooftop.

He should climb down, call it in, get Scene of Crime out to comb it all over.

But he had to know.

A few more steps took him up onto the roof. It wasn't big—about half the size of a tennis court, maybe—and well over-looked by the much taller hotel across the street. That's what the tarp would be for. Petrie wouldn't have wanted anyone but Logan to find what lay beneath.

He kept his distance at first, scanning the area around the plastic sheet for anything obvious.

It was no distance at all from this roof to the upper floor of the car park below, and yet the din of Glasgow had softened, like the city was holding its breath. Like it remembered what had taken place here last time, and was now watching and waiting to see what would happen next.

A breeze swirled around Logan, nudging his coat around his knees, and crackling the tarpaulin. Even that—even the whistling of the wind—was familiar.

No, not familiar. The same.

He closed his eyes, and the world was ten years younger. Shapes heaved in the darkness behind his eyelids. Figures thrashed and fought.

And fell.

Logan snapped his eyes open, shook his head, and focused his attention on the here and now.

It had rained since the tarp had been placed down. Water gathered in its crinkles and crevices, and pooled in puddles on the uneven tiles of the roof.

Very little for him to accidentally compromise, then.

He approached the tarp quickly, the earlier leaden feeling replaced by an urge to just get this over with. Get it done, and find out what he was dealing with.

Carefully, he moved aside one of the bricks that pinned down the tarpaulin, then took hold of the material's edge.

He took a breath. Held it. Exhaled.

And then, he lifted the plastic sheeting away, and stared into the unblinking eyes of horror.

LOGAN LEANED against the bonnet of Detective Superintendent Hoon's BMW, sipping a disappointing coffee from a paper cup.

The whole of Cambridge Street, where the car park stairs were, and Hill Street, where the vehicle entrance was, had been cordoned off. Flashing blues painted the grey rendered walls of the multi-storey, and danced in the windows of the hotel opposite.

The Scene of Crime team were up there now, doing their thing. Getting what they could from the site, and from Ramesh's body.

Or what was left of it, anyway.

He had been tortured. Extensively. His eyelids were missing. Most of his teeth and fingernails, too.

Pathology would have to confirm, but Logan was putting the cause of death as the bloody great indent in the doctor's skull, just above his hairline. The positioning of it wasn't coincidence, Logan knew. The injury was in the exact same spot as the one Petrie had sustained the night Logan had caught him.

The night he fell.

The torture couldn't have been done at the scene—someone would have seen or heard—and it was a safe bet that he'd been killed elsewhere, too. Which meant Petrie had somehow managed to get his body up onto the roof.

Presumably, he'd done it under the cover of darkness, so as not to risk being spotted by someone in the hotel. It wouldn't have been easy, but then the bastard had never exactly been lacking in conviction.

The SOC lot would do their best, but it was pointless, really. They knew who the killer was, and there would be nothing up there that would point to his whereabouts.

And, besides the body, the only other thing of interest at the scene was currently tucked out of sight in the inside pocket of Logan's coat.

"How's the coffee, Jack?" asked Snecky, appearing around from the back of the Beamer.

"Shite."

The other DCI appeared mildly offended, like he'd ground the beans himself, rather than just sending the nearest Uniform to the closest available petrol station.

"Aye, well. Better than nothing," Snecky replied.

This, Logan thought, was debatable.

Snecky joined Logan in leaning against the bonnet. The moment his backside touched the metal, a horn blasted, and he leaped forward like he'd been fired from a catapult.

"Get your fat arse off my fucking car!" Hoon ordered, sticking his head out of the driver's side window. He had a phone pressed to his ear, and a scowl fixed to his face.

Snecky glanced around, hoping no one had seen him throwing himself skyward like he'd been electrocuted. Half a dozen Uniforms and a couple of detectives all looked away as his eyes swept over them, little smirks tugging at the corners of their mouths.

"Sorry, sir," Snecky said, lowering his head in a show of deference and submission that obliterated any last shreds of respect Logan might have had for the man.

The other DCI made a point of glaring at the point where Logan's body met the front of Hoon's car, but the Detective Superintendent had pulled his head back inside the vehicle now, and the window was sliding back up with a faint electronic hum.

"I must be in his good books," Logan said. He used his sleeve to wipe the spot on the car where Snecky had attempted to sit. "If it's any consolation, it won't last."

Going by the look on Snecky's face, this wasn't much consolation at all, but he said no more about it, and instead indicated the roof of the car park with a jab of a thumb.

"How'd you know?" he asked. "Where he'd be, I mean."

Logan's eyes pointed up at the spot where he'd found the body, but he wasn't looking there. Not really.

Or, maybe he was looking *there*, he just wasn't looking *then*.

"It's where I caught him," he said, although it wasn't immediately clear if he was talking to Snecky or just reminiscing out loud. "I chased him down. He ran up to the roof. Aye, where the cars are, I mean. Thought he was going to jump off. Thought he had, in fact. There's a drop into bushes on the far side. We assumed he'd gone over."

"But he hadn't?"

Logan shook his head. "Hid himself up on the very top. Lay down flat. Don't even know what made me look. I didn't check the cars, didn't wait for Uniform to check the bushes, I just... knew. Like a fucking homing beacon. I knew the bastard was up there."

"Then what happened?" asked Snecky.

Logan blinked and looked away from the roof. He drained his coffee, winced, then stood up. "Then he attacked me, and then he fell, mashed his skull, and had everyone convinced that he was a turnip." He grunted. "Almost everyone. And now, here we are."

The Beamer rocked as Hoon got out and shut his door. He joined the DCIs up front, checked the hood of the car for damage, then nodded vaguely at the organised chaos surrounding them.

"All in hand?"

DCI Grant practically curtsied as he delivered his report. "Got my team over at the hotel talking to staff. Once we've got a solid idea of time of death, we can see about getting a list of guests in the overlooking rooms. See if anyone saw anything."

"I assume no bastard's getting in or out of the car park until our boys have had their fucking way with it?" Hoon asked.

"All cordoned off, sir, yes," Snecky confirmed. "It'll ruffle a few feathers when folk realise they can't get their cars out, but we'll deal with that when we have to. A wee bit of inconvenience is a small price to pay when a man's life has been—"

"Aye, aye, I wanted an update, no' a message from fucking Hallmark," Hoon snapped, cutting off the end of the sentence. "I spoke to the Assistant Chief Constable. She's going to try to get the jump on the press. She says she'll stick her foot down their fucking bile-ducts and out their collective arses if she has to. I mean, no' in so many words. I'm paraphrasing, but that's the general gist. This does not get out into the fucking wild until we say so. None of it. Ramesh. Petrie. Fuck all. Understood?"

Snecky nodded obediently. Logan didn't bother. The question hadn't been aimed at him. He and Hoon shared very similar views on the men and women of the media, although only one of them had ever threatened 'a fucking press genocide' on live TV.

The fact that the Detective Superintendent hadn't lost his job after that press conference was testament to how highly his superiors thought of him. Or, as he himself insisted, how shit-scared they were.

"You can count on me, sir," said Snecky, overcompensating for Logan's lack of response. "And I've taken the liberty of adding Jack to the team inbox. His knowledge and experience will come in handy. Aye, just on this particular case, I mean," the DCI added, lest anyone should think for one second that he wasn't up to the job.

"No need. I'm not hanging about," Logan said.

He crumpled up his coffee cup, looked around for somewhere to dispose of it, then handed it to Snecky. The other DCI accepted it, stared at it in confusion for a moment, then shoved it into the pocket of his jacket.

"You're... what? You're not? I thought... You know, given the circumstances?" Snecky said.

"No. I'm going to head back up the road," Logan replied. "I'll take a lift, sir, if it's going."

Snecky's face was all crumpled up with concern. He side-eyed Hoon, but found no support lurking there.

"You're... you're heading up the road?" he asked. "But, I mean, I thought you'd be sticking around to... assist. I thought you'd want to help collar the bastard."

"I do. And I will," Logan said. He turned to Hoon. "You said it yourself, sir. He'll come after me. And if that's going to happen, I'd rather it happened on my home turf."

"Thought this was your home turf, Jack?" Hoon replied.

Logan looked up at the car park, then around at what he could see of the city's towers and spires.

"Once-upon-a-time," he admitted. He thrust his hands into his pockets and pulled his coat tighter around himself. "But no' anymore."

CHAPTER FOUR

THERE WERE TWO THINGS LOGAN INSISTED HE HAD TO DO before starting the journey north. This had earned him a barrage of abuse from Hoon, and several comments along the lines of how the Detective Superintendent was, "No' a fucking taxi service."

But Logan had held firm, and Hoon had eventually relented to the DCI's requests.

The first stop was the easy one. Logan just wanted to put his head round the door and look into the eyes of Hoon's counterpart while he broke the news about Dr Ramesh. He wanted to see the reaction, up close and first-hand.

Of course, the bastard already knew by the time Logan got to his office. Snecky had gone scuttling into his office the moment the call had come through.

Detective Superintendent Gordon Mackenzie—the Gozer, to pretty much everyone on the force this side of Hadrian's Wall—was sitting back in his chair, fingers steepled in front of his mouth, when Logan went barging in without knocking.

There was a tiny freeze-frame of alarm on the Gozer's face

when Logan came striding in, then it was swept away by a look of distinct disapproval.

"The general idea is you knock and wait until I tell you to come in, Jack," he said. "It's sort of traditional."

"Your old golf buddy's dead," Logan told him, wasting no time. "Dr Ramesh."

The Gozer's chair squeaked as he adjusted himself. Or, given the circumstances, it may have been his arse.

"Yes. I'm aware of that," he said. "And, he wasn't my 'old golf buddy.' I mean, yes, he was, but... I barely knew him."

"He had your phone number, didn't he? Was quick to come running to you after I'd been in to see Petrie."

"My personal number, yes. Not work. I'm the club secretary. Everyone has my number," the Gozer said. "Manan was no different."

"First name terms, though," Logan said. "Cosy."

"For Christ's sake, Jack. We knew each other socially. I'm hardly likely to call him 'Ramesh.' That's generally considered rude out in the real world. Maybe if you visited it once in a while, you'd know."

The Gozer leaned forward, his expression hardening. "Look, if you've come here to accuse me of something, spit it out. But if I were you, I'd be careful of what I said, Jack. I'd be very fucking careful, indeed."

Logan ground his back teeth together, the muscles in his jaw clenching and unclenching as he stared the older man down. The Gozer, to his credit, didn't blink. Not once.

"We found him on top of the car park. Cambridge Street."

From the look on the Gozer's face, Snecky hadn't considered this detail important enough to share.

"Jesus," the Detective Superintendent whispered. "How bad?"

"Bad. Tortured. Head caved in." Logan tapped a spot on his skull. "Here."

"He couldn't have known what he was getting himself into," the Gozer muttered. "He couldn't possibly have known."

"He knew only too fucking well," Logan snapped. "Your pal was playing the long game. He'd been talking to Petrie for years prior to working at Carstairs. Did a PhD on the bastard. He knew him better than most, and he helped him escape. So, forgive me if I don't shed a tear for him."

The Gozer nodded, albeit with some reluctance. "No. No, you're right, of course," he said. "The ACC was in here earlier. She'd been talking to Bob Hoon...." A look of concern briefly creased the lines of his face. "...for some reason. Not really his patch, but... Anyway. The thought is to keep it low profile for as long as we can. Hopefully, catch Petrie before the press can get wind of it. Last thing we need is to drag it all back up with a fresh barrage of Mister Whisper headlines."

That thing lying coiled in Logan's gut tightened again at the mention of Owen Petrie's nickname. He hadn't chosen it himself. The tabloids had come up with it, based on the description of his voice one of the kids who'd managed to get away from him had given. But, it had become so indelibly linked to the bastard that even now, the merest mention of it still made parents run off to check where their kids were.

"Aye. Makes sense," Logan said, although he wasn't entirely comfortable with it. The last thing he wanted was to get the press involved—to give them the bloody satisfaction of whipping the country into a state of panic.

But, maybe the country should be in a state of panic. Maybe parents should be keeping their kids inside. Maybe going public would help stop him sooner. Maybe it would save lives.

"We'll review it in a day or two," the Gozer said, as if reading the DCI's mind. "See where we are. With any luck, we'll have caught him by then."

"Aye. Maybe," Logan said. He shoved his hands deep down

in his pockets and, for a moment, considered mentioning the thing that was tucked in the inside of his coat.

If anyone would understand, it was the man sitting across the desk. He'd been there, after all. He'd been there on the ladder when Petrie fell.

"Was there something else, Jack?" the Gozer asked.

And like that, the moment was gone.

"No. Nothing else," Logan said. He turned for the door, opened it a fraction, then stopped. "Wait."

The door closed again. Logan turned back to the Detective Superintendent.

"Ramesh. When did he join? The golf club, I mean."

The Gozer's nose wrinkled as he thought back. "Couple of years. Two and a half, maybe."

"And how was he? Any good?"

"Not particularly. Think he was pretty new to it when he joined up. He paid for quite a lot of coaching to get his game up to..."

The DSup's voice tumbled away into silence. He ran a hand through a hairline that wasn't so much receding as beating a full-scale retreat.

"You don't think..."

"That he joined the club to get access to you?" Logan finished. "Like I said, looks like he was playing the long game, so I wouldn't put it past him."

He stepped closer, the floorboards creaking beneath the carpet tiles. The Gozer's eyes darted left and right, like he was scanning through his memories of Ramesh, looking for clues as to his motive.

"I told you Petrie was phoning me," Logan said. "And not just the mobile. He got office numbers. Direct lines. No way he could do that without someone on the inside."

The Gozer's head snapped up. "What the hell are you implying, Jack?"

"Implying? Nothing, sir," Logan said. He took another step closer, forcing the Gozer to lean back to maintain eye contact. "I'm coming right out with it. Someone on the force fed Owen Petrie details of where to find me. The only viable way they could do that—that we know of—is via Dr Ramesh. Your golf buddy."

"I told you, he's not my..." the Gozer objected, but the protest got off to a weak start, and quickly died away.

"I'm not accusing you of anything, sir. Not yet. Not without evidence," Logan said.

"Oh, well that's very bloody generous of you," the Gozer spat.

"What I'm saying is, is it possible that Ramesh compromised you in some way? Got into your computer somehow? Maybe your phone?"

"No. No, can't see it. Got the impression he was a bit of a Luddite. Always forwarding on those bloody round robin things. 'Share this with six people to help cure this kid of cancer.' That sort of thing. That and bloody jokes. YouTube videos. Pain in the arse, if I'm honest." The Gozer shook his head. "So, no. He's far from a computer genius. I mean, half the links he sent to things didn't even work."

The silence that followed that sentence was deafening.

Logan didn't know much about technology, beyond what he needed to. He knew that switching things off and back on again was usually a safe bet. He knew that phone batteries didn't last nearly as long as he wanted them to.

And he knew never to click a link from an untrustworthy source. And Dr Manan Ramesh, as far as Logan was concerned, was up there among the least trustworthy sources of all.

"With all due respect, sir," he groaned. "You're a fucking idiot."

"I beg your pardon! What did you just say?"

"Turn it off. Your phone," Logan instructed. "Turn it off. Now!"

A number of emotions went swooshing across the face of the man behind the desk, starting at *fury* and progressing through to *horrified realisation*.

"Shite!"

Springing to his feet, he hurried over to where his coat was hanging behind the door and searched the pockets until he produced a phone in a slightly battered wood-effect case. He turned it over in his hands, fumbling for the button, then pressed it down until the freshly illuminated screen went dark again.

The Gozer tossed the phone onto his desk, then stepped back, like it might explode at any moment. "Fuck. Shit. *Fuck*," he said, ejecting each word with more passion than the one before. "You don't really think...? Fuck!"

"Give it to the tech boys. They'll be able to tell," Logan said. "But aye, if you clicked the links he sent, then I think there's a very good chance that he's put something on there."

"Oh, shit. *Shit*," the Gozer hissed. He clutched his head in his hands, like he was trying to stop it blowing itself to bits.

"It's your personal phone though, right?" Logan said, indicating the handset on the desk. "You said he had your personal number. Not work. That's what you said."

"Yes. Yes, my personal number. Not..." the Gozer began. He chewed his lip and swallowed, visibly building up to something. "But there were emails, Jack. And I..."

His eyes went to the PC sitting on his desk, then came darting back to the Detective Chief Inspector. Logan groaned.

"Oh," he said. "Well, is that no' bloody marvellous?"

THE SECOND STOP Logan wanted to make was far less enjoyable than the first, and that hadn't exactly been a barrel of laughs.

Still, give him a barney with the Gozer any day over this.

Dylan Muir had been the first of Owen Petrie's three victims. The first child to be taken by the bastard, and the only one whose remains had never been found.

Logan now knew why, of course, but the couple sitting on the couch across from him didn't know. Would *never* know, if he had anything to say about it.

They were in hell wondering what had become of their son, but even that—even the endless misery of not knowing—would be better than the truth.

But he had to tell them this. And he had to tell them in person.

"Escaped? What do you mean, 'escaped'? How can he have escaped?"

It had been twenty years since Aisling Muir had lost her son, and every second of that time had been carved into the lines of her face.

She'd been a young mum—just eighteen when Dylan had been born—which made her... what? Forty-one now? She looked older. A decade older, maybe more. Her hair was greying at the roots, and cut into a shapeless sort of bob that sat flat against the sides of her head.

Logan had stopped in a few times over the years, delivering updates—or a lack of them—to Aisling and her husband, Jerry.

Dylan's dad was a couple of years older than his wife, and was holding up no better. He'd been a larger-than-life type when Logan had first met him—tall and broad, and with a vigour that had driven him to spend hours on end searching the streets for his boy, rallying neighbours, organising awareness-raising events, and generally doing anything and everything he could to bring Dylan home.

His energy had seemed limitless. His drive, remarkable. It took a lot to impress Logan, even back then, but Jerry Muir had done it day in, day out.

The shape slouched on the couch across from Logan now was like a shrunken version of that man. A memory of him that had been fading further every time the DCI had visited, and which was now little more than a ghost.

"Jack?" Aisling prompted. She had a cigarette clutched between two boney fingers. Smoke circled her head like a wreath. "What are you saying? Escaped?"

Logan set his cup down in his saucer. They'd made him tea when he'd turned up, like they usually did, but he hadn't touched it. He wasn't sure, given everything, that he'd be able to keep it down.

"He killed an orderly. Took a nurse hostage, and killed her, too," Logan said. There was no point in sugar-coating it. Not to them. "We don't currently know his whereabouts, but we're making a concerted effort to—"

"Don't fucking talk like that," Aisling snapped. She sucked on the end of her cigarette like it was a blast of pure oxygen. "Not to us. Not after everything."

Her face had hardened, but that didn't last. It couldn't. Her eyes softened first, becoming wide and pleading.

"Please. Don't. Just tell us straight."

Beside her, her husband gave her hand a squeeze, but said nothing. He'd spoken less and less each time Logan had visited, and now the DCI got the impression that Jerry didn't tend to say very much.

"We're looking for him. Everyone. We're not going to the press yet, but it's a full-scale manhunt," Logan said. "We're telling the other parents, but I wanted to tell you personally."

"But... but how the fuck could he escape?" Aisling demanded. "He was a vegetable. You all said he was a vegetable!

That's why he couldn't tell you where our Dylan's body was. That's what you all said!"

"I know, Aisling, but—"

"Then how the fuck can a vegetable escape from a secure hospital? Hmm? Tell me that, Jack!"

Logan placed the cup and saucer down on the coffee table. Through the glass top, he could see the shelf below, still stacked with kids' books and colouring pencils.

They'd told him during a visit six or seven years ago that they hadn't changed Dylan's room. They hadn't mentioned it again since, and he'd never been able to bring himself to ask.

"I know this must be difficult for you. Both of you," he said. "But we're going to catch him. We're going to get him, and we're going to put him where he belongs."

"You can get him to tell you what he did with Dylan," Aisling said. Her voice shook as she said it, a blend of anger and grief. "You can make him. Can't you? You can let us bury our boy."

Logan glanced down at the floor by his feet. The carpet was the same one he'd first walked on when he made his first visit. The couch was unchanged, too, and the same pictures of Dylan Muir smiled down at him from the walls.

The house had been frozen in time, while its occupants had withered and aged.

"I'm going to do everything I can. I'm going to stop him. You have to trust me on that."

Jerry spoke then. His voice was flat. Detached. His eyes, which had been glassy and distant, came briefly into focus.

"Like we trusted you to bring our boy home, you mean?" he said.

"Jerry, I—"

"I think you should go, Jack," Aisling interjected. Her face had hardened to solid steel. Jerry squeezed her hand like he was feeding her his strength. "Please. Just go."

CHAPTER FIVE

HOON WAS IMPATIENTLY DRUMMING HIS HANDS ON THE steering wheel of the Beamer when Logan emerged from the Muir's block of flats and came plodding along the pavement through the orange puddles thrown down by the streetlights.

The DSup spoke even before the DCI had reached to open the door, raising his voice to be heard through the glass. "Well, going by the state of your face, I'm guessing that wasn't a roaring fucking success?"

Logan said nothing until he was sitting in the car with his belt on. "No, but I had to tell them. They deserve to know."

He looked back at the flats. There were eight of them in the block. The Muirs lived second up on the left. Aisling watched him from the window. He raised a hand, giving her a wave. She reached a hand up, and for a moment, Logan thought she was going to wave back. But then, she pulled the curtains closed with a jerk, shutting out him and the rest of the world.

"I want Uniform keeping an eye," he said. "Low profile."

"Think the fucker'll come here?" Hoon asked.

Logan shook his head. "No. But no harm in keeping watch."

"Well, you can phone it in," Hoon said. He pushed a foot

down on the clutch and jabbed at the button that started the engine. "I want to get us the fuck up this road before midnight."

Logan cleared his throat. "Uh, aye, about that, sir," he said, turning in his seat.

Hoon's hands gripped the wheel. His bottom jaw locked into place, lower teeth protruding in front of the upper set. He turned his head. Slowly. Dangerously.

Logan offered up a hopeful smile and raised his eyebrows. "Any chance we could make a couple more quick stops first?"

VANESSA'S FACE went through its entire emotional repertoire in the first two seconds after opening the door, before settling on something halfway between anger and fear.

"What?" she demanded, looking the man on her doorstep up and down. "What's happened?"

Their marriage had been a good one, right up until it wasn't. He wished he could blame her for it. Or that he could say it was a mutual thing. *Two people, just falling out of love.*

But it was his fault, of course. All of it. Him and—

"Petrie," he said. "It's... it's Petrie. He's out."

The anger slipped away, leaving only the fear behind. A hand went to her mouth. Tears came to her eyes. She stepped aside without a word, and Logan stepped over a threshold he hadn't crossed in a very long time.

Given their history and the circumstances, the conversation went better than Logan had been bracing himself for. Vanessa listened. It had been a while since that had happened. She just listened, not interrupting, not shouting him down, not calling him out on any of it. She just sat there on her big leather couch, listening as she worked her way through a sizeable glass of red wine.

And, with everything she heard, her fear grew.

"You think he'll come here?" she asked, once Logan had brought her up to date. "Why would he come here?"

"To get at me," Logan said. "To hurt me."

Vanessa snorted. "Christ. He's well off the mark then, isn't he?"

"Don't say that," Logan told her. "I got that call. Remember? The one I phoned you up to warn you about. He asked how you were. No one believed it was him—"

"How could we?" Vanessa asked.

"But, I knew. I knew," Logan said. "And if he asked about you then, there's a good chance he'll come for you now. And, well, differences aside, I'm not having you get hurt. I won't." He swallowed. "I can't."

"So, what are you saying, Jack?" Vanessa asked. There was no aggressiveness in it. Nothing confrontational for once. "What should I do?"

"I want you and Maddie to come with me to Inverness. We'll put you somewhere safe. Just until this is over."

"Jesus, Jack," Vanessa sighed. "Why Inverness? Isn't there somewhere down here we can go?"

"Because... Because I want you both close," he admitted. "If anything happens, I want to be there."

"Christ Almighty." Vanessa looked to the ceiling, shook her head, then faced him again. "Fine."

Logan straightened a little in the armchair, not quite believing what he was hearing. "Fine? What... just like that? Just... fine?"

"What the hell else do you expect me to say?" Vanessa asked him. "You know Petrie better than anyone. You know what he's capable of. If you think we're in danger, then I've got no choice but to believe you, have I?"

She drained the last glug from her wine glass, swished it around in her mouth, then swallowed it as she got to her feet. "Give me ten minutes to pack some things and phone Maddie. Will I tell her you'll pick her up on the way?"

"Aye. Good. Aye, do that," Logan said, also standing. He glanced out of the window at the black BMW parked along the leafy suburban street. "Although, I should point out, it won't be me driving."

EIGHTY-ODD MINUTES LATER, Detective Superintendent Hoon was practically growling as he powered the BMW up Loch Lomondside, his full-beam headlights driving the darkness away from the narrow, twisting road.

Occasionally, another car would appear around a bend ahead. Hoon gave the oncoming driver approximately a fifth of a second to dip their lights, before ejecting a, "Fuck's sake!" and furiously flashing the high-beams.

It had taken a bit more convincing to get Maddie to drop everything and head north, but Vanessa had done much of the heavy lifting, and she'd eventually seen sense. Both women sat in the back of the Beamer, hands gripping the handles above the doors, and occasionally reaching down to check that their seatbelts were fastened correctly.

Even without Hoon there, conversation would likely have been awkward. Given the DSup's presence, though, and his frequent foul-mouthed outbursts, much of the journey had been spent in a solemn, stilted sort of silence.

The rain started at the Crianlarich bypass, an inoffensive smir at first, that was a downpour by the time they stopped for a pee at the Green Welly in Tyndrum.

Technically, the toilets were closed at that time of night, but after Hoon unleashed both barrels of his persuasive charm at the poor bugger behind the counter in the petrol station, a key was quickly sourced.

Realising he hadn't eaten since leaving Canna that morning, Logan grabbed a sandwich, a bag of crisps, and an iced coffee from the petrol station, only for Hoon to make it very clear that he wasn't 'eating any of that shite' in the Detective Superintendent's car.

While Hoon sat revving the engine on the forecourt, Logan wolfed down two big bites of the sandwich, forced it down with the cold coffee, then shoved the crisps in his coat pocket for later.

That done, he jumped back in the car, and Hoon screeched off up the hill towards Rannoch Moor and the darkened hills and valleys of Glen Coe.

THEY ARRIVED in Inverness a little after one in the morning. Logan wanted to keep the safe house as secret as possible from the rest of the force—it was likely that the Gozer had been the one inadvertently leaking information to Petrie, but the DCI wasn't ruling out the possibility of other rats—so the fewer people who knew, the better.

Unfortunately, this meant arranging it all himself, and that would take hours.

He'd invited Vanessa and Maddie back to his flat, although had warned them that they'd have to share the bed, and that the place hadn't been aired in a few days.

They had, unsurprisingly, declined, and Hoon had taken them to the Premier Inn out by Raigmore Hospital, where they'd managed to book a twin room for the night. Logan had insisted that he pay for it. Vanessa had insisted that he didn't.

After thanking Hoon, and receiving an ear-bashing in response, Logan had accompanied his daughter and ex-wife up to the room and started to talk them through what they could expect to happen the next day.

Hotel check-out was at eleven. He'd have the safe house sorted out for them by then, he promised. It wouldn't be a palace, but it would only be for a few days. Petrie would show himself before long. It would all be over soon.

"Dad," Maddie said, during his second run-through of all that information. She covered her mouth as she yawned. "We get it. You're going to sort it out. Can we sleep now?"

Logan nodded. Smiled. "Aye," he said. "Aye. Get some sleep. We can talk about it all tomorrow."

He opened the door and stopped there, half in the room, and half out in the corridor.

"And I'm sorry. About all this," he said. "I know it's..."

"A pain in the arse?" Vanessa said.

"I was going to say 'difficult,' but aye. Yours is more accurate," Logan said.

He looked back at them both, standing there together. There was so much he wanted to say to them. So many words tumbling around in his head. Too many for him to be able to choose.

"Goodnight," was the one he settled on, and then he stepped all the way out into the hotel corridor, and pulled the door closed behind him.

LOGAN WAS PAYING for the taxi outside his flat when the front door of the building opened, and a young woman came hurrying down the steps, a rucksack swung over her shoulder, a look of grim determination fixed on her face.

"Tanya?" Logan said, stepping into the path of his downstairs neighbour. "What's the matter?" He looked past her to the front door of the close, and the steps leading up to the flats above. "Has something happened? Has he done something?"

Tanya blinked a few times, like she was struggling to recognise the bear-sized figure towering above her.

"Jack," Logan said. "From upstairs. With the polis."

"Oh. Aye. Aye," Tanya said. She wiped her nose on the sleeve of her denim jacket and tried to arrange her mouth into the shape of a smile. Judging by the result, she'd forgotten what one was supposed to look like. "Fine. I'm just... I'm getting out."

"But it's your flat. If..." Logan clicked his fingers a few times, searching for the name. "What's he called?"

"Bud."

"Bud," Logan said, his nostrils flaring like he resented having to dirty his mouth with the word. "If you want me to get him out, I can. It's no bother."

It would be a source of tremendous personal pleasure, in fact, but he stopped short of saying so.

Tanya shook her head. She was in her early twenties, but looked younger. Much younger right now, in fact, with the rings of red around her eyes, and her hair tied back in a ponytail.

She had a pyjama top on under her jacket. A fluffy pink thing with a unicorn on it. She wore a pair of dirty combats on her bottom half, but the waistband of her pyjama bottoms stuck up over the top, and the bottom of one leg had fallen out at her left ankle and snagged on the heel of a trainer.

"I've just... I'm sick of it. Him coming in pissed. Bringing randomers back every night. He's drinking with some new mate of his in there now, and I just looked at him, and I thought... fuck this. I'm done. I've had it."

Logan looked up at the flat below his own. Lights burned in all the windows, and he could hear a series of muffled noises that were presumably meant to be music.

"You shouldn't have to leave your own flat, Tanya," he told her, positively itching to go up there and kick off on her behalf. "Come on, away back inside."

Tanya pulled away from him, like she was worried he might

try dragging her back up the stairs. "I've spoken to my mum. I'm going to go there," she said. She gritted her teeth, fighting off the cracks that had appeared in her voice. "I just... I want my mum."

There was a *clunk* as the taxi driver put the car into gear. Logan turned and slapped the flat of his hand on the roof. "Hold up," he said.

"I've no' got money. I'll just walk," Tanya said. "It's not that far."

Logan opened the back door. "You're fine," he said, urging her inside with a nod.

She eyed him warily for a moment, then swung her bag down off her shoulder and got into the back of the car.

"Tenner cover it?" he asked.

She nodded, and watched in silence as he took the money from his wallet and held it out to her.

"Why are you doing this?" she asked, regarding the folded-up note with suspicion.

"Because I'm a mug," he said. He stretched forward with the money until she took it. "Now, away and get a hug off your mum."

Tanya scrunched the note up in a fist, then looked past the DCI to the light in the windows above. "You're not going to hurt him, are you?" she asked.

"Only if I have to," Logan said, then he closed the door, knocked on the taxi roof, and watched it until it vanished around the corner.

It had been a long, unpleasant day. One of the longest and most unpleasant he could remember, actually. It had been a succession of low-points, with very few highlights to speak of.

Until now.

"Right then, *Bud*," Logan said, rubbing his hands together. "Let's you and I have a little chat."

CHAPTER SIX

BUD YANKED THE DOOR OPEN AFTER THE THIRD ROUND OF hammering, letting the god-awful din of his music flood out onto the landing. He stood there, eyes blazing in the dark hollows of their sockets, greasy hair plastered flat against one side of his head, and sticking up like *Oor Wullie*'s on the other.

He was drowning in a big black jumper that trailed down to his knees, food-stains down the front, thumbs sticking out through holes in the sleeves. His teeth were turning so yellow they'd started to come out the other end into brown. They were so squint, so higgledy-piggledy, that it looked like they'd been scattered into his mouth at random, and probably from a great height.

It had been a few months since Logan had first introduced himself to Bud. The wee scrote still had a kink in his nose to remind him of it, and he instinctively traced it with a fingertip when he saw the DCI looming out on the landing.

Given that so much time had passed, Logan was immensely satisfied by the flash of panic that made itself known as it passed across Bud's face. Obviously, he'd made an impression on the lad beyond the physical one.

"The fuck you want?" Bud demanded, but there was no conviction in it. No venom. He was playing the role he expected of himself, no doubt against his own better judgement.

"I saw Tanya," Logan said.

Bud turned and looked back over his shoulder towards the source of that bloody music. Logan clicked his fingers a couple of times, drawing his attention back.

"She's no' there. She's gone."

This appeared to be news to Bud, but he shrugged and carried on. "And?"

"And, I'd much prefer her as a neighbour than you. So, tomorrow morning, you're going to gather up your stuff, you're going to clean the place from top to bottom, and then you're going to go."

Bud opened his horrible little mouth to object, but Logan wasn't done.

"I don't care where you go. Ideally, it'll be a long way away. But you're going to go." He laid a hand on the smaller man's shoulder. The weight of it almost buckled Bud at the knees. "One way or another, you're going to go. Is that clear?"

Bud regarded the hand like it was a poisonous spider for a few seconds, then he pulled away and squared up to the man in the doorway.

"That a fucking threat, like?"

Logan smiled genially and shook his head. "No. No, son, I wasn't threatening you," he said. The shape of the smile didn't change, yet it suddenly became something much more dangerous. He leaned forward, bringing himself closer to Bud's height. "Would you like me to?"

He waited for an answer, knowing he wouldn't get one but hoping he would.

"No, thought not," he finally said, straightening. "Tomorrow morning," he reiterated. "Get up and get cleaning."

Bud started to close the door, but Logan slammed a hand

against it, easily holding it. "And turn that fucking racket off," he barked. "Or I'll turn it off for you."

And with that, he stepped back and let the door swing shut. He stood there, hands in his pockets, counting down from twenty in his head. He reached thirteen before the music stopped. Then, with a nod of satisfaction, he turned and plodded up the stairs.

His flat was exactly as he'd left it, aside from a smattering of mail on the front mat, and the smell which was noticeably worse. He'd forgotten to open the curtains the morning he was called over to Canna, and the living room felt like it was withering through lack of sunlight. Still, no point in opening them now.

He checked his watch. Ten to two. He should eat, he knew, but it was late, and the worst of the smell was coming from the bin in the kitchen, so he didn't much fancy the idea of going in there to cook.

Instead, he flopped down into his armchair, leaned left a little to compensate for the slouch in the base, and took the bag of crisps from his coat pocket. He tore the top of the bag open without paying too much attention, and shoved a handful in his mouth.

He was two chews in when he winced at the taste, and checked the front of the bag. "Tomato and basil?" he read out loud. The packet was a near-identical red to the *Ready Salted* he'd been aiming for.

He peered inside the bag and gave the crisps a look that suggested they had personally betrayed him in some way, then grabbed another couple and horsed them down.

Logan made sure he'd eaten every last crumb before he allowed himself to think about the other thing in his pocket. Some part of him hadn't stopped thinking about it since he'd found it there, placed neatly in the cold, dead hand of Dr Ramesh. Left there for the DCI to find.

He folded up his crisp packet, rolled it into a thin strip, then tied it in a knot and sat it down on the coffee table beside a mug that was growing a wee furry blue lifeform at the bottom.

That done, he got up, went to the bathroom, and washed his hands. The little box of rubber gloves he kept in his pocket was empty, so he was forced to venture through into the kitchen to get the spare box he kept in the drawer.

The smell was pungently sweet, with rich notes of rot and decay that coated the lining of his nose and oozed down the back of his throat. He remembered the chicken he'd burned the arse off the night before his Canna trip and recalled how he'd chucked the inedible bits—most of it—in the kitchen bin, fully intending to take it out next day.

Holding his breath, he lifted off the plastic lid of the bin, unhooked the top of the bag, and scrunched it together to trap the stench inside.

"Right," he grunted, and he headed for the door, kicking the mail aside so as not to trample on it.

He was back in the kitchen a minute later, cracking open a window to try to air the place out.

The landing had been quiet when he'd passed the downstairs flat. Just as well for Bud, or the bastard would've found himself the recipient of an all-you-can-eat chicken buffet.

With the window open and fresh air tentatively making its way inside, Logan rummaged in the kitchen drawers until he found the box of gloves, then returned with it to the living room.

He sat in the sloping armchair, pulled on a pair of the gloves, then reached into his inside pocket for the rectangle of card he had tucked there.

It had been a message, in the most literal sense of all. A postcard, written in handwriting he'd recognised at first glance. Handwriting he would *always* recognise, and which would always make his mouth go dry, and the hairs on the back of his neck stand on end.

The message was simple. Direct.

'Jump,' it read. 'And I'll turn myself in.'

There was a smiley face below that, and then another sentence further down still.

'Don't, and everything that happens next is on you.'

He'd signed it 'M.W.'

Not 'Owen.' Not 'Petrie.'

M.W.

Mister Whisper.

Logan turned the postcard over. There, on the front, was a photograph of Loch Ness, with a badly Photoshopped head and neck rising from the water. He recognised it from a dozen different racks outside tourist shops all through the city. A bright red caption emblazoned across the sky above it read: 'Look Out For the Monster!'

He placed the postcard back in his pocket and rubbed his eyes with the thumb and forefinger of one gloved hand.

Poor Snecky had looked like someone had pissed on his chips when Logan had told him he wasn't sticking around. Had it not been for the postcard, he probably would have.

But what would be the point of staying there now? Petrie wasn't in Glasgow. Petrie was coming here. Coming for him.

And there was no way Logan was going to hide from the bastard.

He checked his watch again, groaned at the time, and got up from the chair, pulling off the gloves as he stood, and tossing them onto the table with the rest of his life's debris.

It took him less than five minutes to get ready for bed—an eminently satisfying slash, a cursory brush of the teeth, and then he headed through to his bedroom, kicking his clothes off on the way.

The bed was made. Or as close to 'made' as it was ever likely to get, anyway. After he'd last woken up in it, he'd hooked the fitted sheet back on at that one corner the bloody thing kept pinging off at, and thrown the top of the quilt roughly in the direction of the pillows. It was far from hotel standard—and he'd kipped in some ropey hotels in his time—but he'd at least made an effort.

Albeit, not a very big one.

He had just pulled off the second of his socks and tossed it into a corner with the first, when he pulled back the covers and saw what had been left for him.

A badge.

A name.

Jack Wright.

The orderly at Carstairs.

The twenty-six-year-old with the wee one at home.

The dead man in the doorway.

CHAPTER SEVEN

LOGAN WAS IN HIS OFFICE AT THE BURNETT ROAD STATION before the rest of the team started to show up. His early arrival was no real surprise, of course, given that he hadn't slept a wink. How could he, knowing that bastard had been in his house? In his damn bedroom.

"Jesus, Jack, you look like death warmed up," DI Ben Forde called through from the Incident Room, as he took off his jacket and hung it over the back of his chair.

Ben jabbed the button that turned on his computer monitor, then came strolling into Logan's office and sat himself down in the seat across from the DCI.

"And here I thought the fresh island air would've taken years off you," Ben said.

An evidence bag *clonked* onto the desk between them. Ben reached for it, turned it over in his hands, then read the name on the front of the badge. "Jack Wright. Who's that?"

"That, Benjamin, is Owen Petrie's fourth victim," Logan said, then his jaw tightened and he gave a barely noticeable shake of his head. "Or... third, technically."

Ben looked from Logan to the badge and back again. "Petrie? What are you talking about?"

"Hoon didn't say?"

Ben shook his head. "Say what?"

Logan sighed, ran a hand down his face, then sat forward in his chair. "Four days ago, Owen Petrie murdered an orderly and a nurse at Carstairs. He got in a car, and he escaped."

"Escaped? How could—?"

"It was an act. Like I've been trying to tell everyone for years. His whole loss of memory thing, his whole, 'Look at me, I'm a cabbage,' act was just that. A sham," Logan said. "Petrie got a doctor at the hospital on side. A Dr Ramesh. He helped the bastard set up the escape. Then, Petrie tortured him and smashed his skull in."

"Charming," Ben muttered. He set the evidence bag down between them again. "But... *Petrie?*" he said, still not convinced. "The medics had him written off."

"They did, but I knew, Ben. I knew. This? Now? This was always coming. This was always just a matter of time," Logan said. "The badge there. Petrie took it off the man he killed. Took it with him."

Ben peered down at the bag over the top of his glasses. "How'd you manage to get your hands on it?"

"Because he left it for me," Logan said. "In my bed."

Ben's gaze snapped up and met the DCI's. "In your *bed?*"

Logan nodded. "Got home last night and found it. He'd been in my flat."

"When?"

"I don't know. It's no' like he clocked-in," Logan replied. "But recently, obviously. Yesterday at some point, I'm guessing."

"Jesus. You should get SOC in there, get them going over it."

"No point. He won't have left anything useful," Logan said. "Besides, I'm fucked if I'm having Sex Pest Palmer going through all my stuff."

"Aye. Fair point. But still..." Ben said. He picked the badge up again, studied it for another few seconds, then replaced it on the desk. "Bastard, eh?"

"Aye. He's that, alright," Logan said. He thought about the postcard in the pocket of his coat, hanging by the door. "There's something else, too."

"Christ, what now?" Ben asked.

Before Logan could answer, there was a *thunk* from out in the Incident Room as the door swung open and closed.

"Morning!" called DC Hamza Khaled. "Anyone for tea or coffee?"

"I knew there was a reason I missed you, Ham," said another man's voice, as the door swung open again. Logan could practically hear the grin on the face of DC Tyler Neish. "Tea. Milk and two."

"Doesn't matter. We'll talk later," Logan told Ben, then he raised his voice and shouted through to Hamza. "Aye, cheers, I'll have a coffee, if it's going."

"Better make it a strong one," Ben added, looking the DCI up and down. "And maybe ask them if they can do it as an IV drip."

"So, you're not sacked then, boss," Tyler observed, once Hamza had returned with the teas and coffees. DC Neish's voice was a little more nasal than usual, the beating he'd received on Canna having now blackened his eyes and swollen the bridge of his nose.

They were all sitting out in the Incident Room, chairs turned to face the middle. The fifth chair stood at another desk, its back to them. Logan had barely been able to bring himself to look at it since it had become empty.

"I wish," Logan said.

"Sacked?" asked Ben. "What would you be sacked for?"

"Burning down Bosco Maximuke's office," Tyler announced. His gaze darted to the DCI. "Shite. That's probably not meant to be common knowledge, is it?"

"Bit late for that. Every bugger knows," Ben said. "CID's probably arranging a whip-round for you as we speak."

"Thought the Detective Superintendent might have a few things to say about it, though, sir," Hamza said.

Logan shook his head. "Other things on his mind," he said, then he took a swig from his coffee, set the paper cup down on the desk beside him, and broke the news. "Owen Petrie—Mister Whisper—has escaped from Carstairs."

Tyler, who had been mid-sip of his tea, coughed hot liquid out through his nose. "Fuck," he wheezed, drying his face on his sleeve.

"How's that possible, sir?" Hamza asked. "Is he not meant to be...?"

"A cabbage. Aye. Key phrase there, 'meant to be,'" Logan said. "Turns out, he's been putting it on."

"Didn't his head get caved in though, boss?" asked Tyler. He was still recovering from the tea-down-nostrils ordeal, and his voice was far higher-pitched than usual.

"Obviously, not enough," Logan said. "But aye. I'm no' saying he's in the prime of his life or anything, but he's been exaggerating the damage for years. Bastard's been biding his time. And now, he's out."

"Shite," said Hamza, and there was a general consensus in the room that this was an accurate summary of their feelings on the matter.

Logan decided to steer them off the subject of Petrie for now. The bastard was consuming enough of his own head without infecting the others, too.

"What's the latest on our haul from Canna?" he asked.

"Oh aye! Meant to say, quite the bloody haul you brought us yesterday," Ben remarked. "Well done, Jack."

"Aye. Well, I couldn't have done it without Detective Constable Neish," Logan said.

Tyler perked right up at that. "Seriously, boss?"

"No. No' really," Logan said. "I mean, you nearly killed a man by running him over, and I seem to recall you spending much of your time covered in vomit. So, all things considered, you were probably more of a hindrance."

"Wait, wait, wait," said Hamza. "What's all this? Nobody said anything about him being covered in vomit."

"I'd say 'covered,' is a strong word..." Tyler objected.

"Dripping with it, he was. Head to bloody toe," Logan said. He turned to Ben. "How did you get on with them all?"

"Mixed bag," Ben said, wrinkling his nose. "But dealt with. We got the murder confession pretty much right away. No real prompting required. Everything else was proving a bit trickier, but it's all CID stuff, so we've passed it over. They'll be extraditing your man with the international arrest warrant. The rest, they'll sort in-house."

"Bloody hell. You can be efficient when you want to be," Logan remarked.

"True. But such talent brings its own problems," Ben said. "Alice wasn't happy." He looked across at the Detective Constables. "The wife."

"Aye, we know, sir," Hamza said. "I've, eh, had the pleasure of her on the phone before, checking when you'd be home."

"You have my condolences, son," Ben offered.

"What's up with her this time?" Logan asked.

From way back when, he and Alice had never exactly seen eye-to-eye. Their relationship had taken a further turn for the worse when Logan had accidentally smashed a ceramic hedgehog called Harry Pricklepants, which Alice had been particularly fond of, despite the fact that it was a hideous bastard of a thing.

"Royal visit yesterday, wasn't it? Opening the castle after the refurb," Ben explained. "And not just any royal visitor. Oh no. None of your Dukes of... whoever. The Queen. Her Majesty herself. Queen Elizabeth the Second, scissors in hand, cutting the ribbon. Waving. The works."

Logan frowned. "She wasn't happy that the Queen was here?"

"On the contrary, Jack. She was bloody delighted that the Queen was here. What she was less delighted about was me no' turning up to drive her in to see said Queen in action," Ben said. He winced at the thought of it. "She had to get the bus. All dressed up in her nice outfit, too. By the time she arrived, it was chock-a-block. She tells me she caught a glimpse of a hat, and that was it."

"That's all you need, surely?" Logan said. "You ask me, the hat's the best bit."

Ben sucked in his cheeks. "Aye. Well, I maybe wouldn't go saying that to Alice when you next see her, eh? For both our sakes."

A phone rang on Ben's desk. His face fell.

"Christ, see if that's her..." he whispered, his eyes darting around the room as if searching for a bugging device.

He signalled for Hamza to take the call, then took a big swig of his tea while the DC leaned over and picked up the handset.

"Major Investigation Team. Detective Inspector Forde's desk. How can...?"

He reached for a notepad as the person on the other end spoke. It was a woman's voice but not, to Ben's relief, the short, clipped tones of his wife. He, Logan, and Tyler sat in silence, watching Hamza scribble down the details as they came down the line.

"Right. Aye. Thanks. We'll follow up," he said, once the

message had been conveyed. Then, he hung up the phone and sat back in his seat, still writing the end of the message in the notepad.

"Well?" Ben asked. "What's up?"

"Body found behind the Premier Inn," Hamza said.

Logan was on his feet in an instant. "What? Where? Which one? Who?" he demanded, all in one breath.

"Uh, out at the West End. The one with the Beefeater," Hamza said, startled by the DCI's reaction. "Junkie, by the looks of it. Probably an OD, although they say he's a bit of a mess."

Logan's legs gave way and he thumped back down into his chair. "Right. Good," he said. "I mean, not good, but... Doesn't matter. Forget it." He looked between Hamza and Tyler. "You two get over there, check it out. Ben, get Scene of Crime rounded up and dispatched, and warn Shona Maguire at Raigmore that she's got incoming."

Ben smirked. "You no' want to give her a call yourself?" he suggested, but Logan wasn't in the mood.

"I've got to see a man about a house," he replied cryptically. "But tell her I'll come see her this afternoon to see what she's got for us."

"What about Petrie, boss?" Tyler asked. From the way Hamza and Ben both looked at the DCI, it was clear they'd been wondering the same thing.

"Petrie..." Logan began. He thought about the postcard in his pocket in the office next door. "He's not our concern. Central Belt's after him. He won't get far. This," he said, pointing to the notepad in Hamza's hand. "This is our case. We'll let someone else worry about Owen Petrie."

Tyler nodded. He and Hamza both got to their feet. "Right, boss. Sounds good."

"We'll give a shout when we know what we're dealing with," Hamza added, then both DC's gathered up their jackets, drained the last of their drinks, and hurried out of the Incident Room.

It was only then that Logan turned to Ben. The DI had been watching him for several long seconds, a curious look on his face.

"Got something to say, Benjamin?"

"You're letting someone else worry about Owen Petrie, are you?" Ben asked.

"Aye. Well," Logan said, getting to his feet. "There's a first time for everything, I suppose."

CHAPTER EIGHT

"I MEAN, I'M NO EXPERT," SAID TYLER, GAZING DOWN AT the body in the grass. "But I'm going to go out on a limb and say I'm not pegging this one as an overdose."

"You reckon? What was your first clue?" asked Hamza.

Tyler gestured down to the lifeless lump sitting propped against the back of the hotel. His head was angled sharply backwards, so the top of his skull was jammed against the wall.

"Take your pick," he said.

Most of the man's face was missing. Some of it—a lot of it, in fact—was stuck to the roughcasting over on his right, suggesting he'd been repeatedly dragged along it until most of the flesh had been torn off.

It didn't need an X-Ray to tell them that his jaw was broken. It hung open, as if stuck mid-scream, revealing a series of black and bloody chasms where his teeth should have been.

He was dressed in what would have been a pretty nice suit, were it not for all the dirt and the blood. The top button of the shirt was done up, but he was missing a tie. Although, all things considered, that was the least of his problems.

They spotted the tie a moment later. It was red, so had

blended in with all the many other red patches that covered the body like varying shades of camouflage. The tie was wrapped around the man's wrists, pulling them tightly together. This would have made it difficult for him to get his hands out, were it not for the fact that he no longer had any.

"Pretty fucked up this, eh?" Tyler remarked.

"Aye," Hamza concurred. "That's one way of putting it."

They were keeping their distance from the body until SOC turned up, and while they couldn't see the missing hands sitting in the grass nearby, there was no way of telling if he was sitting on them until the body was moved.

Thankfully, neither of them would have to get involved in that part.

Chances are they wouldn't be there, of course. Missing teeth, missing hands, and a face that had been mangled almost down to the bone suggested someone had been determined to hide the man's identity.

The smell of all the assorted bodily fluids at the scene had started Tyler's saliva glands working overtime. He turned away to get a breath, just in time to see a female uniformed officer climb out of one of the four squad cars currently gathered at the scene.

Constable Sinead Bell smiled and waved at him, and Tyler let out an involuntary little yelp of delight. She started to make her way over, but he held a hand up and shook his head.

"I wouldn't. He's honking," Tyler advised, wafting his other hand in front of his face. "And the dead body stinks, too."

"Haha. Funny bastard," Hamza said. He rolled his eyes, gave Sinead a wave, then turned his attention back to the corpse.

Taking out his phone, Hamza snapped off a couple of pictures while Tyler headed over to meet Sinead. He checked them over, winced at some of the gorier close-ups, then sent the whole lot over to the team inbox.

The lack of face made it difficult to judge the man's age. He had a decent head of hair, and none of it was grey, so probably not very old, but anything beyond that would require a closer look than he was prepared to give.

The length of the sleeves made the suit look a little on the large side for him. Although, they might well have appeared shorter had he not been missing everything below the wrists.

Hamza's eyes went to the man's shoes. They were battered trainers, not in keeping with the rest of the outfit. Size twelve or thirteen, he guessed. Big buggers of things. Well worn on the sole. Badly scuffed on the one side that he could see from where he was standing.

He snapped off another couple of pictures, mailed them to the inbox, then turned and headed for the cordon tape, where Tyler stood talking to Sinead.

"Was filling her in on the state of our boy over there," Tyler said, as if justifying the conversation.

"No hands, I hear," said Sinead.

"Largely missing a face, too," Hamza said. "Hi, by the way."

Sinead smiled. "Hi."

"I mean, technically he's not exactly missing a face," Tyler said. "It's all there. It's just that it's spread out across several feet of wall beside him."

Sinead gave an involuntary shudder. "Who the hell does something like that?"

Tyler puffed out his chest. "That's what we're going to find out," he said. "That's why they pay us the big bucks."

"They don't," Hamza reminded him.

Tyler deflated. "Oh. Aye. Fair point. 'That's why they pay us an absolute bloody pittance' hasn't got quite the same ring to it though, does it?"

There was a honk from a horn as a large white van pulled into the car park at the rear of the building and crunched to an abrupt stop at the cordon tape. A red-faced man in a white paper hood wound down the driver's window and leaned his head out.

"Bloody shift, will you?" the Scene of Crime team's Geoff Palmer bellowed at the closest uniformed officer. "Some of us have got jobs to do."

Logan marched along the hotel corridor, an overnight bag in each hand, enduring the ongoing flashback that was the sound of his ex-wife complaining.

"Good Night Guarantee, my backside," she said. "That traffic goes on all night. And the heat. We couldn't get the heat turned down, could we, Maddie?"

From right behind him, Logan heard their daughter eject the tiniest of sighs. Had he not been listening for it, he wouldn't have heard it. The fact that he did gave him immense pleasure. That sigh, barely audible as it was, was the highlight of at least the past forty-eight hours.

"It was warm, Mum, yeah," Maddie agreed.

"We should get our money back," Vanessa said. "That's what they offer, isn't it? The guarantee? If you don't sleep?"

Logan gave a non-committal sort of grunt and shouldered open the door that led to the stairs. He held it long enough for Maddie to take the weight of it, then continued on. Vanessa barely missed a beat as she ducked under Maddie's arm and followed Logan down the stairs.

"How much was it, anyway? I mean, it can't have been much, but still. It's the principle, isn't it? 'Good Night Guarantee.' I know I didn't have a good night. Did you, Maddie?"

"Definitely not," Maddie muttered, although the way she said it suggested that wasn't so much the fault of the hotel as the company.

"There you go, then," Vanessa said. "We can ask for our money back. It's in their adverts."

"We're not asking for the money back," Logan said without turning.

He reached the bottom of the stairs. The door here had a pull handle, so he stepped aside to make room for someone else to open it.

"Why not?" Vanessa asked.

Logan indicated the door with a nod. She grabbed the handle and yanked it open, eliciting a little scream from the hinges.

"Why not?" she asked again, as Logan, then Maddie trudged into the hotel's reception area.

A woman in her fifties rose from behind the front desk and smoothed down her purple uniform with a smile. "Good morning!" she chirped, and Logan felt a pang of sympathy for her over what was to come. "Checking out?"

"They are, aye," Logan said, hoping he might be able to keep Vanessa quiet if he just jumped in quickly enough.

No such luck.

"Yes, that's right," she said, slapping the plastic card keys down on the desk as if disposing of a losing poker hand. "And not a minute too soon, I'm sorry to say."

The woman behind the counter's face fell. "Oh! Was there a problem?"

"Problems. Plural," Vanessa said.

Logan closed his eyes and whispered a, "Christ's sake, here we go," beneath his breath.

"Mum..." began Maddie, clearly sharing her old man's sentiment, but Vanessa wasn't for backing down.

"For starters, the traffic. I know it's not your fault. But, I mean, who builds a hotel between a dual carriageway and a busy hospital? Without triple glazing?" Vanessa complained. "And then there was the heat. How do you switch it off? *Can* you switch it off? Is that possible? We were cooking in there, weren't we, Maddie?"

"That's a bit of an overstatement," Maddie said. She shot the receptionist an apologetic look. "It was just a bit warm."

"You do the guarantee thing, don't you?" Vanessa demanded. "I've seen it in the adverts."

Logan side-stepped in front of his ex-wife and addressed the receptionist directly. "Could you give us a minute?" he asked, indicating the office behind her with a nod of his head.

The woman behind the counter blinked, frowned, and smiled all at the same time. "Uh, yes. Of course," she said, then she retreated into the room like she was backing away from a wild animal, and closed the door with a *click*.

"Do you bloody mind?" Vanessa hissed. "I was in the middle of—"

"Shut up, Vanessa," Logan said. He took no pleasure from it, or for the look of shock that spread quickly across her face.

OK, maybe a *little* pleasure.

"What did you say?" she asked him, hackles rising. He knew the warning signs. He knew this could turn explosive. But, right at that moment, he didn't care.

"Do you know what the words 'low profile' mean, Vanessa?" he asked. He was still carrying both overnight bags, and the handles *creaked* as he tightened his grip. "Do you understand the concept of hiding?"

"Don't patronise me, Jack," she spat.

"I wouldn't dream of it. It's a serious question. Do you understand what I mean when I say that you—the pair of you—weren't here for a wee holiday. This isn't a pleasure break."

"You don't have to tell me that!" Vanessa bit back.

"This was for your safety. That's why I paid in cash. That's why, when I filled in your details on the wee machine there, I didn't use your real names. Low profile. That's what we're aiming for."

He glanced to his right, where Maddie was saying nothing. From her expression, though, she had grasped all this already, even if her mother hadn't.

"Low profile does not mean kicking up a fuss at reception," Logan continued. "It does not mean complaining about the heating, or the bloody windows, or anything else for that matter. And, it certainly doesn't mean filling out a form to get me my money back."

Vanessa had no response to that beyond a tut and a shake of the head. Both those things used to wind Logan up no end, but he ignored them now, and his voice took on a softer edge as he spoke again.

"I don't want my money back, Vanessa. I want both of you safe," he said. "That's all that matters." He smiled hopefully. "Alright?"

Vanessa held his gaze for a few seconds, then sighed. She picked up the keycards. "Fine," she muttered, then she dropped both cards into the return slot on the desk, and gestured towards the hotel's sliding front door. "Lead the way."

"No, after you. And good. Great. I'm glad you saw sense," Logan said. He waited until Vanessa had passed him, then winked at their daughter as they both shared a smile. "Besides, if you think this was bad, just wait until you see the next place."

DESPITE THE WARNING, the safe house wasn't too shocking. It was a two-bedroom mid-terrace on Murray Road, in the Smithton area of the city.

From the outside, it could be generously described as 'functional,' and was unlikely to win any design awards. There was a small garden at the front from which you could look out across the Moray Firth. Aye, you'd need a sturdy ladder and a decent pair of binoculars, but it was out there somewhere.

The back garden was slightly larger and well enclosed on all sides by tall fence panels. There was a wee shed at the far end, but even if Logan had known where the keys for the padlock were, the mechanism had rusted shut long ago.

Inside, the house was basic, but functional. Couch. TV. Assorted cooking appliances. Everything they could possibly need, Logan had told them. Which, Vanessa had replied, spoke volumes about how he chose to live his life.

The beds hadn't been made up, but the bedding was all there in bags in one of the upstairs cupboards. There was one double, and two singles. Vanessa, of course, had claimed the double without actually saying so. She'd just placed her bag in that room, right behind the door, and the message was understood.

There was no food in the place, but Logan had stopped in at Tesco before picking them up at the hotel. He'd brought in four big bags of shopping from the car. He'd got staples like bread, milk, eggs, and cheese, mostly, but there was some chocolate, a multi-pack of *Wotsits*, and a couple of bottles of wine in there, too.

"Who the hell were you catering for?" Vanessa had asked, standing with a bottle of Merlot in one hand, and a three-pack of *Freddos* in the other. "Alcoholic toddlers?"

Logan had suggested she make him a list for next time. Not that there'd be a next time, he'd quickly added. The Petrie thing would be cleared up in no time. This would be a temporary inconvenience, nothing more. He was certain of it.

Or he hoped he'd sounded certain, at least.

The place was used as an Airbnb. Different people came and went all the time, so the neighbours wouldn't think twice about them staying there. Still, probably best not to talk to them. Or anyone, for that matter.

"You're lying low," he stressed, mostly for Vanessa's benefit.

"No shopping trips. No nipping to the pub. No long walks in public. You need something, tell me, and I'll get it."

"Actually, Dad, you could get me, um, sanitary products," Maddie said.

Logan's face didn't know what to do with itself. The eyes widened, narrowed, then blinked, while the mouth attempted a sort of parted-lip smile that wandered dangerously close to grimace territory.

"Right. Aye. Of course. Is it... uh... urgent?" he asked.

"No. I'm fine for today," she replied. "I'll send you a photo of the box so you know what to get."

"Aye. OK. Good," Logan said, nodding on each word like his head was connected to his voicebox by a pulley system. "You do that."

He said his goodbyes then, and headed for the door. He was just stepping out onto the front path when Vanessa appeared in the hallway behind him.

"Jack?"

He tried very hard not to sigh, and instead turned to her, all smiles. "Vanessa."

Vanessa stayed inside the house, but looked both ways along the street before focusing her gaze on her ex-husband. "Thanks," she said.

Of all the words Logan had expected to come out of her mouth, that one had been way down the list.

"Thanks? For what?" he asked.

"Well, for this. Obviously. Maddie. Both of us," Vanessa said. "I know you wouldn't do it if we weren't... If you weren't worried. I know all this... with Petrie... it must be hard on you. But, well, I appreciate it, is what I'm saying. You looking out for us."

"Aye. Well," said Logan, not quite sure of what else to add. "Uniform will keep an eye. They won't know who you are, but they'll keep a watch on the house. You'll be safe. You'll both be fine."

"I'm sure we will," Vanessa said. She smiled. It was, he thought, the first time she'd smiled at him in a very long time. "I mean, we've got cheesy *Wotsits* and wine. How could we not be?"

"That's the cornerstone of any nutritious diet right there," Logan said. He looked past her into the house. "I know I don't need to tell you, but look after her."

Vanessa nodded. "You're right. You don't need to tell me," she said. "And good luck. With Petrie. I'm sure you'll get him."

"Not me," Logan said. "Petrie's no' my case."

Vanessa snorted. "Oh, yes. Sure, Jack," she said. She smiled at him as she started to edge the door closed. It was a thin and sad-looking thing. A smile not so much for the here and now, but for a life that could have been. "Just you go ahead and keep telling yourself that."

CHAPTER NINE

MUSIC WAS PLAYING BEHIND THE DOOR OF THE downstairs flat when Logan passed it. It wasn't blaring out. Had it been anyone else, in fact, he might not even have noticed it, but as it was, he gave the door a dunt and shouted, "Turn that racket down!"

There was no response at first, then a sullen voice replied with a, "Fine," and the music dropped in volume.

Three black bags were stacked up outside the door to the flat. Logan poked one with his foot and was able to tell that there were clothes inside.

Logan was about to shout a reminder that he expected Bud to hurry up and fuck off, when a hoover coughed into life somewhere further inside the flat. He decided to leave him to it, and trudged on up the stairs to his own place.

He found his old holdall in the cupboard next to the bathroom, and spent the next few minutes gathering up the essentials—underwear, socks, a couple of shirts, and his shaving gear —and bundling them into the bag.

He'd had a good look around after finding the badge, of course. Checked all the obvious spots for cameras or microphones. Chucked out everything in the fridge, in case Petrie had poisoned it, and binned his toothbrush in case the bastard had shoved it up his arse.

But even as he'd given the place the all-clear, he'd known he couldn't stay there. Not now. Not knowing that Petrie had been there in his bedroom—that he'd come and gone without smashing a window or breaking the lock.

It wasn't even the thought that he might come back that bothered him. God knew, he *wanted* him to show face again. It was the thought that he'd been here. The thought that he'd contaminated the flat with his very presence. He'd haunt the place until he was caught, and that was one flatmate Logan was not prepared to put up with.

He'd bed down at the office for a few nights. Wouldn't be the first time, and probably wouldn't be the last. If Petrie was caught in the next few days, then great. If not, he'd sort out something longer term. That Premier Inn had seemed alright.

The thought of the hotel led onto another one. After zipping up his bag, Logan checked the shared team email inbox from his phone, and was immediately presented with a close-up of a faceless corpse in a suit.

"That's one hell of an overdose," he muttered, swiping through the other images.

Once he'd gone through them all, he sighed, picked up his bag, and cast his gaze around the flat.

"Never rains but it pours, eh?" he asked of nobody in particular, and then he turned and left, and locked the door behind him.

———

"Well?" asked Tyler, when the man in the white paper suit had come striding over to the cordon line where he and Hamza were waiting. "What have we got?"

"The hell happened to you?" Palmer asked, practically recoiling in horror at the sight of Tyler's bruised and swollen face. "Plastic surgery go wrong, did it?"

"Something like that, aye," Tyler said.

Geoff Palmer looked both DCs up and down, his displeasure written on the pudgy circle of his face that stuck out through the hole in the paper hood. "Look at the pair of you. Where's Logan? He sending the bairns in to do his dirty work now, is he?"

"Bit rich that, Geoff," Hamza said. He made a circular motion with his finger, indicating Palmer's face. The elasticated seam of the hood was tight and squeezed in on both his cheeks. "Considering you look like you're in the process of being born before our very eyes."

Tyler held a fist low at his side. Hamza bumped it without looking.

"Aye, very good," Palmer tutted. "Have your wee jokes. I'm sure Big Chief Shitting Bull will be very impressed. You're both a chip off the old block."

"Who's Big Chief Shitting Bull?" Hamza asked.

"And is that no' a bit racist, Geoff?" Tyler wondered. "You'll want to be careful saying stuff like that. Cultural appropriation. Maybe even hate speech. You'll want to watch yourself."

Palmer sighed. "God Almighty. I think you might actually be worse than he is. Do you want to know the story, or don't you? No skin off my nose." He tipped his head back in the direction of the body, which was in the process of being covered up. "No pun intended."

Hamza took out his notebook. "Aye. Go for it. What have you got?"

"A lot more than he's got, let's put it that way. No teeth, no hands. No sign of either laying around the scene. We're going to extend the search around the perimeter of the hotel, but beyond that, it's on you. You might need to bring the dogs in. See if they can sniff out the missing bits."

"Right. Aye. What else?" Hamza asked. He held his pencil poised, ready to start writing just as soon as Palmer said something worth taking note of.

"The suit's not his. Or, I suppose it is now, no other bugger's going to want it. There's a charity shop label on the tag, though. British Heart Foundation. Four quid."

"Bargain," Tyler remarked.

"Not his trainers, either. Far too big. I'd put him about a size seven. They're thirteens. Laces were around his feet to hold them on. Even then, they were hanging off."

"Probably couldn't have walked far in them, then," Hamza reasoned.

"No. Feet were manky, too. Bruised and cut. There were a lot of wee stones sticking to them and insides the shoes, so he walked barefoot for some distance before the shoes were put on. We're having a look for fingerprints on the trainers, but nothing turning up so far."

"And on the rest of him?" Tyler asked.

"Nothing yet. With all that blood, I'd expect to see stray prints somewhere, but nothing showing up at all so far. Killer probably wore gloves," Palmer continued. "Also, before you ask, there was no wallet, no keys, no ID of any kind."

"But then where would be the challenge in that?" Tyler asked.

"Killed at the scene, do you think?" Hamza asked.

"Looks like it, given the amount of blood, aye. There's a puncture wound to the neck that would've sprayed. That matches the spatter on the wall and ground. Can't say if the face was done before he bled out, during, or after. Hands were done after, though, I'd say. Teeth, I've got no idea. Pathology will be able to tell you more. We'll take the clothes and shoes for testing. We've also taken a cast of a print that's been left in the grass."

"Fingerprint?" Tyler asked. It was out of him before he could stop it, and he fully accepted the withering looks the question earned from both Hamza and Palmer.

"Footprint, obviously," Palmer said. "Doesn't match the trainers, so might be your killer. It was near the scene, as opposed to at the scene, though, so it could be from anyone."

"Great," Hamza said, scribbling in the pad. "Anything else?"

"Nothing startling. Obviously, the death was violent. There's bunching on the back and front of his clothing that suggested he was dragged, probably when they mashed his face into the wall," Palmer said. "The guy's probably nine stone soaking wet, so it could've been one attacker, and most likely was, given how little the ground around him was disturbed. Killer took the weapon with him, or disposed of it somewhere we haven't been able to find it yet."

"What about time of death? Any idea?" Hamza asked.

"Recent. Very recent," Palmer said. "He wasn't warm when we got to him, exactly, but not stiff enough to have spent the night here. Blood was still wet, too, and hadn't fully soaked into the grass."

He bent his wrist back and glanced at the watch he had tucked between where his paper sleeve ended and his rubber glove began.

"What are we on now? Quarter past one? I'd say... Six this morning? Thereabouts. Obviously, there's a bit of leeway in that either way."

"He was found just after half seven," Hamza said. "Young lassie on her way into work found him. Poor thing."

"Sinead's with her in one of the hotel offices," Tyler told the other DC. "I said I'd go in and have a chat."

"No bother. We're nearly done," Hamza said. He raised his eyebrows and looked over the top of his notepad to Geoff Palmer. "Anything else?"

"Jesus Christ, son. What else do you want?" Palmer asked. "The killer's name and address?"

"That'd be handy, if you've got it," said Logan, ducking under the cordon tape and striding over to join them. "Save us a bit of time and effort."

"Alright, boss?" Tyler asked.

"Got my emails, then," Hamza added.

"Aye. Bit of warning next time would be nice. Lucky for both of us, I hadn't bothered with breakfast," Logan replied. He turned his attention to the man in the paper suit. "So, what have we got?"

Palmer scowled and gave a dismissive wave in Hamza's direction. "Your man here's got it all. We'll finish up in the next couple of hours and I'll get the full report sent over. But, I think we can all safely agree that you're looking at a homicide. You'll need to get a move on, Jack," he said, with a self-satisfied smirk that was crying out for a belt in the mouth. "You'll be building up a backlog soon, between here and Canna."

"Canna's done," Logan said.

Palmer's forehead furrowed beneath the hood. "Done? Already?"

"Full confession," Logan said.

He watched the expression settle on Palmer's face. The bastard actually had the brass neck to look annoyed.

"Well... good work, I suppose," the Scene of Crime man said.

"Aye, well, I only do it to earn your praise, Geoff, so thanks. That really means a lot," Logan replied.

Palmer looked from Logan to the two DCs who now flanked him on either side. With a tut, a sigh, and a shake of his head, he pulled off a crisp about-turn and announced he was getting back to it.

"Right, so, what have we got?" Logan asked, once Palmer had joined the rest of his team over by the body.

Hamza opened his mouth to reply, but Tyler interjected before he had a chance to speak.

"I'm going to go talk to the lassie that found him. Sinead's waiting inside with her," he said.

Logan regarded him with something treading the line between confusion and disbelief.

"Unless... Do you want to do it, boss?" Tyler asked, unable to miss the look the remark had earned him.

"No. It's fine," Logan said. "You go. Shout if you need us."

"Will do. Cheers, boss," Tyler replied, all smiles again. He ducked under the cordon tape, fired off a finger-gun at a passing Uniform, then went strutting around the side of the hotel in the direction of the front door.

Logan waited until he was out of sight before turning to Hamza. "Did he just...? Did he just use his initiative?"

Hamza glanced in the direction the other DC had gone. "He might've done, sir. Aye."

"Bugger me. Wonders will never cease," Logan mumbled. He tapped Hamza's notepad with the end of a finger. "Now, talk me through it, and let's see where we are."

CHAPTER TEN

THE GIRL WAS UPSET. BUT THEN, WHO WOULDN'T BE?

She was sitting hunched in a wooden chair in something that might have been an office, but equally could have been a storeroom. Packs of toilet paper were stacked six high at one end, while reams of other—probably much less vital—paper overflowed from an in-tray that stood on a desk at the other end.

Constable Bell was perched forward on another chair, saying soft, soothing things when Tyler knocked and entered. Both women looked up at him as he stepped through the door, although only one of them looked even remotely pleased to see him.

"Detective Constable. We've just been talking about you," Sinead said.

Tyler visibly struggled with where to pitch his comeback. On the one hand, there was a young woman in the room who'd just found a dismembered corpse. On the other hand, his natural instinct around Sinead was to flirt for all he was worth.

In the end, he settled for something that erred on the side of professionalism without, he hoped, making him sound like a humourless twat.

"Thought my ears were burning," he said. He reached a hand out to the young woman in the chair. She looked squarely in her teens. Seventeen, maybe? "Hi. I'm Detective Constable Neish. Call me Tyler."

"Kerri," she said in a voice that was just a half-decibel or so above a whisper.

"With an 'i'," Sinead added.

"Nice," said Tyler, smiling at the girl. "Fancy."

He looked around for another chair but found none. Sinead started to get up, but he motioned for her to stay seated, and instead grabbed a couple of packs of toilet paper, placed them on the floor in front of Kerri, and sat on those.

"You've had a rough morning, I hear," he said.

Kerri drew in a breath through her nose. Her eyes widened a little, like she'd just managed to forget what she'd seen, and had now had it brought rushing back.

"Not the best," she said. Her accent was local, not the Eastern European that Tyler realised he had been expecting.

"I'm sorry you had to see that. Must've been rough."

"Not the best," she said again. "What happened to your face?"

"Hmm? Oh," Tyler said. He very carefully traced the bump in his nose with his fingertips. "Got into a fight. You should see the other guy."

"He's largely unharmed," Sinead said.

"Key word 'largely'," Tyler said. "He's not *completely* unharmed."

"Just mostly."

"Aye. Just mostly," Tyler confirmed, and Kerri managed half a smile at that.

Even smiling, she had a haunted look about her. One of the worst Tyler had seen, in fact. He'd have said she looked like she'd seen a ghost, but it was more than that. She looked like she'd accidentally spilled a ghost's pint, and it was now drunkenly threatening to kick her teeth in. It was the mask of the shell-shocked, and she was wearing it well.

"Did we call her parents?" Tyler asked Sinead.

"There's just my mum," Kerri said, answering before the constable could. "She's in Glasgow all week. Training."

"Oh. Right."

"She's a dog groomer," Kerri said.

"Wow. Cool."

Kerri rolled her eyes, and for a moment looked a bit more like a normal teenager, and a bit less like someone who was going to need therapy for the rest of their life.

"It's really not."

This was clearly a conversational route she was more comfortable with. Tyler indulged her, wandering along it with her. They chatted about dogs for a while. Then about jobs. Then about parents, and their many embarrassing qualities.

"You think your mum's bad? My dad's a doctor. A GP," Tyler said. "When I was in... I think second year in high school, maybe? Guess who came in to do the sex talk in SE."

Kerri sat up straighter in her chair. "No way!"

"Yep. There he is, front of the whole class, banana in one hand, condom in the other, and I'm sat up the back looking at the window thinking, 'It's only four floors. Maybe I'll survive the impact.'"

Kerri slapped a hand over her mouth and groaned. "Oh, God. I can't imagine," she said, then she turned to PC Bell.

Sinead felt her heart plunge into her stomach. She battled valiantly to keep her smile fixed in place, but she knew what was coming. She could see it approaching, like a set of headlights powering along a darkened road towards her. Unavoidable. Inevitable.

"What about you? What do your mum and dad do?" Kerri asked.

"They, uh..." Sinead could feel Tyler's gaze on her. Could

feel his sympathy burning into the side of her face. "You know, this and that. Nothing much."

Kerri's brow creased into the start of a frown, like she was about to press the constable further. Tyler quickly steered the conversation back onto more pressing matters before she had the chance.

"So, do you mind taking me through what happened this morning, Kerri?" he asked. "Just in your own time. There's no hurry."

The girl's body language drew itself tighter again. She pulled the heels of her feet up onto the chair, her bent legs like a barrier between her and the officers.

"Eh, yeah. OK," she said. Then, after a few deep breaths and a couple of false starts, she took them through it.

She usually got a lift in from her mum, but had walked that day, due to the aforementioned dog clipping training down in Glasgow. She'd left sharp, to be on the safe side, and so had turned up almost half an hour early for her morning shift, which was due to start at eight. She'd nipped around the back of the hotel for a fly blast of her vape before she clocked in.

And that was when she'd found him.

At first, she'd thought it was another staff member on a smoking break. Then, as she'd got closer, she'd thought it was someone lying drunk.

It was only when she'd put on her glasses, that she'd realised the full terrible truth of what she was looking at.

"Did you go over to it? The body?" Tyler asked.

Kerri's expression made it very clear that no force on Earth would've been able to drag her over to that man propped up against the wall.

"No. I just turned and ran inside and found Cathy."

Tyler side-eyed Sinead.

"Assistant night manager," the constable clarified.

"She called the police. I didn't go back out," Kerri said. She wrapped her arms around her legs, hugging them. "I didn't want to see it again."

"That's understandable. And you absolutely did the right thing, Kerri. Well done," Tyler said. "Now, I need you to think, was there anything else you saw that seemed... out of place, maybe?"

Kerri shook her head. "No. Just... that. Him."

"Take a minute. Don't rush," Tyler urged. "Think. Could there have been anything else, anything at all, that struck you as odd? Or not even odd, necessarily, just different?"

Kerri's eyes flitted left to right, like she was rewinding and replaying film footage of the event inside her head.

"No," she finally said. "No, I don't think... wait."

Tyler straightened on his stack of toilet paper. Kerri looked from him to Sinead and back again.

"Now that I think about it, there was one thing."

———

"A VAN?"

"That's what she said, boss. Small transit. No markings on the side that she noticed, but she can't be sure," Tyler said. He turned his chair away from his desk so it was facing Logan's, then sat in it. "Passed her coming out of the car park about quarter past seven. She went inside, dropped her stuff, then went around the back for a smoke and found the body."

"Hotel car park. Could've been workmen staying," Logan reasoned. "Not uncommon for vans to be coming and going."

"No, I know, boss. But..." Tyler sat back and gestured for Hamza to take over.

"Guests have to log their vehicle reg at reception. I got the list for last night and ran through them."

Logan sat forward in his chair, becoming more interested. "No vans, I take it?"

"No vans," Hamza confirmed.

DI Forde had been prodding away at his keyboard while the conversation had taken place, but leaned out from behind the monitor now to chip in. "Delivery maybe?"

"I thought about that, too," Tyler said. He exchanged a look with Hamza, then shrugged. "Alright, technically Sinead thought that, too. So, we checked. Nothing."

Logan drummed his fingers on the desk. "So, we've got a van. What's the camera situation around there? I know there's nothing at the hotel, but anything nearby?"

"Afraid not, sir," Hamza said. "CCTV's mostly just city centre. We could put out an appeal on the radio for dashcam footage. Paper's out late tomorrow night, too. We could get something in there."

"Aye. Do that. Maybe someone saw something," Logan said. He sucked air in through his teeth. "Still, pretty thin, though. A van."

"Better than nothing, boss."

"Aye. Barely," Logan said. He stood up. He hadn't bothered to take his coat off since coming in last time, and his hands instinctively found their natural home in his pockets. "But keep at it. I'm heading to the hospital."

"No' the prostate exam is it, boss?" Tyler asked. He grinned, despite the thoroughly unamused expression that had settled on Logan's face. "Man of your age, and all that."

"Did anyone ever tell you you should've been a comedian, son?"

"No' yet, boss."

Logan shook his head. "No. Didn't think so," he said. "Ben, hold the fort. Call me if anything comes in. I'm going to go check in on the post-mortem."

"Right, Jack. No bother," Ben said. "And for God's sake, be careful."

Logan stopped by the exit. "Aye. Well, you know me, Detective Inspector," he said, then he pushed through the swing doors, and was gone.

"I do," Ben muttered. "And that's what bloody worries me."

"Haw! Fannybaws!"

Logan stopped a pace or two past Detective Superintendent Hoon's open office door, then backtracked until he was filling the doorway.

"Sir?"

"Don't fucking, 'sir,' me. Come in," Hoon urged.

Logan contemplated objecting, then stepped into the office.

"Were you born in a bastarding barn?" Hoon asked.

Logan closed the door behind him without a word.

"Good. Right," Hoon said, indicating the chair across from him. "Got some reports in from the fuckers down the road. Petrie case. Thought you'd want to be kept up to date."

"Honestly, sir?" Logan began. "I'm not sure that—"

"Just shut your fucking piehole and listen," the DSup snapped. He clicked his computer mouse, and his eyes went to the top right corner of the screen. "Right. Hang on. It's... fuck. Hang on."

He clicked a few more times. Each time he did, something else on the monitor caught his attention, until his gaze was moving left, right, up, and down like he was following the ball in a game of *Pong*.

"Jesus Christ. They make these things so fucking complicated. How do I get back?"

"Back where?" Logan asked.

Hoon shot him a foul look. "I was thinking out loud, for fuck's sake. Was that no' obvious? I don't expect you to fucking know what I'm... Aha. Here we go," he said, double-clicking something and then sitting back in his chair. "Post Mortem report on the doctor. Best estimate is he was killed within five or six hours of Petrie escaping Carstairs. Judging by his injuries, those five or six hours would not have been pleasant ones."

"Aye. He was a mess," Logan said.

"You don't know the fucking half of it," Hoon said, staring at the screen. "Eyelids cut off. Teeth and fingernails pulled out. Not all of them, but enough that you'd well and truly fucking smart."

He continued to read, turning the mouse wheel with a fingertip as he scrolled down the page.

"Signs of strangulation. Burns to chest and stomach from some fucking corrosive material they've yet to identify. In the mouth and stomach lining, too, so he made the poor bastard drink it," Hoon continued. "Ribs cracked. Fingers and toes broken. Thumbs completely fucking detached."

His face screwed up and he tucked his own thumbs into his palms. "Ooyah bastard," he remarked, before turning his attention back to the report. "Rectal damage suggests something was forcibly rammed up there. Doesn't say if it was implement or cock."

He scrolled down a little further.

"No. Tell a lie. Wasn't a cock. Don't know if that's better or worse," he muttered. His eyes went to the next paragraph and he flinched. "Fuck me! Worse. Something hooked or barbed, they reckon."

"Aye. That's worse," Logan agreed.

"Long and the short of it is, he might've had a stiffy for Mister Whisper, but the feeling clearly wasn't mutual. Petrie fucked him over the first chance he got."

"No great surprise there," Logan said.

Hoon grunted, neither in agreement nor disagreement. He sat back until he was almost reclining in his chair, and rested his hands on his stomach, fingers interlocked.

"They've got their eyes peeled down the road, checking his

old haunts, likely places the fucker might hide. The usual," the DSup said. He pinned Logan to his seat with a sharp, piercing stare. "No sign of him. But then, they probably won't find him, will they?"

"I hope so, sir," Logan said.

"Cut the shite, Detective Chief Inspector," Hoon told him. "You and I both know, that if you thought Owen fucking Petrie was knocking about in Glasgow, there's no' a snowball's chance in Hell you'd have fucked off back up here so soon."

Logan said nothing. He didn't have to.

"You think he's up here, don't you?" Hoon asked. "No, you fucking *know* he's up here."

"He might be. He's hard to predict."

"Fuck off! 'Hard to predict.' Who the fuck do you think you're talking to, son? I was doing this job while you were still hanging off yer mammy's tits."

Part of Logan wanted to point out that the Detective Superintendent was barely more than ten years older than him, but another part—the part that concerned itself with his personal welfare—thought it best not to mention it.

"If you want to fuck around obsessing over that sick bastard, fine. I don't care. Let him cut your eyelids off and shove whatever pronged devices he likes up your arse," Hoon said. "But I'm sure I don't need to remind you, Jack, that you've already lost one good officer recently."

Logan's chair gave a low, ominous groan as the DCI adjusted his position.

"If I find out you're putting anyone else at risk by withholding information, I will engulf you in a whirlwind of shit. I'll be the vengeful fucking Thunder God of Faeces. A maelstrom of steaming hot excrement, and you'll be at the eye of the fucking storm. You won't have to worry about Petrie ramming stuff up your arse, because I'll be in front of him in the queue wi' an electric whisk and a foot pump. Is that clear?"

"I wouldn't do anything to put my team in harm's way," Logan said.

"Aye, well. They're my fucking team, too, and believe it or not, I care about their welfare," Hoon said. "I mean, maybe no' the mouthy wee prick wi' the hair. I'd gladly punch his fucking mouth loose. But the rest of them. Understood?"

Logan nodded. "Understood."

"Good. And, I mean, maybe I've got it wrong. Surely you can't be too fucking concerned about him coming up here, or you wouldn't have brought your daughter up here, would you? The ex, aye. That I can see. But your wean? What kind of monster'd do something like that? Eh, Jack? Knowing what we know?"

Several seconds passed, both men staring the other down. It was Logan who eventually broke.

"I brought them here to keep them safe," he said.

"Right. And I should hope so, too. Now, go. Fuck off and get back to it," Hoon said. "And, if you think of anything—any reason you might have for believing that fucker's somewhere up this way—then you be sure to let me know."

"I'll rack my brains, sir," Logan said.

"I'll rack your balls, if you're no' careful," Hoon warned. He waved a hand, dismissing the DCI. "Now, get out of my fucking sight."

CHAPTER ELEVEN

IT WASN'T FAIR!

The first day—maybe the only day ever—that he'd been allowed to go out by himself, and nobody else was coming out to play. Not Michael upstairs, not Adam from the flats next door. Not even Lisa from the houses round the corner, which he was secretly a bit relieved about, because she always talked about kissing and wanted to hold his hand when they walked round to the park.

He had no one to hold his hand when he walked round to the park today.

Him and his mum always went to the park together at the same time, but he'd been excited about the idea of going out on his own one time. He'd harped on about it for weeks, in fact.

"Michael's already been out *twice* by himself," he'd said. "And he's nearly a whole month younger than me!"

She'd said, "No way," at first. A lot of times, actually. Sometimes laughing about it, sometimes serious.

Once, after she'd been working late the night before, she'd shouted at him so sharply that he'd burst into tears on the spot, and gone running into his bedroom. She'd come in a few minutes later with a bar of chocolate and an apology, snuggled up with him on his bed, and told him she just worried about him. Told him he was still very young, and that she'd be scared if he went out on his own. Told him she hoped he understood, and that one day—someday—he'd get to go out by himself.

That had been yesterday. This morning, when he'd asked, she'd sighed, shaken her head, and told him he could go, but only if he didn't go further than the park so she could at least watch him from the window.

He'd tried to protest, but it was that or nothing, she'd said. Take it or leave it.

"My way, or the highway."

He knew better than to argue. This was the best deal he was likely to get. And so, he'd given in. Fine. She could watch him if she *had* to, but she wasn't allowed to shout over and embarrass him in front of his friends.

No chance of that now.

The park was empty. The swings creaked and groaned on their chains as they were nudged back and forth by the breeze, all swinging at different times.

He'd seen the bigger kids play games like that before, where they'd start the swings going, then try to run through the middle of them without getting hit.

He'd always thought the whole thing looked scary, and when Alice Something-Or-Other from the other side of the estate had misjudged a run and had her nose smashed open by one of the baby swings, he'd made the decision never to try it for himself.

He went to the roundabout first, put one foot on the wooden base, and pushed himself around with a series of drawn-out screeches of metal on metal. It had never turned properly since Wee Sid had got the front wheel of his bike stuck under it that time, and after four slow revolutions his legs were aching too much to keep pushing.

Cupping his hands to his eyes, he looked over at his block of flats. He counted the windows—three from the bottom, two in from the left—and squinted to try to see his mum. The sunlight was reflecting off the glass, so he wasn't sure if she was there. He waved, anyway, and in that moment felt a little pang of regret and wished she was here with him.

He trudged over to the swings, jumped up onto the rubber seat, and reached with his feet to try to touch the ground. Some of the other kids could get themselves started just by swinging their legs, but he'd never been able to manage it.

Groaning with the effort, he stretched his legs as far as they would stretch, pointed his toes straight out until the tips of his shoes brushed against the safety mat. It was half-covered in stones, and most of the little holes were clogged up with weeds. He wasn't sure just how safe it would be to land on if he fell, but he wasn't planning on going high, anyway.

Just a wee swing. Just for a minute, so he could say he'd done it, then he could go home. His mum might play a game with him. Maybe she'd do hot-dogs for lunch.

Clinging to the chains with both hands, he slid his bum to the edge of the seat. His toe touched the ground. He tried to kick back, but instead just sort of hopped and finished in the exact same position, poised like a ballerina.

He tried again. Push. Hop. *Thump.*

He really hoped his mum wasn't watching. She'd never let him out on his own again if he couldn't even get a swing started.

One more try. That would do it. One more big push, and...

He cried out with the effort of the kick, clutching the chains and throwing himself backwards as he put his full weight into the shove.

For a moment—a glorious, perfect moment—he felt the swing start to climb. But then, he buckled. His nerve gave out, and he slipped forward off the seat, pain jarring up his legs as both feet thudded flatly onto the mat.

Shame burned at his cheeks and pricked at his eyes. He couldn't look over at the window now, in case he saw her looking back. He hoped she wasn't there. He hoped she hadn't seen him failing so spectacularly. He hoped nobody had.

"Hello there."

The voice came from behind him, making him jump.

A man was there, smiling at him. He had a woollen hat pulled down low on his head, but not quite low enough to hide the bottom of the scar that was above his eye.

The man stepped forward and spoke again. His voice was soft and gentle. A murmur.

A whisper.

"Would you like me to give you a push?"

CHAPTER TWELVE

DR SHONA MAGUIRE WASN'T IN HER OFFICE WHEN LOGAN turned up. The lights were on through the back, though—the room where all the post-mortem unpleasantness took place—and he could hear her singing Alice Cooper's *School's Out* to herself as she went about her work.

Logan shuffled from foot to foot in the outer office doorway for a few seconds, not quite sure if he should interrupt. He certainly didn't want to go marching into the back room unannounced. His constitution was pretty rock-solid, but the body had been in a grim state even before Shona had got at it. He wasn't sure he wanted to wander in there and find him with his stomach pinned open and his intestines piled up on a set of scales.

He settled for announcing his presence with a cough and a shout of, "Hello. Just me. Take your time."

The singing stopped. "Me who?" came the reply.

"It's, uh, just... Jack."

"Jack who?"

Logan felt like he'd taken a punch to the chest. Before he could reply, the door swung open enough for Shona's head to appear through it. She wore a visor over the top part of her face, and a mask across the bottom, but he could tell she was grinning at him.

"Just kidding. Hiya. Give me a couple of minutes," she said, then she vanished back into the mortuary, only to appear again a second later. "And stick the kettle on."

Logan looked around the untidy outer office until he found the kettle. It was tucked behind a stack of paperwork on a stainless steel countertop, the cable trailing to a bank of sockets on the end of a long extension.

A spaghetti of wires ran from the other plugs connected to the extension. At least three of them were charges for various electronic devices, and the other stretched up to a smart speaker that teetered ominously on the edge of a shelf.

Logan picked up the kettle, swished it around to gauge if there was enough water in it, concluded there was, then set it back down and switched it on.

He conducted a cursory search for cups, but found only one sitting beside the PC. As it was crawling with enough mould to repopulate Mars, he decided to leave it be. No point disturbing it. That might make it angry.

Turning away from the boiling kettle, Logan caught sight of his reflection in the glass of the office's outer door. Christ, he looked tired. Old, too. He ran a hand down his face, like he might be able to magically wipe away the five days of stubble and the two decades of bags under his eyes.

No such luck.

The kettle had just clicked off when the mortuary door opened. Shona pointed to a box that sat on the closest table. "Masks and gloves are in there," she said. "If you fancy taking a wee swatch at your man?"

Logan couldn't say he did particularly fancy it, but he grabbed the protective gear anyway, and pulled it on before squeezing past Shona into the much colder room beyond.

The faceless figure had looked bad in the photographs, but was even more unsettling up-close and in person. He was mostly covered by a sheet, with only his head and feet poking out at either end.

"OK, victim was a Caucasian male, mid-to-late-twenties, best guess. And, well, I'll say this about you, Jack, you keep things interesting. You bring me some crazy stuff," Shona remarked. "I mean, you see a lot in this job—too much, some might argue—but this is a first for me."

"How so?" Logan asked.

"Well, I'm not sure if you've noticed, but someone's gone and scraped all his face off," Shona said. She stood at the head of the body and cupped her hands at either side, as if presenting the prize-winning entry in a baking contest. "Ta-daa."

The face was mostly sinew and gristle, but worn down enough that patches of skull showed through on the cheeks and forehead. The jaw hung impossibly wide, making the face look even more monstrous than it already did.

The teeth had been removed. "Smashed in and ripped out," Shona explained. "While alive, I'd say. There's clotting around some of the front sockets, which were probably the first to go. There's also bruising on his arms and shoulders that would suggest he was held down, and that he tried to put up a fight. Someone, it is safe to say, was not a big fan of this gentleman."

"Jesus Christ," Logan muttered.

"Nah. I doubt he's the culprit," Shona said. "He's more the 'turn the other cheek' type than the 'grind both cheeks against a roughcast wall until they fall off.'"

"That must've taken a lot of force," Logan remarked, flicking his eyes down to the victim's face. "Before or after he died, you think?"

"Hard to determine," Shona said. "Either right before, or immediately after. Given that it's a reasonably public place, and there'd be a *lot* of screaming involved, I'd say after. Or, at least, that he was unconscious during it."

"That's something."

"Yeah. Although, that said, he was stabbed in the back. That's what killed him. Multiple downward strikes with a reasonably short blade. Four, five inches maybe. Hard to be precise on the number of times he was stabbed, but somewhere between twelve and fourteen. They were clustered tightly together, so there's a lot of overlap."

"How tightly together?" Logan asked.

"About that," said Shona, using the forefingers and thumbs of both gloved hands to indicate a circle the size of a small orange. "I've got pictures I can send you."

"Doesn't suggest someone panicking and just stabbing wildly, then," Logan said. "That's controlled."

"Yeah, that fits," Shona said. "And, in the back, downward strikes suggest the killer was standing over him."

"So, he could've had his face against the wall then. Down on his knees," Logan said. He thought back to the photos Hamza had sent him. "Pretty sure there were grass stains on the knees of his trousers, now I think about it."

"Right. Well, that's what makes me wonder if maybe the face was..." She gestured down at the body, at a loss for words. "...*rubbed off* while he was still alive."

Logan looked at her over the top of the corpse. "Best guess?" he asked.

Shona scratched the back of her neck. "If you're putting me on the spot, it was done after. I think it went teeth—done elsewhere, not at the scene, judging by the clotting and the whole *scream factor* I mentioned—then he's shoved up against the wall on his knees, stabbed repeatedly, and then, while he's still bleeding, the face is dragged back and forth across the wall."

"Then his hands are cut off?" Logan asked.

Shona looked a little disappointed behind her mask. "Aw,

you knew about that? I was going to leave it as a surprise. Just, like, whip the sheet away and... Boom. No hands." She stared in silence at the DCI for a few seconds, before clearing her throat. "Which, now I say it out loud, would've been inappropriate. But yes. Hands last. He'd lost a good percentage of his blood before then."

Logan nodded and looked the body up and down, focusing more on the feet-end, and less on the face, which was like something out of a nightmare. "Anything else?"

"I'd say you're looking at more than one attacker. At least two, probably more. The shape of the bruises on his arms and shoulders would suggest a couple of people held him," Shona reasoned. "If it was while his teeth were being pulled, then someone else would've had to have been on pliers duty. Strong, too. The ones holding him, I mean. Big hands."

"Anything in his system? Drink? Drugs?"

"Too early to say. I've already sent samples off to Toxicology, but it'll take a while. He's a habitual drugs user, though. Track marks on his arms, and a couple on his legs and feet. Varying ages, going back a few weeks up until the last few days."

"How long's a while?" Logan asked.

"For the full report? Days for preliminary. Could be a month waiting for the full spectrometry at the minute. I'm told there's a backlog at the lab. Funding cuts."

"Great," Logan grunted.

"If it helps, I did a basic alcohol blood test—not easy, given the amount of blood loss—and he'd definitely been drinking. I can tell you that, at least. How much or when? Can't say for sure. But there was alcohol in his system."

"Right. Hopefully, the full Toxicology report will clarify," Logan said.

"It should. Oh! I almost forgot," Shona said. She pulled back the sheet to reveal the victim's left arm. There was a deep gouge that ran almost from his shoulder to the crook of his elbow, the skin hacked away until only the flesh beneath it remained. "He also had this."

Logan joined her on the other side of the table, and leaned in for a closer look at the wound. The edges were neat, so whatever had been used to carve out the chunk of flesh had been sharp. The exposed muscle was a sickly pale shade of pinkish-grey, not the meaty-red Logan would've expected.

"Done after he was dead," Shona said. "Big chunk of skin and flesh just cut right out of him. Another trophy, I'm guessing."

Logan straightened and shook his head. "My money's on a tattoo," he said. "Common placement for one, and if you're going to the trouble of taking the hands and teeth to hide the guy's identity, you don't want a distinctive tattoo to make it all pointless."

"Of course. Yeah. Should've seen that," Shona said, and she seemed genuinely irritated that she hadn't.

"It's an educated guess. I could be talking shite," Logan told her. "Only mentioned it because I've seen the same thing before."

"No, it makes sense," Shona said. She bumped him with her hip. "On another note... It's good to see you, by the way. You're looking well."

Logan snorted. "I am bloody not."

"Well, I mean, forty percent of your face is covered, and the only thing I've got to compare you to is him," the pathologist said, indicating the body on the table. "So, I guess it's all relative."

She smiled at him behind her mask. "You hungry?"

Logan glanced down at the mutilated corpse. "Not particularly," he admitted.

"Oh," said Shona, a little crestfallen.

Logan shrugged. "But, I'm sure I could eat. You know, just ideally not in this room."

"Excellent!" said Shona, brightening immediately. "Because... You know how we've been talking about lunch, or dinner, or whatever for... Well, forever?"

"Aye," said Logan. "We may have mentioned it once or twice."

"Right. Well, I was fed up of it never happening, so I decided to take matters into my own hands," Shona said. She headed for the door, already pulling off her rubber gloves. "Come with me. I've had a bit of an idea."

IT WASN'T the lunch date Logan had been hoping for. Not by a long shot.

He'd never admit it, of course, but he'd had a plan for it. A nice restaurant. Some wine for her, a soft drink for himself. Music, maybe, not so loud that it interfered with their conversation, but a nice accompaniment.

That was the lunch he'd been hoping for. That would've been perfect.

What he got fell short of that ideal by some distance.

His *Pot Noodle* sat steaming on the stainless steel worktop beside him. It was chicken tikka flavour. "A new one!" Shona had excitedly announced, as she'd ripped the foil lids off both pots and poured in the boiling water with meticulous care and precision.

"You don't want it runny," she'd explained. "Too much, and you've got chicken tikka noodle soup, and who wants that?"

She'd slid Logan's to him along the worktop, like an Old West barman sliding whisky along the bar. He'd caught it with only the most minimal sloshing of scalding hot liquid, and had begun jabbing at it with his fork to break up the still hard-packed noodles.

"What are you doing?" Shona had demanded, practically

snatching the pot back out of his hands. "Leave it two minutes, *then* stir. Jesus, what are you, some sort of Philistine?"

"Oh. Sorry," he'd replied. "I generally just bash it into submission."

Shona had smirked at that. "Interesting insight into your psyche there, Detective Chief Inspector," she'd said, her amusement evidenced in the musical lilt of her Irish accent. Then, she'd set his pot down next to her own on the counter and hopped up onto the stool beside his.

"Well, this is—" Logan began, but Shona held a finger up for silence.

"Alexa!" she barked, with such sudden ferocity that Logan nearly jumped off the stool. Shona smiled apologetically and lowered her voice to a whisper. "Sorry. I'm sure the bitch ignores me on purpose."

She glanced back over her shoulder to make sure the top ring of the smart speaker was glowing blue, then spoke again.

"Play *Come on Eileen*."

There was a momentary pause, before an electronic voice replied: "Playing *Come on Eileen* by Dexy's Midnight Runners on Spotify."

She turned to Logan and grinned as the opening bars of the song played from the speaker.

Not too loud. A nice accompaniment.

"Good choice," Logan said. "You remembered."

"I did. And don't say I'm not good to you. Sure, it's an awful bloody song."

Logan leaned back on the stool in a show of mock outrage. He pointed to the smart speaker. "This?"

"Aye."

"What are you...? Are you even listening? Do you have ears?" Logan asked. "This is the greatest... Well, no, it's no' the greatest song ever written, but it's up there. Top ten. Top five, maybe."

"You're deluded," Shona laughed.

"Shh," said Logan. "Appreciate."

They listened, holding eye contact through the first verse and into the chorus. Shona shook her head. "Nope. Not getting it," she said. "You know who I feel sorry for?"

"Eileen?" Logan guessed, which brought a snort of laughter from the pathologist.

"Well, yes, obviously. Poor cow. But no. Duran Duran."

Logan frowned. "Eh?"

"Duran Duran. *Save a Prayer*. Clearly a better song by any conceivable standard, but this shite robbed it of getting to number one."

"It's not a better song!" Logan countered. "It's dreary guff."

"It's a far better song. There's not a metric available by which it isn't. And it was kept off number one by this and by... and I'm going to guess that you'll approve of this... *Eye of the Tiger*."

"A classic," said Logan, very much approving. "From *Rocky*."

Shona shook her head. "No."

"It bloody is," Logan told her.

"It's from *Rocky* 3," she told him.

She picked up her *Pot Noodle*, stirred it, and indicated for Logan to do the same.

"Oh. Is it? I always thought it was the first one. Is three the one with the big Russian fella?"

"That's *Rocky* 4. Dolph Lundgren. Three's the one with Mr T." She scowled and adopted her best Mr T voice. "I'll kill you, sucka!"

"Aye. So it is," Logan said. "And that was eerily accurate, by the way. Well done. Shut your eyes, and maybe, you know, cover your ears nearly all the way, and you'd swear it was him."

"I thank you. I'm a woman of many talents," Shona said, taking a little bow.

Logan finished stirring his noodles, then began twisting them around his fork.

"Jesus Christ," Shona sighed. "You've still to put the sauce in and leave it another two minutes. Seriously, have you never had one of these before?"

"Plenty," Logan replied. "But I'm no' a big one for following instructions."

Shona shook her head reproachfully. "There's nothing big or clever about slapdash *Pot Noodling*," she told him. She pointed to the little square sachet sitting on the counter next to the container. "Sauce."

Logan obediently tore open the sachet and stirred in the sauce.

"Now, leave it be," Shona told him. "Let it mature."

Logan chuckled at that. "*Mature*. It's no' a fine wine."

"No, it's better," Shona said. She shot the pot a slightly worried look. "Although, new flavour. This could all go horribly wrong."

Logan wanted to reply that, as lunch dates went, it hadn't exactly gone particularly right so far, but he couldn't. The fact of it was, this was... nice. Good.

Not perfect, obviously but how could it be? When had anything in his life ever come close to perfection? When had anything in anyone's?

The final few bars of *Come on Eileen* echoed around the office, then faded into silence.

"Right. You want to hear a real song?" Shona asked. She raised her voice without waiting for his response. "Alexa! Play *Then You Can Tell Me Goodbye* by Bettye Swann."

The smart speaker replied to confirm, then an acoustic guitar began to play. They both listened as a simple, sultry female voice started to sing. Logan watched Shona as she first hummed, then quietly sang along with the lyrics.

"Come on," she said, stepping down off the stool. She held a hand out, but he baulked at it.

"What? No."

"You don't dance?" Shona asked, her hand still outstretched.

"Not if I can possibly avoid it."

She reached over and took his hand. "Well, you can't," she told him, and he gave a resigned little grunt as he let her pull him up onto his feet.

The fingers of her right hand interlocked with his left, and her other hand went to his chest. Logan tensed at her closeness, suddenly filled with the type of self-consciousness he hadn't felt in years. Decades, maybe.

He began to shuffle in time with the music, one hand on her waist, her eyes gazing up into his.

"Wow," she whispered, staring up at him.

Logan felt himself blush. "What?"

She bit her bottom lip, fighting back the urge to laugh. "You really can't dance, can you?"

He spun her around with one hand, then caught her as he leaned her back. "Who says I can't?" he said, his face close to hers, breathing the same air.

"Well, aren't you just full of surprises?" Shona said. Her smile fell away, as her eyes searched his face.

Logan held her there, nestled in his arms, as the music continued to play.

He maintained that this wasn't the perfect lunch date. How could it be?

But it was, he reckoned, close enough.

His phone rang. Of course, it did.

He saw his own disappointment mirrored on Shona's face, and for a moment he considered ignoring it. Just letting it ring.

At any other time, he would've. But not today. He couldn't today.

And like that, the moment was gone.

He straightened, lifting Shona back up onto her feet.

"Sorry," he told her, reaching into his pocket.

"No. It's fine," she said. "Duty calls."

He took out the phone, and Ben Forde's name flashed up at him from the screen. Logan sighed. Never a bloody cold caller when you needed one.

"Ben?" he said into the handset. "What's up?"

"Where are you? You still at the hospital?"

"I am. Just... looking over the pathology findings. Why?"

"We've had... an incident. It's, eh... We think it's Petrie. There was a boy at a park. You should come in."

Logan turned and looked at Shona. She was back on her stool now, stirring her *Pot Noodle*. She read the meaning in the look without him having to say a word.

"It's fine," she whispered. "Go!"

Logan managed a thin-lipped smile, silently mouthed a, "Sorry," then turned and marched towards the door. "I'm on my way," he said into the handset. "What is it? What's happened?"

Shona watched the door swing closed behind him, then looked down at the steam rising from the abandoned plastic pot on the countertop.

"Alexa! Stop," she said.

The music cut off, and silence flooded the office.

But only for a moment.

"Playing *Stop* by The Spice Girls," Alexa announced.

"No, I don't..." Shona began, but then she rolled her eyes and shook her head. "Fine. Whatever."

As Ginger, Scary, Baby and the others began their tuneless caterwauling, Shona twisted her fork around in her noodles, blew on them to cool them, then slurped them down.

Alone.

CHAPTER THIRTEEN

LOGAN SAT AT ONE END OF A CORNER COUCH, TALKING TO the anxious, drawn-out looking woman perched at the opposite end.

He could hear Sinead rattling around through in the kitchen, hunting for mugs as the kettle came rolling to the boil.

"Miss Thomas... Louisa. I know you've already spoken to my officers, but if you could just take me through it again one more time, that would be really helpful," the DCI said.

Louisa Thomas was sitting forward, balanced right on the front edge of the cushion. One leg bounced up and down, shaking the couch all the way around to Logan's side.

"I don't know what... What else can I tell you?" she asked.

"I know it's upsetting to go over it again, but if you can go from the start, that would really help me out," Logan told her. "You were watching your son... Jaden. You were watching Jaden out of the window?"

Louisa nodded. She was young—mid-twenties or so—and lived alone with her boy. Her lips stretched out, becoming thinner as her eyes shimmered behind a wall of tears that had been building since Logan's arrival.

"He'd never been out on his own before," she said, her eyes going past Logan to the room's only window. "I'd told him no, but he kept going on and on. Everyone else did it. 'It's fine, Mum. It's safe.'"

She pressed a crumpled tissue to her mouth, cleared her throat a few times, then exhaled slowly and continued.

"So, I let him. I let him go. Told him not to go any further than the park. You can see it from the window."

Logan got up, crossed to the window, and looked out. The playpark was roughly two hundred yards away. Two squad cars were parked on the grass beside it. Their flashing blue lights reflected off the slide, and the swings, and the cordon tape that billowed on the breeze.

"I was watching him. I swear, I was keeping an eye on him," Louisa said behind him. "I just looked away for a couple of minutes. That was all."

"You can't blame yourself," Logan said, turning his back on the window. He returned to the couch, sitting a little closer this time. "None of this is your fault, Louisa."

She sniffed into her tissue and nodded, but she clearly wasn't convinced.

"Any sign of that tea, Sinead?" he called into the kitchen, giving her a moment to compose herself.

"We're working on it!" Sinead replied. "Just a sec."

Logan turned his attention back to the woman on the couch. "You looked away," he said. "Then what?"

"I looked back and... I couldn't see him. Not at first," Louisa said. "The sun was... It was bright, it made it tricky to..."

Her voice cracked. She sat up straight, drawing in a deep breath that pushed her chest out.

"You're doing brilliantly," Logan assured her. "I know how difficult this is."

"And then... And then..." Louisa pressed on, like she had to get it out now, had to be free of it. "I saw him on the swings, and there was a man there, and... and... he was grabbing Jaden by the... He had him by the arm. And he was pulling him. He was pulling him towards the exit! He was taking my son!"

The words were like an exorcism for all the fear and hurt churning around inside her. She sagged in the middle and flopped back onto the couch like her spine could no longer hold her upright.

"Davey saw it all. His front window looks out onto the park," she said.

"Davey?"

"Neighbour. Across the way," Louisa explained. "If he hadn't seen... Well, it doesn't bear thinking about."

"Tea's up," Sinead announced, opening the door to the kitchen and letting a boy go through first, proudly carrying a plate of chocolate digestives. "Jaden helped sort out the biscuits. He tells me he knows all your hiding places, Mum."

Louisa sat up as Jaden carefully placed the biscuits on the table.

"Oh, I know he does!" she said.

She beamed at the boy and pulled him onto the couch beside her. He snuggled in, wrapping an arm around hers and clinging to it like it was all that was anchoring him in place.

"Jaden had a big scare today, sir," Sinead said, handing Logan his tea and sitting on the couch beside him. "He's been telling me all about it. Haven't you, Jaden?"

Cooried up beside his mum, Jaden gave a quick single nod of his head.

"I've been hearing all about it," Logan said. "But he's back safe with his mum. No one's going to hurt him now."

"That's what I said, sir," Sinead replied. "And you'll never guess. Jaden's only done a picture of the man he saw at the park."

"Brilliant!" said Logan. He smiled at the boy. "Can I get a look, Jaden? You gonnae show me?"

Jaden looked up at his mum for reassurance, and she gave it with a nod and a smile. "Go get it. It's really good."

"It'll be a big help, Jaden. It'll help us to catch the bas—" Logan stopped short just in time. "It'll help us to catch the bad man who grabbed you."

Jaden slid off the couch like he was melting onto the carpet. He rummaged under the coffee table until he found a sheet of A4 paper. Logan watched as the boy clutched it in both shaking hands and stared at the drawing he'd done. Fear blazed behind his eyes, the image representing the worst, most terrifying moment of his young life.

"Mind if I see, son?" Logan asked. He held a hand out, and Jaden was only too eager to be rid of the thing.

Logan studied the sheet for a moment, then flicked his gaze to the boy still sitting on the floor. "You never did this! It's really good," he said, which brought a flighty, tentative smile to Jaden's face.

The image wasn't going to be hanging in any galleries anytime soon, but for a five-year-old, it was a solid effort. It showed a man with dark rings around his eyes, and a vile, twisted leer that contorted the lines of his face.

There was something on the ground next to him that looked like a bobble hat. The head that the hat should have covered had hair on one side, and a jagged, angular dent on the other, which the boy had added zig-zag red lines to.

"What's this bit?" Logan asked, pointing to the lines.

Jaden squirmed on the floor, like he didn't want to think about it again.

"Tell him, pet," his mum urged.

"He had a sore bit," Jaden said.

"Was he bleeding?" Logan asked.

Jaden shook his head.

"Was it an old-looking sore bit?"

Jaden nodded.

"And did he speak to you, Jaden?" Logan asked. "Did he say anything?"

"Sort of."

Logan frowned. "Sort of? How do you mean?"

"He said stuff, but he didn't speak properly," Jaden said.

The boy took a biscuit from the plate, then climbed back up onto the couch and tucked himself in at his mum's side. He was so far back that Logan could barely see him.

"How did he speak?" Logan asked.

Jaden took a bite of his biscuit and chewed it before replying.

"He whispered."

LOGAN STOOD at the Big Board, Jaden Thomas's drawing held in one hand, a photograph of Owen Petrie in the other.

Even without the additional details the boy had provided, the resemblance was there. The big dunkle on the skull was the biggest giveaway, but the boy had nailed the bastard's eyes, too. Dark. Soulless. The eyes of evil itself.

He pinned both images close together on the otherwise unmarked board, then turned to face the rest of the room. Ben, Hamza, and Tyler were sitting at their desks, chairs angled to face him. Sinead had joined them, but sat slightly apart from them, like she felt she didn't quite belong.

It was also, Logan thought, a deliberate attempt to put distance between herself and Tyler, because she was too professional to do otherwise.

They all watched him in silence, waiting for him to deliver some words of wisdom, or genius insight that he didn't possess. He couldn't give them those things, but there was one thing he could give them.

The truth.

Or, most of it, at least.

"Owen Petrie—Mister Whisper—is in Inverness," he announced. "I have... suspected he might be since yesterday evening, after I found this."

He deposited an evidence bag on Ben's desk with a *thunk*. Everyone except Ben himself leaned in for a closer look.

"It's a badge," Logan explained. "It belonged to the orderly Petrie killed while making his escape from Carstairs."

"Where'd you get that, sir?" Hamza asked.

Logan rolled the response around in his mouth, like it was resisting him.

"In my flat," he eventually said. "In my bed."

"What the fuck, boss?" Tyler gasped. "He was in your flat? In your *bedroom*?"

Logan nodded. "Aye. Looks like."

"How did he know where you live?" Sinead asked.

"From what we can tell, he was working with a doctor at the hospital. That doctor compromised the phone and PC of a senior officer down in Glasgow," Logan said. "I think that's most likely where he got the information."

"He was in your room last night, and you're only telling us now, sir?" asked Hamza. There was a touch of outrage about it, like the DCI had betrayed them in some way. "Why didn't you say anything earlier?"

"He did to me," Ben said, shooting the DC an admonishing look. "The Detective Chief Inspector is not obliged to share every piece of information with junior officers."

"No, I know that, sir, but this is—"

"That's enough, Detective Constable," Ben warned.

"No. He's right, Ben," Logan said. "On this, I should've said."

He took a deep breath, gave a shake of his head, then tapped the photo of Petrie with a knuckle. "You've all heard of Owen Petrie. You all know what he did. Only... you don't. No' really,"

Logan said. "Without being there, without seeing it, you couldn't possibly comprehend what the man is capable of. The things he did. To them kids."

Logan shook his head again, more firmly this time, like he was trying to chase away the mental pictures that were gathering there like hungry wolves.

"Just be grateful you weren't there. That you didn't see," Logan muttered. "And pray to God that you don't."

"What's the plan, boss?" Tyler asked. "How are we going to catch the bastard?"

"*We're* not. I am," Logan said.

"Eh?" Ben ejected. "What you talking about, Jack?"

"Petrie's here for me. He's after me, and he will kill anyone he thinks stands in his way," Logan explained. "I can't put you at risk."

"At risk?" Ben said, his voice climbing higher.

"Your job—all of you—is to focus on the body found this morning. Someone somewhere has lost a son, or a father, or a husband, or whatever he may be. We need to find out who he was, and then—"

"Hold on just a minute, Jack," Ben said, pushing back his chair and standing up. "Obviously, we're going to work on the murder. That's a given. But you're not going after Petrie on your own."

"I didn't say I was going after him," Logan said. "He'll come to me."

"Well, he'll find us all bloody waiting for him," Ben replied.

Logan looked the Detective Inspector in the eye. How many years had they known each other now? Eighteen? Twenty? Ben had just been out of the army when they'd met—older than Logan, but newer to the force. They'd hit it off almost immediately, and their friendship had only grown since.

Which was why he couldn't let him get involved. Not in this. Not Owen Petrie.

"I'm perfectly able to look after myself, Benjamin. But thank you for your concern," Logan said.

"Bollocks to 'concern,' Jack!" Ben protested. "Anyway, this isn't just about you. A wee lad was nearly taken today. We both know what would've happened to him, you and I better than most. This isn't just about you now. It's about the kids out there. It's about his next victim."

"I'm going to take care of it," Logan assured him. "There'll be no more victims."

"How the hell can you possibly know that?" Ben demanded. "He could be out there grabbing a kiddie off the street right now for all we know!"

"You'll just have to trust me."

"I trust you on most things, Jack. I'd trust you with my life. But, you've never seen straight on Petrie. The bastard's always gotten under your skin. On your own, you'll make mistakes. You might not see him coming. Together, with all of us, we can—"

"That's enough, Detective Inspector," Logan said, raising his voice to silence the older man.

"Enough? I've no' even got started—"

"I said, that's enough!" Logan roared. The ferocity of it took the whole room by surprise. "I am the senior investigating officer here. I decide what resource is allocated where, and you—the lot of you—are working on this morning's homicide. Is that clear?"

He glowered at them—Ben in particular—daring any of them to object.

"I said, *is that clear?*"

"Clear, sir," said Hamza.

"If that's what you want, boss," Tyler added.

Sinead just gave a nod, while Ben stood eyeballing the much larger man standing before him.

"Crystal, Jack. Just crystal," DI Forde said through gritted teeth, then he more or less threw himself back into his chair and folded his arms across his chest.

Turning, Logan tore down the pictures he'd stuck to the Big Board and tucked them under his arm. "Petrie's mine. He's nothing to do with you. You're not involved. None of you. I'll take care of him myself. DI Forde's lead on the homicide, reporting directly to me. I want the body ID'd, then I want to know who killed him."

He glared around at them, making sure there were no further objections, then went storming towards his office.

"Good," he said. "Now, get on with it."

IT WAS three whole minutes before one of them knocked on his door. Logan had expected Ben to follow him into the office for an almost immediate round two, but he hadn't. Nobody had, and Logan was just starting to think they'd gotten the message when there was a rapping on the glass on the other side of the blinds.

"What?" he called.

The door opened, revealing Sinead in her uniform. "Got a minute, sir?"

Logan sighed, deliberately suggesting he very much did not have a minute, but he motioned for her to enter and sat back in his chair, waiting for her to speak.

There was a *click* as she closed the door behind her.

"What can I do for you, Constable?" Logan urged. "As you know, we've a lot to be getting—"

"That was out of order, sir," Sinead told him.

Logan blinked in surprise. His chair let out a low moan as he shifted forward in it, leaning his elbows on the desk as he fixed Sinead with one of his better glares.

"It was, was it?"

"Yes, sir," Sinead said, not flinching. "They all care about you. *We* all care about you. We want to help."

"Ben put you up to this, did he?"

Sinead shook her head. "He told me not to. But, I thought, if anyone's going to fire me for it, it'll be you, not him."

She sat on the chair across from him, the rubbing of one finger against her thumb the only indication of her nervousness.

"I don't know about the Petrie case. Not really. Only what I've heard. But I know how it affected you, sir. Your relationships. You told me yourself, how it made you drive everyone away. Your wife. Your daughter."

Logan's face remained impassive as he listened in silence.

"And, well, I know I'm out of line, sir, but it seems to me like that's what you're doing again. Pushing people away. People who care about you. And, well, I don't think you should. If you ask me, that's the last thing you should be doing." She smiled sympathetically. "I know you don't believe it, but you need people around you. People you can trust. Now, more than ever, sir."

Logan ran his tongue across the back of his teeth, then clicked it against the roof of his mouth. "You done?" he asked.

A look of shock flitted like a shadow across Sinead's face, then was gone. She nodded. "I've said my bit, sir."

"Good," Logan said. "Then get out of my office and get back to work."

She was hurt by that. He saw it in her eyes. But, she nodded, stood, then pushed the chair in and headed for the door.

"Sinead," Logan said, as her fingers touched the handle.

She turned. "Sir?"

Logan contemplated his next sentence for a long time before coming out with it. There were so many things he wanted to say.

But so many things he couldn't.

"I appreciate the concern," was all he said in the end. "Please close the door behind you on your way out."

CHAPTER FOURTEEN

"TOLD YOU," SAID DI FORDE, AS SINEAD EMERGED FROM the office. "He's a stubborn bugger. Although, I have to say, I'm impressed you made it out in one piece. He must think very highly of you."

Sinead gave a thin-lipped smile. "I said my bit, sir. All I could do." She cleared her throat and straightened her back. "And sorry for disobeying your order. I understand if you want to start disciplinary action."

"Och, away you go," Ben told her. "All that paperwork? How about you just help us out here? Reckon that should be punishment enough for you."

"Sounds good, sir," Sinead said. "And thanks."

She glanced back at Logan's closed door, then looked from Tyler to Hamza. Tyler was rocking back in his chair, twiddling a pencil, while Hamza was staring at his computer screen, eyes flitting left to right as he read.

"Anything you want me working on?" Sinead asked.

"I'd say you can help Tyler, but he appears to be doing bugger all," Ben replied. "What *are* you doing, DC Neish?"

Tyler stopped twiddling his pencil, then reached over and

clicked his mouse a couple of times. "I'm, eh, just..." He knew the charade wasn't standing up to scrutiny. "Nothing yet, boss. You didn't give me anything."

"Jesus Christ, son. How about you try using your initiative for once?" Ben sighed. "There's plenty needs doing. Pick one and get on with it."

"YES!" Hamza roared, thrusting both hands into the air. All eyes turned his way, and he quickly dropped his arms again. "Shite. Sorry. It's just... the roadworks being done at the new roundabout on the A82, they've had a load of stuff nicked off site recently."

"Magic!" Tyler cried, emulating Hamza's upwards arm thrust. "But in what way is that good news?"

"Because, ya fanny, they installed CCTV on-site three days ago."

Tyler still had his hands held above his head. He lowered them and frowned. "Still not getting it."

"The new A82 roundabout," Hamza began, turning his monitor for the other DC to see. "Is right by the entrance to the Premier Inn where the body was found."

"The van!" Tyler exclaimed.

"The van," Hamza confirmed. "If the van headed into the city, their camera will have got it. Hell, depending on where it's set up, whichever way the van went, the camera might have got footage."

"Bloody hell, nice find, Ham."

"Let's not get too excited yet," said Ben. "One of you go over and check it out. Get them to show you it."

"They sent a link to the footage with their reply, sir," Hamza replied. He clicked to download, then clicked again to confirm. A timer appeared in the middle of the screen. "I'm getting it now. Be done in five, ten minutes."

He reached for his mug, looked disappointed when he

found it empty, then held it out for Tyler. "Your turn on tea run."

"What? How is it my turn?" Tyler asked.

"Because you didn't find the CCTV footage," Ben told him. "And because you're doing nothing else."

Tyler tutted. "Aye. Fair enough," he said, reluctantly dragging himself to his feet. "Boss?"

"Don't mind if I do," Ben said, offering up his mug. It *chinked* against Hamza's as Tyler threaded his fingers through both handles.

"Want a hand?" Sinead asked. She turned to Ben. "Unless you need me here, sir?"

"I'm sure we can spare you for five minutes," the DI told her. He raised a finger and pointed to them both. "But no funny business."

TYLER HEADED for the fridge while Sinead put water in the kettle and switched it on to boil. The DC squatted down, recoiling from the smell of an egg sandwich some selfish bastard had decided to contaminate the place with.

"Shit," he said, after checking in the shelf on the inside of the refrigerator door. "We're out of milk."

"What's that there?" Sinead asked, pointing to a tall plastic bottle with a green lid.

"That's CID's. They go batshit if we take that," Tyler said. He tapped the top of a smaller bottle. Blue lid, this time. "And that's Detective Superintendent Hoon's. Apparently, we're welcome to use it, but he gobs in it. He made a point of telling us that *after* we used it last time."

He closed the fridge, leaned past Sinead, and clicked off the kettle. "There's the vending machine. We can try that. Boss won't be pleased, but if it's that or Hoon's saliva, he'll take the machine."

Tyler brushed his hand against hers, then quickly stepped back when the door to the staff canteen opened and one of the Detective Sergeants from CID came in.

She stopped just inside the doorway, regarding them both with suspicion.

"Alright, Sarge?"

The DS looked them both up and down. "Yous'd better not have touched our milk."

"Haven't been anywhere near it," Tyler replied. "Scout's honour. We were just heading to the vending machine."

The Detective Sergeant pulled a mildly horrified face. "Aye. Well. Good luck with that," she said, then she held the door open and motioned for them both to go.

———

A FEW MOMENTS LATER, Tyler stood pumping coins into the vending machine, with Sinead by his side.

"You think Logan's going to be OK?" she asked as she passed him another pound coin.

"The boss? Oh. Aye. He's pretty much indestructible by this point, I'd have thought. Like the Terminator, but bigger, and with less emotional range."

"Ha. Aye. Maybe," Sinead said.

"What time you finish?" Tyler asked, feeding more money into the machine's slot.

"Eh, not sure. Thought I'd hang on until the DI kicked me out. So, whenever, really."

"Nice one. What about your brother? Who's getting Harris from school?"

"Auntie Val. She's picking him up and watching him until

I'm done," Sinead said. "Or maybe overnight, depending on when I get done."

"He'll be alright with that, will he?"

"Alright? Aye. You can say that again."

"Auntie Val? Can I get another drink?"

Harris lay on his front on Val's big leather couch, fingers frantically prodding at the controllers on the side of the Nintendo Switch console. Val had bought it especially for his visits, along with a stack of games that Sinead had complained must've set her back a fortune.

"Another one?" chuckled Val, poking her head around the doorframe. "Your bladder's going to burst at this rate. Coke?"

"Yes, please!"

"Right you are," Val said. She smiled as she watched him jabbing furiously at the buttons. "And I'll see if I can rustle up a wee slice of cake."

Tyler finished putting in the money, then thumbed one of the buttons. A red light flashed up on it, indicating the dispenser was empty.

"Oh, for fuck's sake," he grumbled, pressing the button several more times in case the machine just wasn't looking hard enough.

"What's it out of this time?" Sinead asked.

Tyler leaned in closer to check the position of the light. "Water, apparently."

"How can it be out of water? Is it not plumbed in?"

"No idea," Tyler said. He jabbed in the button that was supposed to spit his money back out.

It didn't.

"What a heap of shite," he complained, giving the thing a dunt with his shoulder. "This is what happens when you use your initiative. You get your money nicked."

"Want me to go across the road and get takeaway?" Sinead suggested.

Tyler winced and smiled. "Would you mind?" he asked. "I'd go, only…"

"You can't be arsed."

"Basically, aye."

She grinned at him, then they leaned in and kissed so quickly Tyler wasn't quite sure it had actually happened. He decided to try for a second helping, but Sinead blocked him with a hand on his chest.

"Go. Detect," she told him, then she wheeled around and set off along the corridor. "And if you're lucky, I might bring you back a cake."

"AND A COFFEE, PLEASE," Sinead said. "Black, two sugars."

The man behind the counter at the takeaway barely qualified as a fully-grown man at all. He was sixteen or seventeen, she guessed, and while his fingers flew across the touch screen till with a speed and grace that suggested he'd been born for the job, any part involving anything resembling conversation seemed to be beyond his grasp.

He'd already addressed her by three different titles – miss, ma'am, and—a bit worryingly—sir. She'd have said it was the uniform that made him nervous, but she'd been three back in the queue when she arrived, and he'd been just as awkward with the other customers, too.

"Thanks," he said, once he'd finished tapping her order into the touchscreen.

She waited for him to say more. He stared back at her with a blank, vacant sort of expression that suggested his mind was an open book. And probably a picture book, at that.

"Something wrong?" he asked her.

"How much is that?" she replied.

"Oh. Aye. Sorry," he said, looking down at the screen.

He had just formed the first syllable of the price when a thought hit him. Physically, given the way his head snapped back and his eyes widened in shock.

"Wait. Are you with the police?" he asked.

Sinead resisted the urge to look down at her uniform, or the word 'Police' on the Velcro badge above her left breast.

"I am. Why? Everything alright?"

"No. I mean, yeah. It's just, there was a guy who wanted to pay for your coffee."

"What guy?" she asked. "What did he say?"

"Just... a guy," the boy said. "He might still be in."

Sinead turned her attention away from the counter. The takeaway was attached through an archway to a small family restaurant. Most of the tables were empty, but a man in a flat cap sat hunched at one in the far corner, his back to the counter.

"Is that him?" she asked.

The boy scrutinised the man's back for a painfully long time, then nodded. "I think so, aye. Maybe. He said he wanted to buy coffee for the next police person that came in."

"Officer," Sinead said, still staring at the man in the hat.

"Eh?"

"Police officer. Not person," she said.

"Right. Sorry. Want me to take it off his money? He left twenty quid."

Sinead stepped away from the counter. "Give me a minute, will you?" she said.

Then, before the cashier could answer, she squeezed past a

woman with a buggy and headed through the archway into the restaurant.

The man was gazing out of one of the big windows at the police station across the road. There was a large coffee on the table in front of him, steam rising from the tall glass mug. The hair she could see below the back of his hat was a salt and pepper of whites and greys. It stopped just above the collar of his battered-looking beige raincoat.

There was background music playing in the restaurant—Radio 2, Sinead thought—but she could hear him humming to himself as she approached, his fingertips dancing on the table like he was practising the piano.

"Uh, hello?" she said, when she was right behind him.

His fingers stopped. The humming died in his throat. He turned slowly in his chair and looked up at her from below the peak of his cap.

"Hello?" he said. His voice was dry, like Autumn leaves being crushed underfoot. "Is there a problem?"

"Did you... Did you leave money, sir?"

"Money?" He flitted his tongue across his lips, wetting them. "How do you mean?"

"Someone left money to buy us coffee. The police, I mean. The cashier thinks it might have been you."

"Ah. Yes. That was me," he said. "I thought... they do such an important job, and they just don't get the thanks they deserve. It's not much. A gesture, that's all."

"Right. OK. Well, thank you," she said. "It's very much appreciated."

"And you're very much welcome, Constable," the man replied. "You and all your colleagues."

"Yes. Well... thanks again," she said.

She started to turn away, but then stopped, her eyes drawn to the man's cap.

"Was there something else?" he asked her.

He was about the right age. Similar build, from what she'd seen of him. The peak of the hat was shadowing his face, making it difficult to make out clearly.

The hat would reveal the truth, of course. Or, what lurked beneath it would.

"Uh, odd question. Your hat, sir. Would you mind removing it?"

The man tilted his head to one side and peered up at her through the veil of shadow.

"Removing it?" he echoed. "My hat? Why?"

Sinead was suddenly aware of all the children in the restaurant. Laughing. Playing. Colouring in their menus.

She was also painfully aware of the knife and fork on the table, well within easy grabbing distance for the man sitting before her.

"We're looking for someone who matches your description, sir," she said. "If you take off your hat, I'll be able to confirm."

"I don't like to take my hat off if I can avoid it," the old man told her. He shifted his gaze around at the parents and children dining in the restaurant, then dropped his voice into a low, hushed whisper. "It's rather embarrassing, you see."

"Please remove your hat, sir," she said, more forcibly this time. "You can do it here, or you can do it at the station."

"I'm no lawyer, Toots, but I'm fairly confident you can't arrest me for wearing a hat," the man said. His eyes seemed to twinkle in their deep pools of shadow. The only part of his face that was clearly visible was his smirk.

She could feel the eyes of the other diners on her now. The low murmuring of conversation had faded into an expectant hush.

Sinead stole a look out the window at the station, hoping to see back-up sauntering over, but nobody was coming. She was on her own.

She stared back into those shadowy depths.

"Sir, I'm going to ask you again one more time. Please remove your hat."

"This is the thanks I get, is it?" He sighed. "Try to do a nice thing, and this is the thanks I get."

He got up slowly, his movements careful. Meticulous. He wasn't as tall as Sinead, but there was a presence about him that made him seem larger than his physical frame suggested.

The man dabbed at his mouth with his napkin, cast his gaze around at the other diners, then gave a resigned shrug. "Fine. Whatever you say, officer."

Sinead felt the world go into slow motion as his hand came up and caught the peak of his cap. Her eyes remained trained on it, but she stepped back, buying herself space in case he tried to make a grab for her.

And then, with a self-conscious cough, he lifted the hat, revealing a perfectly smooth, undamaged skull. His hairline had receded all the way up his head and set up camp there in an unflattering straight line that crossed the summit on a slightly diagonal angle.

It was, Sinead thought, the most unfortunate case of male pattern baldness she'd ever seen.

"Happy?" he asked, eyes darting around with shame and embarrassment. "Can I...?"

"Sorry. Yes. Sorry," Sinead said. "Sorry, I just... Sorry. I'm really sorry."

The man gave an unhappy little scowl, then pulled his hat low on his head and sat back down at the table. Turning his back on her, he reached for his coffee with a shaking hand.

Sinead turned, and the eyes of almost everyone in the building darted down to their food, or across to the person sitting opposite. Her journey back to the counter was accompanied by hushed words and murmured whispers which she did her best to ignore.

"Here's your drinks, sir." The lad behind the counter tutted and shook his head. "Miss. Ma'am. Sorry."

"Thanks," said Sinead. She reached into the front pocket of her vest and took out a bank card.

"I thought the old boy was paying for it?" the cashier said.

Sinead glanced back at the old man at the table. "Yeah," she said with a wince. "I think he'll probably be asking for his money back."

CHAPTER FIFTEEN

TYLER REGARDED THE STACK OF PRINTOUTS THE uniformed officer who stood over him had deposited on his desk. It was about half a ream's worth of paper, divided into about fifteen card folders.

"Eh, what's this?" he asked, looking up at the female officer. She was in her mid-forties, with a fierce look about her that suggested she didn't suffer fools gladly. Or, at all, for that matter. "Sarge," he hastily added when he saw the stripes she wore.

"Missing persons," she told him. "You wanted to see if anyone matched the description of your body."

Tyler sized up the pile on his desk. "Oh. Right. Aye," he said. He leaned past her and looked over at DI Forde. "Initiative. See?"

"It doesn't count if I have to tell you to do it," Ben replied, not looking up from his PC.

Tyler tutted, then fixed on his most winning smile—the one he saved for special occasions—and took aim with it at the sergeant. "Thanks for this. It's just... I thought you were going to go through it for me."

The sergeant let out a derisory snort. "Aye. Well, you

thought wrong. Keep dreaming, son," she said. "They're all yours."

She gave Ben a nod of recognition and left the Incident Room before Tyler could offer any further objections.

"Shit," Tyler muttered.

He shot a sideways look at Hamza. DC Khaled was sitting back in his chair, watching the CCTV footage on his monitor and crunching noisily on a packet of *Polos*.

"Want to swap?" Tyler asked.

"Nothing ventured, nothing gained, eh?" said Hamza, not turning. He shook his head. "But no. Definitely not."

Tyler tutted and sighed. "Can I have a Polo, then?"

Still not taking his eyes off the screen, Hamza tore the paper and silver foil of the packet just enough for a single mint to protrude, then offered it out to Tyler.

"Cheers," Tyler said, taking the mint and popping it in his mouth.

"They're the sugar-free ones," Hamza said.

Tyler physically recoiled, like the other DC had just told him the sweets had been dipped in dogshit.

"What? *Why?*" he asked.

"Calories," was Hamza's only explanation. He gestured to the screen. "Now, shut up, I'm trying to concentrate."

Tyler moved the sugar-free Polo around in his mouth with the tip of his tongue, bouncing it from tooth to tooth like he was deliberately trying not to taste it.

With a groan, he reached for the uppermost folder on the pile and opened it on the desk in front of him. A woman in her thirties stared sullenly up at him from the page. She had a haunted, hunted look to her, and Tyler immediately concluded that she'd killed herself.

"Nope."

He placed the printout to one side, then looked into the eyes of a man who'd gone missing seven years previously. Considering he was in his late-eighties at the time of his disappearance, Tyler reckoned the chances of finding him fit and well now were slim.

"Not you..."

"You're not going to say something for every single one, are you?" Hamza asked. He still had his eyes trained on the screen, watching black and white traffic go trundling by.

Tyler sniffed. "I might."

"Can you say it silently, then?" Hamza asked. "Because you're only two in, and it's already getting on my tits."

Tyler rattled the Polo around inside his mouth. *Clack-clack-clack.*

"Fine," he said. He glanced at the pile of reports, then rolled his chair closer to the other DC's and groaned. "Aw, come on, just swap."

Hamza looked back over his shoulder at Tyler. "No. I'm not swapping. I came up with the lead. I got the footage. I'm going to sit here and watch it until—"

"There," Tyler said, stabbing a finger past him at the screen.

Hamza's head snapped back to the screen. "What? No. What?" he yelped. The footage showed a car and a bus go trundling south on the A82. "You winding me up?"

"No. Rewind. Honestly," Tyler urged.

Hamza eyed him suspiciously, then scrubbed backwards through the footage a few seconds.

"Play from there," Tyler said.

"Aye, I know," Hamza said, suddenly defensive. "I've been watching that for bloody ages, see if you've come swanning in and..."

"There. See it?" said Tyler, pointing to the screen again.

Hamza tutted. "Of course, I see it. It's a big van."

"You would've missed that, if it wasn't for me," Tyler crowed, sitting back in triumph.

"Would I bollocks! It was your fault I turned around. I'd have been looking right at it if you hadn't come trundling over."

Tyler patted the other DC on the shoulder. "Aye. Keep telling yourself that, Ham. You've got to help me with the missing persons files now, by the way. Fair's fair."

"How's that fair?!" Hamza protested. "You literally looked over my shoulder for two seconds!"

"Fair's fair, Detective Constable. Come on," Tyler said, adopting a smug expression and superior attitude that would, in almost any other company, have earned him a smack in the mouth. "I helped you, you can help me. I scratch your back, you scratch mine. *Mi casa, su casa.*"

"I don't think that means what you think it means," Hamza said.

"Whatever. Which half do you want?"

Hamza glowered at him, then turned away and straightened to look over the top of his monitor. Ben sat at his own computer, pecking at the keys with two fingers.

"We've got the van, sir," he announced.

"Well, 'we' is being a bit generous," Tyler added, then he wheeled back in his chair and narrowly escaped getting a dead leg.

"Can you get a plate off it?" Ben asked.

Both detective constables looked at the screen. "Bit fuzzy," Hamza reported. "But I could maybe try to sharpen it up, only DC Neish wants me to help go through the missing persons files."

"DC Neish is perfectly capable of going through those on his own," Ben said.

"But I found the van!" Tyler protested.

"Right. Well, do you want to try using your technical wizardry to sharpen up the CCTV footage, then?" the DI asked him.

Tyler looked from Ben to the image on screen, then to

Hamza. Finally, he tutted and rolled his chair all the way back to his own desk. "Fuck's sake," he muttered. "I'll go through them myself."

"Go through what yourself?" asked Sinead, appearing by his desk with a cardboard tray laden with paper cups.

Tyler grinned up at her. "Ah, Constable Bell," he said. He picked up roughly half of the folders and set them down beside the rest. "Just the very woman I was looking for."

"COME IN."

Sinead eased open the door to Logan's office, the cup of coffee held in front of her like a shield.

"Brought you a drink, sir."

He was sitting behind his desk, his sleeves rolled up, a notepad beside him cluttered with increasingly frantic-looking scribbles.

"Oh. Thanks," Logan said. He pressed on his eyes with finger and thumb and rubbed, then blinked a few times, clearing his vision. "Bloody computer screens."

Sinead searched the desk for a clear path to put the cup down on, then decided it was safest just to hand it to him. "Anything I can help with?" she asked, as he took the drink from her.

"No. Just going over some old stuff. Jogging the memory on a few details," Logan replied. "That's all."

"Right, well, if you do need anything, you know where we are."

"Aye. I know," Logan said. "And thanks for the coffee."

"There was only Detective Superintendent Hoon's milk in the fridge," Sinead said, and Logan pulled back from the drink like it was a cup of poison. "No, I mean... I went and got them across the road. So that we didn't have to use his."

"Thank Christ for that," Logan said, then he frowned.

"Hold on. What am I saying? I stopped taking milk months ago. And now, you know why."

Sinead laughed. "Makes sense," she said. "Well... bye for now, then, sir."

"The suit," Logan said, as the constable turned to leave.

"Sir?"

"The suit came from a charity shop."

Sinead nodded. "Aye. DI Forde's got Uniform..." She looked down at how she was dressed herself. "I mean, he's got some officers checking the British Heart Foundation, where it was bought, to see if anyone remembers anything."

"He kept the tag on," Logan said.

"I believe he did, sir, yes."

"Why would someone keep the tag on their clothes?" he asked. He said it like a teacher might who already knew the correct answer.

It took just a second or so for Sinead to work out what that answer was. "So they could return it."

"Right. They buy it, they wear it to some party or event, and then they return it and get their money back," Logan said. "So, what sort of one-off event might a fella with a history of drug abuse find himself having to attend that would require the wearing of a suit?"

"Court! A court date."

Logan raised his cup to her. "Worth a look, I'd have thought."

"Definitely. I'll get checking," Sinead said.

"Do that. And take the credit for it," Logan urged. "You practically worked it all out, anyway. I just nudged you along."

Sinead shook her head. "No, sir, it was you who—"

The phone on Logan's desk rang. He reached out and grasped the handset, but made no move to lift it yet.

"Please. Take the credit, Sinead," he said, and there was a

note to his voice that made it sound less like a request and more like a direct order. "You deserve it."

His eyes went to his ringing phone, then to the door, but she'd already taken the hint and was halfway through it. "OK. Well... will do, then, sir. Thanks again."

Logan waited until the door had closed before lifting the handset. "DCI Logan."

There was silence from the other end, but it was soft and muffled, like someone had accidentally dialled his number from their pocket.

"DCI Logan. Who's this?" he asked.

The silence shifted at the other end of the line. Definitely a pocket-dial, he thought.

He was about to hang up when the voice came creeping out of the dark.

"You didn't jump, Jack," it whispered. "On your head be it."

"Petrie!" Logan hissed. "Owen, listen to me, you need to—"

There was a click, then a hum and the line went dead. Logan squeezed the handset until his knuckles went white, then replaced it on the base unit.

Then, after a moment, he picked it up again and slammed it back down three or four times in rapid succession until there was a *crack* of breaking plastic.

"Fuck!" he spat at the world in general.

Grabbing the phone's base unit, he dragged it closer and fumbled through the menu options until he found the list of incoming calls. The latest was listed simply as 'unknown'.

Of course, it was.

He added to his previous *fuck* with a couple of *shits* and a particularly venomous *bastard*.

Then, the phone rang again and he pounced on it like a tiger on its prey.

"Petrie?" he hissed.

"Aye, in your fucking dreams, ye cock-thumbed bawbag," snarled the voice of Detective Superintendent Hoon.

He usually sounded angry—it was pretty much his default setting—but he was positively foaming-at-the-mouth-level seething now.

"Get your fat, useless arse through here to my office," he ordered. "Right. Fucking. *Now*."

CHAPTER SIXTEEN

"THE FUCK'S THIS I'M HEARING, JACK?"

Logan stood in Hoon's office, making a point of saying nothing until he knew exactly what had driven the Detective Superintendent into such a rage.

He had been standing at the window when Logan had entered, bent low, furiously trying to suck the fresh evening air in through the narrow opening allowed by the window's safety catch. He'd spun with surprising speed and grace, given the size of him, and had it not been for the desk blocking the way, Logan was sure the DSup would've come windmilling at him, fists flying.

Instead, he'd kicked his chair aside, slammed both hands on the desk, and asked the question again.

"Eh? What am I fucking hearing, Jack?"

Logan thought of the postcard in his coat pocket.

At least, he hoped it was still in his coat pocket. It had been a while since he'd checked.

His gaze did a quick sweep of the desk but saw nothing incriminating there.

"Is it all your blood whooshing about, sir?" Logan asked. "Because your face has gone quite red."

A stapler clattered against the wall on Logan's left.

"Do I look like I'm in the fucking mood for jokes here?"

Logan had to admit that no, he did not.

"Who's Jaden Thomas?" Hoon demanded.

"Jaden Thomas is a boy we spoke to earlier today," Logan said, trying very hard to hide his relief. This was fine. This, he could deal with. "He was at the park, and someone tried to grab him."

"Someone," said Hoon. It wasn't a question. It was more like he was drawing the DCI's attention to the word and inviting him to circle back to it.

"A man, sir. He... matched the description of Owen Petrie."

"And there it fucking is," Hoon said. "There's the topsy-fucking-turvy world we find ourselves in. Mister Whisper gets up to his old shite in my fucking town—in broad daylight, no less—and my own DCI doesn't feel that it's worth his bastarding time to tell me."

"I was compiling a report, sir. It would all have been—"

"Close that toothy fucking wound in your face until I say you can speak, Detective Chief Inspector," Hoon seethed. "Or maintenance'll be Vaxing you out of the fucking carpet."

He flexed his fingers in and out like he was counting up in tens, rapidly at first, then slower as he breathed in through his nose and out through his mouth. He made Logan think of Dr Jekyll trying to hold back Mr Hyde. Bruce Banner struggling to contain the Incredible Hulk.

Finally, he stopped flexing, clasped his hands together, and sat in his chair.

"Tell me the boy's alright, at least."

"He's alright. Freaked, obviously, but safely back home. Parents are split, but his dad's coming to stay over for a few nights," Logan said. "We've got Uniform checking in and keeping an eye."

"How'd he get away?"

"Neighbour intervened," Logan replied. "We spoke to him. Same description. He tried to give chase, but Jaden was upset and clung to him, so he couldn't. Petrie—assuming it *was* him—disappeared into the housing estate that borders the swing park. Uniform did a sweep, but he'd have been long gone by then."

"Well, obviously," Hoon said. "He's hardly going to hang about."

His voice was a lot softer following his breathing exercises, and the redness of rage had faded from his face. It wasn't gone completely—it never went completely—but he no longer looked like he was about to pop open like a pimple and fill the room with brains and pus.

"You want to know how I know about Jaden?" Hoon asked. He was smiling. This, Logan knew, was rarely good.

"How, sir?"

"Because I know fucking everything, Jack. That's important. I want you to remember that. I want you to keep that at the forefront of your fucking mind from here on in. *Hoon knows everything*. That's what I want you to be thinking at all times. Morning, noon, and fucking night," the DSup said. "And I'll know if you're not. Because, to reiterate, I know everything. Where this place is concerned, I am fucking omnipotent. Got that?"

"Got it, sir," Logan said.

"Specifically, though, you want to know how I found out about wee Jaden's run-in with the most notorious fucking child-killer in this nation's modern history, Jack? Because this'll surprise you. This'll blow your shrivelled wee brain out through your arsehole."

Hoon's smile was wider now. Bordering on manic. This did not bode well.

"How did you find out?" Logan asked.

"Because Louisa—Jaden's mum? She's my fucking niece, Jack," Hoon said, his eyes just about bulging out of their sockets with the effort of containing his rage. "Wee Jaden's my great-nephew. And he *is* a great nephew. I mean, I wouldn't fucking want him on my team at a pub quiz, but he's a great wee lad, so he is. Kind. Thoughtful. And now, oh-so-fucking-terrified."

Logan's head was spinning. Petrie trying to snatch one of Hoon's relatives couldn't be a coincidence, could it? What were the chances?

"I can see you and I are of a similar train of thought, Detective Chief Inspector," Hoon said, reading Logan's mind through his expression alone. "Of all the weans knocking about up here, what are the fucking odds he goes after the only one of the snottery-nosed wee bastards that's directly related to me? Not high, I'd have thought. No' unless it was fucking deliberate."

"Seems unlikely, sir, aye," Logan agreed.

"I'm glad we're in agreement, Jack," Hoon said. His hands were still clasped together, but the white spots forming at each of his knuckles revealed he wasn't as calm as he was trying to make out. "Now, keeping in mind what I said a moment ago about my all-seeing, all-fucking-knowing omnipotence.... Is there anything else you'd like to tell me?"

Logan stood his ground, uncowed and unblinking. He should tell him about the orderly's badge, of course. That was bound to get back to him before long. But, if he found out Petrie had been in Logan's room—that the bastard was acting on the vague threat scrawled across the poor bastard's chest back at Carstairs—then he might take him off the case before he was even officially on it.

And Logan wasn't about to let that happen.

"No, sir, I don't—"

Hoon leaned forward sharply a finger raising to silence the DCI.

"Wait!" he said, the word ejecting out with enough kinetic force to shift the paperwork around on the desk. "I want you to think very fucking carefully about the next words out of your mouth, Detective Chief Inspector. *Very* fucking carefully, indeed."

Logan's lips parted to speak. Hoon jabbed the finger at him again.

"At-at! *Very fucking carefully*, I said," Hoon reminded him. "And, just to make it a wee bit easier on you, if your answer doesn't contain the words, 'the bastard left a badge in my bed,' you'll be on immediate fucking suspension."

Logan's heart sank. *Shite*. So much for that plan.

The Detective Superintendent eyeballed him for a few lingering seconds, then lowered his finger, clasped his hands across his belly, and reclined in his chair.

"Now, on you go, Jack," he said, that dangerous smile twisting up the corners of his mouth and showing an uncomfortable number of teeth. "In your own time."

Logan's explanation took just a couple of minutes. The bollocking he received for it lasted considerably longer.

Eventually, though, Hoon's rage burned itself out. He dropped back into his chair, surrounded by scattered paperwork and broken stationery, ran through his breathing exercises again, then muttered something that might have been a calming mantra, but just as easily might have been a voodoo curse.

"Right. So. The badge. We've got that. Tick," the Detective Superintendent said. "You say you showed it to the team, and it's being logged. Fine. Would I have liked you to have told me about it sooner? Too fucking true, I would."

He took a breath again, catching himself before his temper could escalate. He pressed a finger against a spot on his wrist, taking his pulse, then continued.

"But, realistically, would me knowing have made any difference to anything? To wee Jaden? No. It probably wouldn't,"

Hoon said. "What it would've done was made me happy. And believe me, Jack, you want to keep me happy, if at all fucking possible. So, one more time—is there anything else I should know about?"

Logan thought of the postcard in the pocket of the coat currently hanging behind his office door.

He thought of the phone call that had come right before Hoon's own.

You didn't jump, Jack.

On your head be it.

"No, sir. Nothing else."

Hoon glowered at him, his stare so sharp it threatened to stab the DCI's eyes clean out of their sockets.

Logan held it. Calm. Composed.

A stark contrast to everything churning around inside him.

"One more time, Detective Chief Inspector," Hoon said, leaning forward in his chair. "Is there anything else you'd like to tell me?"

Logan couldn't tell him about the postcard. No way. He'd taken evidence from the scene of a crime. He wouldn't just be off the case for that, he'd be off the force.

"No, sir," he said again. "There's nothing else I'd like to tell you."

Hoon's gaze kept boring into him for a few more seconds, before the DSup grunted and sat back.

"Right. Good," he said. "Well, as it happens, I've got a fairly fucking juicy piece of gossip for you."

"Oh?"

"Dr Manan Ramesh. The prick who helped Petrie escape?"

"What about him?"

"Nonce."

Logan frowned. "Ramesh?"

"Computer's fucking overflowing with the stuff. Dates back years. Taskforce down the road has gone through some of it, but the sick fucker had tens of thousands of images on there. Abuse. Posing. Torture. You name it."

"Jesus."

"Aye. Taskforce has seen some of them before. Stuff that's been circulating a while. Kids who've already been identified," Hoon said. He had taken a pencil from the pot on his desk and was rolling it around between finger and thumb with enough force to make the wood groan under the pressure. "But there are images in there they've never seen before. New stuff. Recent, going by the fucking... codes. Whatever it's called. Data. In the picture. I don't fucking know."

The pencil snapped. He looked down at both halves in surprise, like he hadn't realised he'd picked the thing up in the first place, then returned them to the pot.

"There are other pictures there, too, Jack," Hoon continued, and he sounded almost apologetic. "The kids Petrie... took. Ramesh had photos of them. New ones. Well, not new, obviously. Unseen."

"Petrie shared them? How?"

Hoon shook his head. "No, not Petrie. Not directly. There's a suggestion that he and Petrie might have been part of the same group. A fucking ring of the dirty bastards. From what they can glean from his computers, Ramesh has been in with the fuckers for four or five years."

"Petrie could've told him about it when he was in doing his interviews," Logan said.

"Aye. Very possible," Hoon said. "We're hoping to get more, but they've hit a bit of a dead-end, tech-wise. There are no direct connections to other members of the ring, it was all done through... fucking... I don't know. The dark web. Fuck knows. However these fucking nonces do their thing."

"What about the other kids? Have they been identified?"

"I said we've got a taskforce working on it, Jack, no' fucking

Batman. These things take time," Hoon said. His tone softened. "But they're working on it. They'll keep us updated.

"Well, anything I can do to help..."

"You can help by getting the fuck out of my sight and back to work," Hoon said. "Oh, and from now on, I want to know everything that's going on in that Incident Room of yours. I want every fucking iota of information you have."

"I'll make sure we keep you in the loop, sir."

"Fuck keeping me in the loop. From here on in, I *am* the fucking loop, Jack. Every decision gets run through me. Every choice you're faced with, I'll be the one doing the choosing. I don't want you taking a shite without my prior fucking approval. Got that?"

Logan said nothing. There was no point trying to argue with Hoon when he was like this. Easiest just to ignore his orders and hope he didn't find out.

"I've got a call scheduled with the Gozer in the morning. I'll see what Snecky's come up with. Probably a big heap of fuck-all, knowing that useless bastard, but you never know," Hoon continued. "Oh, and we're getting CID in on this. The more the fucking merrier. And, we need to get a warning out to parents, pronto."

Logan would've gasped, but he wasn't really a gasping sort of man. Instead, he mostly just glowered, with a single eyebrow raised in surprise.

"You can't be serious, sir? We're not going public on Petrie, are we? We'll be hoaching with the bastards of the mass bloody media before we know it. They'll be crawling all over the place."

Hoon blew out his cheeks and shook his head. "I don't like it either, Jack. You know me. The only time I want to hear the words 'mass' and 'media' in the same sentence is when the words '*murder of every fucker working in the*' is jammed between them."

He gestured to the window, and to the darkening city beyond.

"But, funnily enough, much as I hate those wankers in the press, I dislike children being kidnapped and murdered even more. I mean, don't get me wrong, it's a close-run thing, but that one just takes it by a nose."

"What if we don't say it's Petrie? Not yet. Just say someone's making a grab for kids. Buy us some time before the vultures descend."

Hoon drummed his fingers on the desktop, considering this.

"You know what'll happen, sir. It'll be a zoo. It'll slow down the investigation, and put more kids' lives at risk," Logan said. "And, knowing Petrie, we'd be giving the bastard exactly what he wants. It'll be 'Mister Whisper' front pages on every rack. He'll be revelling in it."

The thought of Petrie basking in his notoriety was clearly too much for the Detective Superintendent. He threw himself back in his chair and stabbed a finger up at Logan.

"Fine. No names, just the warning. For now," he said. "But we both know, we can't contain this for long, Jack. Some bastard'll get wind of it. We've got to find that fucker and get him banged up before it all kicks off."

"Aye. Agreed, sir," Logan said

"Then why the fuck are you still standing there? Hoon asked. "Go. Find him. Do your fucking job while you've still got it."

"I have a request first, sir."

"A fucking *request*?!" Hoon said, almost choking on the word. "You winding me up?"

"Vanessa and Madison."

"Your wife and daughter? What about them?"

"Ex and... Aye." Logan cleared his throat. "With Petrie up here. I'd like to get them protection. Someone to keep an eye."

"I bet you fucking would," Hoon said. He leaned forwards

in his chair. "But first, I want you to answer me a question. Honestly."

Logan shifted his weight from one foot to the other. "What's that then, sir?"

"Your family. Your ex and your daughter... You didn't know he was going to come after you when you brought them up here, did you? Beyond the 'Hi Jack' message, I mean?"

Hoon was scrutinising the DCI, watching every movement of his face, every flicker of emotion that passed there.

"You didn't know they'd be in more danger up here than they were down the road when you packed them into my car? Did you?" he asked.

Logan's hesitation was fleeting, but it was there. He couldn't tell if Hoon had picked up on it or not.

"No, sir," he replied, with an emphatic shake of his head. "I did not."

Hoon's glare lingered for several long, uncomfortable moments, then he sat back. "I can arrange Uniform to keep an eye on the house." He checked his watch. "But it'll be tomorrow, now."

"Tomorrow?"

"Take it or fucking leave it, Jack."

Logan nodded. "Thank you, sir," he said. "Tomorrow will be fine."

CHAPTER SEVENTEEN

BEN FORDE LOOKED UP FROM HIS COMPUTER WHEN LOGAN returned to the Incident Room.

"Well, you've no' got your balls in your hands, so unless he's made you eat them, I'd say that must've gone pretty well," the DI remarked.

"Not the best. Not the worst," Logan conceded. "He wants all decisions in the Petrie case to go through him first. He is the loop, apparently."

"Aye. Well. Might be good to have a more objective viewpoint," Ben said. "Or... detached viewpoint, maybe. Aye. Detached. I'm no' saying you're no' objective, I'm just—"

"I get it, Benjamin, thank you," Logan said, cutting him off. "And aye. Maybe. He wants to bring in CID now that Petrie's made a move. Also wants us to put word out to the public."

Ben's eyebrows crept higher up his forehead in surprise.

"We're not naming him. Not yet, anyway," Logan explained. "But he wants parents aware that there's someone trying to nab kids off the street. The wee one who was nearly grabbed... Jaden."

"What about him?" Ben asked.

"He's Hoon's great-nephew. The mother's his niece."

Constable Bell and DC's Neish and Khaled all turned in their chairs at that.

"Bloody hell," Hamza remarked.

"I didn't think he had any relatives," Tyler added. "I thought he'd just been, like... *made* at some point. Like... built by the government."

"Coincidence?" asked Ben, ignoring both comments.

"Highly doubt it," Logan replied.

"Well, looks like we'll be getting involved whether you like it or not, Jack," Ben told him. "I mean, if he's getting CID to chip in..."

"We'll see," Logan said.

"Jack..."

"For now, your priority's the homicide."

"Aye. Well, we thought we had a bit of a breakthrough with that, actually," Ben said. "Sinead came up with a pretty clever theory about why the fella had the tag in his suit."

"Did she?" Logan asked, turning to the room's only uniformed officer.

Sinead blushed. "Didn't pan out, sir," she said. "Dead end, unfortunately."

"Well, worth a try though, I'm sure," Logan told her.

"Aye, it was solid detective work, alright," Ben confirmed. A knowing smile curved the lines of his mouth. "Worthy of yourself, even, Jack. She'll go far, this one."

Avoiding Ben's gaze, Logan looked over to the Big Board. It stood off to one side, like an unwelcome guest at a party, bare and untouched.

"You not putting anything up?" he asked.

Ben and the others exchanged glances.

"Didn't have the heart to, sir," Hamza said. "Didn't think we'd do it justice."

"I mean, we tried with the Canna case," Ben added. "But it just... It wasn't the same."

"No. You made an arse of that, right enough," Logan said. "No offence."

"None taken," Ben said. "I just don't have the knack for it."

Over at her desk, Sinead quietly cleared her throat. "I, eh, I could have a bash at doing it. You know, if you want." She looked across their faces. "It won't be as good as DS McQuarrie's. I mean, obviously. But..." She looked to Tyler for help. "I know you said having it laid out visually helped you. Didn't you?"

Tyler nodded. "Yeah. It did. It does. It's handy to have."

Logan gestured to the board. "If you think you can do it justice, by all means, have a bash."

"Right. OK. I will do then, sir," Sinead said.

Nobody moved.

"I'll, eh, maybe not do it with everyone watching, though," she said, her face reddening. "I'll hang off a bit and get it set up tonight."

"And then, we can all take the piss out of it in the morning," Tyler said, rubbing his hands together in gleeful anticipation.

Sinead gave him two fingers, but it was good-natured. Mostly.

Logan checked his watch. "Unless there's anything urgent you're waiting on, I'm going to suggest we call it a day," he announced. "Tomorrow could be a big day, and if Petrie tries anything, we might all be called in tonight. Best get some rest while you can."

Tyler quickly flipped closed the missing persons folder he'd been working through and got to his feet, already reaching for his jacket. "Sounds good to me, boss."

Hamza clicked the refresh button on his email inbox, and watched as absolutely nothing whatsoever happened.

"I'm waiting on word from DVLA. Got a partial plate match for a van seen near the hotel around the time we're interested in. Hoping they can give us something." He shrugged. "It'll come to my phone, if there's anything. I'm sure the wife won't complain if I'm home early."

"No doubt mine will," Ben said. He switched off his screen, then got to his feet. "But she'll just have to like it or lump it."

Logan nodded. "Good. Right. Well, I'll hopefully see you all in the morning, and not before."

"Night, boss," Tyler said, and the others chipped in with their own farewells before Logan retreated into his office to get his coat.

DC Neish hung back with Sinead while Ben and Hamza left the Incident Room.

"Sorry about the dig earlier," he said. "Force of habit."

"Aye, well, you won't be laughing when you see how good my Big Board is," Sinead teased. "You'll be blown away."

"Want me to stay and give you a hand?"

"No chance," Sinead said. "And have you take all the credit?"

"I wouldn't!" Tyler protested. He maintained the lie for three-fifths of a second, before conceding with a nod. "No, you're right, I totally would do that."

He stole a glance at Logan's door, then quickly leaned in and kissed her. It lingered for a second or two, before the squeak of the door opening made them both spring apart.

"Want me to come over later?" Tyler asked, as Logan came trudging towards them.

Sinead shook her head. "Better not tonight. By the time I get Harris back from Val's, it'll be late. I'll see you tomorrow."

"This man annoying you, officer?" Logan asked

"Constantly." Sinead grinned. "Don't know how I put up with it, sir."

"Either you've the patience of a saint, or you're filled with self-loathing. I haven't quite decided yet," Logan told her.

He looked over at the Big Board and let his gaze stare there for a long time.

"Right. Good luck," he eventually said, then he turned to Tyler and motioned towards the door. "After you, Detective Constable. Let's let the lady work."

Sinead watched them go, Logan walking behind Tyler, ushering him out the door with the weight of his presence alone.

Once they'd left, she turned to the Big Board, and perched herself on the edge of a desk, sizing it up. The blank emptiness of it seemed to look back at her, taunting her, daring her to cover it. Daring her to try.

She held her gaze on it, like she was trying to stare it into submission, and took her phone from her pocket. Her fingers moved on instinct, navigating to the phone screen and tapping on the face of her Auntie Val without breaking eye contact with the Big Board.

The Big Board, for its part, remained just as defiant as before.

The phone rang six or seven times before Val answered.

"Sinead. Hello! How you getting on?"

"Aye, not bad, Val. How's you two?"

"We're fine," Val replied down the line. "I mean, I'm run ragged, but you know me. I wouldn't have it any other way."

Sinead bit her lip before asking the next question. "Any chance he could stay over tonight? I think it's going to be a late one."

"Of course! I already told you, it's no problem," Val said. "It's a pleasure, actually. He'll probably eat me out of house and home by the morning, but he's a growing lad."

"Thank you so much, Val. I really appreciate it," Sinead said. "Is he there? Can you stick him on?"

Val's voice became simultaneously louder and quieter as she

leaned away from the handset and shouted. "Harris! Sinead wants a word."

There was a shouted reply that Sinead couldn't quite make out.

"He's coming," Val said, her voice closer again. "What about you? Have you eaten?"

"I'm fine, aye. Thank you," Sinead said.

"Make sure you get plenty to eat and drink. And take your breaks. You're entitled to them," Val said. "Oh. Here he is. Hang on."

There was some rustling as the phone was handed over, then Harris's voice was right there in her ear.

"Hiya. What's up?"

"Hey. How's it going?"

"Good. Auntie Val got me *Let's Go Pikachu* on the Switch."

Sinead heard an urgent mumbling in the background, and Harris quickly retracted his previous statement.

"Wait. No. She didn't."

Sinead smiled. "Tell her she's too bloody good to you. You OK staying there tonight?"

"Yeah. But my homework's at home, so I can't do that. You'll have to do me a note."

"Aw. You must be gutted. I know how you love your homework."

Her gaze hadn't shifted from the Big Board throughout the call. She could feel it pulling at her now, asking her to show it what she'd got.

"Right, I'd better run. I'll get you after school tomorrow. Be good, OK? Tell Auntie Val just to phone if there's anything."

"OK. Night."

"Night, Harris. Love you."

"Eugh," was Harris's disgusted reply, then the call was ended.

Sinead slipped the phone into her pocket and slapped her hands on her thighs.

"Right then," she announced. She grabbed a stack of *Post-Its* from Hamza's desk, and the sharpest pencil she could find. "Let's give this a bash."

CHAPTER EIGHTEEN

DC NEISH WHISTLED TO HIMSELF AS HE MADE HIS WAY across the car park to where he'd left his car. Logan, who held one of the cherished reserved spaces close to the entrance, had already gone sweeping past in his Volvo, blasting his horn right as he passed Tyler, and subsequently almost causing the detective constable to lose bladder control.

"Cheers for that, boss," he'd called after the car, earning a quick flash of the hazard lights in reply, before Logan hung a left onto Burnett Road and was absorbed into the evening traffic.

Tyler's car *chirped* happily as he tapped the button on his key fob. He was still whistling when he reached the driver's door and opened it, but spun suddenly on his heels when another vehicle skidded to a stop behind him, gravel crunching beneath its wheels.

"Fuck's sake, Ham," Tyler spat, lowering the fists he had instinctively raised. "I thought I was about to be abducted."

"Who'd want to abduct you?" asked Hamza, his side window gliding down. "I can't think of anything worse."

"Shut up. I'd fetch a pretty penny on the black market, I'll have you know," Tyler insisted.

"Aye, well, good luck with that." Hamza held up his phone and waved it at the other DC. "Just got an email from DVLA with a possible match for the van."

"Did you?" asked Tyler making very little effort to hide his almost total lack of interest. "Cool. Well done."

"You not going to ask what they've come back with?"

"I hadn't planned to, no," Tyler said. "But, I'm guessing you're going to tell me, anyway."

"Bosco Maximuke," Hamza blurted, unable to keep it to himself any longer.

Tyler perked up at that. "What? Seriously?"

"Aye. Van belongs to him. Registered to his company. I mean, that's if the plate says what I think it says, but I can't see what else it could be. So, yeah."

Tyler closed his car door and leaned against it, considering the ramifications of this new information. Bosco Maximuke was well-known to the team, and to Logan in particular. Bosco and the DCI went back years. Logan was the reason the Russian had moved his business out of Glasgow and up the road to Inverness.

Maximuke was a big player in the Scottish drugs scene. Everyone knew it. Finding a way to prove it, however, had thus far escaped them all. The man was either 'coated in Teflon' or 'a slippery fat bastard'. It depended on who you asked.

To say there was no love lost between Logan and Bosco was a fairly substantial understatement. Logan held the Russian at least partly responsible for the death of DS McQuarrie, and it was only a few days ago that he'd taken matters into his own hands and burned Bosco's Portakabin office to the ground.

Had Maximuke made an official complaint, Logan might well have been looking at the end of his career. Fortunately, given his understandable reluctance to have the polis snooping around his business, Bosco wasn't likely to be picking up the phone to the Complaints Commission anytime soon.

"So... what do we do?" Tyler asked. "Think we should forward it on to the boss tonight?"

Hamza shrugged. "Not sure. Which one? Ben, maybe. Think the DCI's probably got enough on his mind. And, if he thinks Bosco's responsible, he might go storming round there, and given everything that happened recently..."

"Probably not the best idea, no," Tyler agreed. "Maybe just sit on it until the morning? I mean, Bosco's not going to up sticks and leave town, and the victim's unlikely to get any deader overnight." He nodded like the decision had been made. "Aye. Leave it. Do the big reveal in the morning."

Hamza smiled with relief. "Great. I thought the same, but wanted to run it by you. Promised Amira I was on my way home. If I got dragged into something else..."

"God, no. Leave it. It'll keep until the morning," Tyler urged. "Get home. Tell her I said 'hello.'"

"What, and spoil her night?" Hamza replied. He chucked his phone into the dooket beneath the stereo. "See you tomorrow."

"Aye. Night," Tyler said, waving him off.

DC Neish got into his car, shoved the keys in the ignition, then pulled on his belt.

He looked back at the station, at the window of the Incident Room, where Sinead would no doubt be stressing over the Big Board, thinking she'd bitten off more than she could chew.

Come tomorrow morning, she'd blow them all away with it, of course. He had no doubts whatsoever.

Tyler drummed his hands on the wheel, beating out a tune-less rhythm. Beyond the car park, night was creeping in across the city. He should go home, grab a bite to eat on the way, maybe. Get some rest.

And yet...

"I'll show you bloody initiative," he muttered, then he

turned the key, crunched the car into reverse, and pulled out of the parking space.

MADDIE STOOD in the hallway near the front door, not yet reaching for the handle. There was a creak from behind her as Vanessa crept out of the kitchen, and Maddie motioned for her mother to stay back.

"Hello?" she called, adjusting her grip on the weapon in her hand. "Who is it?"

"It's me," came the reply, and both women sighed with relief.

"I thought you were going to phone ahead?" Maddie said, opening the door to reveal Logan standing out there on the step. Her brow creased when she saw his expression. "What is it? What's wrong?"

"Nothing. Nothing, it's... Can I come in?"

Maddie looked down at the threshold, as if only just realising she was blocking it, then stepped aside for him to enter.

"Nice frying pan," Logan remarked. "You'd do some damage with that."

"Don't tempt me," Maddie replied. She stole a glance out at the darkened street, then closed the door and turned the snib to lock it.

"Jesus Christ, who were you expecting?" Logan asked, noticing the long, serrated knife that was currently in the clutches of his ex-wife. "Jack the Ripper?"

Vanessa glanced down at the knife, then passed it from one hand to the other. Her face reddened, either through embarrassment or anger, it was hard to say which.

"It's late," she said. "You didn't phone ahead. We didn't know who it was."

"Aye. Well... good. Better safe than sorry. Well done." He eyed Vanessa warily. "But, eh, you can put it down now."

Logan headed for the living room while both women returned their respective weapons to the kitchen. He sat on the arm of the couch, decided it was better if he stood, and was barely back on his feet when Maddie appeared in the doorway.

"Want tea? Kettle's on?"

"Eh, no. No thanks."

"Bloody Hell," called Vanessa from the hallway behind her. "Must be serious."

"Can you... Can you both come in? I need to talk to you about something," Logan said.

Vanessa followed Maddie into the living room. Concern was etched across her face. "Shit, it is something serious, isn't it?" she asked.

She folded her arms and leaned all her weight on one leg, pushing out her hip. It was a stance Logan knew only too well. It meant she was anticipating an argument, and that she was bloody well ready for it.

"Well?" Maddie asked. Her body language was less aggressive than her mother's. More worried than soon-to-be-angry. "What is it?"

Logan had rehearsed the speech all the way over in the car. Or... no. Not *speech*. *Confession*. He'd carefully picked the right words, honed their order to minimise the fallout and the number of casualties. It had been right there in his head as he'd come striding up the path, on the tip of his tongue when he'd knocked on the door.

Now, though, it was nowhere to be seen. Now, all he had was a head full of nothing, and a weight in his coat pocket that he swore was dragging him down at one side.

"Oh, for God's sake, Jack, don't leave us in suspense!" Vanessa urged. "You're not announcing the winner of the bloody *X-Factor*. Spit it out."

"It's, eh..."

He had to tell them. They had to know what he'd done. To know how he'd put them at risk.

The postcard in his pocket felt hot against his chest, like it was spewing out radiation that was rotting away his insides.

He had to tell them. They had to know. They deserved that much, at least.

"It's, eh... It's nothing, really," he said, and the weight in his pocket almost pulled him to the floor. "It's just... We've got reason to believe Owen Petrie's in Inverness."

"Jesus," Vanessa whispered.

"How do you know?" Maddie asked.

Logan rubbed the back of his neck and angled his head back, unable to hold his daughter's gaze. "He tried to take a boy from a swing park. A neighbour intervened. The description we got... Well, it's Petrie."

"How sure are you?" Maddie asked.

"We're sure."

"Well, so much for us being safe up here!" Vanessa spat. "We'd have been better off down the road!"

"He didn't know, Mum," Maddie said. "He couldn't have known this would happen."

Logan continued to stare up at the ceiling, his fingers massaging the back of his neck. He could say it. Now. Right now. He could just come out with it. Tell them the truth. Tell them what he'd done.

How he'd used them as bait.

"No," he said. "You're safe here. I'd never let anything happen to you—either of you, believe it or not—but, now that we know he's here, maybe we should think about getting you back down the road."

"Home! Yes! I agree," Vanessa said. "Let's do that."

"Not home," Logan told her. "You can't go home yet. He's up here now, but the road goes both ways. He could be down there in a few hours." He shook his head. "No, if you go down the road, you're going to another safe house."

"Then what's the point?" Maddie asked. "I mean, if we're going to be stuck in another safe house, then why not stay in this one?"

"Because Owen Petrie's here," Vanessa said. "You might not remember him, but I do, and—"

"I remember him. Of course, I remember him," Maddie said, and there was an accusing tone to her voice. "How could I not remember?"

She stared at her mother, almost daring her to speak, then turned her attention back to her dad.

"It's like you said, road goes both ways. If he wants to get to us, he will. And, honestly? I feel safer knowing that you're around."

Logan hadn't been prepared for that. "You do?"

"Of course, I do."

"I don't. Just for the record," Vanessa was quick to add. She winced at how the comment sounded. "Meant to be a joke," she clarified. "I suppose, on balance, all things considered... So do I. A bit. A tiny bit."

Under any normal circumstances, Logan would've enjoyed the moment. Enjoyed his family—broken as it was—telling him he made them feel safe.

But how could he enjoy it now? When he knew the real truth of it.

When he'd deliberately put them in harm's way.

"Aye, well... I want you both to be careful," he told them.

"I almost clanged you with a frying pan, and she nearly fucked you up old school with a bread knife," Maddie pointed out. She smiled at him. "I'd say we've got 'being careful' pretty much covered. Wouldn't you?"

He conceded that she had a point but stressed the importance of keeping the place locked down, and only opening the door to him, to Ben, who they both knew, or—at a push—to a uniformed officer.

He was going to arrange extra patrols, he told them, try to get Uniform to keep a close eye on the place. Their safety was his number one priority. Not Petrie. Not this time. He'd learned that lesson, he said.

They didn't believe him. He could see it in their eyes.

He couldn't blame them.

CHAPTER NINETEEN

THE STAIRWELL LEADING UP TO LOGAN'S FLAT HAD A clinical, bleachy sort of smell to it when he entered and started up the stone steps.

Tanya, the downstairs neighbour, was digging around in her pocket for her keys outside her front door, a holdall slung over her shoulder.

"Hey. You're back," Logan remarked. "He gone, then?"

Tanya nodded, smiled, and brushed a strand of hair back over her ear. "Yes. Thankfully. He texted this morning, said that was him out. Said he'd cleaned the place from top to bottom. He mentioned you'd... had a word."

Logan gave a non-committal tilt of his head. "I mean, I may have *gently* suggested he consider moving on."

"Thanks. Really," the girl said. "Mum was totally doing my nut in."

"Aye, they do that," Logan said.

"Aha!" Tanya cried, finding her key in the back pocket of her ripped jeans. "Got it."

"Right, well, I'll leave you to it. Good to see you back. If he turns up again, I probably won't be upstairs, but you've got my number."

"You going away somewhere?" Tanya asked, suddenly concerned. "You're not leaving, are you?"

"No, just... work-related. Be back in a day or two. But I'm around. So, if there's anything..."

Tanya exhaled with relief. "I'll call you. I'm sure it'll be fine, though."

"I'm sure it will be," Logan agreed. "So, I'll just—"

She flung herself at him, arms wrapping around his broad chest and barely meeting at the back. Her head pressed against him, and she squeezed for a moment, then quickly released and stepped back, all bluster and embarrassment.

"Sorry. Sorry, I just... Thanks. For everything you've done. It's good to have someone looking out for me."

"Aye. Well. You're welcome," he said, then he gave her a nod and headed for the next flight of stairs.

He was halfway up them when he turned back. The girl had the key in the lock, and the door ajar.

"Oh, Tanya," he called down to her.

"Yeah?"

"Do me a favour, and don't open the door to any strange men."

Tanya blew air out through her mouth, making a sound like a horse. "No worries there. I've had enough of strange men to last me a lifetime!"

"Good. Well, if you see anyone... odd poking around, call me. OK?"

That look of concern fell like a veil over Tanya's face again. "Sure. OK," she said.

And then, with a final nod, Logan continued up the steps, stopped outside the door to his flat, and pulled on a pair of rubber gloves.

He'd checked the place over at the time, but mostly for

camera and microphones. Given the amount of adrenaline that had been flooding his system at the time, and the gnawing urge he'd had to get the fuck out of there as quickly as his legs would carry him, it was possible he'd missed something.

He could've ordered a full forensic sweep of the place—and it might come to that—but for now, the thought of Geoff Palmer poking around in his pants drawer was almost as bad as the thought of Petrie doing it.

There were a couple of other letters sitting on the mat near those he'd kicked aside on his last stop by the place. Both looked like marketing shite, and he swept them into the corner with his foot to join the others.

The flat felt stuffier than it had last night, having had another seventeen or so hours to stew in its curtained-off lack of sunlight.

The smell of the bin was no longer the first thing you noticed when you stepped inside, though. It was still lingering, but it was background noise now, not the full-scale assault it had previously been. That was something, at least.

"Right, then," Logan said to the empty hallway. "Let's see what we've got."

———

HAMZA DROPPED his bag in the hallway, hung his coat on the peg, then followed the smell of Mexican food into the kitchen.

"Well, well, wonders will never cease," said his wife, Amira. She turned away from the stove to give him a peck on the lips, then got back to stirring the contents of the pan. "Live case, and you're home before midnight? That DCI of yours must be losing his touch."

"It was his idea, actually," Hamza said. "He sent us home."

"Wow. Really a day of miracles, then," Amira said. "We're having fajitas, by the way."

"I noticed," Hamza said. "Want me to do anything?"

"You could get out of my road," Amira suggested.

Hamza raised his hands and backed away. "Consider it done," he said.

"Kamila and I made lemonade. It's in the fridge."

"Oh? Nice one," Hamza said. He opened the fridge and there, standing proudly in the centre of the meticulously organised shelves, was a plastic bottle of a very faintly yellowish liquid.

He took the bottle out, gave it a shake, opened the lid, then sniffed it tentatively. There was a definite scent of lemon in there, and so he brought the bottle to his lips and sipped.

"I wouldn't," Amira told him, glancing back over her shoulder.

Hamza's cheeks almost collapsed inwards into his head, even as his head jerked back, desperately trying to get away from the liquid in the bottle.

"We forgot to put sugar in."

"Oh... fuck," Hamza wheezed. His face was scrunched up like a ball of paper, and he was sure he could feel the enamel being stripped from his teeth. "What did you use instead? Nitric acid?"

"She wanted to leave some for you to try," Amira said.

"Does she hate me? Is that it?" Hamza asked, screwing the top back on the bottle.

Amira laughed. "Count yourself lucky. She gave me a whole cup of the stuff."

Hamza turned to face her, eyes wide. "A whole cup? You'll be dead by morning! You'll dissolve."

"I didn't drink it, obviously. Turns out, you don't need a lot of sleight of hand to fool a three-year-old."

"That's a relief," Hamza said. "I couldn't face having to mop you up first thing in the morning." He held the bottle over the sink. "Down the drain?"

Amira nodded. "Might clear them."

Hamza glugged the liquid down the sink, being careful not to spill any of it on the wooden worktop, in case it burned clean through.

Once it was empty, he swirled the bottle under the tap a couple of times, then set it on the draining board to dry out.

"She sleeping?" he asked, wiping his hands on a piece of kitchen roll.

"Yes. Just down. She didn't nap today, so she was exhausted." Amira turned, wooden spoon raised like a weapon. "If you go in, *don't* wake her up!"

"I won't."

"I mean it! She's been a headwreck all day. I just want us to be able to sit down and have a nice dinner for once."

"I won't wake her up," Hamza said. He dodged around the spoon and kissed his wife on the forehead. "Promise."

The door to Kamila's room was two along from the kitchen. It was mostly in darkness, aside from the strip of light that came in through the gap where Amira had left the door ajar.

Hamza tiptoed the last few steps, edged the door open just enough to peek through, and looked down at the bed where his daughter lay.

Should've lain.

His body reacted before his brain could, heart fluttering into a higher gear, stomach clenching, like it was bracing itself for the worst. His blood became hot in his veins. His breath froze in his lungs.

The bed was empty, the covers pulled back.

She was gone. Kamila, his daughter, was—

"Daddy!"

Hamza pushed the door all the way open, and the light flooded in. Kamila ran to him from the window, arms wide, pyjamas so long they were almost tripping her, smile brightening the room better than any lightbulb ever could.

He dropped to his knees and caught her, pulling her in close. She felt so tiny against him, so vulnerable. The feeling of her in his arms—and the adrenaline of those few terrifying moments—brought tears springing to his eyes.

"I made you juice," Kamila told him. He felt her little hand patting against the back of his neck.

"I know. And it was delicious!" he said. "I drank it all."

Kamila leaned back and looked at him, delight widening her already big brown eyes. "Every single drop?"

"Every single drop," Hamza said.

"So much for not waking her," sighed a voice from the doorway. Amira stood there with a plate of food in each hand.

"Mummy!"

"Hello, you. You're meant to be sleeping."

"It wasn't my fault. She wasn't in bed," Hamza was quick to explain. He turned back to their daughter and wagged a finger. "Why weren't you in bed, young lady? Hmm?"

"I was talking!"

"Talking?"

Kamila nodded. "To the man."

Hamza glanced up at his wife, then back to their child. "What man?"

"That man," Kamila giggled. "The man out there."

And then, she turned and pointed to the gap where her bedroom curtains hadn't quite met. Her other hand rubbed against her forehead, just above her left eye.

"The man with the boo-boo."

"Don't be silly, Kamila—" Amira began, but Hamza was already on his feet, already racing to the window, already throwing the curtains all the way open.

The back garden was empty. The open gate *clacked* gently against the latch, shifting back and forth on the breeze.

"Stay here," Hamza said. Storming to the door and pointing

to their daughter. "Watch Kamila. Don't open the door to anyone but me."

"What's going on?" Amira asked. "There's nobody there. She probably imagined it."

"Amira, please," Hamza said. He stopped in front of her, just for a moment, and the look on his face told her everything she needed to know.

"Kamila, come here. Come with Mummy," she said, setting the plates down on the bed and taking her daughter's hand. "How about we go play Hide and Seek with Daddy? We'll hide. Together. OK?"

Kamila danced with excitement, her grin showing off the big gap between her two front teeth. "Yay! Don't come until we're ready, Daddy!"

"I won't," Hamza said. He shot his wife another look, then hurried out into the hallway and headed for the door.

He made a brief detour via the kitchen, grabbed the dirty chef's knife from the countertop where Amira had left it, and headed outside to face the darkness.

CHAPTER TWENTY

THE SMELL OF SMOKE STILL HUNG IN THE AIR AROUND
Bosco Maximuke's yard.

Tyler had seen the old Portakabin over the fence on the
drive down the hill that led to the yard's entrance. There wasn't
a lot left of it, and under the insipid glow of the streetlights, the
blackened frame made him think of dinosaur bones.

The big vehicle gates at the front of the yard were locked,
but he blasted his car horn on the street outside until a stony-
faced skinhead in a black bomber jacket emerged through a
smaller gate a few yards along from the main two, and came
storming over to the vehicle.

"What is problem?" the skinhead demanded. He leaned in
through the open side window, slapping his hands on the door
of the car with such force he made the whole vehicle shake.

His face was bruised, like he'd recently taken a kicking, and
his accent was either Russian, Latvian, or—because Geography
had never really been Tyler's strongpoint—from any country
remotely in that neck of the woods, none of whose names he
could remember.

"What you want?" he barked. "Why you fucking *beep-beep?*"

"I'm here to see Bosco," Tyler said.

The skinhead's sneer remained fixed in place.

"Maximuke," Tyler added, just in case there was more than one Bosco knocking around inside the yard's high fences. He didn't think there was, but it'd be embarrassing if he ended up being brought to the wrong one, so no harm in specifying.

"We're closed," the skinhead replied. He jabbed a thumb back over his shoulder. "See? Closed."

Tyler produced his warrant card and held it up like it was a party invitation. "DC Tyler Neish. Police Scotland, Major Investigations."

"So?"

Tyler side-eyed his ID, making sure he was showing off the right thing. "So... I'd like to ask Mr Maximuke a few questions."

"You have warrant?"

"Warrant?" Tyler snorted. He leaned back against the car's headrest and laughed. "Do *I* have a warrant?"

"Do you?"

"Well, I mean... Not on me, no," Tyler said. "Look, I'd just like—"

"Shh."

"Sorry?"

"Shut fuck up."

The skinhead straightened and held a hand up for silence. A finger of his other hand pressed against one ear, and Tyler spotted the coil of wire running down the side of the man's thick, sinewy neck.

"Wait," he ordered, firing a look of utter contempt in the DC's direction. He turned and entered the yard again via the same gate he'd come out through.

Tyler sat in the car, the engine running, waiting to see what would happen next. This had all seemed like a good idea back at the station. A solid demonstration of using his initiative.

He'd become less convinced of it on the drive over. And now that he was sitting there alone outside the lion's den, he was starting to think it was up there with the worst ideas he'd ever had.

Thankfully, it wasn't too late to back out. The skinhead seemed to have gone, and the road behind Tyler's car was clear of vehicles. He could turn around. Go home, maybe via KFC. He could come back tomorrow with back-up.

Aye, that made much more sense. Back-up. Daylight. Even just someone somewhere knowing where he was.

That sounded like a plan.

He'd just slipped the gearstick into reverse when the double gates opened. At first, Tyler thought he was looking at some sort of mirror system, as both gates were being pulled back by the same hulking, baldy-headed bastard. It was only when they both caught the full-beam of his headlights that he realised they were two different, albeit near-identical-looking, people.

A third man came striding into the space left by the gates. Tyler thought he was the guy he'd been speaking to a few moments before, but they all looked so bloody similar, it was hard to be sure.

"Bosco says you can come in," he shouted. He made an urgent beckoning motion with one hand. "Hurry up."

Tyler sat there with the car in reverse for a few long, uncertain seconds. Then, with a quiet sigh and a plastered on smile, he slipped the gearstick into first and went crawling in through the open gates.

The skinheads on both sides glowered at him as he eased through the gap and passed them. Tyler watched as, reddened by the glow of his tail lights, they pushed the gates closed behind him, and slid the large metal latch closed with a *clunk*.

LOGAN HAD SEARCHED THROUGH MOST of the rooms in turn, starting with his bedroom and working through to the kitchen via the bathroom and living room.

In each room, he'd stand as close to the middle as furniture allowed, and slowly turn on the spot, searching for anything that looked out of place.

In each room, he'd seen nothing.

Then, he went through them all more thoroughly, checking under the bed, in the drawers, in the toilet cistern, inside the washing machine—anywhere Petrie might feasibly have left something for him to find.

Still, he'd found nothing.

By the third time around, he was growing more impatient. He yanked up the sofa cushions and tossed them on the floor so he could dig down the sides. There was only one picture on the wall—a bland-looking winter landscape that had been there when he'd moved in. He unhooked it, checked behind, then removed the back in case there was anything hidden away in there.

Nope.

The fourth pass of the flat essentially just involved him kicking random pieces of furniture and swearing at them.

He shoved the couch cushions back into place, then slumped onto them, lay back, and stared up at the ceiling.

What had he expected to find? He had no idea. Something. That was all he'd hoped for. Something, anything, that might point him to Petrie's whereabouts, or give him some clue as to what he was planning to do next.

But there was nothing. He was no further on than he had been an hour ago, and there was no saying what the bastard had been up to in that hour.

"Hoon's bloody nephew," he spat at the light fitting above him. He'd ransacked that bloody thing, too, but there had been nothing hidden in it.

What were the chances of Petrie targeting Hoon's nephew by accident? It *could* be a coincidence, of course, but it felt unlikely. Although, that said, Logan hadn't even known that Hoon had siblings, let alone other relatives. If someone had deliberately targeted the kid, then it would've taken a lot of dedication and research.

And why Hoon? He'd been around at the time of the original case. He'd even pitched in from time to time, but he hadn't been involved enough to warrant a revenge play from Petrie.

The Gozer? Aye, he could see him being a target. The Gozer had been right there with Logan all the way through it, but Hoon? It didn't make sense.

He let his mind go for a wander, skirting around the edges of the case, where sometimes the view was clearer.

Dr Ramesh had been closer to Petrie than they'd first thought. A 'nonce,' Hoon had called him, but he was something even worse than that. He hadn't just collected those images. It wasn't just a case of him having enjoyed them, in whatever sick and twisted way he had—although, that was bad enough.

More than that, though, he'd sought out and helped the man responsible for some of the worst of them. He'd deliberately helped him escape, so he'd be free to do those things again.

Petrie was a monster, no doubt, but Ramesh was almost as bad, and in some ways even worse. Logan would not be mourning the bastard's death, only the loss of opportunity to question him. Ideally, in a soundproof room with no cameras.

But Ramesh was just the tip of the iceberg, it seemed. There was a ring of them out there, sharing that stuff, egging each other on.

That was hardly news, of course. Rings like that popped up

all the time. But to have Petrie as a member? That had to be the nonce equivalent of having DeNiro join your drama club.

How long had he been a member? Pre-arrest, obviously. Which begged the question, how much did the rest of his little group know about what he was up to? He wouldn't have needed much egging on, but if they had, then weren't they an accessory to everything that happened to those boys?

Logan pushed the thought away. One thing at a time. Catching Petrie was the main priority. After that, they'd have a long chat about his circle of friends.

He smiled grimly at the thought of having Petrie sitting in an interview room, all that pretence of his brain damage stripped away, so there was only the two of them and the truth between them.

As he lay there on the couch enjoying that thought, the exhaustion of the last few days came creeping up on him. He caught his eyes closing and forced them open again.

No. No time for that. Not tonight.

Swinging his legs down from the couch, Logan stood, gave himself a shake, and retrieved his coat from the corner where he'd chucked it.

As he pulled it on, he felt the weight of the postcard in the pocket. He thought about taking it out to look at it again, but what would be the point? The message was etched there —*burned* there—on his brain. Indelible. Permanent.

Jump, and I'll turn myself in.

Don't, and everything that happens next is on you.

Logan took one last look around the living room from over by the door, then clicked the light off and went stomping along the hall.

He had just turned the latch and started to pull the front door open, when his toe brushed against one of the marketing letters that had been waiting for him earlier.

A sweep of his foot sent it skidding across the carpet, and Logan left the flat.

Then, a few seconds later, there was a rattle of keys and the door opened again. The DCI leaned inside, and his eyes crept down to the several days' worth of mail that lay piled up in the corner.

CHAPTER TWENTY-ONE

HAMZA PAUSED IN THE SHADOWS AT THE GABLE END OF THE house long enough to swallow down a couple of steadying breaths, then he peered around the corner into the back garden.

Light spilled out in overlapping rectangles onto the neatly tended lawn, but the area by Kamila's bedroom window was cloaked in darkness.

The tall back gate groaned at him as it shifted incrementally on its rusting hinges. Hamza listened for any other signs of movement—anything to indicate someone else was there with him in the garden—then crept across the grass, avoiding the pools of light as best he could.

The shed stood between him and the gate. He checked the door, but the padlock was in place, and there were no signs of forced entry.

He had a better view of Kamila's window from there, and with his eyes adjusting to the gloom he saw the patch of garden outside her bedroom was empty.

Hamza had just started to make for the gate when the light in his daughter's bedroom flicked on. The curtains were pulled aside, revealing a figure silhouetted on the other side of the glass.

His grip tightened on the handle of the knife.

The figure raised a hand, knocked on the window.

"See anything?" Amira asked, shouting to be heard through the glass.

Hamza breathed. "Fuck," he whispered, then everything inside him clenched as the bedroom door edged open behind his wife.

"Amira!"

She turned at the sound of footsteps, then bent and picked up Kamila. Hamza let out a sob of relief as he watched his wife reprimand his daughter, and watched his daughter hold her own. Their voices were too muffled for him to hear, but he could imagine them.

"You were supposed to be hiding."

"But, Mummy, so were you!"

The gate *clacked* behind him, and he turned knife raised as a man came stepping from the gloom of the footpath that ran between the back of the house and the one across the way.

"Wait, wait! It's me! It's me!"

"Shite. Jim. Sorry," Hamza said, hurriedly lowering the knife.

His neighbour—the other half of the semi-detached—stepped back, eyeing him with concern. Jim was pushing eighty, but he had more energy and drive than most people half his age.

He'd cut Hamza's grass an embarrassing number of times, and had even fixed a couple of tiles that had slipped loose in a storm a few months back. Hamza had only been aware of the problem when he'd returned home from work one day to find Jim teetering atop a ladder with tools in hand.

"Everything alright, Hamza?" Jim asked.

Hamza forced a smile. "Fine, Jim. Aye. Fine."

"Right. It's just... you've got a big knife."

Hamza looked down at the knife, then tucked it out of sight behind his back. "Sorry. Yeah, it's... There was—"

"Is it about that fella who was hanging about?"

Hamza took a step closer. "Fella? What fella?"

"Saw him from the kitchen window," Jim said. "Coming out of your garden a couple of minutes ago. Thought to myself, 'That's strange,' I thought. 'Who's that, and what's he up to?' Looked shifty, see?"

"You got a good look at him?"

Jim's nod was a firm, definite one. The way he wrinkled up his nose lessened his air of certainty, though.

"Yes. No. A bit. I mean, it's dark, isn't it? I've been onto the council umpteen times about getting a light for the alleyway. They could stick it on the side of Sandra's house, if they didn't want to put a pole in. It'd make a right difference to—"

"Jim," Hamza implored.

"Oh. Right. Yes. Well, he had a hat on. He was about my height, I'd say, based on... well, the size of him. Came strolling out, too, casual as you like. Not a care in the world."

"You didn't see his face?"

"No," Jim admitted. "Now, if we'd had a light..."

While Jim continued to bemoan his lack of response from the Highland Council street lighting officials, Hamza looked past him along the alleyway. It branched off in the middle, joining a maze of other passages that ran through the whole estate. Given his head-start, finding him in there would be almost impossible.

"...had no idea what he was up to, and then he got up again and hurried off."

Hamza blinked, snapping back to the present moment. "Sorry? What?"

"I was just saying how he stopped and bent down," Jim said. "And I thought to myself, I thought, 'Hello. What's he up to now? Odd, that,' I thought. And so, when he was gone, I came out, and looked, and that's where I found it."

"Found what?" Hamza asked.

Jim held up a soft toy. It was a ragged, threadbare looking teddy-bear. An envelope had been stapled to its paws.

"This ugly bugger of a thing. It's hard to read what it says on the front—again, a light would be handy—but I was able to make it out. It says, 'Open me,'" said Jim. "Surprise inside."

Bosco Maximuke sat in a high-backed leather chair, naked from the waist up.

The office Tyler had been brought to was in another Portakabin, with the window looking across to the burned-out remains of the old place. The room was stiflingly hot, and rivulets of sweat trickled through the forest of curly hairs on the Russian's sagging chest.

There had been a young girl sitting in the corner of the office, staring at an iPad screen with headphones on. Bosco had sent her out of the room when Tyler had been brought in, and she'd glared at the DC as she passed, like she despised him for this tiny interruption to her arduous viewing schedule.

"My daughter. Olivia. Apple of my eye, light of my life," Bosco said, once the girl had slammed the door behind her with enough force to shake the whole hut. "She is charming girl, really. So I hear, anyway. Please, excuse her manners."

"It's fine," Tyler said. Bosco's Russian accent was thicker than the DC had been prepared for, and he was having to recalibrate his hearing to pick up what the other man was saying.

"And, excuse my bareness," Bosco continued, indicating his upper half with a wave of both hands. "Fucking heater is stuck on. Crazy, yes? Run fucking building company, can't get electrician to come fix heater."

"Aye. Well, we've all got our problems," Tyler said.

"Ha!" Bosco ejected. He waved a finger in Tyler's direction.

"This, you can say again, my young friend. From you? Now? This is... what is word? Apt. Apt? That is word, yes?"

"It's *a* word, yes," Tyler confirmed, although he chose not to dwell too much on what it meant in the context of him or his being here.

He glanced back over his shoulder at the two hulking skinheads who flanked the door. They weren't blocking it, exactly, but then they didn't have to. The way they loomed there in silence made it very clear that he wasn't going anywhere until the semi-naked Russian behind the desk decided he was.

If he survived this in one piece, Tyler thought, he was never using his initiative again.

"What is it you want, *Detective Constable?*" Bosco asked. The way he spoke Tyler's rank made it sound like he found it amusing. Like it was the punchline to some private joke he wasn't prepared to share. "It is late. Business hours are over. And—maybe I am wrong—but I do not think you here for construction work. Yes?"

"One of your vans was spotted leaving the scene of a crime this morning."

Bosco's brow furrowed, as if in concern. He ran a hand down his chest and over the ripples of his naked belly, smearing the sweat into polish-like sheen.

"Oh? This is most concerning," the Russian said. "What van? What crime?"

"It's, eh..."

Shit, shit, shit. What was the reg? Why hadn't he written it down?

"We ran the registration, and it's one of yours. Transit-type. Unmarked. Was seen leaving the Premier Inn at the West End early this morning."

"Going to hotel is not crime. Unlimited breakfast buffet." Bosco slapped his stomach, making everything from his neck to his waistband wobble. "Is good."

"A body was discovered at the scene. We have reason to believe foul play was involved."

Bosco chuckled at that. "You have *reason to believe*? So, you don't know for sure?"

"No, we know," Tyler said. "I just—"

"And what van? Tell me registration. I have many vans, going many places. All the time. In, out, roundabout. You check CCTV across city, across country, there I am. My vans."

"Well, yes, that might be the case, but—"

"Who was body? Dead man. Who?"

Tyler picked up on the Russian's mistake and jumped on it.

"I didn't say it was a man."

"You didn't say it was not. And... how do you say it? Numbers?" Bosco shook his head. "Statistics say, murder victims most likely men. By three to one. In Russia, four to one. It says much about us, does it not? Men."

"I mean—"

"Am I wrong? Was victim woman?"

"I'm not at liberty to disclose that information," Tyler said.

Bosco waved a hand in irritation.

"Then, you have come here to bother me with nothing, *Detective Constable*." He said Tyler's rank in that same amused way, and this time both skinheads let out single, simultaneous snorts of laughter at it. "You have come to tell me a van—a van you say is mine, but that you cannot identify for me—was seen near a hotel that serves delicious breakfast buffet."

Tyler said nothing. He wished he could argue. He wished he could pull out some firm piece of evidence that would wipe the smile off the bastard's face.

Then again, if he did that, he might well not walk out of there alive.

Bosco slapped out a rhythm on his belly. It wobbled hypnotically, and Tyler found his eyes briefly drawn to it.

"What are we to do with you?" the Russian wondered aloud. "Hmm? What are we to do?"

Bosco jammed a finger in his belly button, wiggled it around, then brought it out and gave it a tentative sniff.

"Did Logan send you?"

Tyler shook his head. "No."

"But he knows you are here?"

Tyler was about to shake his head again, when he thought better of it. "Yes."

Bosco cocked his head to one side and studied the DC. A smile spread, tooth-by-tooth, across his face.

"Liar, liar, pants are on fire," he said. "He would not let you come here alone. Not after what he did. You see my old office? Burned. Ruined. He did this. And now, I stuck here in too-fuck-ing-hot other office, sweating like a... like a..."

He grasped for an appropriate word or phrase, then gestured to one of the men behind Tyler.

"Valdis?"

"Like a fat whore?" suggested Valdis, the man who had met Tyler at the gate.

"Yes! Perfect! I sit here, and I sweat like fat whore, because our mutual friend burn my fucking office to the ground."

There were no amused tones woven through Bosco's words now. His smile had gone, replaced by a cold, menacing scowl.

"Cannot even open fucking windows. So here I sit, and boil like a pig. Because of Jack Logan."

The back of Tyler's shirt was sticking to him with sweat, and only partly because of the temperature in the room.

"I don't know anything about that," he said. "You'll have to take it up with him."

"Oh, I will. I will get own back, yes?" He glanced at the chunky gold watch on his wrist, and his mouth curved upwards at the edges again. He winked and lowered his voice until it was a conspiratorial whisper. "In fact, maybe I already have!"

"What does that mean?" Tyler asked.

"You think you know him. Jack Logan. You do not. Not like I do," Bosco said. "You have not seen him as he truly is. You see... fake news. You see disguise that he hides behind. Mask that he wears. You think he is good man? He is not good man."

"Again, you'll have to take that up with him," Tyler said.

"How is Ruth?" Bosco asked, changing the subject with a carefree smile.

His hands tapped out a beat on his belly again. This time, Tyler didn't look.

"Ruth?"

"Yes. You know. Ruth. Your mother. How is she?"

Tyler tensed his jaw, only just managing to stop it falling open.

"Her and your father still separated?" Bosco continued. "Must be a worry for you. For her. Living all alone."

Tyler's fingers curled inwards, forming fists. Behind him, the floorboards of the Portakabin squeaked as both men shifted their weight.

"What is she? Fifty-eight. Attractive woman, for her age. Fine, handsome woman. Looks after herself. Jogging. Every morning. Without fail. Up and down road. Always the same."

"Shut your fucking mouth," Tyler hissed, which drew a booming outburst of laughter from the man across the desk.

"I am just being... what is word? Complimentary, *Detective Constable*. That is all." Bosco wiped the sweat from his chest, then flicked it onto the desk between them. "You see, I know everything that happens in this city. Top to bottom, side to side. I have eyes and ears beyond those you see here on my face. Out there. Everywhere."

Tyler's whole body was trembling now, as he fought the urge to dive across the table and smack the fat Russian bastard in the mouth. It would be suicide, of course, but it would be a thoroughly satisfying one.

"This is why our friend, Logan, he comes to me over the years. Asks me for favours. Turns a blind eye if one of my men should accidentally find themselves in trouble. We go back, he and I. Way back. We have been mutually scratching for a very long time."

Bosco opened his arms like he was offering up a hug. "And I can scratch your itches, too, *Detective Constable*. My nails are very sharp. And maybe, once you are older and a grown-up, you can help me, too. Win-win. Scratch, scratch."

His eyes darted to Valdis. Tyler uncurled his fists as he heard the door opening behind him.

"Please, see yourself out," Bosco urged. His smile crept higher on his face, becoming something twisted and wrong. "And, please, give my regards to Ruth when you next see her."

He curled his forefinger and thumb together, then smacked his lips off them in a chef's kiss. "Tell her she is looking very beautiful."

HAMZA STOOD IN HIS KITCHEN, well back from the countertop where the teddy bear sat nursing its dirty envelope.

Jim had been spot-on with the words of the message, although he'd got the order of the sentences themselves jumbled up.

'Surprise inside,' had been typed first, the letters varying in weight and darkness, like they'd been hammered out on an old manual typewriter.

'Open me,' was a couple of line-spaces below it, indented so it was almost but not quite centred beneath the previous sentence.

It was eerily similar to the bear and the envelope that had been left on the doorstep of Connor Reid's parents back in Fort William all those months ago.

And to the bears and the envelopes that had been left for the parents of Petrie's original victims so many years before that.

He heard footsteps beyond the kitchen door. "Stay there! Don't come in!" he barked. An order, not a request.

Usually, Amira would have given him an earbashing for talking to her like that, but these were not normal circumstances.

"Just... shout if you need me," she replied, then the footsteps receded along the hall.

"I will," he replied, but he knew his wife couldn't help him. Not with this.

Only one man could help him with this.

Still eyeing the bear like it might be about to explode, Hamza slipped a hand into his trouser pocket and took out his phone.

CHAPTER TWENTY-TWO

LOGAN DESCENDED THE STAIRS FROM HIS FLAT WITH A bagged-up envelope clutched in one hand, all the colour missing from his face.

The door to Tanya's flat was closed, but he could hear music playing quietly from one of the rooms beyond. It was light and poppy. Some boy band or other. Shite, in other words, but a far cry from the thunderous din her ex had been pumping out at top volume.

He had just left the close and was marching back to his car when his phone rang. He fished in his pocket, saw DC Khaled's name on screen, and answered with a tap.

"Hamza? What's up?"

A couple of paces later, he stopped walking. He stood there, in the middle of the darkened pavement, listening to the words coming rushing at him down the line. Listening to the fear and the worry in the DC's voice.

"Text me your address, son. I'm on my way," Logan said.

And the postcard in his pocket felt heavier than ever.

FOURTEEN MINUTES LATER, Logan stood in Hamza's kitchen, glaring down at the teddy bear like he was trying to intimidate a suspect.

Hamza himself had backed away so he was leaning against the opposite worktop. He sipped a glass of water he'd poured himself from the tap, washing down a couple of painkillers he'd had Amira bring him for the headache he could feel building behind his eyes.

"And it was left on the window?" Logan asked, not turning away from the stuffed animal.

"No. In the alleyway. My neighbour found it," Hamza said. His voice shook as he said the next sentence, the breaths coming in all the wrong places. "Petrie was at the window. At my daughter's window. She... she spoke to him."

Logan turned at that. "What did he say?"

Hamza shrugged. "Amira asked, but didn't get much. He said he liked her room. And he said..."

The DC's voice failed him completely, and he necked a big gulp of water while he tried to steady himself.

"He said she was pretty."

The crags and furrows in Logan's face deepened. "I'm sorry, son. How is she?"

"Kamila? She's fine. She doesn't understand." Hamza looked at the vile thing on his worktop. "How could she?"

Logan nodded. "It's probably overkill, but I think maybe—"

"Amira's already packing," Hamza said, anticipating the rest of the DCI's suggestion. "They're going to go to her brother's. Big family, mostly grown-up. Lot of adult nephews. She'll be safe there. Her and Kamila will share a room."

"Good. You going to take them?"

"No. Her brother's coming over. Be here shortly."

Both men turned their attention back to the soft toy. One of its glassy black eyes dangled from a loose thread, so it was resting on a threadbare cheek. The other stared defiantly back at them, like it was urging them to follow the instruction on the envelope.

"What do we do with it?" Hamza asked.

Logan bent forward, bringing his head to the same level as the bear. The moment he'd stepped into the kitchen and seen it, his every instinct had told him to run. To go. To get out. To not go back to this. Not this.

Anything but this.

He'd seen too many bears with too many envelopes. Too many children lost to a monster.

Too many.

But no more.

"Do you have a knife?" Logan asked.

Hamza picked up the knife block from the counter behind him and offered it out to the DCI. Logan gloved himself up, then picked the smallest handle from the block.

He approached the bear cautiously as if it were a real wild animal that might attack at any moment.

Holding the top of the envelope, he inserted the blade of the knife and slid it sideways, creating an opening.

Sitting the knife down, he prised the envelope open, and felt a bubble of panic rise in his throat when he saw a small stack of Polaroid photographs inside.

His brain rebelled. Screamed at him. He shouldn't look at those images. *Please, God, don't look*. Not this. Not again.

But, his legs were now tree trunks, their roots buried in the floor. He was going nowhere.

Taking great care, he teased the photographs out of the gap at the top of the envelope. There was a moment of relief, that was quickly replaced by confusion.

The first image was not one he'd expected. He'd been braced for another child in another chair, tears cutting grooves through the blood and the filth on his face.

Instead, the image showed the window of a house. The

curtains were drawn, blocking all but a thin gap at one side, where a strip of the room could just about be made out.

Beneath the image, on the thickest part of the white border, the word 'driveways' had been written in black pen. Whoever had written it—presumably Petrie—had pressed so hard and gone over it so often the word was practically carved into the glossy paper.

He fixated on the word for a few moments, contemplating its possible meaning. A connection was made in his head. A confirmation of something he'd been almost, but not quite, certain of.

Logan turned the photograph over, found nothing on the other side, then placed it in an evidence bag and set it on the counter next to him.

Hamza stepped closer and leaned over so he could see the image.

"*Driveways?*" he said, but Logan was already focused on the next picture.

It was of the same window, but taken closer, so the gap was more prominent. It was just about possible to make out part of something that might have been a couch, but could have been a bed. The word 'toast' had been written beneath this one, in the same demented, scratched-in style.

Logan flipped quickly to the third and final image. This one was taken from right outside the window, the lens pressed up to the gap so only a suggestion of the curtain and the window frame could be seen at opposite edges of the photograph.

It was a couch. That much was clear now. Someone lay on it. Young, Logan thought, judging by how far their feet reached.

Their arms were up like they were holding something, but whatever it was had been cut off by the edge of the window frame, along with their head and neck.

Logan's gaze flitted momentarily to the word 'nature' which

was etched into the border, then back to the unknown child in the unfamiliar house.

"Who's that?" asked Hamza, looking over his shoulder. "Is that... is that a kid?"

Logan said nothing, just stood there staring at the image.

"That's... shite. Who is that? We need to get this out. If he's going after that kid, we need to stop him, sir. We need to warn... whoever."

"It's too late."

The words hung there in the air between them, surrounded by the stifling silence of the kitchen.

"Whoever it is, it's too late. Petrie's already got them."

———

"AUNTIE VAL, can I get something for supper?"

Harris lay on his back on the couch, gaze fixed on the screen of the Nintendo Switch he held directly above him, his fingers frantically jabbing at buttons and flipping the little joysticks.

It had only been a few minutes since Sinead had phoned, but he'd been quick to settle into the idea of spending the night at Val's. She always had the best sweets, and didn't ration them out like Sinead did.

Supper back home was toast or cereal. At Val's, it was cookies, or cake, or freshly-baked scones with butter and jam. Sometimes, if he was hungry, she'd make chips, even if it was after ten o'clock!

She wasn't as strict on bedtime, either. She was far more relaxed and laid back about it, like Sinead had been after their mum and dad had died. She'd let him stay up nearly all night once, and they'd quite often just fall asleep on the couch together, watching stuff they'd recorded off the telly.

Yes, it was fun spending the night at Auntie Val's, and he

couldn't wait to see what she was going to serve up for supper tonight.

She hadn't replied to him, so he shouted again, louder this time.

"Auntie Val?"

He jabbed at buttons for a few more seconds, waiting for the response, then glanced over at the living room door to see if he could see her out in the hall.

When he didn't, he paused the game, swung his legs down onto the floor, and sat on the edge of the couch.

"Auntie Val?" he called again.

Somewhere in the house, a floorboard creaked.

Harris set the console down on the coffee table, got up, stretched, and went padding through to the kitchen. The lino floor was cold on his bare feet, and he tiptoed over to the big drawer where Val kept the biscuits and chocolate.

She was probably in the bathroom, he thought. She'd be out in a minute.

His eyes fell on the kettle, and he decided he'd surprise his aunt with a cup of tea. She'd been running about after him for most of the day, making sure he had everything he could possibly need.

A cup of tea and a biscuit. That's what he'd get her. When she came out of the bathroom, he'd tell her to go put her feet up, and he'd bring it through to her.

He lifted the kettle off the base, filled it at the tap, set it back on the base, then wiped up all the water that had sprayed onto the worktop around the sink when the tap had come blasting on like a fire hose.

He pressed the button that started the kettle boiling, then searched in the cupboards until he found the cups. If he stretched, he was *just* able to get a finger to a big red mug and with a bit of effort, he was able to pull it close enough to the front of the high cupboard for him to be able to lift it out.

Harris stood swinging the mug by its handle on one finger, his other hand scratching the top of his head.

"Teabags," he muttered, looking across the rest of the work-top. "Teabags, teabags, teabags..."

He spotted three metal canisters tucked in under the windowsill, and was just reaching for one when he heard the whispering of the wind outside. It seemed loud in the otherwise quiet kitchen, and he assumed the window must have been left open.

Crinkling the metal blinds, Harris reached through them and felt for the window handle. To his surprise, he found it closed. Shut tight, against the darkness outside.

The whispers came again. Louder, this time.

For a moment, he could've sworn they said his name.

But, if they weren't coming from outside, then...

Slowly, his bare feet slapping on the cold lino, Harris turned around.

And the big red mug shattered against the floor.

CHAPTER TWENTY-THREE

LOGAN INDICATED THE TEDDY BEAR ON HAMZA'S KITCHEN worktop, while the other hand tapped his phone awake and swiped to his contacts.

"Bag it up. I'll get Ben, tell him his night off's just been cancelled," Logan said. "Yours, too, I'm afraid."

"Of course," Hamza said, making for the door. "I've got bags through in the spare room."

Logan nodded, then winced at the voice that answered the phone. "Alice? Hello. I was, eh, I was looking for Ben."

"I'll bet you bloody were," said the voice from the other end. "He's barely in the door. He's away for a shower."

"Could you get him to call me when he's done?" Logan asked.

Alice's sigh was so loud and forceful it made the line crackle. "I don't see why I should. You know there's a law about working hours, don't you? How long you can work in a day, and how many days. How many breaks you need. That sort of thing. You know that, don't you, Jack?"

"I do, but—"

"And, let's be honest here, he's no spring chicken," Alice

continued. "He's knocking on now. Sure, he'll tell you he's fine, but you don't see him when he comes home. Exhausted he is, some days. Can barely put one foot in front of the other, so—"

"It's a child, Alice," Logan said. She stopped talking at that. "There's a child's life in danger."

Alice sighed again, but this one wasn't for his benefit.

"I suppose I'd better go make him a flask of coffee, then," she said, and then there was a *beep* in Logan's ear as she hung up the phone.

Hamza grabbed gloves and an evidence bag from the computer desk in the spare room and turned to leave. Amira stood in the doorway with a sleeping Kamila in her arms. They both had jackets on, Kamila's so puffy it made her upper body look twice the size it actually was.

A small wheeled suitcase sat patiently in the hallway behind them.

"You all set?" Hamza asked.

Amira gave a tiny tilt of her head. "Yes. I mean... I think so. We might have to send for more things. Depends how long we'll be away for."

"Not long," Hamza said. "We'll get him. I promise. It won't be long."

He leaned in and kissed their daughter on the forehead. She rumbled in her sleep, peeled open one eyelid, then gave a half-smile before flaking out again.

He kissed Amira, too. His wife put a hand on his face, holding him close to her, even after the kiss had broken off.

"Be careful," she whispered. "Please."

"I will," Hamza said. "I promise."

There was a knock on the front door. "Amira?" a concerned voice called. "Everything OK?"

"That's Usman," Amira said. "We'd better go."

Hamza reached past her for the suitcase, but she beat him to it. "It's fine. It's on wheels. I've got it."

She kissed him again, then trundled the case over to the front door and opened it. Her brother smiled warmly and hugged her, being careful not to crush the sleeping Kamila between them.

"Thank you for this," Amira said, but Usman dismissed it with a shake of his head and the wave of a hand.

"Shut up, sis. We're all looking forward to it. We can't wait to have Kamila running about the place," Usman said. "You, we can take or leave, but her..."

Amira kicked him playfully with the side of her foot. "Hey, watch it. You might be bigger, but I can still kick your arse."

"Ha! I don't doubt it," Usman said.

He looked past his sister to where Hamza stood in the hall. A look passed between them. A nod. A moment of understanding. And Hamza knew that his family would be safe.

"Thank you, Usman," he said. "I'll call you in the morning, Amira."

And with that, he headed into the kitchen to join his DCI.

Logan had just hung up the phone when Hamza returned, and let out a big breath as he swiped back to his contacts.

"Jesus, that woman can fair give out an earbashing," he remarked. "Don't know how Ben copes with it."

"Love, sir, I suppose," Hamza said. He picked up the teddy bear and slid it into the evidence bag, then listened to the sound of Usman's car driving off. He thought of his wife and child, and what they'd gone through tonight. "It makes you put up with a lot of shit."

"Aye, so I hear," Logan said. He pointed to the bagged up bear and the Polaroids. "Can you take that into the office? Ben'll meet you there, and I'll try to get hold of Tyler. Tell Ben I said to get cracking. Better notify Hoon, too. See if there's been any reports of kids going missing. If not, work on trying to identify them from the photos. Go public, if you have to."

Hamza sat the bear down beside the photographs. "What about you, sir? When are you coming in?"

"I'm not," Logan said.

Hamza's eyes widened. "What?"

"I'm following up another lead," Logan told him. "On Petrie."

"What other lead?" Hamza asked. It snapped out of him, not a request for information but a demand.

"Another lead. That's all you need to know for now," Logan said.

"Bollocks it is, sir," Hamza said. "That bastard was here. He was at my house. He was talking to my daughter in her bedroom! I've never met the man, never been involved with him, but he's targeting me. My *child*."

"I know it feels that way, Hamza, but this is to get at me. I'm the target."

"You? Then why the fuck was he outside *my* daughter's window?!" Hamza demanded.

His voice had been growing louder, the tone turning more and more sour. He took a breath and brought it all down a notch.

"I think I deserve to know what's going on," he said.

"You're right. You do," Logan conceded. There was no anger in his reply, just a heavy sort of weariness that almost made Hamza regret his outburst. "And you will. If it turns out to be anything concrete, you will. But for now, your focus is on finding that child."

"And what about you?" Hamza asked, and the venom was back in his voice again. "What's your priority, *sir*?"

DC Neish sat behind the wheel of his car, watching as the identikit skinheads heaved open the big double gates of Bosco's yard.

He glanced in his rear-view mirror, saw the semi-naked Bosco watching him from the window of the Portakabin, and quickly averted his gaze.

"Come on, come on," he muttered, as the Russian's men slowly walked the gates into the fully wide position.

Just as they got them all the way open, and Tyler put the car into gear, there was a sharp knock at his window. Valdis, the first man he'd encountered, signalled for him to wind the window down, and Tyler slid it down a few inches, then stopped.

"You want advice?" Valdis said. "Stay away. You come back here, we will not be as welcoming. Yes?"

He banged a hand on the top of the car, making the DC jump. A toothy grin cracked open the bottom half of his face.

"Get fuck off our property, little mouse," he hissed, then he stepped back from the car, and Tyler quickly drove out through the open gateway.

He was halfway along the street, heading back up the hill, when his phone rang over the car speakers, making him jump again. He spat out a, "Shit!" as he corrected his jerk of the wheel, then stabbed at the button on the radio that answered the call.

"Uh, yeah? Hello?" he said, and his voice sounded different, like it had lost something.

"Tyler?"

Logan sounded confused, like he wasn't sure he'd come through to the right person.

"Eh, aye. Aye, it's me, boss," Tyler said.

"You sound weird."

"I'm... I'm in the car."

This seemed to satisfy the DCI.

"That's handy. We need you back into base. There's been a development."

Tyler checked his mirrors, half-expecting to find an unmarked van following him up the hill. The road, to his relief, was empty.

"You there?"

"Aye. Sorry, boss. Here," Tyler said. "Development? Which case?"

Logan's reply was short and to the point. "Petrie."

Tyler indicated right at the next junction and turned in the direction of Burnett Road. "Right, boss," he said. "I'm on my way."

SINEAD STEPPED BACK from the Big Board and was just weighing up her next move when the door to the Incident Room opened. She turned to see Tyler come shuffling in. He smiled at the sight of her, but it was a thin, hollow thing that she saw through immediately.

"What's wrong? What's happened?" she asked, hurrying over to him.

"Eh... nothing. Nothing," Tyler said. "Just... the boss phoned. Wanted us back in here. Some sort of development in the Petrie case. Ham's going to fill us in."

"Right." Sinead looked the DC up and down. "You sure you're alright? You look shellshocked, or something."

Tyler shook his head, and diverted more energy to the smile, trying to make it more convincing. "Honestly, I'm fine. Was just looking forward to putting my feet up." He gestured past her. "Big Board's looking good."

The hasty change of subject did not go unnoticed, but Sinead decided to go with it for now. "It's getting there," she said. "It's harder than I thought. I was half-thinking of scrapping it and starting over again."

"Don't you bloody dare."

Tyler and Sinead both turned to see Ben Forde standing just inside the doorway. He had a small rucksack on his back, and a big Thermos in one hand. His thinning hair was light and fluffy, and stood up as if full of static electricity.

"It's good work. It'll come in very useful. You've done Caitlyn proud," Ben said, plodding over to his desk.

Swinging the rucksack down, he dumped it on the desk and pulled open the zip. With a bit of effort, he wrestled two large Tupperware boxes out, sat them down one beside the other, then pulled the lid off one to reveal a large stack of assorted sandwiches.

"Anyone for a piece and ham?" he asked. "There's cheese spread and tuna, too. Alice was worried I might get hungry."

"What does she think you are, sir?" asked Sinead, looking down at the mound of bread and fillings. "A horse?"

Ben's eyes twinkled mischievously, but then he gave a curt shake of his head. "Was going to make a joke there, but realised it would've been inappropriate," he said, clearing his throat. "Aye, she's a feeder alright. You think that's bad?"

He pulled off the lid of the other box to reveal a hefty Victoria sponge with an inch-thick layer of jam and cream.

"Check out this brute of a thing."

"Ooh, very nice," Sinead said. "I'll be happy to take a bit of that off your hands, sir."

Ben turned to DC Neish. Tyler hadn't spoken a word since the DI had arrived. That was over a minute now, which had to be some sort of personal record.

"Fancy a bit of sponge, son?" Ben asked.

"Eh, maybe later, boss. I'm no' that hungry."

A frown troubled DI Forde's brow, but before he could ask

the younger officer what was wrong, the door swung open for the third time in almost as many minutes.

They could tell right away from Hamza's expression that something had happened. Something serious. Something awful.

"What is it, son?" Ben asked. "What's going on?"

Without a word, Hamza sat the evidence bags he was holding down on the desk next to the one with the cake and sandwiches. All three of the other officers stared down at the threadbare teddy bear, and its one good eye stared back.

"Oh God," Ben whispered. "Oh God, no."

LOGAN STARED at the darkened screen of his phone, willing it to light up.

"Come on, come on," he muttered, drumming a finger on the steering wheel of the Volvo in time with each word.

He tapped the phone awake, and saw his own message sitting there on the screen:

Just checking in. Everything OK?

It had been sent almost a full minute ago now. How long did he wait for a response? How long could he afford to give it?

Logan looked out through the windscreen at the terraced house a hundred yards along Murray Road, squinting like he might be able to see right through the walls.

There was no sign of anyone outside. The lights were on in the living room and an upstairs room. Hallway, too, he thought, judging by the glow through the mottled glass in the door.

He checked the phone again.

Nothing.

"Damn it, Maddie," he muttered, reaching for the door handle.

His phone buzzed just as he got the door open.

Fine, thx. U?

He closed the door again, texted out a quick reply and wished her goodnight, then plugged the phone into the charging cable and set it in the holder on the dash.

Reaching into the carrier bag beside him, he took out the sandwich he'd picked up at the Tesco petrol station on the drive over. It was cheese and onion—not something he'd normally go for, but at this time of night the range had been pretty limited—and the smell of it filled the car almost the moment he broke the seal on the packet.

Next out of the bag came a four-pack of Red Bull. He tore one from the cardboard, cracked the ring-pull, and gulped the liquid down. His face contorted at the taste of it, but it wasn't the flavour he'd bought them for, it was the caffeine.

He took a bite of his sandwich, fixed his gaze on the safe house door, and settled in for a long, uncomfortable night.

CHAPTER TWENTY-FOUR

BEN AND THE OTHERS STOOD IN A VAGUE SEMI-CIRCLE around the teddy bear. To anyone walking in at that moment, it would've looked like the soft toy was holding court, telling its audience of some horrendous tragedy that had befallen it.

Certainly, that would explain the long faces of the officers, and the looks of trepidation in their eyes.

"It was in the alleyway behind my house," Hamza said. His voice was low and flat, like he was afraid he might scare the teddy bear away if he spoke loudly or with too much inflection. "Petrie had been talking to Kamila. My little girl."

Tyler put a hand on the other DC's back for a moment, saying nothing.

"I called the DCI. He came over and opened it. There were pictures inside. Polaroids."

The sound Ben made at the back of his throat was quiet, but it was raw and primal, like an animal in pain. He picked up the evidence bag containing the photographs, and fanned the glossy squares out inside their plastic protector, but didn't look at them yet. He gave himself a moment to prepare first.

Over the years, Ben Forde had seen things that would have broken most other men.

Teenage rape victims. Bruised and bloodied, but too afraid to let anyone near them to help.

Murder victims. Beaten, burned, bludgeoned, stabbed, strangled, sliced from end to end.

Car accidents. Parents sobbing up front, demanding to know why they couldn't hear their littles ones crying in the back, but in no right mind to hear the answer.

And that was just since joining the polis. Before that, when he'd been serving in Northern Ireland during the Troubles, he'd seen worse still. Far worse.

He'd thought he had faced the darkest aspects of humanity. He thought he had seen the worst.

And then, he'd seen the Mister Whisper photographs, and he'd realised how wrong he was.

He took a breath and forced himself to look at the images in the evidence bag.

They were not, to his relief, what he'd been expecting. The Mister Whisper photographs of old had been close-up, post-abduction images that showed his young victims tied to a chair, faces twisted in agony and terror.

He had hand-delivered them to the parents, leaving them on the doorstep in the arms of a threadbare teddy bear not unlike the one that sat glaring up at them all now.

The words scratched into the bottom of the pictures was a new touch, too. *Driveways, toast, nature.* Christ knew what all that was about. Not his immediate concern, though.

There was a child in the last picture, although—mercifully—not bound to a chair.

Not yet.

"Who is this? Do we know?" Ben asked, looking across at Hamza.

"No, sir," Hamza said. "DCI reckons he—or she, it's hard to tell—will already have been taken."

Ben handed the photographs to Tyler, then looked past him to Sinead. "Anything come through about kids being taken, do you know?"

"I've been flat-out on the board, sir," Sinead replied. "Want me to go check?"

"Please," Ben said.

Sinead turned away just as Tyler moved to hand her the photographs. He held onto them, instead, staring blankly down at the kid on the couch.

"What do you make of it?" Ben asked.

Tyler looked up from the images, then back down. "It's... I don't know, boss. It's a kid."

"Astute observation, Detective Constable," Ben said. "Identifying this child is top priority. Maybe Logan's right and Petrie's already nabbed them, and maybe he isn't. We need to know, and we need to know now. Hamza, go through and talk to CID. We'll need to bring them in on this."

Hamza nodded. "Yes, sir. The DCI wanted me to keep Hoon informed, too."

"Christ. Did he?" Ben said, wincing. "Aye. Aye, I suppose so," he conceded with a sigh. "I'll do that. Don't you worry about him. Tyler."

DC Neish was back to looking at the photographs again. Ben had to say his name a second time before his head snapped up.

"Hmm? Sorry, boss. What?"

Ben motioned for Hamza to leave. "Go see CID, will you?"

"On it, sir," Hamza said, heading for the door.

Sinead was talking on the phone, her back to the two men. Ben dropped his voice so she wouldn't hear.

"Look, I don't know what's up with you, son, but you need to shake it off. A child's life is at stake here. I need you firing on all cylinders, not moping about." He glanced over at Sinead. "If you two have had a falling out, then leave it at the door."

"What? No. It's nothing like that, boss," Tyler said. "It's..."

He wanted to tell him. About Bosco. About everything the Russian had said. Even about how scared he'd made him feel.

But now wasn't the time. Now wasn't about him.

"I'm fine, boss," he said, straightening his shoulders. "Just tell me what you need me to do."

Ben tapped the evidence bag in Tyler's hand. "I want you to find the child in that photograph," he said. "Because I'm afraid I don't have the first bloody clue as to how we're going to do it."

LOGAN WAS two cans of Red Bull down, but he could still feel sleep prowling around him like wolves around a campsite, searching for a gap in his defences. He contemplated cracking open the third can, but that would leave just one to see him through the rest of the night, and so he opened up the family-sized bag of *Maltesers* he'd brought along and got ripped into those, instead.

The street was quiet. A few cars had come and gone. A dog walker or two. A woman on a bike. Nothing out of the ordinary.

As he watched, his mind kept drifting back to Hamza's kitchen. To the look of fright on the face of his wee girl when Logan had been let inside.

And to the fear in Hamza's eyes when he thought of that bastard being right there at his home.

Logan drew in a sharp breath, and almost choked on a Malteser. He hacked and coughed it back up as he opened the Volvo's glovebox. An evidence bag slid out, and he caught it just as he managed to crunch the sweet between his back teeth and swallow what was left of it.

Sitting upright, Logan spread the evidence bag across the

steering wheel, flattening its contents. With all the drama at Hamza's, he'd almost forgotten what he'd found in his flat.

There was no saying it had come from Petrie. It wasn't his style. It was a plain white envelope with Logan's name and address printed neatly on a rectangular sticker on the front. He'd barely have glanced twice at it, were it not for the fact that it didn't have a stamp or a postmark on it.

He'd opened it carefully, and had found three separate sheets of paper inside. Each one contained just a single word, printed in a sans-serif typeface in the middle of the page.

Mentions.

Idealist.

Info.

Three words, apparently all random. It hadn't been until he'd seen another random word—*driveways*—scribbled onto one of the photographs that had been left at Hamza's that he became sure of the Petrie connection.

This wasn't like him, though. Riddles were never his thing. Mind you, ten years in a secure mental hospital pretending to be brain-damaged would no doubt change a man. He'd certainly have had plenty of time on his hands.

Logan took pictures of the pages on his phone, then emailed them to the central team inbox.

Less than a minute later, Ben Forde's name flashed up on the phone's screen, and Logan swiped the button to answer.

"Ben."

"Jack. Where the bloody hell are you?" DI Forde demanded.

"Following up on another Petrie lead," Logan said.

"Aye, Hamza said something along those lines," Ben replied. "What lead?"

Logan thought about pulling rank and giving Ben the brush-off, but he knew the older man would never let him get away with it.

"I'm watching the safe house. Where Maddie and Vanessa are," he said. "I'm thinking Petrie might try something."

"What makes you think that?" Ben asked.

Logan adjusted his position in the seat. Half his arse and most of his left leg had been falling asleep for the past ten minutes, and it had reached the point where he had to do something about it.

"Just a feeling."

"A feeling? How would he even know where it was?" Ben asked. "I don't even know which one you're using."

"I don't know. Because the bastard knows things. He's been in at the Gozer's phone and computer."

"The Gozer wouldn't have that information though. It's held locally. There are very few people with access, and Owen Petrie certainly isn't one of them."

"Aye. I know. It's just... I've got a feeling. I can't explain it. I think he'll come here. I think..."

"You think what?" Ben asked after Logan let the sentence die away.

Logan almost spoke the terrible truth of it. *I think I hoped he'd come here. I think that's why I brought them.* But how could he say it? How could he confess to using his daughter and ex-wife as bait? How could he admit that to Ben? To anyone?

"I just think he's going to turn up," he said in the end. "That's all."

"And what? You're just going to hang around and catch him in the act, are you? That's your big plan?"

"It's the best one I've currently got, aye," Logan admitted. He sighed, and the warmth of his breath fogged the edges of the cold windscreen. "I brought them here, Ben. I can't let anything happen to them. Hoon's going to get surveillance sorted for tomorrow, but I can't leave them tonight. And, if he does show up, this is our chance to nab the bastard."

The grunt Ben gave suggested he wasn't happy with any of it, but knew better than to push too hard.

"What's this in the inbox?" he asked.

"Found it in my flat tonight. Put through the door. I wasn't sure it was Petrie, but the random three words thing ties it to the photos left for Hamza to find. See if anyone makes anything of it, and I'll get the originals in as soon as I can for Forensics to go over," Logan explained. "You given them the other stuff yet?"

"Not yet," Ben said. "We want to go through it all with Hoon and CID first, see if it sparks anything, then we'll hand it all over. Sinead's checked the nine-nine-nine logs. No reports of missing kids tonight, so we're hoping it's a warning or something, and that he hasn't actually nabbed anyone."

"Aye. Maybe," Logan said. "But I wouldn't count on it. Keep me posted."

"Will do," Ben said. "Oh! Jack!"

"Still here. What's up?"

"Not the Petrie case, but thought you'd want to know. Hamza ID'd the van."

"Van?"

"The one CCTV caught driving away from our murder scene," Ben said. "At the hotel."

"Oh. Aye. And?"

"You'll never guess who it belongs to."

Logan wasn't in the mood for guessing games. He puffed out his cheeks and shrugged. "Pass."

"Bosco Maximuke."

Normally, Logan would've had some sort of reaction to that. Tonight, though, with Mister Whisper on the prowl, his family sitting in a safe house just along the road, and half a litre of Red Bull buzzing around in his system, his focus was elsewhere.

"Interesting," he said. "I'll follow that up once all this has settled down."

"Aye. Well. Just thought you'd want to know," Ben said. "Keep in touch."

The screen lit-up as the call was ended, then dimmed again.

Ben hadn't sounded happy. No surprise there. Logan would have to go some to make all this up to him later. Hamza, too.

He fished out another handful of Maltesers and turned his attention back to the safe house. Almost the precise moment he did, his phone rang again. An incoming video call this time. The name on the screen made him sit up straighter, despite the protests from his dead arse.

He caught himself checking his hair and teeth in the rearview mirror, reprimanded himself with some muttered swearing, then answered the call.

Shona Maguire's face filled the screen. Logan couldn't see anything of the background, but he could tell by the way her hair was hanging in loose ringlets that she wasn't at work.

"Hey!" she said, all smiles at first, then frowning. "Where are you? You're all dark?"

"In the car," Logan said.

"Shite, you're not driving, are you?" she teased. "I don't think you're allowed to video call and drive. You could get into trouble, and I hear the police in this town are a right bunch of dicks."

"Aye, I've heard that a few times myself," he agreed. "I'll keep my eyes peeled."

"You do that," Shona said.

There was an awkward silence as Logan tried to decide if it was his turn to speak.

"Is, eh, is everything alright?" he asked, filling the void with the first thing that came into his head.

"Fine, aye. Just relaxing after a hard day's cutting people into wee bits. That Pot Noodle was pretty rank, by the way," she said. "You didn't miss much."

"Oh, well. That's good to know," Logan said. "But it was... fun. Lunch, I mean."

"It would've got way more fun, too," Shona said, then her face fell. "I don't mean... I'm not saying... I had chocolate eclairs in the fridge."

"Those weren't a weird flavour too, were they?"

"What, like Spaghetti Bolognaise? No, cream, chocolate, and that pastry stuff. What's it called."

"Choux?"

Shona smirked. "Bless you."

It wasn't a funny joke. Not by a long-shot. Logan found himself chuckling, anyway.

"You get the report on our mystery man?" Shona asked.

"Uh, yeah, I saw it," Logan lied. "Haven't had a chance to go over it properly yet."

"It's pretty much what we discussed," Shona said. "Any luck IDing him?"

"Not yet. It's sort of slipped down the list of priorities a bit. We've had something come up."

"Ah. Is that why you went running out on me earlier?" Shona asked. She gave a little shake of her head. "Sorry, none of my business."

"No. Aye. I mean, it was just a..."

He wanted to say 'work thing.' He wanted to play it down, to avoid her being soiled by Owen Petrie like everything else in his life had been.

But that wasn't fair.

He took a deep breath, looked her in the eye, and told her the truth.

"Owen Petrie. Mister Whisper. He escaped from Carstairs a few days ago. He's up here now. He's targeted the kids of two officers I work closely with."

"Jesus. He's taken them?"

"No. Didn't manage. Got disturbed both times. But he's sent

pictures of another kid, taken through a window. Like he was watching them."

"Christ Almighty, that's creepy," Shona said, visibly shuddering. "Another officer's kid?"

"No. I mean, I don't know. But none of the others I work with have..."

The rest of the sentence stuck in Logan's throat. He choked, coughed, and sat forward, grabbing for the phone.

"Shona, I have to go. I'm sorry."

The look of surprise on her face was only there for a moment before he terminated the call and frantically swiped to recent calls.

"Come on, come on," he muttered, as he waited for Ben to answer. The line clicked. Logan spoke before Ben had a chance to. "Has Sinead seen the photos?"

"Sinead?" Ben sounded confused. But, when he said the PC's name a second later, Logan could hear the same dawning horror in the DI's voice as he felt himself. "Sinead. Shite."

"Show her. Put me on loudspeaker so I can hear."

There was some clunking and clattering from the other end. Logan set the phone back in the cradle on the dash and stared at it his leg bouncing on the clutch pedal.

"Sinead, do me a favour, will you?"

"Sure, sir. What do you need?"

Logan bit down on his bottom lip, eyes still fixed on the phone.

"Take a look at these."

There was a rustling of the evidence bag. Sinead's voice came again.

"Are these the photos that..."

Her words fell away into a chasm of silence.

"Sir?" she said, and the breathless whisper of it told Logan everything he needed to know before she said it. "That's Harris. That's my brother!"

"What? What's happening?"

That was Tyler, his voice growing louder as he approached the phone.

"These photos! They're Harris! That's Val's house!" Sinead said, the words coming out as a series of throaty sobs.

"What's the address?" Logan asked.

There was silence from the phone. A sniff. A sob.

"Sinead, what's the address?" Logan asked again.

This time, she gave it. Logan's knowledge of Inverness still had big gaps in it, but he knew roughly where that address was. Close. He could be there in minutes.

"Shite," he spat, shooting a look along the road in the direction of the safe house. He fired up the engine, and the Volvo roared like a lion. "I'm on my way."

CHAPTER TWENTY-FIVE

HE WAS TOO LATE. THAT MUCH WAS OBVIOUS.

The front of the house had been all locked up, but the back gate was open. The back door, too. Logan hurried towards it, not sneaking, or creeping, no thought for his own personal safety. If the bastard was lying in wait in there, he'd deal with it. Let him jump out. Let him spring his fucking trap. See how far it got him.

Logan was halfway along the path when he saw the body of a woman slumped over beside the bins. Somewhere in the distance, sirens wailed.

He hurried over to the motionless woman. Several thin lines of blood ran down her face. They were uneven, unsteady, like they'd been painted on by someone with a shaky hand.

Logan felt her neck. There was a pulse there. Weak, but steady. He fired off a text to Ben, telling him to send an ambulance, and then copied in Tyler and Hamza to be on the safe side.

Removing his coat, he draped it over the unconscious woman and tucked it in underneath her as best he could.

With that done, he pressed on into the house, more cautious

this time than a few moments before, the discovery of poor Auntie Val a stark reminder that it wasn't just his life that he was putting on the line by barging in.

The back door led into a utility room off a good-sized kitchen. The internal door was open, and through it, Logan could see the debris of a broken mug on the floor.

He poked his head around the doorframe, but found the kitchen empty.

The kettle was cool to the touch. If someone had been making tea, then it had been a while ago.

Logan moved on into the hall. He stopped there and listened, but all he could hear was the coming of the sirens. The house itself was silent and still.

The light was on in the living room. Logan entered, and recognised it from the photographs. Same curtains. Same couch. All that was missing was the child.

Blue lights lit up the room, flashing across the walls.

Logan met two Uniforms at the front door, flashed them his ID, then sent them around to the back of the house to look after Val until the ambulance arrived.

His phone rang as he was dishing out the orders, and he reached for it without looking. He automatically swiped the answer button while the Uniforms went hurrying around the back, and it was only as he was bringing the phone to his ear that he realised there was no name on the screen.

The sound down the line was echoey, like the person on the other end of the line was far underground.

"Hello?" Logan said.

He'd expected Petrie to reply. He'd been ready for the bastard's voice.

He wasn't ready for the voice he actually heard.

"H-help me."

A child.

A boy.

Harris.

"P-please."

And with that, the line went dead.

Logan looked along the path, beyond the gate at the front, as another car came skidding to a halt. Sinead was out of the passenger door before the vehicle had fully stopped, leaving the door open as she raced up the path, shouting her brother's name.

"Harris? Harris!"

Logan caught her at the door. "Sinead. Sinead, stop," he said.

Sinead's eyes were wide and blazing with panic and fear. She looked from the DCI into the hallway behind him, her thought process written in the anguished lines of her face.

"Oh God. Is he...? Is he...?"

"He's not here," Logan said. "But he's alive. I spoke to him."

Tyler ran up the path behind Sinead, the wailing of an approaching ambulance accompanying him like a soundtrack.

"You spoke to him?" Sinead gasped. "How could you speak to him? Where is he?"

"I don't know," Logan said. "I got a phone call just a few seconds before you got here. I'm pretty sure... I'm *sure* it was him."

"Well, what did he say?!" Sinead demanded.

Logan shifted uncomfortably. "I'm not sure..."

"Tell her," Tyler interjected. "What did he say?"

Logan tightened his grip on Sinead's shoulders, readying himself in case he had to hold her up. "He said, 'Help me.'"

Tyler was at Sinead's side in one step, an arm around her waist, a hand grabbing for hers. He met Logan's gaze dead-on.

"I've got her," he said. "It's fine."

Sinead twisted, shrugging them both off. "Where's Val? What happened to Val?"

"She's out back. She's hurt, but she's alive. Ambulance is on its... It's here," Logan said, just as the paramedics arrived in a blaze of sirens and lights. He looked from Sinead to Tyler and back again. "I'll take them round, then I'll check the rest of the house."

"You haven't checked it yet?" Sinead asked. She forced past him, voice rising as she projected it into every corner of the building. "Harris? Harris!"

"We should try not to disturb the place if we can—"

"Aye. I know, boss," Tyler said. "Can I get in?"

There was something off about the DC. Something had changed in the way he was looking at Logan, and not for the better.

"Aye. Just be careful," Logan said, stepping aside.

Tyler entered without a word and hurried after Sinead, who had gone running up the stairs, two at a time.

Logan glanced after them, then jogged along the path to meet the paramedics as they climbed down out of the ambulance. "She's round back," he said, pointing them towards the alley that ran around to the back of the house. "And please..." His gaze went to the upstairs bedroom window, where a light had just clicked on. "...hurry."

SINEAD HADN'T EXPECTED him to be up there. Not really. She'd had to check, though. She'd had to know for sure.

His room—and it *was* his room, Val had repeatedly told him, any time he wanted to use it—was empty. A pair of new pyjamas had been sat on his pillow for him, and a hot water bottle—now lukewarm—had been slipped between the quilt and the sheet.

The bedroom spun, the floor rocking like the deck of a boat. Sinead grabbed for the doorframe to support herself, missed, and was caught by Tyler before she lost her balance completely.

"He's gone," she sobbed. "He's gone. He's taken him. Oh, God, Tyler, he's taken him."

"I know, I know. Shh. We'll get him back. It's OK, we'll get him."

"How?!" Sinead demanded, her grief shifting gears into an explosive burst of anger. "How will we get him? *How?*"

"We'll..." Tyler began, then she collapsed against him and buried her face against his chest. He held her as her body was wracked by big silent sobs. "We'll get him back," he said, holding her close. "We'll get him back."

"THE FUCKITY FUCK's going on, then?" asked Detective Superintendent Hoon, appearing in the Incident Room like a demon summoned from the fiery depths of Hell.

His gaze swept across the room like a searchlight, alighting briefly on the faces of DC Khaled and DI Forde.

"You both look like you've recently shat out a walrus. What's happened?"

"A lot, sir," Ben said. "Not one bit of it good." His phone rang. He grabbed it from the desk and checked the screen. "It's Logan," he said, tapping the answer button and putting the handset to his ear. "Jack?"

Ben listened. Hamza and Hoon both watched him, and both saw the way the colour left his face.

"OK. We'll be here."

The DI hung up the call. He dropped the phone back onto the desk like it was dirty, somehow. Infected.

"What happened, sir?" Hamza asked.

Ben felt behind him until he found his chair, then lowered himself into it. "The, eh, the boy's gone."

"Shite," Hamza whispered.

"What boy?" Hoon demanded. "What the fuck's going on?"

"Sinead's... Eh, Sinead Bell. From Uniform?" Ben said.

"What about her?"

"Her brother. Harris. Petrie's taken him."

"Fuck. *What?*" Hoon spat. He looked from one man to the other, his expression darkening with every moment that passed. "Well?" he snapped, at neither one in particular. "Is someone going to explain to me just what the fuck is going on?"

And so, they did. They tag-teamed it, in the end, Hamza filling the DSup in on everything that had happened at his house, and Ben taking over to explain how the photos had led them to discover that Harris was missing.

Once it was all over, Hoon sat heavily in Logan's chair, spun it around once, then loudly announced: "Well, what an almighty clusterfuck this is," before jumping back to his feet and dishing out orders. "Ben, get the press. All of them. Round up every last one of the parasitic wankers you can find. No point trying to fucking contain this when that boy's life's at risk."

"We're going public, sir?"

"Too fucking right we are. Name and shame. Let them all tug each other off in a foamy-mouthed Mister Whisper frenzy. Let's shine a spotlight on the fucker, make sure he's got nowhere to hide. I want pictures of him on every front page tomorrow morning, and every news bulletin within the hour. Wall to wall coverage. I want to see the bastard's ugly mug everywhere I look. Papers, telly, internet. Commemorative fucking tea towels, if it comes to it. I want his face everywhere. Got it?"

Ben nodded. "Right, sir."

"In fact, no. Forget that," Hoon said. He spun on his heels to Hamza. "You. Tweedle-fucking-dum. You do all that stuff I just said. DI Forde, you're going to help me round up the cavalry. Anyone who's off-duty is now officially back on fucking duty as of right now. If they're sleeping, I want them woken up. If they're having a shite, I don't even want them wasting their time wiping. We get them in, and we get them in now. I want all fucking hands on deck for this."

The Detective Superintendent's face had been turning a deeper, richer shade of purple with every word he spat. Now, his whole head resembled a particularly nasty bruise.

"Mister Whisper is not getting up to his old fucking tricks again. Not in my town!"

He looked around at both men, neither of whom had yet moved.

"Well?" he screeched. "What are you fucking waiting for? Jump to it!"

LOGAN PULLED HIS COAT ON, patted his inside pocket to make sure the postcard was still there, then watched as Sinead climbed into the back of the ambulance beside the unconscious Val.

The paramedics had done what they could to stabilise her at the scene, then loaded her onto a spinal board and into the back of the ambulance. She was breathing, which was good, but she was still unresponsive, which wasn't. The longer she remained out, the more chance there was for lasting damage, and she'd been out for a while already.

The house and gardens had been cordoned off with tape as soon as the paramedics had taken Val out, and half a dozen Uniforms were standing guard at various points, because they hadn't been dismissed, and they weren't entirely sure what else to do.

Geoff Palmer's Scene of Crime team was on the way. Logan was hoping to be gone by the time they showed up.

The rear ambulance doors closed, and Logan watched it go speeding off, sirens screaming. He kept watching until it had rounded the corner and vanished out of sight at the end of the road, then turned to find DC Neish standing on the path behind him.

"Tyler," he said. "Didn't see you there. You OK, son?"

"Petrie's nothing to do with us."

Logan frowned. "Eh?"

"That's what you said. Petrie's nothing to do with us. Any of us." Tyler was shaking, like he might be about to burst into tears, or start swinging punches. There was also a very good chance he might do both. "And now look what's happened. Harris. Hamza's wee one. Fucking... Hoon's nephew. You told us to keep away. You told us it wasn't our case, but it looks like nobody bothered their arse to tell Petrie that. Looks like we're all up to our necks in it, whether you like it or not."

"Look, Tyler—"

"And what next? Who next?" Tyler asked. He thought of his mum, and of a semi-naked Russian grinning up from his office chair. His voice came out as a high-pitched croak. "Who else is in danger?"

Logan sighed. It wasn't aimed at the DC. It wasn't even aimed at himself, really. It was just a brief lapse of strength. A sagging of the shoulders. A lowering of the head.

"I don't know, son," he admitted. "I honestly don't know." He looked back over his shoulder in the direction of the fading sirens. "You going to head in to the hospital?"

Tyler shook his head. "No. She doesn't want me there. She wants me out looking for Harris. So, that's what I'm going to do."

Logan looked up at the light burning in the bedroom window of the house. He felt the weight in his inside pocket and thought of the safe house just a few streets away.

At last, he looked DC Neish straight in the eye. He smiled. It was an apology. A peace offering. "Mind if I give you a hand?"

CHAPTER TWENTY-SIX

LOGAN CLOSED THE DOOR TO HOON'S OFFICE, ALLOWED himself a tiny moment of relief, then set off in the direction of the Incident Room.

They were going to be OK. It had taken some persuasion on his part, and two-thirds of a full-scale bollocking on Hoon's, but the DSup was authorising the resource required to put the safe house on twenty-four-seven surveillance.

Aye, that was just a grand way of saying there'd be a Uniform in a car parked along the street keeping watch on the place, but it would do. If Vanessa and Maddie kept their wits about them, then that should be enough.

Please, let that be enough.

He entered the Incident Room to find the place alive with activity. Ben was talking to a couple of officers from CID—a DS and a DC, if Logan remembered correctly, although there was no chance of him recalling their names—while Hamza and Tyler spoke into their phones. Both men were animated, their hands gesticulating as their voices rose, like they were giving serious grief to whoever was proving to be an obstacle on the other end of the line.

Good for them.

The press conference had been scheduled for first thing in the morning. Photos and quotes had gone out to the major media outlets and the locals, and they'd been scrambling to be the first to break the news online.

Hamza had seemed genuinely delighted when the first 'Mister Whisper Strikes Again!' headline had appeared on one of the red tops' websites. Logan had felt a sickness deep in his gut.

Harris's photo would soon be everywhere, sat right next to Petrie's mugshot, forever linking the two in people's minds. Tyler had given Sinead a call to prepare her, but she hadn't answered, and there had been no further updates from her on the condition of her aunt.

Logan sat at his desk and looked over to the Big Board that Sinead had been working on. It was good. Different to how Caitlyn would've done it, but a solid effort. Clear, informative, easy to follow—everything he could've asked for.

He swept his gaze across it, taking in the bigger picture, then something drew him back to the start where Sinead had stuck half a sheet of A4 paper with the words 'Premier Inn' printed on it. To the paper, she'd added a Post-It that simply asked 'Why?'

Logan read both notes again.

Why?

Why there? On the one night in his life that he'd put his own family in an Inverness Premier Inn, a body turns up at another branch at the opposite end of the city.

Connected? Almost certainly not.

But maybe.

He rose slowly from his chair. The others were all still engaged in their conversations. Ben seemed to be about to finish up with the CID lot, but he had a habit of remembering things at the last moment, so it might drag on yet.

Logan approached the Big Board. He touched the 'Premier

Inn' sheet, like physical contact might somehow impart more information, then went over the other information that Sinead had pinned in place.

The photographs of the victim looked like a make-up test for a low-budget horror movie from the eighties, where buckets of blood and visceral gore compensated for god-awful acting and a complete lack of plot.

Sinead had added a Post-It for every notable thing about the body—the missing teeth, the mashed-up face, the lack of hands. That sort of thing.

Below those was another note that listed a few less-interesting details, like his suit with its charity-shop tag.

Logan turned to ask Hamza if anything useful had come back from the British Heart Foundation stores, but he was still fully invested in his phone call. It could wait.

The bottom note also referenced the victim having walked in his bare feet, and his shoes, which were too big for his feet. Logan had been dimly aware of that detail, but his head had been full of Owen Petrie, and it was only now that something about it nagged at him.

Logan stared into the mangled face of the victim. He picked at the skin around his thumbs with his forefingers, the cogs in his brain clanking and whirring into life.

"The shoes," he muttered.

The shoes.

"Do we know what—?" he began, before a wave from Tyler caught his eye.

"Boss. Sinead," the DC said, holding up his mobile phone. He was still on the landline, and he tossed the smaller handset to Logan, who snatched it from the air and brought it immediately to his ear.

"Sinead. Hello. It's Lo... It's Jack. What's the latest?"

Constable Bell sounded shaken. Probably the understatement of the year. Val was in a bad way. Her skull had been fractured, and there was a bleed on her brain. Whoever had hit her had done so with tremendous force.

The next few hours would be critical, the doctors had told her. She was in surgery now, but the damage was severe, and Sinead had been primed to prepare herself for the worst. Even if Val woke up, there was no saying she'd be anything like the person she was before.

Another life destroyed by that bastard.

How many more?

Logan filled her in on the progress so far. It made for slim pickings, so he focused on the effort, rather than the results. They were pulling out all the stops. Officers were being drafted in from across the country. They were going to find him, the DCI promised. They were going to bring Harris home.

"You want me to send Tyler to you?" Logan asked, once he'd brought her up to date.

"No. I want him there helping."

"You shouldn't be on your own, Sinead. Not at a time like this."

"Nor should Harris," Sinead said, and he heard her break as she spoke his name. "So bring him home, sir. Please."

"I will. *We* will," Logan said.

Sinead sniffed and cleared her throat. "I better get inside," she said, and the strain of holding it together was obvious in her voice. "I'll call back."

The line went dead before Logan could reply. He held onto the phone until it went dark, then set it on Tyler's desk.

"One sec," the DC said into the landline, then he pressed the handset to his shoulder.

"Val's in surgery. Sinead is... doing fine, considering."

"Does she want me over?"

Logan shook his head. "She wants us all focused on getting her brother home."

Tyler looked down at his mobile, nodded, then returned to his call.

"Sorry about that. Can you send the link through to my email?" he asked. "Have you got a pen?"

Logan headed over to Ben, the Big Board and the victim whose face was plastered across it forgotten for the moment.

"Call it twenty minutes, will we?" Ben was saying to the CID officers. "Briefing room won't be big enough, so we'll use the canteen. Can you get on that?"

The Detective Sergeant—a thirty-something man with a rugged, outdoorsy sort of look to him—gave a confident nod. "Not a problem, sir. We're on it. Fifteen minutes."

He and the younger DC he'd brought with him about-turned in near-unison and went striding out of the Incident Room.

"What was all that about?" Logan asked, as the doors swung closed.

"Hoon wants a full staff briefing. As many bodies as we can cram in. He wants to bring them all up to speed. Stress the importance of getting the boy home safe," Ben said. "Only, he swore a lot more when he was explaining it."

"Obviously," Logan agreed. "Does he have everything he needs?"

Ben raised a quizzical eyebrow.

"For the briefing," said Logan. "Does he have all the information?"

"Oh, no. You misunderstand, Jack," Ben replied. He gave the DCI a bump on the arm, and smiled. "He's no' giving the briefing. You are."

A SHADE over fifteen minutes later, Logan stood in the canteen, looking out at a sea of officers. Most of them were Uniforms, but there were half a dozen plainclothes officers dotted around, as well as Tyler and Ben sitting in the front row.

Any other day, he'd be bracing himself for the pair of them to start heckling him as soon as he stood up to talk, but not tonight. Everyone's sense of humour had long-since deserted them.

Hamza sat behind Logan and off to the side, the back of his chair pushed up against a stack of trays. Technically, the canteen was still open, but the food had all been covered over, and the lights had been switched off at the serving area for the duration of the briefing.

Detective Superintendent Hoon stood at the very back of the room, directly across from Logan and very deliberately in his eyeline. There was a low murmur of chattering from the audience, but mostly they were staring at him, too.

God, Logan hated doing these things.

He had never been what you might call a motivational speaker. Not unless you counted the threat of a boot up the arse as an acceptable form of motivation.

Even then, that worked much better on a one-to-one basis. In a room this size, with this many people, there were just too many arses to kick. And that meant finding a way to motivate them without the threat of physical violence. Inspiring through words alone.

It had never been his strong point. Fortunately, given what he was about to tell them, it shouldn't take much to get them motivated.

He looked out at the sea of expectant faces. He hardly recognised any of them, and very few of them knew him other than by reputation. A few of them—a lot of them, actually—looked young. Stupidly young. Too young for what they might be about to face.

God, Logan hated doing these things.

But then, he only had himself to blame. It was all his fault.

He had a postcard in his pocket that told him so.

Pushing that thought away, Logan turned and gave the nod to Hamza. With the press of a remote, a boy's face—all dirt and smiles—filled the projector screen beside the DCI.

"Harris Bell. Brother of Constable Sinead Bell, who I'm sure most of you know. He was staying with his aunt tonight in the Viewhill area when she was badly beaten, and he was taken, we believe, by this man."

Hamza picked up on his cue. He moved to the next slide. Logan didn't have to look to know this had happened. The ripple of recognition and horror that spread through the audience told him that the image on screen had changed.

"Owen Petrie. Maybe better known to some of you as 'Mister Whisper.' For those of you fortunate enough to be unfamiliar with him, he abducted and murdered three young boys in and around Glasgow over a decade ago," Logan explained. "He was, until last week, a patient at Carstairs State Hospital. But he got out. And he came here."

"Why?" asked a senior uniformed officer. A Chief Inspector, if Logan remembered correctly. "Why here? What ties him to Inverness?"

Logan briefly met Hoon's eye at the back of the hall.

"I do," he said, in answer to the question. "I was the arresting officer in the original case. I brought him in. He's here because I'm here. I believe he targeted Constable Bell's brother to hurt me and the people I... know.

"But, right now, the why isn't important. We need to know the where. Where is Harris? Where would he take him? Petrie's new to the city, fresh out of Carstairs. We have reason to believe he had access to information on the inside through a doctor who worked there, but he's on his own now. No money, no friends, nowhere to go. But he's gone *somewhere*, and we need to find where."

Logan frowned. A thought darted through his head, then

was gone. He tried to grab for it, but it slipped through his fingers like a dream in the moments after waking.

"He, uh... Historically, he's kept his victims alive for around seventy-two hours," Logan continued. "But in those three days he put those kids through hell. So, we find Harris quickly. Tonight. Even if it means turning the city upside-down. We find that boy. We bring him home. If we can catch Petrie while we're at it, that's a bonus, but the safe return of Harris Bell is our number one focus, and we..."

Is he on his own, though?

The question popped unbidden into Logan's head, throwing him off his stride.

The audience watched in silence as the DCI turned and looked at the projector screen. Owen Petrie's face leered out at him from ten years ago. The scar on his head was still fresh, the skin puckered where the sutures pulled it tight.

This wasn't the face Logan remembered, though. That had been pre-scar. Pre-arrest. Pre-fall. Back when he was leering at him, laughing at him, telling him of all the terrible things he'd done to those kids.

Telling him how much he'd loved it.

"Eh... Jack?" Ben prompted him from the front row.

"Hmm? Oh. Sorry. I just..."

There was a ring of them. That's what Hoon had said. A ring. A network.

A support group.

They'd been assuming he was working alone now, like they'd assumed he was working alone then, but what if he hadn't been? What if he wasn't?

What if he had help?

Shoes.

That word also made itself known without warning or fanfare.

Shoes. The murder victim's shoes had been too big.

How big?

"What size were those trainers?" Logan asked, turning to DI Forde.

Ben frowned. "Trainers?"

"On the victim. At the hotel."

"Oh. Them. Eh... I'm no' sure."

"What the fuck are you two wittering about?" bellowed Hoon from up the back. "Now's hardly the time for a cosy fucking chat. Get on with it."

"Tyler? Hamza? The shoes, any idea?" Logan asked, ignoring the Detective Superintendent. There was some confused murmuring from the audience, as the Uniforms and CID tried unsuccessfully to follow what was going on.

"Not sure, boss. Big, though," Tyler said, which was no bloody help at all, quite frankly.

"Thirteens, sir," said Hamza.

Thirteens.

Thirteens.

No. Couldn't be.

Another coincidence, that was all.

Logan looked down at his feet, and the scuffed boots he wore on them.

"Fuck it," he ejected, then he turned and ran out of the canteen, with the roaring of Detective Superintendent Hoon chasing him along the corridor.

Logan was out of breath when he threw open the doors of the Incident Room. He thundered over to the exhibits desk, where the evidence they'd gathered in the case was stacked in sturdy storage boxes.

He found the trainers in the second box and lifted them out by the corner of their sealed plastic bag. They were battered old Nikes, the rubber of the sole well-worn, the leather, or plastic, or whatever the hell they were made from nowadays, all coated with flecks of dried mud.

Logan hadn't run in years. Not unless he had to. But, somewhere at the back of his mind, he'd harboured the idea that he might again someday. That he might find the time and the inclination to get out there into the wilderness like he used to do.

And so, he'd kept his old running shoes. He'd taken them with him when he and Vanessa had split up, and they'd moved with him whenever he'd relocated to a new place. A new house. A new flat.

Even a new city.

The door opened at Logan's back. A slightly breathless Tyler hurried in and let the door close again behind him. "Hoon's on the warpath, boss. He's charging over, and he's not happy," the DC said. He swallowed, then puffed out his chest. "And, well, I'm not happy, either. We're meant to be discussing Harris and Petrie. What's more important that you go—"

"These trainers," said Logan, holding the bag up for the younger detective to see.

Tyler flicked his gaze to them, then back to the DCI. "What about them?"

"They're mine."

CHAPTER TWENTY-SEVEN

THE MAN HAD GONE. THAT WAS GOOD. HE SCARED HIM. Terrified him. Made him cry, even though he tried so hard to hold it back.

The man had laughed at him. He'd stood over him, and he'd laughed. Then, he'd caught one of his tears on the tip of his finger and he'd tasted it, moaning with pleasure like it was something delicious.

After that, the man had squatted down in front of the chair and put his icy-cold hands on his knees. The man had just stared at him for a while, like he was memorising his face. There had been no expression on his own, just a blank, lifeless stare from eyes that felt cruel and judgemental.

Harris had sat there, saying nothing, his hands tied behind him, his face glistening with tears and snot. A minute had passed. Two. The man just watched him, and watched him, and watched him, until the tension of it all became too much, and Harris sobbed into the rag that had been rammed into his mouth and taped over.

He had wanted to be sick. He had gagged and boaked as the material was forced into his mouth back at Auntie Val's. He had thought he was going to die, right there and then, unable to breathe. But the man had told him to breathe through his nose. He'd guided him, demonstrating with his own breaths.

In. Out. In. Out.

He'd almost seemed kind, but then he dragged the boy out into the garden, and Harris saw Auntie Val lying by the bins. Her eyes were staring. Her mouth moved, making gurgling sounds as bubbles of blood burst on her lips.

Harris had kicked and struggled, tried to scream, but then he was inside the back of van, and the door was sliding shut, plunging him into total darkness.

An engine had roared. A voice had spoken as a whisper in his ear.

"You and I are going to have a lot of fun together."

Everything after that was a blur of panic and fear. A bag had been put over his head. Voices had spoken, muffled and quiet. There had been arguing, he thought, but whispered so he didn't hear it.

And then, there had been hands, and dragging, and carry-ing, and movement.

And then, there had been the ropes, and the chair, and the man standing over him, waiting to taste his tears.

He was gone now, but Harris wasn't alone. He'd left the woman to watch him. She sat in a chair in the darkened next room, only half-visible through the open doorway.

The man had said she was going to watch him, and Harris could see the light reflecting off her eyes. She hadn't said a word since he'd been brought in, but her gaze was fixed on him, pinning him to the spot and daring him to make a sound, to try to escape.

The man was bad, but something about her told Harris that the woman would be even worse.

And so, he lowered his head to hide his shame, and cried big heaving sobs into his lap.

CHAPTER TWENTY-EIGHT

"THIS HAD BETTER BE FUCKING GOOD, JACK!" HOON SPAT, throwing open the double doors of the Incident Room like a gunfighter entering a Wild West saloon. "What's with the fucking vanishing act?"

"The body found behind the Premier Inn was wearing a pair of trainers that were too big for his feet," Logan explained, wasting no time. "They were my trainers. They came from my flat. Petrie must've taken them."

Hoon's forehead furrowed as his brain worked to process this.

"So, what are you saying? Petrie killed that guy?"

"Aye. I think so."

Tyler shot Hoon a sideways glance to make sure he wasn't about to incur the DSup's wrath by speaking over him. "Didn't the Pathology report say he was held down by two or three people when the teeth were being yanked, boss?"

"It did," Logan confirmed, not taking his eyes off Hoon. "You said it yourself, sir. He was part of a ring. He's not working alone on this. He's got help."

"Oh, well that's fucking marvellous news," Hoon ejected, in a tone that suggested it very much was not.

"Bosco."

Both senior officers turned to look at Tyler, and he had to resist the urge to run away.

"*What*?" Hoon asked.

Tyler cleared his throat. "Eh, Bosco Maximuke, sir. His van... one of them... was identified as being at the scene around the time the body was dumped."

Hoon blinked several times, like this information was causing some sort of short-circuit in his brain. "Bosco and Owen Petrie? I can't see it. Bosco's a fucking pain in the arse, but... a paedo? No. Doubt it."

"Bosco goes where the money is," Logan said. "And there's money in filth."

"I just can't see it," Hoon said, shaking his head. "Drugs, prostitution, whatever. Aye. That's Bosco. But him and Petrie working together? No."

"Worth a follow-up," Logan said.

"I don't think it is," Hoon said. "I think we need to focus on finding the missing boy. Forget Bosco for now."

Logan noted that Hoon had gone several sentences now without swearing once. Surely a new personal best?

"With all due respect, sir, this is our only lead on the boy."

"You fucking deaf, Detective Chief Inspector?" Hoon spat, breaking his swear-free run. For a moment, it looked like he was about to launch into one of his usual tirades, but then his shoulders dipped, and he ran a hand down his face from top to bottom. "Fine. No, you're right. Worth a look. Ben can finish the briefing. I think it's a waste of time, but I've been wrong before."

"Very big of you to admit it, sir," Logan said.

"Aye, well. It was once, when I accepted your fucking transfer request," Hoon replied.

"We all make mistakes."

Hoon nodded. His head seemed heavy, like he was struggling to hold it up. "Aye. That we do, Jack. That we do." He drew himself up to his full height and headed for the door. "And remember, I am the fucking loop. Alright?"

"Got it, sir," Logan replied, just as Hoon vanished out through the double doors again. He watched them for a while, wondering what the hell all that was about, then turned to Tyler. "Fancy a trip to see Bosco Maximuke?"

Tyler shifted on the balls of his feet. "I, uh, I'd better check in with Sinead, boss. I mean, I would, but... I should probably..."

"Aye. Makes sense. If she needs you there, go," Logan said. "Soon as I know anything, I'll be in touch.

"Cool. Good. That's..." Tyler's tongue flicked across his lips, which had gone dry. "I mean, you two know each other, anyway. Don't you? Bosco and you, I mean. You go... back. A while."

"We're no' exactly best pals," Logan said. "I did recently burn down his office, you might recall? But aye, for better or worse I've been dealing with the Russian bastard for a while."

"You never pegged him as being connected to Petrie?"

Logan shook his head. "No. Not a pair I'd have put together, but... Christ knows. We'll see."

"Yeah, boss." Tyler nodded. "I guess we will."

LOGAN MADE a quick diversion via the safe house on the way to Bosco's yard and was satisfied to see a squad car parked just along the street, a burly male Uniform watching the house from the driver's seat.

One less thing to worry about.

When he reached the Russian's yard, it was locked up. Hardly surprising, given the time of night, but a few long blasts of his horn brought an irritated looking skinhead scuttling out through the front gate.

The smell of burning Portakabin still lingered in the air, but the rain—never far away—had started to fall on the drive over, and it dampened the odour down. The steady downpour did nothing for the demeanour of the skinhead, though, who scowled up at it like he was angry with the gods themselves.

Logan recognised Valdis, mostly from the bruising the skinhead had sustained when the DCI had elbowed him in the face just a few days earlier. Judging by the way Valdis's mouth curled into a sneer, he had no problem recognising Logan, either.

"It's you. Should have guessed," Valdis spat. "What now?"

"I'm here to see Bosco," Logan said. He pointed at Valdis's bruises and twiddled his finger around in a circle. "How's your face, by the way? On the mend, I hope."

"Face is fucking not your business. And Bosco is not here."

"Where is he?"

"Not here. That is all I know." Valdis held up a finger. "Wait. No. I know something else, too."

"And what's that?" Logan asked.

"I know you are not fucking getting into yard without warrant," Valdis said. There was venom in it, and he looked Logan up and down like he was a giant cockroach who'd just come climbing out from behind the fridge. "You fucking police pigs. I am sick of you coming here, throwing weight around. If it up to me, you go fuck yourself."

"That's no' very friendly now, Valdis," Logan said. He nodded back in the direction of the gate, and a droplet of rainwater fell from the end of his nose. "How about you run along and tell Bosco I'm here? Be a good lad."

Valdis squared his shoulders. He gave the DCI another once-over with his eyes, sizing him up this time.

"I wouldn't, son," Logan warned. "Or have you forgotten what happened last time?"

"Fucking take me by surprise last time," Valdis said.

Logan chuckled. "I took *you* by surprise? If memory serves, son, you were the one trying to jump me from behind. I just defended myself."

The DCI's smile remained fixed in place, but the look in his eyes became a sharp and dangerous thing.

"How do you fancy your chances face to face?" he asked.

"No problem," Valdis said, after just a moment's hesitation. His sneer became a grin far broader than Logan's own. "How you fancy chances three against one?"

Over the sound of the rain, Logan heard the scuffing of a footstep behind him. He looked back, first over his left shoulder, then his right, and realised he was in the centre of a triangle of angry bastards.

"Now, here is my advice," Valdis said. "Go. Get fuck out of here. Bosco is not here. I will—if I fucking feel like it—tell him you came when I see him tomorrow."

Logan nodded slowly. "And if I choose not to follow that advice?"

"Then... This would be regretful for you," Valdis replied, and there was no mistaking the meaning behind it.

Logan glanced around at all three men again, calculating his chances. He came to the conclusion that they weren't great. He might be able to take down one or two of them, but the men were younger than he was, faster than he was, and no doubt had come tooled up. It was not a fight he was going to win.

"Maybe you can pass on a message for me, then?" Logan asked.

Valdis seemed annoyed by the suggestion. "What is message?" he demanded.

"Tell him I hadn't put him down as a nonce. Tell him I know he's helping Owen Petrie. Tell him if either of them harm a hair on that boy's head, I will hunt them down, I will find them, and I will turn them inside-out. Slowly. Along with anyone else who helped them. And I will enjoy every fucking moment of it."

He looked from face to face. The men behind him were stoic and impassive, but there was a subtle shift in Valdis's expression that he couldn't quite identify.

"You got that?" Logan asked. "You want to write it down, maybe, so you don't forget?"

Valdis tapped the side of his head to indicate that the message was locked in, then gestured to the Volvo abandoned outside the yard's double gates.

"Now, get in car and fuck off."

"You don't want to get involved in this, Valdis," Logan said. "Child abduction. Child murder. This isn't what you signed up for. If you know where the boy is, tell me, and we can make sure you—none of you three—get the rap for it."

There was an exchange of looks between the points of the triangle surrounding the DCI, and Logan almost let himself believe the skinheads were going to take him up on the offer.

But then, Valdis had to go and open his mouth and ruin it.

"We know nothing about any boy," he said. "Now, get fuck out of here before we make you."

Logan thought about just going for it. Taking a kicking would almost be worth it, if it meant getting another crack in at Valdis. That smug fucking look wasn't going to wipe itself off.

But, no. He needed to be in one piece for whatever came next. He couldn't find Petrie from a hospital bed, or worse, the bottom of the Moray Firth.

He settled for eyeballing all three of the baldy-headed bastards in turn, then muttered an, "I'll be back," that was worthy of the Terminator himself, before climbing back into the Volvo and getting the hell out of there.

CHAPTER TWENTY-NINE

HAMZA WAS ONTO SOMETHING. HE WAS SURE OF IT.

It would require a spreadsheet, though. And, ideally, a few people with some data entry experience.

Granted, it was a bit of a stretch, and Hoon had made it very clear that until such times as he had evidence that backed up his theory, he was on his own. By then, of course, there would be no point in the additional manpower. He'd have cracked it.

He opened a spreadsheet, typed the numbers one, two, and three in the top left columns, and was about to start working his way through the next hundred or so rows when Logan returned to the Incident Room.

From the look on his face, his meeting with Bosco had not gone well.

"Uh, alright, sir?" Hamza asked. He was the only one in the Incident Room, and felt like he should extend some sort of greeting. "How'd you get on?"

"Shite," Logan said. "No sign of Bosco at the yard. I'm going to pull a home address for him, if we've got one. Last I checked, his address was still registered as being in Glasgow. Don't think we've got a new one for up here, but worth a look. My gut tells me we won't get to speak to him until tomorrow, though, and even then we might be lucky. If he's involved, he may well have done a runner already."

"I think CID went round to speak to his ex-wife at one point, sir. They should have an address for her. She might know where to find him."

"Good to know. I'll get that checked out," Logan said. He looked around. "Where's everyone else?"

"The DI's in with the Detective Superintendent, and Tyler's off to the hospital."

Logan stopped with his coat half on and half off. "What's happened?"

"Nothing. Nothing bad, anyway. Sinead's aunt's stable, they reckon. They're keeping her in an induced coma to give her brain a chance to heal," Hamza said. "So, Sinead doesn't see the point in sitting around there."

"Makes sense. Best to get home and get some rest."

"Aye, you'd think, sir," Hamza said.

Logan finished taking off his coat this time before replying. "She's not coming in, is she?"

"Apparently, aye. Wants to help. Understandable, I suppose."

"Still an' all," Logan said. "This could get rough. Very rough. I'm not sure she should be on the front line for it."

"Good luck trying to stop her, sir," Hamza said, to which Logan could only grunt and nod.

"Fair point," he conceded.

Sinead was young, but she'd had to grow up fast. She was determined to the point of stubbornness, and a bloody good officer to boot. If she wanted to be at the coal face on this one, then someone else would have to discourage her, because Logan wasn't prepared to.

"I've, eh, I've maybe got something," Hamza said. "But it's... tentative at the minute."

Logan hurried over to the DC's desk. "Tentative? I'll take 'almost impossible' at the moment. What is it?"

"It's the words, sir. On the photos and in that envelope he left for you. I've been thinking about them," Hamza said. He glanced down at his notepad. "Mentions, idealist, info. Driveways, toast, nature."

"And?"

"I was trying to think of a way they linked together. Or to see if they made a message. Like, 'driveways toast nature,' could be some sort of environmental message, or whatever."

Logan side-eyed the younger detective. "He's a child killer, Hamza, no' fucking Greenpeace. I mean, I know you said it was tentative..."

"Aye, I know. I decided against that, and started thinking about what else it might be," the DC continued. "You heard of an app called 'what3words,' sir?"

The creases on Logan's forehead made it clear that he had not.

"Right, well, it's like a map thing. Every square metre on Earth is represented by three random words. You put a location into the app and it spits out three words that you can share with people so they can find you. RAC is using it, I think. There was a mountain rescue case down in Fort William recently where a climber was—"

"I don't need the backstory," Logan interrupted. "So... did you try?"

"I did, sir," Hamza replied.

"And?"

"I started with the first three words. From the photos left at my place. Driveways, toast, nature."

"And?" Logan urged again. "Did it work? Is it a place?"

"It's a place, sir, aye."

Logan flopped down into the nearest chair, wide-eyed. "Bloody hell! Seriously?"

"But it's in Alaska."

"Jesus Christ," the DCI sighed, his sudden surge of optimism leaving him like air from a shrivelled balloon. "What about the other one?"

Hamza winced, ever so slightly, before replying. "Switzerland, sir."

"Great," said Logan slapping his thighs and standing up. "So, either he's in Switzerland, or he's near the Arctic bloody Circle."

"Aye, but... they might be jumbled up, sir," Hamza said. "They might not be in the right order. Nature, driveways, toast, for example. That's Norway."

"I highly doubt he's there, either," Logan said. "But... How long to go through them all?"

"A wee while, sir. By my reckoning, there are about a hundred and twenty combinations, if we use all six words. I'll go through them as there original groups of three first, and... I mean, it might turn out to be nothing, obviously, but..."

He ran out of steam then, and finished with a shrug and a vaguely embarrassed look.

"Worth a try," Logan told him. "And good thinking. It's not something I'd have ever come up with. Crack on, and see what you get." He looked at the door and puffed out his cheeks. "I suppose I'd better go rescue Ben."

DI FORDE WAS NOT in Hoon's office when Logan knocked and entered. The Detective Superintendent sat alone, gazing out of the office window at the city beyond.

It wasn't much of a view, really. From Hoon's seat, it was all car showrooms and dual carriageways. Aye, if he got close to the window and got the angle right, he might be able to get a glimpse of the building that housed *Iceland* and *Home Bargains*, but that hardly seemed worth the effort.

"Sorry, sir, I was expecting Ben to be here," Logan volunteered. He wondered if he could just leave now without any fuss. From the look of him, Hoon would probably quite like to be alone. Maybe he could just back out into the corridor again and close the door.

"Sit down," Hoon said, not yet turning.

Damn it.

Logan wheeled one of the other chairs out from the DSup's desk and took a seat across from him. Hoon still hadn't turned away from the window, the lure of the Longman Industrial Estate clearly proving too much of a temptation.

"I sent Ben home," he said.

Logan repeated that last word, but in a higher, somewhat incredulous register. "Home?" he said. "Why did you send him home?"

"Because he's dead on his bloody feet," Hoon said, finally walking himself around in his swivel chair to face the DCI. "He's no' as young as he once was, and I know what a nebby cow that wife of his can be."

Logan had to admit that Ben had looked exhausted. And he couldn't really argue with the 'nebby cow' part, either. Still, given what they were facing, he'd have expected the DI to hang it out a little longer.

"I gave him a choice," said Hoon, appearing to read Logan's mind. "He could go home and rest for a few hours, or he could be suspended. He did not go willingly."

Logan nodded, pleased to hear this. "No. I wouldn't imagine he would've."

"Exhaustion breeds mistakes. You're tired, you miss things. We've all seen it," Hoon said. "And look at the state of you. When did you last sleep?"

Logan had absolutely no idea when he'd last slept. Not

without grabbing a bit of paper and a pencil and doing some sums.

"Not too long ago, sir," he lied.

"Then see a fucking doctor, man, because you look like a sack of shite," Hoon told him.

The swear words jumped out at Logan. Usually, the Detective Superintendent poured on the cursing like salt on a chip shop fish supper. It was rare for him to make it through a sentence without effing and blinding at least once. It was how he expressed most of his emotions—anger, rage, fury, contempt, and, very occasionally, begrudging respect.

For the second time tonight, though, he was being oddly subdued with his language, and it made Logan uneasy.

"What happened with Bosco?" Hoon asked. His fingers were drumming on the arm of his chair. Fast, too. Another odd change in behaviour.

"Couldn't find him. He wasn't at his yard," Logan said.

Hoon nodded, like this had confirmed something. "Well, it's late. Got a home address?"

"No, sir. But we're digging up one for his ex-wife. They have joint custody of the daughter, so she'll likely know."

"Right. Right. Good," Hoon said. "And what's your gut telling you about him and Petrie? You think that's a thing?"

"I do, sir," Logan said.

Hoon frowned. "You sound very confident."

"Aye. I know the shoes were in my cupboard before I went to Canna. I saw them when I was packing. Petrie was in my flat when I was away—or someone was in there for him—leaving the name badge. Presumably, they took the shoes at the same time, and stuck them on the victim."

"But we don't know Bosco had anything to do with that," Hoon said. "The murder. Do we?"

"We don't know very much, no. But we can put one of his vans leaving the scene just after the time we believe the victim was done in. And we know he's a dodgy bastard who's had people killed before, even if we've never been able to make anything stick."

"But this? Petrie? That's different," Hoon said. "I mean, aye, we know he's big in the drugs scene, but if he's killed anyone before it's been some other shady bastard. Crooks killing crooks. I'm no' saying I approve, but... it isn't kids."

"I still hold Bosco responsible for Detective Sergeant McQuarrie's death," Logan said, and the tone of his voice suggested that, senior officer or not, Hoon was skating on some very thin ice.

"I'm no' saying he's one of the good guys," Hoon said. "And believe me, I'd love to take the bastard down. I've tried often enough. But, my point is... Bosco. Petrie. I just... I don't see it."

"Well, I do, sir," Logan said. "And I think it would also go some way to explaining what happened with your nephew. Jaden."

Hoon's head snapped up at that. "What the fuck are you talking about?" he asked, some of his usual fury spluttering into life behind his eyes.

"It's how Bosco operates, isn't it? Threaten the family. Usually veiled enough that we can't charge him for it," Logan said. "He tried it with mine a few years back."

"What happened?" Hoon asked.

"I stabbed him through the hand with a fountain pen," Logan said, matter-of-factly. "The point is, I don't think Petrie was ever going to take Jaden. I think it was a warning. Same with Hamza's wee one."

"Then why take the other kid? PC Bell's brother?"

"That, I'm not sure of," Logan said.

Hoon leaned forward and clasped his hands on the desk. "So, then maybe Petrie is working on his own, like we first thought. Maybe he did try to grab Jaden and DC Khaled's daughter, but was interrupted. Maybe you're overthinking all this."

"How would he know where to find everyone?" Logan asked. "If he was on his own?"

Hoon shrugged. "The Gozer's phone and computer were hacked, you said. Maybe—"

"They were, but he wouldn't have got Hamza's address from that. Or your niece's, for that matter," Logan reasoned. "I mean, aye, maybe he's working with someone else—someone who's not Bosco, I mean—but I think it's a safe assumption that Petrie is not on his own. He's only been out a few days, nowhere near long enough to get this established on his own. And Bosco knows everything that's going on in the city. He's got eyes and ears everywhere. We know there's got to be at least one leak in this building."

"What makes you say that?" Hoon asked.

"The stuff he knows. When he ran me off the road on Loch Ness-side a while back. Only way he could've got set up for that is if someone told him where I was going." Logan said. "The man is bloody everywhere. He'd know where to find your niece's kid. He'd know where Sinead's aunt lives. And he'd know..."

Logan stopped. There had been a knot building in his stomach for the past few hours. A niggle worming its way around inside his brain that only now popped to the surface.

He knew everything. How to find everyone.

He threatened families. That's what he did.

He'd threatened Logan's own.

Logan was on his feet in an instant. He looked out of the window at the city, like some sort of telescopic vision might let him see all the way to the Smithton Area.

To the house on Murray Road.

And to his ex-wife and daughter hiding away inside.

CHAPTER THIRTY

VANESSA LURKED IN THE CORNER BEHIND THE DOOR, THE handle of the frying pan held tightly in both hands. She gave the nod to Maddie, confirming she was ready, then braced herself for whatever was coming next.

Maddie, for her part, held the kitchen knife low at her side, but angled so she could stab upwards should the need arise. She hoped it wouldn't. God, she hoped it wouldn't. But if it came to it, she'd do it.

Wouldn't she?

Edging closer to the door, she peered through the peephole, but the darkness outside made it impossible to tell who was out there. The knocking had roused them both from their rooms, although neither of them had been able to sleep.

There was a light on the porch, but switching it on would alert whoever was out there to their presence. Still, better that than opening the door to a serial killer.

Holding her eye to the peephole, she reached for the switch and clicked it on. A uniformed officer on the front step was momentarily taken aback by the sudden illumination. The rain had been pooling on top of his flat cap, and it came pouring off as he leaned in a little closer to the door.

"Hello? Is someone...? I just got a call from base. DCI Logan believes the location of the house has been compromised. He thinks you're in danger. I'm to take you to him at the station."

Maddie shot a sideways look at her mother. Vanessa's only response was an unhelpful shrugging of her shoulders.

"Give him a call to verify, if you like," the officer said. "I can wait until you've spoken to—"

From outside came a short screech of tyres skidding to a stop, and a muttered, "Shite," from the policeman on the step.

Maddie pressed her eye to the peephole again, and saw headlights blazing just beyond the garden gate. Three doors opened then slammed. A trio of figures appeared silhouetted in the glow of the full beams.

The officer grabbed for the radio on his shoulder, but he fumbled with it, unable to find the button in his growing panic.

"Shit," Maddie hissed, then she unlocked the door, pulled him in, and slammed it again.

The constable almost jumped out of his skin when he saw Vanessa hiding in the corner. His eyes, like most of his face, were in shadow beneath the brim of his cap, but they darted anxiously to the knife in Maddie's hands.

"Uh, best watch what you're doing with that," he began, then a hammering on the door became a bigger priority for all of them. "Is there a back door?" the officer whispered, as they all backed off along the hall.

"There is," Maddie confirmed.

"Right, then let's use it, get to my car, and get the hell out of here."

THE VOLVO SCREECHED to a stop nose to nose with the squad car on Murray Road, its headlights flooding the inside of the smaller vehicle.

Empty.

Logan jumped out without switching off the engine and ran to the car. The driver's side window had been lowered, and there was blood on the glass and down the white paintwork of the door.

A man lay slumped in the back seat, naked apart from a blood-soaked shirt and a pair of boxer shorts. There was a gaping hole where his throat should have been, the flesh there pinkish and raw.

His eyes were open and staring at the seat in front of him, like he'd known it would be the last thing he'd ever seen, and he'd wanted to memorise it, hang onto the image for as long as he possibly could.

"No, no, no," Logan said, each one louder than the one before. He threw himself in the direction of the safe house, top half leading the way, legs pumping furiously as they tried to keep up.

He had his phone in his hand by the time he reached the gate, was calling Maddie's number before his shoulder connected with the front door. It held firm, and pain went rattling through his skeleton as the sound of Maddie's voice came tinnily through the speakers.

"Hi, this is Maddie."

"Maddie!" Logan cried, but his daughter's voice spoke over him.

"I can't come to the phone right now..."

Shite!

He hung up, hammered on the door with one hand, while scrolling to Vanessa's name in his contacts with the other.

"Maddie! Vanessa! Open up, it's me!" he bellowed.

There was no movement from the windows. No twitching

of curtains, or switching on of the lights.

He put his shoulder to the door another couple of times, then brought his foot up and kicked it. Once. Twice. Vanessa's voicemail greeting played from his phone's speaker.

"No, no, no!"

Sirens approached. He'd put the shout out on the way over, hoping someone was close enough to beat him there, but most of the station was focused on Harris, and doors were being knocked on all around the area he'd gone missing from.

Logan searched the garden for a rock, or a bit of loose paving —something light enough for him to lift, but heavy enough to obliterate the window at the side of the door.

He found nothing, but spotted the smiling wee face of a garden gnome peeking over the wall at him from the garden next door. A big concrete bastard of a thing it was, with a jolly red hat and a chin like a baby's arse.

That'd do it.

He vaulted the wall, grabbed the gnome, and was halfway back to the front door when the neighbour shouted at him from an upstairs window.

"Put that back! What do you think you're playing at?" he bellowed, but Logan wasn't listening.

Charging for the door, he raised the gnome above his head and launched it at the glass. Both window and garden ornament exploded into shards of glass and concrete, and the neighbour exploded into a foul-mouthed tirade that Logan barely caught any of.

He was inside the house a handful of seconds later, charging along the hall, calling out for his daughter and her mother as he searched the downstairs rooms.

Empty.

He was headed for the last of the downstairs doors when he felt the draft blowing through the gap beneath it.

Throwing the door wide, Logan stumbled into the kitchen.

The toe of his boot collided with something heavy on the floor, and sent it skidding across the lino. It hit a kickplate with a metallic clang.

A frying pan.

And there, on the counter by the open door, a knife. Blood dotted the metal of the blade, like paint on a non-porous surface. More of it pooled on the worktop beneath it, and a bloodied handprint was smeared on the wall next to the door.

The postcard in his pocket howled at him, screamed at him, as he pulled the back door open all the way and went racing out into the garden.

"J-Jack?"

Vanessa lay on the grass, blood marking her face like camouflage. Her breathing was fast and shallow, each breath accompanied by a whimper or a sob.

He was at her side in an instant, and immediately saw the hands she held pressed against her thighs, and the blood that came pumping up between her fingers.

"Vanessa! What happened?"

Aside from the vibrant red of the blood, Vanessa was sepia-toned, like she'd stepped out of a photo in some old book. She was shivering, her body wracked with violent shudders as it went into shock.

"It was him... It was Petrie. He was in uniform, he... he..." Tears choked her, forcing her to gulp and gasp for breath. "He took her," she sobbed, when she could speak again. "Maddie. He took Maddie. He stabbed me. My legs. And he... and he... he said I should wave. He said I should wave goodbye."

Logan looked over to the back gate. It stood open, creaking gently as it was nudged back and forth by the breeze.

"When? How long ago?" he asked.

"I don't... Ten minutes. Fifteen. I don't k-know.

She hissed, as pain radiated through her. The cuts in her legs were deep, the one on the right worse than the one on the left. She had a dressing gown on, so Logan pulled out the belt cord and wrapped it around the right leg, a few inches above the wound.

"What are you d-doing?" she demanded. "Go. Get her. Not me, get her."

"Vanessa, if we don't stop this bleeding—"

She lashed out at him, slapping at his arm, her hands leaving bloody prints wherever they made contact. Her face was all twisted up with grief and rage.

"Fucking... go! Go, get her. Not me! I don't c-care!"

Pain tore through her again, arching her back on the grass. When it passed, all the venom had left her, and her voice was a pleading wheeze.

"Save our baby girl, Jack. Please."

"Police. Don't move!" barked a voice from inside the house, and Logan felt a surge of relief when he saw a surly-looking female constable glaring at him from the back door.

"DCI Jack Logan," he replied, turning and blinking in the beam of the officer's torch. She held the light on him for a couple of seconds, then angled it away.

"Sorry, sir, didn't recognise you in the dark," she said.

Logan jumped up and pointed to Vanessa. "Get an ambulance. Apply pressure to her injuries until it arrives. And put a call in, Owen Petrie is in this area. He may be wearing a uniform. There's a dead constable in a car out front."

The officer stared at him, her torch angled limply down at the grass. Her mouth moved, like she was reciting everything Logan had told her over again in her head, not quite able to process any of it.

"Get a fucking move on, Constable!" the DCI barked, which jolted the officer into life. He met Vanessa's wide-eyed look of terror again. "You're going to be OK."

"Just go, Jack. Hurry," Vanessa whispered. "And bring her back safe."

CHAPTER THIRTY-ONE

LOGAN'S LUNGS BURNED AS HE RACED ALONG THE PATH that led past the back of the safe house. It was flanked on both sides, gardens to the right, a high wall and a small forest of trees on the left. Pools of weak orange spilled from the streetlights dotted along the way, the night sky overhead too choked with cloud to offer any light of its own.

"Maddie!" he called as he ran, forcing what little breath was left in his lungs to carry her name ahead of him into the gloom. He spat *his* name out, too—"Petrie!"—but neither one brought any response.

And so, he ran. Ran faster than he'd ever run before. Ran like his daughter's life depended on it.

Some time later—probably not long, but it felt like a lifetime —he came stumbling into a car park beside a modern-looking church.

There were no cars there. No signs of life. No Owen Petrie.
No Maddie.

"Fuck!" Logan roared, just as a clap of thunder went rolling across the sky. He shouted her name again. Screamed it. "Maddie!"

What had he done? God, *what had he done*? This was his fault. He'd brought them here. He'd known this might happen, that it was at least a possibility.

An ambulance whizzed past, lights flashing, headed for the safe house.

What was he going to tell Vanessa? How could he break it to her?

How could he say he'd lost their little girl?

No. He wouldn't. He couldn't.

He'd find her. He'd get her back. That was what he did.

Logan ran in the direction the ambulance had gone, reaching for his phone as he did. Hamza answered on the third ring.

"Sir?"

"Bosco's ex-wife's address," Logan said. "Did you get it?"

"Aye. Are... are you alright, sir? You sound out of—"

"Text it to me," Logan ordered, then he hung up.

He reached the Volvo after a few minutes of running, stared at the ambulance parked outside the safe house for a few moments, then yanked open the driver's door of the car and jumped in.

His headlights filled the interior of the squad car parked in front of him. He muttered an apology to the dead officer in the back, then crunched the car into gear and floored it.

As he went speeding along Murray Road, he caught a glimpse of one of the paramedics moving through the house, and then he was turning onto Tower Road, tyres squealing in protest at his cornering speed.

Hamza's text arrived with a *bleep*. The address was in the Crown area. Close to the city centre, but plush. Made sense for a gangster's ex-wife.

It wasn't the sort of place the polis got called to frequently, and Logan wasn't overly familiar with it, but he knew it was near the Eastgate Centre enough for him to be able to find his way there. The night traffic was thin, so he didn't need to announce his arrival by sticking on the lights or siren.

If Logan was lucky, Bosco would be at the house. He doubted that, though. At best, he'd get a home address for the bastard, or some insight into where he might be.

One way or another, whatever it took, Bosco would lead him to Petrie, and Petrie would lead him to Maddie and Harris.

One way or another.

Whatever it took.

HAMZA GOT up from his chair and hugged Sinead. She leaned against him, grateful for the temporary support, then flopped down onto a chair when he stepped back and let her go.

"Stupid question, I know, but... how you doing?" he asked her.

Sinead shrugged. Her mouth formed a variety of shapes, testing out several possible responses. In the end, she settled on, "I don't know."

"You want coffee, or tea, or...?"

"Tyler's getting it. Thanks."

"No, no. Don't... It's fine," Hamza said, turning his seat to face her before sitting down.

She was still wearing her uniform. Its short sleeves showed crisscrossing red lines on her forearms, where she'd been anxiously scratching while waiting for news.

"How's your aunt?"

Sinead shrugged again. "Not great. But still with us." She looked down at the floor, took a breath, then forced herself to look up again. Her eyes were filled with some new emotion, some mix of dread and hope. "Anything on Harris?"

"Uniform's doing a huge push. Door to door across the

whole area," Hamza said. "Got a press conference scheduled for tomorrow, but it's already out on the web and social media."

"So, no, then."

Hamza could only offer a sympathetic smile. "We'll find him. I'm looking into..."

He thought better of saying more. No point getting her hopes up. So far, the three-word combinations he'd tried had taken him all over the world, but none of them had brought him even close to Scotland, much less Inverness. He was barely a third of the way through, but he was starting to suspect he was wasting his time.

"You're looking into what?" Sinead pressed.

"It's probably nothing. I shouldn't have—"

"Hamza." The hope was draining from Sinead's face, leaving only the dread behind. "Please."

"Right. OK. But, like I say, it's probably nothing," Hamza began, and then he launched into the explanation he'd offered Logan earlier.

Unlike the DCI, Sinead was familiar with the what3words app, and was already reaching for her phone by the time DC Khaled was approaching the main thrust of the explanation.

"Have you got a list?" she asked, tapping the App Store icon with her thumb.

"Spreadsheet, aye," Hamza said.

"Let's see it, then."

Hamza spun his chair back to his computer, clicked back to the spreadsheet, and showed Sinead the list of all the possible alternatives he'd compiled.

"I can share it with you," he said.

"Tyler, too," Sinead instructed. "We'll split up what's left and work through it."

Hamza nodded. "OK. Just... like I say, it might not work."

"But it might," Sinead said. She bit on her bottom lip, like she was stopping tears from coming. "I have to do something."

"Right. Well, let's get it done, then," Hamza said, clicking the 'share' icon.

He had just filled out Sinead and Tyler's email addresses when the door to the Incident Room opened and a shocked-looking DC Neish came charging in. He hadn't brought any coffee with him. Probably just as well, given how much his hands were shaking.

Announcing his arrival with a cry of, "Fucking Hell," Tyler stopped by the first available desk and leaned on it, supporting himself.

"What? What's wrong?" Sinead asked, already on her feet, already fearing the worst.

"Just heard. Boss's daughter's been taken. Wife's being rushed to hospital," Tyler said, tripping over the words as they came tumbling out of his mouth. "Constable who'd been watching the safe house was murdered. Fucker took his uniform. A PC Lindsay?"

"Ross Lindsay?" Sinead gasped.

"Maybe, I'm not sure. Little fella, I think. Aye, I mean, no' a dwarf, but..."

"We were at Tulliallan together," Sinead said. "Fuck. Nice guy, too."

"Where's Logan now?" Hamza asked.

Tyler shook his head. "No idea. Nobody seems to know."

Hamza glanced down at his phone sitting on the desk beside his computer. "Eh... I might," he said. "And he might be going to do something stupid."

THE FORMER MRS BOSCO MAXIMUKE lived in a mock-Tudor place with a garden you could've held a five-a-side tournament in. There was a set of iron gates at the front, but the wall that surrounded the grounds was barely waist-height, so Logan abandoned the Volvo in the street and vaulted over it.

A downpour had accompanied the latter half of his drive over, but it had dialled back enough that only the occasional fat drop of rain went flecking off him as he hurried across the damp grass.

Spotlights illuminated high on the walls, and around the path as the sensors detected his approach. From an extension on the right that had probably once been a garage, a couple of large-sounding dogs began to bark and growl.

Shielding his eyes from the glare of the lights, Logan ran the last few yards to the front door. It was a heavy old wooden thing, with enough ironmongery bolted to it to build a Spitfire. He rattled the heavy round knocker, hammered on the wood with a fist, and then gave the doorbell half a dozen jabs for good measure.

After almost a minute of this, and with an increasing number of lights appearing in the windows of the houses across the street, a lock *clacked*. The door opened, and Logan found himself staring into a hallway with a sweeping staircase, yellowing wallpaper, and shelves laden with enough tacky ornaments to put Alice Forde's collection to shame.

What he did not see was a person. At least, not until he adjusted the angle of his gaze.

Bosco's daughter stood on a 'Please Wipe Your Feet' mat just inside the door. She was bare-footed, dressed in Christmas-themed pyjamas, and carried a sizeable axe in a way that suggested she wasn't only prepared to use it, she was actively looking forward to it.

Logan had not been prepared for this. He'd been expecting Bosco's wife, or some other adult he could shout at or threaten. He couldn't exactly threaten a ten-year-old, though. Axe or no bloody axe.

"What do you want?" she asked.

Christ, what was her name? Bosco had mentioned it a few times...

"Olivia," Logan said, trying not to make it sound like a question. She did nothing to confirm or deny the name, so Logan pressed on. "I'm looking for your dad. Bosco."

"I know what my dad's name is," Olivia replied. She looked the DCI up and down. "Why?"

"I just... I need to talk to him," Logan said. He looked past her into the house. "Is your mum around? Or someone else I can talk to?"

"Mum's sleeping," Olivia said. "She took her pills. She won't wake up until about lunchtime tomorrow."

"*Lunchtime?* What did she take, a horse tranquilliser?"

Olivia frowned, not getting the joke. "No. Sleeping pills."

"Aye. Fair enough. So... what? You're on your own?" Logan asked.

Olivia rolled her eyes and hefted the head of the axe onto her shoulder. She kept her grip on it, though, and it wouldn't take much for her to throw the blade forward and hack a chunk out of Logan's crotch.

"No, my mum's here. She's just sleeping," Olivia said. She spoke slowly and deliberately, like she'd come to the conclusion the DCI had learning difficulties. "And I don't know where my dad is."

"You know his home address, though."

Olivia looked him up and down. She took her time about it, not even remotely unnerved by the towering detective on the front step.

"You're the one who beat up Valdis and set my dad's office on fire," she said.

Logan fumbled for a response to this, ideally one that wouldn't immediately make her slam the door.

"That was... There was a misunderstanding," he said. "I shouldn't have done what I did."

"It was pretty awesome," Olivia said. "I liked watching it burn." She rubbed her cheek idly against the side of the axe's blade. "Fire's cool."

She gave him another once-over with her eyes, then sighed and dropped the axe to her side. "Wait here."

The door closed. Logan turned and looked up at the neighbouring houses. Three faces watched him from three different windows. At least one of them was talking into their phone, probably calling nine-nine-nine. He waved, then turned back to the door as it opened.

Olivia thrust a torn-out notebook page into his hands. "There. That's where he lives."

Logan looked down at the address. Out of town, but not too far.

"Thank you," he said. "I won't tell him you gave it to me."

The girl shrugged. "I don't care. It'll be funny," she said, then she slammed the door, and Logan heard the *clunk* of the lock sliding back into place.

"Jesus. She's going to be one to watch," he remarked, then he turned and jogged back across the grass.

He was just vaulting over the wall when a car pulled around the corner and onto the street. The headlights blinded him, forcing him to shield his eyes with an arm. He stuffed the address in a coat pocket, freeing both hands up for what might come next.

"Boss?"

Logan peered through the glare and saw a well-maintained head of hair emerge from the driver's side window of the car, followed by the head itself.

"Turn the fucking lights off," he growled.

"Shite, aye. Sorry, boss."

The lights went out, leaving only the spots they'd created swimming in the air before Logan's eyes.

"What are you doing here?" the DCI demanded, as Tyler stepped out onto the street.

It was hard to tell with all the glowing yellow orbs still dancing in front of his face, but DC Neish had a shady look about him, like he was hiding something.

"Just, eh, wanted to check if you needed back-up, boss," he said.

"Bollocks. You thought I was going to tear the place apart looking for Bosco," Logan replied.

Tyler smiled warily. "I, eh, we heard what happened. With your daughter. I'm sorry, boss. We just thought... We didn't want you burning this place to the ground, too."

"Aye, well, no need," Logan said. He produced the piece of paper from his pocket. "I got the address. I'm going to go check it out. If I need support, I'll call for it."

Tyler clicked his fingers a couple of times, playing out an anxious little rhythm. "Aye. Right. Just... don't do anything stupid, boss. I mean, not that you would... Just..."

"Thanks for the advice, Detective Constable," Logan said, pulling open the driver's door of the Volvo. "But I've got this. Does Hoon know?"

"I, eh, don't know, boss. I'd imagine so, given that he seems to know pretty much everything, but I haven't seen him."

If Hoon knew that Petrie had Maddie and that Logan was on the warpath, he'd be duty-bound to intervene. Whether he actually would or not, Logan wouldn't like to speculate. Best not give him the opportunity.

"If he asks where I am, you don't know," Logan said.

Tyler hesitated, wrestling with something, then he gave a nod. "Right. OK. But, I don't like this, boss. It feels... I don't know. I've got a bad feeling about it all."

"Aye. You and me both, son," Logan said. "You and me both." He started to get in the car, then stopped with one hand on the roof. "How's Sinead?"

"She's coping," Tyler said. "Her and Hamza are going through some spreadsheet of... like addresses, or something? It's keeping her busy, which is what she needs."

"It is," Logan agreed. "Keep an eye on her. She's strong, but... Keep an eye."

"I will, boss," Tyler said. He looked down at his feet, took a breath to compose himself, then came right out with the question that had been gnawing at him over the past few hours. "We're going to get him, aren't we?"

"Petrie?"

"Harris," Tyler said. "I mean... You know Petrie better than most. If we find him... *when*... Harris is going to be alright, isn't he? Sinead's already been through so much, boss. With her parents. And now Val, and... If anything happens to Harris..."

"He'll be fine, son," Logan said. He had nothing to base this on, of course. Whatever game Petrie was playing now, it wasn't the same rules as before. But he knew what the DC needed to keep going, and so he gave him it. "Harris will be fine, if we catch this bastard soon."

Tyler seemed to grow an inch or two. "Right, boss. Best get to it, then," he said.

"Aye. Best had," Logan said. He tapped the roof of the car a couple of times in farewell, then dropped the rest of the way into the driver's seat.

Before he could even start the engine, his phone rang. It wasn't the usual ring, and it took him a moment to recognise it.

Video call.

Bringing the phone from his pocket, he saw Shona Maguire's name emblazoned across the screen. He hesitated with his thumb over the answer button, then swiped to reject the call.

She'd be checking on him, that was all. A friendly social call, to make sure he was OK after he'd ended things so abruptly last time.

The phone was halfway back to his pocket when she called him back. This time, he tapped the other button.

This time, he answered.

And there and then, in that car, in that moment, everything changed.

CHAPTER THIRTY-TWO

PETRIE WAS THERE. LOGAN COULDN'T SEE HIM, BUT HE could hear his voice. That hoarse, scratchy rasp that had earned him his nickname. That same voice that had been goading him on the phone of late.

"Is that him?" Petrie said. "Has he answered?"

On screen, Shona nodded. There was blood on her top lip, and her cheeks shone with tears and thin black rivulets of mascara that she hadn't got around to taking off.

"J-Jack," she said. Her voice was shaking, but she was doing her best to hold it together. "It's him. It's Petrie."

"You don't have to tell him. He knows it's me. Don't you, Jack?"

Logan flashed his headlights several times, then held up a hand, signalling for Tyler to wait.

"Owen. You need to stop this," Logan warned. "You need to stop before you make it worse for yourself."

"Worse? This isn't worse, this is *great*. I'm loving life again, Jack," Petrie hissed from the other side of the phone. "After all those years locked up, these last few days... well, I'll be honest, they've been a bit of a dream come true. And, the best part is, we're just getting to the good bit!"

The footage was handheld and shaky, and Logan caught a glimpse of a movie poster on the wall at Shona's back.

They were still at her place. Logan thumbed the microphone mute button and beckoned Tyler over, as Petrie's voice continued to seep from the phone's speaker.

"Rule one. You come here, and you come alone," he said. "If you want her to live, you come alone. If you call it in, I'll know about it."

"Wait," Logan told Tyler, signalling for him to stop.

"Jack? I can't hear you. Do you understand rule number one?"

Logan activated his phone's microphone again. "I understand, Owen. But, why are you doing all this?"

"Why am I doing this?" Petrie asked, and his tone, which had been light and taunting so far, took a darker turn. "Why do you fucking *think* I'm doing it, Jack?"

"We can talk about this, Owen. We can sort—"

"Rule number *two*," Petrie declared, shouting him down.

The video footage swept across the walls and ceiling as the phone was turned around. A quarter of Petrie's face filled the screen—an eye, part of his scarred forehead, and a direct line of sight up one flared nostril.

"Get here quick," he urged. He kept the camera on himself as he walked behind Shona and caught her by the hair. He yanked her head back with enough force to make her cry out in pain, then lowered his head so they were side by side, like lovers in a photo booth. "All that time rotting in that hospital you put me in means I have a tendency to get bored easily." He ran a hand through Shona's hair and grinned. "And, believe me, neither of you wants that."

And then, before Logan could say a word, the call was ended.

"Shite!" Logan spat, tossing the phone into the dooket beneath the dash.

"Boss?" Tyler asked, cautiously approaching the car. "What's going on?"

"It's Petrie. He's got Shona."

Tyler looked at him blankly, then realisation registered on his face. "The Pathologist? Where?"

"Her place," Logan said.

"I'll call it in," Tyler said, reaching for his phone.

"No! If we call it in, he'll kill her," Logan said. "I'm going. Alone."

"Jesus, boss..." Tyler began to protest, but a look from the DCI cut it dead.

Logan jumped out of the Volvo, fished in his pocket, and thrust the notebook page into Tyler's hands. "Bosco's house," he explained. "Go, see what's what. But quietly."

"Bosco's house?" Tyler repeated, looking down at the address.

"Drive by. That's all," Logan instructed. "Scope the place, but do not engage with the fucker if he's there. Don't even let him see you. Drive past, look, drive on. Repeat, if necessary. Do not approach without backup. That clear?"

Tyler was still staring down at the address. A shout from Logan kick-started him again.

"*Is that clear*, Tyler?"

"Yes, boss. Sorry, boss. I'm on it," the DC said. "Bosco's place. Drive by only. Don't engage."

Logan clapped him on the arm. "Don't fuck this up."

Tyler smiled grimly. "Aye," he said. "You, too, boss."

A TEXT HAD COME through a minute or so later, Shona presumably having explained that Logan didn't have her address. He'd been vaguely aware that it was somewhere near the Kessock Bridge, but he'd assumed it was on the Inverness side.

He'd also assumed it had been a flat, so when he pulled up outside a ramshackle whitewashed cottage looking out onto the Beauly Firth, he had to double-check to make sure he had the right place.

There were four windows visible from the front, two downstairs and another two which looked like relatively recent additions in the loft space. The curtains were drawn in all of them, and all but one were in darkness.

Logan spent a few seconds staring at the upper left window, where the light had been left on. Were they in there? Was it a trap?

Of course, it was a trap. Petrie was hardly going to confront him one-on-one. But, trap or not, he had to go in and face whatever was waiting for him.

The front door was unlocked. It was an old, heavy thing, and badly in need of a coat of paint. He'd expected it to creak ominously when he opened it, but it glided smoothly on its hinges, and he clicked it quietly closed again behind him.

The hall was oddly shaped, with three doors leading off it and a steep set of wooden stairs leading to a landing above. The ceiling was not so low that Logan bumped his head, but low enough that he felt sure he was going to. He ducked a little as he approached the steps, and listened from the bottom.

There was no sound from upstairs. No squeaking of floorboards, no chattering of voices, no sobs, or cries.

Nothing.

The steps were essentially a large wooden ladder with elongated rungs. Theoretically, it was probably possible to go up them without using your hands, but given his size and the width of the hatch above, Logan felt it best not to try.

While the well-oiled door hinges had been a pleasant

surprise, the steps completely betrayed him. Each one creaked out a different note as he placed his weight on it, and any hopes of keeping the element of surprise completely evaporated.

He stopped with his head just below the hatch and looked up and around at the darkened landing, in case Petrie was waiting to brain him. Seeing nobody lurking near the edge, he hurried up the last few steps and found himself in a space not much bigger than a large cupboard. It would hold two people at a push. One, if they were both Logan's size.

A poster promoting the film, *Lethal Weapon 2*, hung from one wall. It was in a frame, and had two signatures in silver pen below the names of the main stars at the top of the image.

Beside it was the door that led to the only room with the lights on. The door stood ajar, letting the light seep out through the gap.

Logan edged it open cautiously, eyes darting up and down to check for traps or tripwires. He doubted Petrie would bother with such things, but he'd rather not find out the hard way.

The room he entered was a small bedroom, with a neatly-made single bed along one wall, a small bookcase against the other, and not a lot else to write home about. It didn't strike Logan as being to Shona's taste at all. Spare bedroom, he guessed.

Not only was it lacking Shona's design taste, it was also lacking Shona herself.

Logan was about to leave, when he spotted the glossy squares spaced regularly on the bed. At first, he'd thought it was just the design of the quilt cover, but as he turned towards the door, he saw them more clearly.

Polaroid photographs. Dozens of them, neatly presented for him to find.

His legs wouldn't move. Not at first. They rooted him to the spot, unwilling to take him closer, unwilling to let him see.

But he had to look. He had to know.

They relented at last, and he went stumbling over. He didn't see any one particular image, but rather got an impression of them all. Pain, suffering, and fear emanated from the display. The pictures ranged from garish, wide-eyed close-ups with too much flash, to wider shots filled with deep pools of darkness.

They showed Harris.

They showed Maddie.

Both tied up. Both in different locations, he thought.

Both crying. Both bleeding.

But both alive.

There was a thump from downstairs. Logan spun around and raced for the steps. He slid backwards down them—a clumsy descent, followed by an even clumsier landing that drew a hiss of pain through his teeth.

The sound he'd heard had come from directly below, so he turned to the door on his right, placed his palm flat against it, then pushed it open.

From the darkness, there came a muffled sob. *Shona*.

Logan found the light switch and clicked it on. Shona winced in the sudden brightness of it, recoiling and screwing her eyes shut in shock, which meant she didn't see the look of horror that crossed Logan's face before he could chase it away again.

Shona sat in the centre of the room, tied to a chair. This was bad, but it was not the worst part.

She had been beaten, her face already bruised, her bloodied nose crusting on the gag that was tied tight across her mouth.

This was not the worst part, either.

The worst part, by some considerable margin, was the bomb.

"Oh," muttered Logan, as the device on Shona's chest gave a *whirr* and a *click*. "Shite."

CHAPTER THIRTY-THREE

DI FORDE LAY ON HIS SIDE WITH THE COVERS PULLED UP under his chin, listening to the toilet flushing for the third time that night.

"Sorry, but I've a weak bladder," was Alice's go-to excuse whenever her midnight micturitions roused her sleeping husband. Ben had tried suggesting she maybe not neck those six cups of tea in the two hours before turning in, but Alice was having none of it. It was a genetic condition, she insisted. Her mother was the same.

Tonight, though, she hadn't disturbed him, because he hadn't been to sleep. He'd been trying since Hoon had sent him home, but it continued to evade him. How could he sleep when that boy was out there somewhere? How could he sleep when the others were still trying to bring him home?

"Did I wake you up?" asked Alice, sliding into the bed behind him. She snuggled up to him, siphoning off some of his warmth. "It's my bladder. You know what it's like."

"Aye, I know," Ben said, his voice partly muffled by the pillow. "But, no. I wasn't sleeping."

"Well, you should be," Alice said, raising her head to look

him in the eye. "You'll do nobody any good if you're knackered. And they'll all be done-in tomorrow morning. You can go in brand new. Fresh pair of eyes. It'll be useful."

"And what if the boy's dead by then, Alice?" Ben asked, half-turning to look at her.

"Then that would be tragic. Horrible. Just... horrible," she said. "But he's not my concern. You are. Besides, Bob Hoon sent you home. There's no arguing with him. Unless you'd rather get suspended. Which, I'll be honest, I'd be in favour of."

She lay back down again. Ben faced front. The alarm clock sat next to the bed, but he'd turned it around so he wasn't just lying there watching the minutes tick by. Somehow, lying there *not* watching the minutes tick by felt better.

"You've given half your life to that place. You can have a night off. I thought I'd stop worrying when you left the forces, but I worry about you more now, if anything," Alice continued. She yawned, then smacked her lips together a few times as if tasting it. "You're not as young as you used to be, Ben. It's high bloody time you started keeping that in—"

The sentence ended in a snore, and Ben was grateful for it. The last thing he needed now was a lecture on how old and useless he was, even a well-meaning one.

Reaching for the bedside table, he turned the alarm clock around, pulled his covers more tightly under his chin, and went back to watching the minutes creep slowly on.

Bosco Maximuke's gaff was on the north side of the city, and the sight of it made Tyler sick to his stomach.

There were a number of reasons for this. He wasn't going to lie and say that anxiety wasn't one of them. His last encounter with Bosco Maximuke had not exactly gone well for him, and it wasn't something he was in a rush to repeat.

The main reason, though, was the size of the bloody place. It sat on its own, surrounded by high fences on a patch of land he'd need a compass and map to navigate across. Half of the house looked old, but painstakingly restored. That part was all sandstone and pillars, while the other half was a metal and glass L-shape that had been built onto the side and wrapped around the back.

Turf had been laid on the roof of the extension. This had presumably been done in an attempt to make the thing look less conspicuous, but in reality, had the exact opposite effect. Who the hell had grass on the roof?

It was all a bit *Grand Designs* for Tyler's tastes, but he resented it, anyway. The place had to be worth a fortune. A million, easy. Far beyond anything Tyler could ever hope to achieve.

He had driven around it twice now, but had seen no sign of life inside. The windows were all in darkness. The gates and doors were all closed. The house had a driveway out front that could've held a dozen cars, but it stood empty.

The house, as far as he could tell, was deserted.

Tyler stopped his car around the side of the building, at the point where it was closest to the fence. There was a gate there. Unlike the big double set at the end of the driveway, this one didn't have a camera above it, or an intercom button fixed on a pole beside it.

It was... just a gate. Tall, yes, but climbable.

He shook his head, admonishing himself. No. He couldn't go in. He had no warrant, for one thing. Logan had told him not to—that was another very valid reason.

And then there was Bosco himself. If Bosco caught him sneaking around, there was no saying what the Russian would do to him, but he could be fairly confident it would be nothing pleasant.

And, what if he did something to his mum?

No.

It was dangerous. Reckless.

Insane.

But Harris might be in there.

And how could he live with himself if he didn't check?

With a turn of the key, Tyler switched off the engine, unbuckled his seatbelt, and opened the door.

"WHAT ARE YOU DOING? Don't fucking touch it!"

Logan whipped his hand back in fright at the sharpness of Shona's outburst. "Jesus! Don't do that!" he told her. "I wasn't going to touch it."

"You bloody were. You had your hand out," Shona hissed back.

Logan had been expecting her to start crying when he removed the gag, but she'd been remarkably composed, and had mostly just snapped at him whenever he tried to examine the device more closely. He was almost starting to regret taking it off.

"I was looking, that's all," he said.

"Look with your eyes! Don't go pissing about with it unless you know what you're doing."

Logan very much did not know what he was doing.

Sure, he'd come across explosive devices before, but they were usually bodge-jobs with less explosive potential than a disposable barbecue. This one, though? This one looked serious.

It was all metal plates and wires, with a canister taped on either side of a plastic box in the middle, where the *clicking* and *whirring* sounds were coming from.

"Take me through what he said again," Logan urged.

"He said there were new rules," Shona repeated for the third time now. "Rule one, you're not allowed to call the bomb squad, or he blows this thing up. Which, in case there's any confusion, I definitely don't want. Rule two is the same as last time." Her eyes flicked down to the device, then back to Logan. "*Hurry.*"

Logan straightened and stepped back a couple of paces. "And he definitely said 'new rules'?"

"Yes."

"And he definitely said 'bomb squad'?"

"Yes! He definitely said 'bomb squad'!"

"You're sure? It's important."

"I got a sense that it was fucking important, Jack," Shona spat, her Irish accent coming through thicker than ever. She shot the bomb on her chest an anxious look, then lowered her voice to a whisper. "Believe me, I'm not underestimating the importance of any of it."

"Sorry. Aye," Logan said. "Just... just try to stay calm."

"I'm calm," Shona told him. "I'm perfectly calm. Given the circumstances, I think I'm the Sea of fucking Tranquillity, don't you?"

Petrie had shaken her badly, Logan could tell. That was hardly surprising, of course. It was to her credit that she wasn't a gibbering wreck.

The injuries on her face seemed mostly superficial, and she'd dismissed Logan's attempts to check her over more thoroughly, at least until such time as there wasn't an explosive device ticking away on her upper torso.

Logan ran a hand down his face, his fingers rasping across his stubble as they passed over his mouth and down to his chin. He sighed then, shot the window a glance, and laid out the options.

"OK, assuming the bomb squad warning is right, and we can't call them, we've got two choices," he said.

"And they are?" Shona asked, sounding like she didn't like any of them already.

"One, I cut this off, chuck it out the window, and we both hope for the best."

"I'm not a big fan of that one," Shona said, after a nanosecond's contemplation. "What's option two?"

"Ben," Logan said.

Shona frowned. "Ben?"

"DI Forde. He's ex-military. Worked with bomb disposal for a big chunk of that time. Landmines, mostly, I think, but he might be able to have a crack at this."

"Might? What the fuck's *might*?"

"Will. He'll know what to do," Logan said.

Shona bit her lip. Aside from the blood and the bruising, there was no colour left in her face.

"Shit. I don't know, Jack..." she said.

"He's not the bomb squad. That's Petrie's rule. I can't call the bomb squad. Well, I wouldn't be. I'd be calling Ben."

"But he said you couldn't call for back-up," Shona reminded him. It was clear from her expression that she wasn't a fan of this plan, either. Unfortunately, there were no others left for her to choose from.

"'New rules.' That's what he told you. That means the old rules don't apply. If I call Ben, I'm sticking to the rules," Logan said. He gave a slightly uncertain tilt of his head. "Technically."

"So... it's a loophole?" Shona asked, her voice rising again. She caught it, this time, before it climbed too high. "How is that a good idea?"

"I'm not saying it's a good idea, but it's the least bad idea we've got," Logan said. "I mean, unless you've got anything better up your sleeve?"

By the looks of her, Shona would dearly love to have something better up her sleeve. Also by the looks of her, she didn't.

"Right, then," Logan said. He turned and raised his voice, addressing the house at large. If Petrie had bugged the place, the DCI wanted to make it very clear what he was doing. "I'm not calling the bomb squad. Like you said. I'm calling DI Ben Forde. He's not involved with any counter-terrorism or explosives-related departments. He's on my team."

There was nothing to indicate that Petrie was even listening, much less that he'd heard. Logan waited a few seconds in case some sort of confirmation came, then turned back to Shona and reached for his phone.

"Right, then. I'm calling Ben," he said, keeping his voice as light and worry-free as possible. "We'll have you out of that thing in no time."

BEN ANSWERED the phone within two rings, jumping on it before it woke his wife up.

"Jack?" he said, after a glance at the caller ID.

"Thank Christ! Ben, I'm at Shona Maguire's. We've... got a situation here. I need you up and dressed and over here, fast as you can."

Ben looked down at his trousers and half-buttoned shirt. He'd concluded that sleep wasn't going to be coming any time soon, and that what Alice didn't know wouldn't hurt her.

"What's the situation?" Ben asked.

"Eh... we've got a bomb."

Ben blinked. "You've got a bomb?"

"Aye."

"Well... can you get rid of it?"

"No. That's what we need you for," Logan explained.

"Then it's no' me you want, it's the bomb squad," Ben said, fastening up the remaining buttons of his shirt.

"Can't. Petrie said if I call the bomb squad, he'll blow it. He must have some sort of remote control on it. But he didn't say anything about calling you."

Ben grimaced and looked back at the door to the bedroom.

He could hear Alice in there, snoring away. She'd be up for another bathroom break soon, and would notice he was gone.

She'd worry.

But then, she always did.

"Text me the address," Ben said, flattening down his collar. "I'm on my way."

CHAPTER THIRTY-FOUR

Tyler ran, doubled-over, across the grass in the direction of the house. It was, to his dismay, further than it looked.

Each scurried step was accompanied by a breathless, "Oh shit," as he scrambled for the cover afforded by the pools of shadow around the darkened building.

After what felt like an inordinately long time, he slammed himself against the sandstone side of the house, and stood there with his back flat against it, gulping down the cool night air.

This was stupid. What was he bloody playing at? He was trespassing at least, but a good solicitor could get that upped to housebreaking without too much difficulty. He could lose his job for this. His freedom, maybe.

Or, if Bosco caught him, his life.

And for what? There was nothing to suggest that Harris was in there. If it came to it, it was allowable to enter a property without a warrant, provided there was evidence that someone inside was in danger.

But, he had no evidence of that. None. And he didn't think,

'Frankly, I just don't trust the shifty Russian bastard,' was likely to stand up to a whole lot of scrutiny.

He was getting his breath back from the awkward, bent-over run. In hindsight, he should've come striding over confidently. If anyone saw him sprinting furiously with his head at waist height, it was likely to arouse some suspicions.

"Walk in like you bloody own the place," Logan had once told him. "Make them feel like they're the ones who shouldn't be there."

That was easy to say when you were DCI Jack Logan. His size alone made most folk sit up and take notice, and his glare would soon grab the attention of those who didn't.

For Tyler, here and now, stealth was the key. He'd find a way to look inside, and then slip out unnoticed. If Harris or the boss's daughter were in there, then...

Well, he'd cross that bridge if he came to it.

For now, the important thing was to find a way inside.

Sliding along the wall, Tyler stopped at the first window he came to. It was a sliding sash design, but firmly locked so he couldn't budge it.

"Not to worry," he whispered. It was comforting to hear the sound of his voice. It meant he hadn't yet been horribly killed.

Or, it would've been a comfort, had he not sounded quite so terrified.

"Plenty more where that came from," he said, then he squatted, did an ungraceful side-shuffle under the window, and straightened up again on the other side.

It was a big house. There were a lot of windows.

This was going to be a very long night.

HAMZA LEANED back in his chair, grabbed a wrist with the opposite hand, then stretched until his back gave a deeply satisfying *clunk*.

He buried his face in his hands as he yawned, then turned his chair to the desk where Sinead was sitting. Her head was raising and lowering as she compared the words on the computer screen with those on her phone.

"Getting anywhere?"

Sinead gave her phone's screen a tap, watched it hopefully, then tutted and shook her head. "Ukraine," she said. "You?"

"Nowhere close yet, and we're over halfway through," Hamza said. As time had ticked on, he'd started to lose faith in the whole idea. He was beginning to see why Hoon hadn't wanted to waste resources on it. "This might be a waste of time."

"Maybe," Sinead said. "But we won't know until we go through them."

Hamza rubbed his eyes with finger and thumb, then stood up. "I'm going to get coffee. You want some?"

Sinead was already back to her computer screen, clicking and scrolling to the next set of possible word variations.

"Hmm?" she asked, when she realised Hamza had spoken to her. "Sorry, I was... What?"

"Coffee," Hamza said. "Want some?"

"Uh, yes. Please," Sinead replied, her eyes pulling back to the screen.

"Any word from Tyler yet?" Hamza asked.

Sinead's gaze flicked to the clock on the wall, then to her phone. "Uh, no, actually," she said. "Should've heard something by now. Shouldn't we?"

"He'll be helping the boss with something. That's all," Hamza assured her.

"Maybe I should phone him."

"I'm sure he'll call when he can," Hamza said, but this didn't reassure Sinead at all. She rubbed her thumb slowly back and forth across the phone's screen like she was stroking it. "Or... maybe give it twenty minutes. If he hasn't turned up then, give him a call."

Sinead gave a nod and set her phone down on the desk. "Aye. Makes sense. I'll do that," she said, then she turned her attention back to her list of words.

There were over twenty-five combinations left on her screen. Checking them wasn't difficult, but it took time.

Time that Harris might not have.

No. She pushed the thought away. They were going to find him. They were going to bring him home.

They had to.

Sinead studied the words on screen, then picked her phone up again.

This was going to be a very long night.

"I'LL GIVE YOU THIS MUCH," said Logan. "It's a hell of a second date."

Shona didn't laugh. Not quite. She still had a fuck-off great explosive device strapped to her chest, after all. But she smiled, and that, as far as Logan was concerned, was good enough.

"Always knew I'd get you back to my place someday," she replied. "Granted, it's not quite what I had in mind..." She let out a sigh. "God, I'd love a cigarette."

Logan turned and scanned the room around him. It was the sort of place an estate agent would describe as 'cosy, with character and charm.' Tiny, in other words, and cluttered with a lot of weird shit.

"Where are they?" he asked.

"Where are what?" Shona asked.

"The cigarettes."

"Oh. No, I don't smoke. I've never smoked," she said. "It's just, I always thought about trying it to see what all the fuss is about. And I reckoned, if I'm going to be blown to bits anyway, lung cancer's probably the least of my concerns."

"You're not going to get blown to bits," Logan said.

"Yeah, well..." she replied, unconvinced. "I'm making a bucket list, just in case."

"'Have a fag,' hardly seems bucket list material," Logan replied.

Shona tutted. "Well, I can hardly go bungee-jumping in my current condition, can I?" she pointed out. "I'll take what I can get."

She had a lop-sided old armchair in the corner of the room, the covering a Frankenstein's monster of different fabrics, where she'd patched it, either through necessity or—and Logan felt this was more likely—by choice. He wrestled it closer to the middle of the room so he could sit facing her.

"What else is on the list, then?" he asked. "Not that you'll need it," he hurriedly added.

He'd hoped Ben would be here by now, but there was still no sign. Keeping her talking was keeping her calm, though, so he was quick to head along this new avenue of conversation.

Who was he kidding? Shona had already managed to get a handle on her panic and was coping well. The conversation was keeping *him* calm. Keeping him distracted from all the thoughts and fears that gnawed hungrily at his insides. Thoughts of what Maddie and Harris might be going through. Thoughts of what Petrie might have done to them. Be doing to them, right now.

Thoughts that, if he surrendered to them, would have him curled up in a ball on the floor.

So, he pushed those thoughts down. Stomped them into the ground.

"Bucket list top five," he urged. "Go."

Shona pursed her lips and moved them from side to side,

thinking this through. "In general, or based on the current situation?"

"Either."

"OK. OK. Current situation, then," she said. "We'll call having a smoke number five."

"That can't be top five. Seriously?"

"Who's bucket list is this?" Shona asked, shooting him a reproachful look.

"Sorry. Go on. Number four," Logan urged.

"Right. Four. And this is a biggie. I would fecking love to go for a pee," she said.

The sombre tone she adopted and the intensity in her eyes brought a burst of laughter from Logan that he wouldn't have thought himself capable of. Hysteria, probably, but he'd take it.

It proved infectious, and Shona joined in, too, much to her apparent dismay. "Christ, don't make me laugh, or I'll be ticking that one off the list right here and now. And I've just cleaned this carpet."

There was also a chance she might explode, Logan thought, although he decided against saying it out loud.

"Right, number three?" he asked, pressing on.

"Number three...?" Shona clicked her tongue against the roof of her mouth. "A comfier chair. This one's got a wicker seat. I don't know what possessed me. That's a lie. I do know. It was cheap."

Logan looked down at the wooden chair she was sitting on. The wiring of the bomb ran around to the back and wrapped around her wrists, holding them together perhaps even more effectively than the wrap of silver tape Petrie had also applied.

"I'd give you this seat, but I'm not sure moving's the best idea," he told her.

"Moving? I'm trying not to bloody breathe, never mind move," Shona replied. "I've accepted I'm not going to tick too many of these off, by the way. Don't you stress yourself. Although..."

Logan raised an eyebrow. "Although what?"

"You could maybe help me with number two." Her eyes widened in horror. "I don't mean... Jesus. On the list, I mean. Number two on the list. You could help me with that."

"What is it?" Logan asked, neatly glossing over any possible misinterpretation of what she'd said in a remarkable show of self-restraint.

"You could scratch my nose for me. Sure, it's driving me up the wall," Shona said. She scrunched her face up, presenting the offending item to him. "Just right on the end there."

Logan leaned closer. "Where? Here?" He reached out a finger and scratched. "That it?"

"Up a bit," Shona said. "Up a—There! Right there!"

She moaned with relief as Logan took care of the offending itch.

"That got it?"

"That got it," she confirmed. "Oh. God. That's better. I so should've made that number five."

Logan sat back. He stole a glance at his watch, then the window, before turning his attention back to Shona.

"Right. The big one. What's top of the list?"

There was some colour coming back to Shona's cheeks now. A slight reddening beneath the blood and the bruises.

"Kiss me," she said.

Logan snorted. "What?"

"Christ, you going deaf in your old age?" she asked with a smirk. Her eyes searched his face. "Kiss me."

"Me? Kiss *you*?" he blurted. "Now? With..." He gestured to the bomb. "...everything?"

"Well, it might be my last chance," she pointed out. "So, yes. Kiss me. Unless..." Her face fell. "Shite. Unless you don't want to. Have I been...? Oh, God. I've been totally misreading things, haven't I?"

"No. No. I mean, you haven't. I mean, I do. Want to," Logan said.

Shona drew in a big breath of relief, then shot the bomb a worried look, turned her head and let the air out slowly again.

"Then, kiss me," she said. "It's number one on the bucket list. You can't say no to a dying woman's last request."

"You're not dying," Logan told her. "We're going to get this sorted."

"Well, whatever," Shona said. "You going to kiss me or what?"

For a moment, Logan didn't move. He wanted to kiss her. He did. He had for a long time.

But now? Like this? With Harris and Maddie out there somewhere? With everything that was going on?

Not to mention the dirty great bomb.

"Bucket list," she reminded him. "Jump to it."

At that, Logan sat forward in the chair. It didn't bring him close enough, so he got down on his knees and shuffled to her. With her sitting and him kneeling, they were at about the same height.

Heads level. Face to face.

"Right, then. Here goes," he said, in what surely qualified as one of the least romantic build-ups in modern history.

He leaned in.

Shona shut her eyes.

There was a knock at the door before their lips could meet. A solid hammering. A polis knock.

"Jack? Jack, you in there?" called DI Ben Forde. "Open the door, it's pishing down out here!"

"Ben," Logan said, holding Shona's gaze.

She smacked her lips together, smiled weakly, and sighed through her teeth. "So close," she lamented.

Logan got up clumsily, using the patchwork chair for support. "I'd better let him in."

"Yeah," Shona agreed. "I suppose you'd better had."

Despite the urgency of the situation, Ben spent a couple of seconds wiping his feet on the mat outside the front door before he stepped inside. Logan closed the door behind him, and shot his friend a grim smile.

"Thanks for coming. I didn't know who else to call."

"Not a problem." Ben indicated the only downstairs room with the lights on. "She in here?"

"Aye." Logan lowered his voice to a whisper. "There's something else you should know."

Ben groaned and raised his eyes to Logan. "God. What now?"

"It's Maddie," Logan said. "He's... Petrie. He's got Maddie."

"Oh, Jack." Ben gripped the DCI's arm. "Oh, Jack. I'm sorry. When? How?"

"Got her at the safe house."

"And Vanessa?"

Logan shook his head.

"Oh, shite. Jack, I'm so sorry," Ben whispered.

"What? Oh, no. She's no' dead. I meant she wasn't taken. She was stabbed in both thighs, though. Not life-threatening. Uniform got her taken into Raigmore."

There was the sound of a throat being cleared from the room next door.

"Uh, hello?" Shona called. "Big bomb in here. Remember?"

"Just coming," Logan replied. He lowered his voice again. "She doesn't know. About what's happened to them. She's got enough to worry about."

"Makes sense," Ben said. He released his grip on Logan's arm and offered a supportive smile. "Right, then. Let's go see what we're dealing with."

CHAPTER THIRTY-FIVE

TYLER HAD DONE ALMOST A COMPLETE CIRCUIT OF THE house when he found the open window. He cursed himself—had he gone left instead of right at that first window, he'd have found this one in under a minute. Instead, he'd spent the best part of half an hour creeping and crawling his way around the outside of the building, checking every possible entrance he came to.

He'd looked inside most of them, too, shining his torch in through the glass when he was sure nobody was lurking within. He'd seen nothing incriminating, unless you counted the ninety-inch curved TVs, and the artworks that probably cost twice Tyler's annual salary.

Bastard.

The open window was another of the sash types, and the gap at the bottom was large enough for him to slide his hands in. The space beyond, from what he could gather, was some sort of utility room, although it had enough washers and driers in it that it might well be a fully-operational laundrette.

The rain rattled on his back and the backs of his legs. He

was already soaked to the skin, and the thought of getting into shelter—even in the house of a Russian gangster, which he had illegally entered—made him throw caution to the wind.

He pushed up on the window. At first, it didn't budge, but a bit of shoving and a fair amount of grunting, and it finally succumbed. The window shot up inside the frame with a high-pitched screech, and banged against the top.

Tyler spun on his heels, pressing himself flat against the wall beside the window, listening for any signs of movement.

Nothing.

The only sounds were the pattering of the rain and the thumping of his own heart inside his chest. As his panic subsided, even his racing heart quietened, until the rainfall was the only sound left.

The house had to be empty. Somebody would've heard that, surely?

He inched out from behind the wall and risked a glance in through the open window. The utility room was still in darkness. The door remained closed.

"This is fucking... nonsense," Tyler whispered to himself, then he reached in through the window, found a handhold on the radiator fixed to the wall beneath it, and slid clumsily inside.

He hit the lino floor with a *thack*, and sat there for another few terrifying moments, listening for any movement within the house.

Satisfied that there was nothing, he got up, dusted himself down, and crept to the door. He opened it just a crack at first and put his eye to the gap. There was a hallway outside the room. Long and narrow, he thought, although he couldn't be sure from that angle.

Nobody moving around, though, so he opened the door enough that he could lean out, quickly glance in both directions, and lean back in.

Empty.

Thank Christ.

Tyler stepped out into the hall, keeping close to the wall. To the left of the door, the corridor ended at a window that looked out onto the grounds at the front of the house.

To the right, it led to a T-junction. A left there would take him through to the rest of the building, he figured, so that was the way he went, tiptoeing along the wall to remain as silent as possible.

It occurred to him a few steps in that he should've worn gloves. He'd have left fingerprints everywhere, and what he was doing was technically illegal.

OK, not even 'technically.' It was fully illegal. He had broken into a man's home on a whim. Even Logan had told him just to drive by the place. Even Logan wouldn't be this reckless.

Would he?

Tyler briefly contemplated going back to the car for gloves, but the damage was already done. Best to press on, do a sweep of the place, and see if Harris or Maddie were here. A quick look, then out. No harm, no foul. No one would ever even know he had been there.

At the T-junction, he looked to the right first. That branch led to another door, much like the one he'd just come through. A bathroom, maybe.

He looked along the branch to the left. The hallway led into a large open-plan living space. The kitchen area, from what he could tell, was bigger than his whole flat, and he could only see part of it.

"Bastard," he said, out loud this time.

He was halfway along the hallway when he heard movement. He froze. There were no doors on either side of him, nothing for him to hide behind. He strained to hear the sound again, but his heart was hammering inside his chest, and all he could hear was the blood surging around inside his head.

Tyler had just taken a backwards step when the dog appeared from around the corner at the end of the hallway ahead. It was, he noted, quite a big dog. As dogs went, this one was exactly the size of a large Doberman. Exactly the same shape and colour, too.

"Oh, shit," Tyler whispered, as the dog's mouth became a showcase for its teeth and gums. It growled, its ears stood up. The short fur on the back of its neck did the same. "Good dog," said Tyler, raising a calming hand.

And with that, the animal launched itself at him, snarling and barking. Tyler spun on the spot and ran, skidding on the polished wooden floor as he threw himself around the corner and powered back towards the utility room.

He caught a glimpse of car headlights approaching through the big window at the end of the corridor, but that felt like a problem for another time. He could hear the dog right behind him now, could practically feel its breath on the back of his legs.

The door was still ajar. He shouldered through it, already turning, and closed the door with a *slam*. There was a thud and a yelp from the other side, then the barking resumed, more furious than ever, as claws scraped and scratched at the door.

From out front, Tyler heard the sound of a car door closing. No, wait. Doors. Plural. Multiple.

Fuck.

"Shh. Shut up," he hissed through the door, but this just made the dog bark louder still. At the rate the animal was tearing at the wood, it would get to him before whoever had just pulled up made it inside.

Time to abort.

Tyler hurried to the open window, stuck a leg through, and sprackled out. He ducked, as another set of headlights swept up the driveway, their glare licking across the lawn ahead of him.

The dog was still barking, but he could hear other sounds from inside the house now. Voices. Raised. Angry.

Shit, shit, shit.

There was nothing else for it. The moment the headlights had passed, Tyler ran, throwing himself towards the gate he'd clambered over. His legs powered like pistons, propelling himself across the endless expanse of grass, putting as much distance between himself and the house as he could.

And then, when he was just past the halfway mark, the inevitable happened. The door to the utility room was thrown open, and the barking of one extremely pissed-off Doberman began to grow exponentially louder as it leaped through the open window and gave chase.

Tyler wasted a lungful of air on a selection of hasty expletives, then he fixed his gaze on the gate, and begged his legs to move faster.

"How you doing there, Shona?" Ben asked. "Holding up alright?"

"I'll be honest, I've had better days."

Ben was already studying the device on her chest, and only half-heard the reply. "Hmm? Oh. Aye. I can imagine. Well, let's see about getting this thing off you, will we?"

"Can you do it?" asked Logan. He was hovering behind the DI, peering over his shoulder and watching him work.

"Maybe if you gave me a bit of room..." Ben suggested.

"Right. Sorry."

Logan took a backwards step. Ben rolled his eyes.

"How about you go get me a cup of coffee?" the DI suggested.

"Is caffeine a good idea?" Logan asked. "Steady hands, and all that."

"Just get me the bloody coffee," Ben instructed, then he turned back to Shona and gave an exasperated shake of his head.

Shona managed a solid three-fifths of a smile. "And I'll have an Earl Grey, while you're there."

Logan's lips drew back in distaste. "Fucking Earl Grey," he muttered, expressing his long-held resentment for a drink he considered nothing more than watery Potpourri.

With a final look at the bomb, he turned and stomped off to find the kitchen. Shona lowered her voice to a whisper once he'd left.

"I don't have Earl Grey," she told Ben. "That should keep him busy for a bit."

Ben chuckled. "I can see why he likes you." He pulled on his reading glasses, balancing them on the end of his nose. "Now, try to keep still, I'm going to have a closer look at this thing and see if we can figure out what we're dealing with."

He brought an ear closer to the device, and listened until it gave its *whirr* and *click*.

"Uh-huh," he said.

"Is that a good 'uh-huh'?" Shona asked.

It didn't sound like a good 'uh-huh.' It didn't sound like a good 'uh-huh,' at all.

"Still figuring it out," Ben said. "You're doing well."

He very gently tapped the canister attached to the left of the device's central hub, then did the same with the one on the right.

"Hmm."

The 'hmm,' sounded even less promising than the, 'uh-huh,' Shona thought, but she didn't say anything. If the news was bad, she wasn't sure she wanted to know. Not just yet.

Ben straightened, then walked around behind her. He knelt down, getting low enough to study the wires that were wrapped around her wrists. One red. One blue. He followed them, and found they connected into the base of the canisters, joining both together.

He returned to the front again, and looked more closely at

the canisters. They were both metal, and both had lids on top. The same red and blue wiring set-up ran from inside each lid to the *whirring* and *clicking* central hub of the device.

"Well, well, well," Ben muttered, and this time Shona couldn't help herself.

"Well, well, well, what?"

"What's happening?" Logan asked, appearing in the doorway behind them with a conspicuous lack of coffee and tea. "What is it? What have we got?"

Ben half-turned so Logan was on his right, and Shona was on his left. His head tick-tocked between them as he told them his findings.

"I've seen a fair few IEDs in my time. All sorts. Nail bombs. but this...? This is a new one on me. I've never seen anything like it."

"Shite," Logan spat.

Shona's eyes were wide with worry again. "Then, what do we do? How do we get it off?"

"Easy," Ben said. "It's fake."

The DCI and the Pathologist both blinked simultaneously. Logan was the first to respond.

"Fake? Are you sure?"

"As sure as you ever can be," Ben replied.

"Which is how sure, exactly?" asked Shona.

"Ninety-five percent," said Ben.

"So, that's one in twenty *not* sure," Shona hurriedly pointed out.

"Ninety-nine percent, then. Ninety-nine-point-nine-nine-nine. It's a fake. I'm certain of it."

"Almost certain," Shona corrected. "*Almost.*"

Ben took off his glasses and tucked them into his shirt pocket. "PIES," he said.

Logan and Shona exchanged glances.

"Pies? What the fuck's 'pies'?" Logan asked.

Ben sat on the arm of the patchwork chair and began to list on his fingers. "Power, initiator, explosive, switch. The four components of a functioning explosive device. PIES. It's a... what do you call it?"

"Acronym," said Shona.

"Yes. Thank you. It's an acronym. PIES."

"And how does it help us?" Logan asked.

Ben gestured to the device strapped to Shona's chest. "At a stretch, let's say those canisters are full of explosives. They're not—I'm sure of it—but for the sake of argument, let's says they are. That's one element. The ticky thing in the middle? That could be the switch. Two. It's got power, because it's making a noise. Three. Is there an initiator? Maybe."

"What's an initiator?" Shona asked.

Logan knew this one. "Like a detonator."

"Right. Basically. It's usually a small amount of explosive that triggers the bigger explosion," Ben explained.

"So... what? It doesn't have one of those?" Logan asked.

"Oh, it might well do," Ben said. "Could be in one of the canisters, or this plastic bit in the middle.

Ben and Shona exchanged another look. This one was even more incredulous than before, and considering that had come after Ben had inexplicably said the word, "Pies," out loud, that was saying something.

"You've lost me," Logan said. "You said it wasn't real, but now you're saying... what? That it is?"

"No, I'm saying it appears to have all the right components," Ben said. "It's meant to fool the layman. No offence, Jack. But it's no' a bomb. It's no' an anything."

Logan remained unconvinced. If the DI was wrong, then things would get very messy, very quickly.

"He said he'd detonate it if you called the bomb squad. Right?" asked Ben.

Logan nodded. "Right."

"How? There's no phone connected. No receiver. How's he going to send the detonate signal?" Ben asked. Logan was almost convinced by that, until the DI continued. "I mean, aye, maybe he's got a small SIM device in the switch. That would work. The key components of the phone without the phone part. I've seen that done."

"For fuck's sake, Ben," Logan cried, throwing his hands up in the air. "Make your bloody mind up. Is it a bomb or isn't it?"

"It isn't. And I'm prepared to stake my life on it."

"You might be staking all our lives on it," Shona pointed out.

"Relax. Trust me. There's more chance of me exploding than that thing," Ben said. He turned back to Logan. "Besides, think about it. Petrie brought you here. He knows you wouldn't leave. Do you really think he'd let you off that easily by blowing you to kingdom come?"

That thought had not occurred to Logan, but it made sense. Petrie was out to torture him. To make him suffer. This would be too quick a death. Too easy a way out.

He took a breath. He met Shona's eye. Something unspoken passed between them, then she nodded. "Just get rid of it," she said. "I just want it done."

Ben clapped his hands so suddenly and loudly that the other two occupants of the room both jumped.

"Jesus Christ!" Logan hissed. "What are you trying to do, give us a bloody heart attack?"

Ben smiled sheepishly. "Sorry." He clapped his hands again, more quietly this time, then rubbed them together, warming up his fingers. "Right, then, m'dear. Let's get this thing off you."

THE BARKING SEEMED to come from behind and on both sides as Tyler thundered across the grass. He could hear voices shouting further back, but the dog was a far more pressing concern.

Tyler tried not to think about its slavering jaws and huge, pointy teeth. He tried, but failed, and a vision of his own grisly death propelled him on.

The dog was close. The gate was closer. He was just a few seconds from it now. A few seconds to prepare. A few seconds to hope the four-legged bastard behind him didn't sink its teeth in at the last moment.

With a banshee yell, Tyler threw himself at the top of the gate, hands grasping for the metal bar. If he caught it, he had a chance. If he missed it, he was done for.

He caught it. Somehow, he caught it. He heaved himself upwards, legs bicycling as his feet tried to find purchase on the narrow metal mesh.

The dog arrived in a fanfare of snarls and barks. Tyler felt its teeth graze against the back of his leg, caught a glimpse of it lowering itself to the ground as it prepared to leap, and then he was tumbling over the top of the gate, and plunging towards the other side.

Just as he registered his concern over the approaching concrete slabs, he hit one, upside-down. The impact fired hot streaks of pain through his shoulder, then his leg flipped over his head and both knees crunched against the neighbouring slab.

Every part of him complained as he bounded to his feet, already fumbling in his pockets for his keys.

He was at the car when he saw the headlights of another vehicle come racing up behind him.

He was in the driver's seat when a van came screeching to a halt in front of him, blocking him in.

"Shite," Tyler hissed.

He grabbed for his phone, opened the contacts, and found Logan's name. Before he could tap it, the window beside him exploded, showering him with diamond-like fragments of glass, and sending his phone tumbling into the passenger footwell.

The business end of a shotgun poked in through the broken window. Tyler looked along it and saw the bruised face of a familiar-looking skinhead.

"Well, now," said Valdis. "Take a look what we have here."

CHAPTER THIRTY-SIX

"And you're absolutely sure about this?" Logan asked. He was looming behind DI Forde, his hands buried deep in his coat pockets.

"Can we ever be absolutely sure of anything?" Ben asked, glancing back over his shoulder. "I'm as sure about this as I've been about anything in my life. Is that good enough for you?"

"Good enough for me," Shona said. "I'm about three minutes away from wetting myself. One, if you do that thing with your hands again."

Ben looked momentarily offended. "What thing with my...? Oh. Clapping. Right. Aye. No, I won't do that." He shot Logan another look. "How's that coffee coming along, by the way?"

"Aye, getting there," Logan replied, showing no signs of moving.

Ben tutted, then turned his attention back to the device. With a click, he slid out the blade of a craft knife Shona kept in a drawer in the kitchen, alongside forty double-A batteries, two screwdrivers, and a head torch.

For a man so confident that the bomb wasn't real, he moved awfully slowly. The top of each canister had been attached with strips of tape. There were three that Ben could see on each one, and probably more around the back of the containers.

He wouldn't be able to reach those without disturbing the device, and an embarrassing amount of hand-to-breast contact, but if he could get the front and side pieces off, those on the back should act like a hinge.

The tape was thin, and the blade was sharp, and he was through them all in a matter of seconds.

Shona's breath came faster as Ben started to slowly jiggle the lid from side to side, working it upwards.

"Here. Look at me," Logan told her, sensing her distress. "Real bucket list. Top five. Go."

Shona's mouth opened and closed, but no words came out. "Um... I don't..." Her eyes were pulled back down to the movement of the canister.

"Pyramids," Logan suggested, drawing her gaze back towards him. "Everyone wants to see the pyramids, don't they?"

Shona gave an absent sort of nod that was sorely missing an accompanying smile. "Suppose."

Ben muttered something quietly below his breath, which earned another worried look from the Pathologist.

"I mean, I don't want to see them personally," Logan continued. "No' really my cup of tea. Just pointy hills, aren't they? And it always looks roasting over there." He shook his head definitively. "No. Not my scene. Always fancied Venice, though. I quite like a wee boat. You fancy Venice?"

"Is... is that an invitation?" Shona asked. Her voice was hoarse, and she was fighting a losing battle against the shakes.

"Almost got it..." Ben remarked.

"Oh, fuck," Shona hissed.

Logan appeared behind her and put his hands on her shoulders. "You're alright. You're doing great."

"Y-you should go," she told him. "Get out. Just in case."

"I'm going nowhere," Logan told her. "DI Forde has my full faith."

Ben glanced up briefly. "Christ. First time for everything," he said, then the canister lid sprang open, and all three of them made involuntary noises in fright.

"See?" said Ben, after a pause. "Nothing to worry about."

He peeked into the canister, then poked around with the craft knife at the contents.

"What is it?" Logan asked.

Ben leaned in closer to the canister and took a sniff. He gave a gentle downwards tug on the wire at the bottom of the container, then pulled upwards at the top.

"It's salt," he said. "And the top wire's just taped to the side. The other end's probably taped inside the bottom, too."

He sat back on his haunches, looking pleased with himself. Had he not known the DI for so long, Logan wouldn't have noticed, but Ben also looked more than a little relieved.

"You can horse it off her now," he said, indicating the harness. "It's fine."

"What about the other one?" Shona asked, looking down at the second container.

"There's not a complete circuit," Ben said. "Even if that one's packed full of explosives—and it won't be—there's no power getting to it. You're fine. If it makes you feel better, though..."

He grabbed the wire at the switch and gave it a sharp tug. It came free without much resistance, and this time Ben looked all-the-way smug.

"Nicely done, Ben. Never doubted you for a minute," Logan said, holding a hand out for the knife.

"Can I get that in writing?" Ben asked, passing the blade over.

Logan unbuckled the straps of the harness and—still being careful—set the device down on the floor. Shona bounced in her chair, agitated, as Logan bent and cut the tape holding her hands, and unwound the rest of the cable.

"There. That's you—"

She was up out of the chair like a sprinter off the starting blocks. "Bathroom. Be right back," she announced, haring out of the room.

Ben flopped down onto the armchair. He'd been hiding it since he'd arrived, but now that the drama was over, Logan could see that Hoon was right. The DI looked exhausted. The kind of exhaustion that penetrated the bones and switched out the marrow for lumps of lead.

"You OK?"

Ben gave himself a shake. "Me? Aye. What about you? I mean, Jesus, Jack..."

"Trying not to think about it," Logan said. "Or... not dwell on it. I'm no use if I'm a basket case."

"That's what he's aiming for," Ben said. "That's what all this is about. He's targeting people close to you. He knows that's how to hurt you."

Logan lowered himself onto the wicker seat of the chair. Shona was right, it was an uncomfortable bugger of a thing.

"How did he know about her?" he asked, gesturing to the door through which the Pathologist had gone running. "I mean... Nobody knows about her. Hell, *I* don't even know what's..."

He sighed and sat back, eliciting a squeak of complaint from the chair's wooden back. "My relationship with Shona is hardly going to be on the Gozer's phone. I mean, it's hardly even a relationship. There's barely anything about it on *my* bloody phone."

"Bosco?" Ben guessed.

"Christ, that reminds me. I'd better check in with Tyler. He's scoping out Bosco's house," Logan said.

Ben frowned. "That sensible?"

"He's keeping his distance. I mean..." Logan shrugged. "I

suppose it has to be Bosco feeding Petrie the info. But how would *he* even know? It's not like I've been popping round here. I've seen her out of work once, months ago, and we both got called away a few minutes into it. The man would have to be bloody psychic or..."

He looked past Ben, his eyes darting back and forth, like he was seeing some explanation written there on the wall.

"Or what?" Ben asked.

"Or... Jesus."

"What? What is it?"

There was the sound of a door opening elsewhere in the house, and Shona returned, looking just as bruised and battered, but far more relaxed than she'd looked when she'd left.

"That's better," she said. "Sorry about that."

Logan and Ben both stood up. "No, you're fine," Ben said. "Understandable. Between you and me, I may have had some light leakage of my own when I was lifting the lid of that container.

"Lovely image there," Logan said. "Thanks for that."

Ben gestured to the armchair, and Shona didn't argue. Her legs practically gave way as she got close to it, and she collapsed into its multi-coloured cushions.

"I'll go get that tea," Logan told her. "Give you a chance to get your breath back before we bombard you with questions."

Shona nodded. "Thanks. I'll tell you everything I can."

Logan took a step towards the door, then stopped when Shona spoke again.

"I don't get it, though," she said.

"Don't get what?"

"Why me? Why come here and do this to me? What have I done?"

Logan backtracked until he was looking directly down at her. "You've done nothing. We think Petrie is targeting people I... have a close working relationship with. It's me he's trying to get at. Not you. He's already targeted the children of three colleagues."

"Bloody hell, that's horrible," Shona said. She turned her gaze to Ben. "Has he done anything to you?"

Ben shook his head. "No. Not me."

"Right. Good," Shona said. She looked between the two detectives. "Because you go way back, don't you?"

"Aye," said Logan. The word came slowly, bringing with it a little knot of dread in the hollow of his chest. "We go way back."

"Decades," Ben agreed. He shifted his weight from one foot to the other. Clearly, he had that same niggling concern that Logan had. "Why hasn't he targeted me?" he wondered aloud.

Logan's heart was in his throat now.

Don't call the bomb squad. That had been the instruction.

But he knew. Petrie knew. About Ben. About his past.

And he knew he'd be the first person that Logan would call.

Logan pulled out his phone, started dialling Hamza's number.

"Oh God," Ben whispered, working it all out just a second or two behind Logan. "Alice!"

CHAPTER THIRTY-SEVEN

EVEN AT THAT TIME OF NIGHT, IT WAS A TWENTY-FIVE-minute drive from Shona's to Ben's. Logan had done it in under fifteen.

Ben was out of the Volvo before it had fully come to a stop. He ran the rest of the way along his street, blue lights spinning through the darkness around him.

He saw the faces of officers he'd spoken to a dozen times before avert their gazes as he went stumbling on towards his house.

Towards his wife.

As he ran, his head was filled with thoughts of her. Memories. Experiences they'd shared.

Their wedding day, the sun filtering through her veil.

Their first house together. Barely a cupboard, but she'd been so proud of it.

Her face when he'd come home from the service for the final time. The hug she'd given him. The touch of her cheek against his, and the tears they had shared.

Their life together.

There was an ambulance right at the end of the driveway, the back doors open, the bed inside empty.

A uniformed sergeant called after him as he clattered past. "Detective Inspector..."

It sounded like an apology.

Ben ignored it. Ran on. Chest heaving.

He saw it on the faces of the Uniforms he passed, in their eyes, in the way they didn't know how to look at him, much less what to say.

He ignored them. Ran on. Heart breaking.

He heard Logan calling to him from somewhere far away. Too far back to stop him. Too far back to intervene.

He was under the tape now. The house was right there. *She* was right there.

He was through the gate.

He was up the path.

He was at the open door.

And then DC Khaled was there before him, eyes wide, hands shaking. "Sir," he said, planting his feet in the doorway. "You can't."

"Get out of my way!" Ben spat, throwing his full weight at Hamza, shouldering, and pushing, and elbowing at him. "Hamza, move!"

"You can't, sir," was all Hamza could say. "I'm sorry."

He jammed himself against the door, absorbed the furious pushing and shoving of the senior officer.

"Get out of the way!" Ben roared, punching and slapping at him now. "Hamza, get out of my way, or—"

He collapsed against the DC, grief hitting him like a hammer-blow. Hamza wrapped his arms around the older man and held him there. Held him close.

"I'm so sorry, sir," he said. "I am so, so sorry."

Logan stood frozen at the end of the path. His head was shaking like he couldn't believe it—like he refused to believe it.

But he knew, of course. He'd known before they'd left Shona's. Petrie was out to hurt him in the most painful ways possible. He'd taken his daughter. And now, he'd broken the heart of his oldest friend.

And he'd made Logan the one who'd called him away. The one who'd made Ben leave Alice alone and unprotected. The bastard had made him responsible.

The flashing blues made the house look different—almost unrecognisable from the place he'd had dinner shortly after he'd relocated up north. Alice had spent much of that night giving him grief about... well, everything.

In hindsight, he'd probably deserved it.

"Ben," Logan said, forcing his feet to carry him along the path. There should have been more after that, he knew. Some words of comfort. Of support. Of *something*. But nothing would come.

What could he possibly say?

"I want to see her," Ben said, pulling away from Hamza and rubbing his eyes on his sleeve. "I'm fine. I'm fine. I want to see her."

Hamza met Logan's gaze over the DI's shoulder. Everything that Petrie had done was written in that look, and Logan felt the hot prickling of tears at the backs of his own eyes.

"Maybe best not, Ben, eh?" Logan said. "Maybe now's not the time."

"I've seen plenty of bloody bodies before!" Ben spat, spinning to face the DCI. "More than you, Jack! A lot worse nick, too!"

"She's no' a body, Ben," Logan said. Softly. Kindly. "She's your wife. She's Alice."

An agonised sob burst from Ben's lips. He leaned a hand on the wall, supporting himself.

He looked past Hamza into the hallway. It had been their hallway when he left the house. His and Alice's. It would never be theirs again. It would never be *his* again. The hallway, like the rest of the house, now belonged to some past version of himself. To the Benjamin Forde who existed before this moment, and who had died along with his wife.

"What am I going to do now?" he asked of nobody in particular, then he cleared his throat, straightened his shoulders, and looked Hamza in the eye. "Where was she?"

Hamza looked uncomfortable with the question. "You should probably try not to—"

"Hamza!" Ben barked. He sighed, his shoulders sloping like that short outburst had drained him of the last of his strength. "Sorry. I just... I need to know where it happened."

Still unsure, Hamza looked to Logan for guidance and received a tentative nod in reply.

"She was... still upstairs, sir. In bed."

Ben tried very hard to put a brave face on it. Tried very hard to pretend that this was normal. That she was some other victim, at some other scene.

"Right," he said, the word barely making it through his constricted throat. "Thanks."

Logan put an arm around Ben's shoulders and beckoned a Uniform over. "We'll get you sat down. Get you that coffee I've been promising."

Ben tore his eyes away from the door. "Aye," he said. "Coffee. That's..."

And then, he ran, pulling away from Logan and catching Hamza off-guard. They both tumbled into the hallway, Hamza thrown off-balance while Ben managed to hold onto his own.

In a second, he was passing the living room. Two Paramedics in there looked up from where they were packing up their equipment as he went charging past, with Logan hot on his heels.

"Ben, no!"

And then, he was on the stairs.

And then, he was at the bedroom door.

And then...

And then...

He stopped, a hand hovering above the handle, not yet touching it. Not yet daring.

Logan clumped to the top of the stairs but came no closer.

"Ben, I know what you're thinking."

"You've got no idea what I'm thinking," Ben snapped back, more savagely than Logan had ever heard him. "This was to get at you. He did this to get at *you*. Not me. Not her. She'd done nothing. Nothing, Jack!"

It was another one of those times where Logan had no reply to offer. Nothing beyond an admission of guilt, anyway.

"Aye," he said. "I know. And I'm sorry, Ben. I'm so sorry. And if you have to go in there, if you have to see her for yourself, then I'm not going to stop you. You're a big boy, you make your own decisions."

Ben's hand rested on the handle, but didn't yet move to turn it.

"I didn't know Alice anything like you did, but I do know that she wouldn't want you seeing her. Not now. Not like this," Logan said.

The house—no, the whole world—hung there in silence around them. Like it, too, didn't quite know what to say.

Ben sniffed and wiped his nose on the back of his hand. He spoke directly at the door, not looking at Logan once.

"She'd... she'd put make-up on. In the morning. Before I was up. Said she didn't want me seeing her looking old." Tears tripped down his cheeks. "But I... I told her. I *loved* seeing her old. Her crow's feet. The grey. Because they were all *ours*. Hers and mine. We were growing old together. The two of us. Me and her."

He leaned forward until his head was resting against the

wood. His shoulders heaved. His hand slipped from the door handle and fell to his side.

"I'm sorry, darling," he whispered, and Logan looked away, shamed by his friend's grief. "I'm so sorry."

———————

LOGAN AND HAMZA stood in Ben's front garden, watching him being led away by a uniformed sergeant, a blanket draped over his shoulders, a cup of coffee from the petrol station along the road clutched in one hand.

"Think he'll be OK?" Hamza asked.

Logan watched Ben getting into the passenger seat of the Volvo, then shook his head. "No. I don't," he admitted.

"He got any family locally? Kids?"

"No. Never had any. Was just him and Alice. Always has been."

He watched Ben for a few more seconds, until the sight of him sitting there staring emptily ahead became too painful, then turned towards the open front door of the house.

"Right. I'm going in before Palmer and his lot get here. One wrong word from that bastard tonight and I'm liable to add to the body count."

Hamza glanced at the upstairs window. "Mind if I... stay here, sir?"

"That bad?"

"It's bad. Not really any worse than some, I suppose, just... knowing who she was..."

Logan patted the DC on the shoulder. "You're fine, son. Stay out here." He turned, then a thought struck him. "Any progress on your three-word thing?"

"Sinead's still on it, back at base," Hamza said. "We're getting through it."

"How is she?"

"She's keeping busy. But about what you'd expect," Hamza said. "How are you doing?"

Logan smiled thinly. "About what you'd expect."

"Did, eh, did Tyler catch up with you?"

"Tyler?" Logan frowned. "Didn't he check back in?"

"Not yet, sir. I mean, maybe. With Sinead. I haven't spoken to her since I left. So, aye. He probably has."

"Phone him, will you? Find out where he's got to," Logan instructed, then he fished a pair of rubber gloves from the pack in his pocket, said "Right, then," for nobody's benefit but his own, and headed back in through DI Forde's front door.

The stairs seemed to go on forever. The closer he got to the top, the more like quicksand they became, pulling him down, trying to get him to stop, to go no further, to turn back before it was too late. Before he saw.

But there was no turning back. There had been no turning back for a while now.

He stopped at the door just as Ben had done, but only for long enough to pull on his gloves and slide shoe protectors on over his boots.

The room was in darkness, but the light from the upstairs landing picked out the thing that had been Alice Forde. It lay on the bed, a torn nightdress exposing its nakedness. It had slashes across its throat, and several others across its breasts and stomach. Its arms, too.

Alice had tried to defend herself. She'd been awake, then. Aware. She'd have looked into the bastard's eyes. She'd have known what was coming.

And she'd fought. Of course, she had. She was Alice Forde. She'd never backed down from an argument in her life.

The bedclothes and mattress had absorbed most of the blood, but some of it had trickled over the edge and onto the floor. A crimson waterfall against the pale blue valance.

There was some spattering on the headboard, less on the

wall above it. A bloodied handprint had clutched at the bedpost at one point. Forensics would have to determine whose, but given that the hands of the thing on the bed were smeared with red, he guessed the prints would be Alice's.

He looked around the room, grateful to no longer be looking directly at the remains.

What else? What else?

The clock had been knocked off the bedside table on the empty side of the bed. The duvet had been thrown off in that direction, and probably clipped the clock on the way over. It hung off the side of the bed now, most of it on the floor, but one corner still trying to cling on.

How had he got in? Window was open, but still on the latch, so he couldn't have come in that way. Through the door, then. He'd have to ask about signs of forced entry downstairs.

What else? What else?

He crossed to the far corner of the room and looked back at the door, taking it all in from another angle. He squatted to see under the bed, and saw the knife there, the blade the colour of a fine red wine.

There were a pair of slippers tucked underneath the bed, too. They were thick, comfy, tartan things, with a white woollen stripe across the front. A single splash of blood pinkened the white at one corner—the only flaw on the otherwise untouched pair.

He left the knife where it was for the Scene of Crime team. The room gave up no further secrets, and Logan headed for the door.

Before he left, he stopped and turned back to the thing on the bed. The thing that had been Alice Forde.

The love of his best friend's life.

"I'll look after him," he said. "I promise."

And with that, he stepped out onto the landing and closed the door.

CHAPTER THIRTY-EIGHT

BEN DIDN'T LOOK UP WHEN LOGAN CLIMBED INTO THE driver's seat of the car. His eyes were instead fixed on the cup of coffee he was nursing in both hands. He'd got as far as removing the lid, but hadn't drunk any of it, for fear of throwing it all back up.

It would only have been a waste, anyway. His senses felt dead. He wouldn't have been able to taste it.

"Well?" he asked.

Logan pulled on his seatbelt before replying. It was a fine line, he knew. Give Ben too much information, and it would haunt him forever. Give him too little, and the images he created in his head would be much, much worse.

"Her throat was cut," Logan said, staring straight ahead at the flashing lights of the various polis vehicles.

Ben nodded slowly, but remained focused on the now-cool liquid in his cup. "And?"

"She fought back. No doubt got a good few licks in."

"Did he rape her?" Ben asked. It was blunt and direct, and he took a big steadying breath after it, like it had taken physical effort to get the question out.

"No. No, nothing like that," Logan said. He wasn't sure of that. He didn't think so, but he couldn't be sure until the post mortem. As he said the words, though, he made damned sure to sound as certain of it as he could.

A tear *plipped* into the cup. Ben's breathing came fast and sudden, like he was hyperventilating. Relief, Logan knew. He'd seen it before under very similar circumstances. All that pent-up fear and dread releasing itself in one go.

"We'll take you back to the station," Logan said. "You can bed down in one of the rooms there. We can talk. Or, you know, there's... support. Mental health."

Ben shook his head. "I've already booked myself into a hotel."

Logan turned in his chair. "A hotel? On your own? I'm not sure that's—"

"I've booked it, Jack. I'm going. You can take me back to my car, or you can drop me off and I can get a taxi out there tomorrow."

"It's tomorrow now," Logan pointed out. "There's no point paying for a hotel for a couple of hours. Come on back—"

"I've made my mind up. I'm booked in. That's that."

"Ben, you're in shock. You shouldn't be in a hotel. You should be with people you know. People who can help."

"People who can *help*? How in God's name can anyone help, Jack? Can they bring Alice back? Can they rewind time?"

"No. They can't," Logan admitted. "Maybe not 'help,' then. Not yet. But you should be with people who care about you."

Ben laughed drily. "People who care about me?" he said, sounding incredulous. "Seems to me, the people that *you* care about all end up hurt. Or dead."

He winced, hearing how the words sounded as they came out of his mouth. His face softened.

"Jack..." he began, and it seemed like an apology was about to be forthcoming. But then he stole a glance back at the house that was no longer his, and the window of the room where his wife's body lay, and his expression firmed up again. "Just take me to the bloody hotel."

———————

THE FIRST FINGERS of sunlight were grasping across the sky when Logan returned to the Incident Room. Four Uniforms and a couple of CID officers sat at desks, talking into phones or typing on computers. They all looked up as Logan entered, nodded to him, then went back to whatever they'd been doing.

Hamza emerged from the DCI's office at the back of the room, and carefully pulled the door closed. The blinds were drawn—something he usually reserved for those occasions where he had to give someone a bollocking.

"Sinead. I told her to get some sleep," Hamza whispered. "She's dead on her feet."

"I know the feeling," Logan said.

Both men asked their next questions at the same time.

"How's Ben?"

"Where's Tyler?"

The look on Logan's face more or less answered Hamza's question, so he volunteered an answer of his own.

"Can't get him, sir. Phone's switched off."

"Sinead's not heard from him?"

"No, sir. I played it down, though. Don't want her getting worried."

"Good thinking. Get a pen, I'll give you Bosco Maximuke's address. Get Uniform round there to suss the place out. See if Tyler's car is anywhere nearby."

Hamza already had pen in hand and notebook open by the time Logan had reached the end of his instructions. He jotted the address down as the DCI relayed it, then went off to arrange the drive-past.

He stopped at his desk. When he turned, there was an apologetic look on his face. "Oh, I almost forgot. Detective Superintendent Hoon wants to see you."

"Does he, indeed?" Logan asked. He shrugged his coat off and tossed it onto the nearest available desk. "That's handy. I want a wee word with him, too."

HOON JUMPED to his feet the moment Logan appeared around his door.

"When the fuck were you planning on telling me about your daughter?" the DSup demanded. "Jesus fucking Christ All-bastard-mighty, Jack! You can't be fucking swanning about like—"

"Sit down, Bob."

Hoon's brow became a series of interlocking lines. His eyebrows met so hard in the middle they practically fused together.

"What did you fucking say?"

Logan's voice had an icy edge to it. "I said: Sit. Down."

Hoon stood his ground. Logan unbuttoned one cuff of his shirt and began to roll up the sleeve.

He was on the second sleeve when Hoon finally caved and sat in his chair.

"I've had quite the bloody night, Bob," Logan told him. "Maddie, you've heard about. Ben's Alice, too, I'm sure. That's bound to have filtered through to you by now. Yes?"

Hoon said nothing, but his head dipped forward to confirm that he had.

Logan finished rolling up his sleeves, then wheeled one of the other chairs back from the desk like he was going to sit on it. Instead, he rolled it over to the corner of the room, out of the way.

"What about Shona Maguire? Did you know about that?" he asked, moving the other chair to the opposite side of the room.

It was clear from the expression on Hoon's face that the Detective Superintendent didn't know about that one, so Logan elaborated.

"Petrie got to her. Strapped a bomb to her chest. Fake, it turned out. She's fine. More or less. But, that's what drew Ben away from home. He used my relationship with her to get me to call Ben. It's thanks to me that Alice was left alone. Which means, it's partly thanks to me that she's dead."

"You can't go blaming—"

"I wasn't finished," Logan said, cutting the Detective Superintendent off.

He glowered at Hoon across the desk. Under any normal circumstances, the DSup would have bitten Logan's head off by now. Possibly literally.

But then, these were far from normal circumstances.

"All through this, I've thought, 'How does he know?'" Logan continued. "How does he know where I live? How does he know where Hamza lives? About Harris? How could he know all that?"

"You said it yourself. If he's working with Bosco, then—"

"But how does Bosco know? To get all that—everything he's had in the past—he'd need half the bloody force on his payroll. Or one very high-up officer with a lot of connections."

Logan left that statement hanging there for a few moments, then leaned forward and placed his clenched fists on the desk.

"How was it you described it, Bob? Your 'all-seeing, all-fucking-knowing omnipotence.' That's what you said, isn't it?"

Once again, Hoon said nothing.

"Until we were in Carstairs, I thought there were four other people who knew about my relationship with Dr Maguire. And then you mentioned—and I'm paraphrasing here—my attempts to 'fire it up that Irish Pathologist bird' and that number grew to five. Four of them, I'd trust with my life. The fifth one? Well..." Logan straightened again. "I'm sure you can figure out who that is."

"If you're saying what I think you're fucking saying, Detective Chief Inspector..." Hoon began, but his heart wasn't in it. The fire was gone.

"Cut the shite, *Bob*," Logan told him. "You owe me that much."

Hoon stared up at him for a few seconds, then opened the bottom drawer of his desk and took out a half-empty bottle of Lagavulin malt. He produced a glass and clunked it down, then raised his gaze back to the DCI.

"You still off it?"

Logan gave a nod, and Hoon grunted his disapproval. He unscrewed the top of the bottle and glugged a couple of fingers into the glass, briefly contemplated replacing the lid, then tossed it onto the desk beside the glass.

"I didn't know," he said, raising the liquid to his lips but not yet drinking. He wasn't meeting Logan's eye, either. "About Petrie. That he and Bosco were... I didn't know. I had no idea."

"Aye. Well. That one came a bit out of left field for all of us."

Hoon took a sip of his drink. His lips drew back over his teeth as the liquid burned down his throat. "I dug into it. After you told me. Couldn't find a link, though. I tell you, I was fucking relieved. I thought... 'That's it, then. It's bullshit. Coincidence, or...' Ach. I don't fucking know."

He gave a little shake of his head and looked up at Logan for the first time since taking out the bottle.

"It isn't, though. Is it? They're connected."

"Aye. I mean... aye. They're connected," Logan said. "I don't know how, exactly, but there's something there. I'll find out what."

There was a knock at the door. It opened half-way, and a secretary popped her head in.

"Give us a minute, will you?"

The look on Logan's face made her hurriedly beat a retreat, and the DCI turned back to the senior officer sitting in the chair. He looked smaller than before, like he was shrinking.

Or like Logan was outgrowing him.

"How did it start?" Logan asked. "Money?"

"No. No, not... Not to start with, Jack. I want you to believe me on that," Hoon said. "Threats. Blackmail. Fucking... photos of my niece. Videos."

"Louisa?"

Hoon took another sip of his drink, and this one burned less than the last. "One of them—Bosco's guys—had got her to do all fucking sorts on a webcam. And I mean *all* sorts. Some of the stuff they got her doing..." He swallowed, like he was resisting the urge to throw up. "Stupid cow."

"What are you saying? You threw us all under a fucking bus so your niece didn't get herself shared around online?"

"It wasn't just that. I mean... it was a part of it. You don't know her, Jack, it would've fucking destroyed her. That girl has been through... Well, she's been through a whole fucking lot."

Logan banged both hands on the desk. "My *daughter* could be going through a whole lot right now, *Bob*. Sinead's brother. How much do you think Alice Forde went through in her final few moments? Eh? Let me tell you, it was a *whole fucking lot!*"

"It wasn't just that," Hoon protested. "The fella. The guy. He'd been chatting to her for weeks. Found out fucking every-thing. About her. About the wee man. Where he went to school. Who his pals were. The whole fucking shebang. They were threatening all sorts."

"You're a Detective Superintendent of the fucking polis, Bob. Or had you forgotten that? Have them arrested!"

"Oh, come on, Jack!" Hoon spat, jumping to his feet. "How

many times have you tried to nail that Russian bastard's fat hairy balls to the fucking wall? How many times have you brought him in? Or one of his guys? They're coated in fucking chip fat, the lot of them. They slide right through our fingers. Every bloody time.

"What, you think they were fucking open about who they were? You think he signed off, 'PP Bosco fucking Maximuke'? They did what they always fucking do, gave me just enough that I knew who they were, but not so much that I could prove it."

He sat down again, the snake that had uncoiled itself in his gut going back to sleep.

"And I tried. Believe me, I fucking tried everything. But I couldn't bring the lot of them in, could I? And if I bring in one or two, what then? What happens to Louisa then? To Jaden?"

"You could've talked to us," Logan said. "Told us."

Hoon waved a hand dismissively. "This goes way back. Before you were on the scene."

"Snecky, then."

"Fuck off! Snecky? I wouldn't tell that bastard the fucking time."

He polished off the last of his drink, then refilled it, glugging more into the glass this time.

"You said, 'Not to start with.'"

Hoon frowned, the glass halfway to his lips. "Eh?"

"I said, 'Money?' You said, 'Not to start with.'"

The Detective Superintendent flinched. He gulped half of the glass's contents, exhaled, then replied.

"I didn't ask for it. Never. And I didn't spend it, either. He just... It started turning up. Wee bundles. Through the post. In the glovebox of my car."

He opened the top drawer of his desk and pointed into it.

"In there, one time. A grand, just sitting there in an envelope with my name on it." Hoon shook his head as he continued to stare into the drawer. "I mean, how the fuck...?" he asked, more to himself than to Logan.

He closed the drawer again. "It's all at home. In shoe boxes. I never touched it. And I told him, I told him I didn't fucking want it. But he said I'd earned it," Hoon continued, and the disgust Logan felt was mirrored by the look on the DSup's face. "And, the worst thing is? He was right. I had."

Logan could feel his back teeth grinding together. He'd heard enough. More than enough.

He'd hoped he was wrong. He'd hoped he'd come in here, throw his accusations around, and Hoon would chew him up and spit him out, and prove him wrong on every one.

But this? This was pathetic.

"Enough with the sob story, Bob. I thought Jinkies was a fucking liability down in Fort William, but at least he was just a useless bastard. But *you*? You knew full well what Bosco Maximuke was. You knew what he'd do with the information you gave him."

"I didn't know he'd do this, Jack. I didn't know he'd do anything like—"

"Shut your fucking mouth!" Logan roared. "I haven't finished talking."

Something flickered behind Hoon's eyes. Some ingrained angry bastard stirred.

But then, it was gone. The fight had left him. The fire had been extinguished.

"You knew what he was capable of. You knew he had it in for me."

"Not to start with," Hoon said, grasping at straws. "He said you'd helped each other. In the past."

The floorboards beneath Logan's feet squeaked as he shifted his weight from foot to foot.

"Aye. Know what? Cards on the table? I turned a blind eye to a couple of Bosco's boys in the past. Nothing major. Nothing we could've put them away for," Logan admitted. "And I called in those favours a couple of times. You know why? To aid me in fucking investigations, Bob. To get bad bastards off the streets. To put killers behind bars. No' for a stack of cash and to save my niece's tits from being plastered all over the internet."

"He didn't ask me for much, either," Hoon said. "Mostly just... wee things. About other bastards we were investigating, half the time. Dealers. Traffickers. Just names and addresses, mostly."

The whole station seemed to go silent then. The air between Logan and Hoon *hummed* like it was alive.

"Was one of those addresses the house where DS McQuarrie was shot?" Logan asked.

"What?" Hoon shook his head. "No. No, it... No. Definitely not. You think I could just fucking sit here if I'd given him that?"

"Aye, Bob. I do. I think you're that much of a coward," Logan replied.

Hoon started to offer up some other objection to that, but Logan raised his voice and spoke over him, cutting him short.

"All I want to know is where to find him. We've got Uniform headed to his house, because DC Neish went round there earlier, and now he's nowhere to be found."

Hoon seemed to shrink another few percent at that news.

"I don't know, Jack. I don't," he said. "I know his yard. That's it. I didn't even know his home address. I swear. He'd always contact me. Well, one of his boys. Never him."

Logan said nothing. He just stared.

"I don't know how to find him. I mean it," Hoon insisted. "Listen, if I did, I'd fucking tell you. I would. I'd spill my guts. What the fuck do I have to lose now?"

"We're a couple of bright lads, Bob. I'm sure, if we put our minds to it, we could think of plenty," Logan said, his voice low and menacing. He leaned forwards again, the knuckles of his clenched fists resting on the table. "If anything has happened to

Tyler, I'll start with your fingers. And, if I find out you were even *remotely* involved in Caitlyn's death... Well, you'll wish I'd started with your fucking fingers."

He pinned him there in the seat with his glare for a few moments, then turned and headed for the door.

Hoon cleared his throat. "Aren't you... Aren't you going to arrest me?"

"I'll get Uniform to notify the Procurator Fiscal," Logan said. He turned and gave the shell of Detective Superintendent Robert Hoon one last look of contempt. "You're no' worth my time."

CHAPTER THIRTY-NINE

BEN SAT IN THE DARK ON THE FOOT END OF THE ROOM'S single bed, his hands clasped limply together, his elbows resting on his thighs.

He hadn't got undressed. He hadn't even kicked off his shoes. What was the point? He wouldn't sleep. Not tonight. Maybe not ever again.

But he'd needed to be alone. Away from Jack and the others. Away from the polis, from the station, from the well-meaning words, and the sympathetic looks. Away from any suggestions of help, or counselling, or support.

Maybe there'd be time for all that. Someday.

Or, maybe there wouldn't.

There was already a hole where she should have been. He could feel it in the space where his heart had been. It tempted him to prod at it, like he might with a newly-removed tooth, but the hole was too raw, and the pain was too great, and even the thought of her name inside his head made his whole body ache.

Alice.

All those happy memories from earlier came rushing back. Their first meeting. Their first date. Their first home.

But, they brought others with them, the pain in his chest dredging up the worst of times, too.

The day they'd lost their unborn baby.

The day she'd started her chemotherapy.

The day they'd found out that she could no longer bear children.

All those tears. All those years. Together.

And now...

He slid off the end of the bed and onto the floor, grasping his head in his hands, the hole where Alice had been threatening to consume him, to swallow him down into the dark.

She must've been so scared. Had she called out for him? Had she wondered why he wasn't coming?

Did she think he'd abandoned her? Left her to die.

Or, God. Worse.

In the dark, did she think it was him? Did she think he was hurting her? Killing her?

"No, no, no, please, no. Please, no."

He rocked back and forth, knees up at his chest, head jammed between them. Pictures came crashing unbidden into his head. Images of Alice. Of a knife. Of a terrified look of betrayal on a face he had forever loved.

'No, Ben! Stop! Why?'

"Please, no, please, no, *please no!*"

He shouted that last one into the darkness. It echoed around the cramped single room and rattled a teaspoon in a mug on the tray by the television.

Ben scrambled onto his hands and knees, grabbed the mug, and hurled it at the wall. It exploded into fragments, but he didn't see. He wasn't looking by then. He was grabbing for the cheap flatscreen TV, pulling on it, tearing the cables out of the wall.

He threw it to the floor, but it wasn't enough, so he stamped on it, drove his heel into the screen—again, again—lashing out, finding an outlet for his pain and his grief.

Alice stared back at him from the bed, her face a finger-painting daubed in blood.

Why hadn't he been there?

Why hadn't he saved her?

Why was he hurting her?

"It wasn't me!" he sobbed, dropping to his knees beside the bed. He buried his face in the floral patterned quilt, muffling the roar that erupted from somewhere deep within him. Somewhere deeper than he had ever thought possible.

There was a knock at the door. He ignored it and just knelt there, face down on the bed, hands twisting knots in the covers.

"It wasn't me, sweetheart," he whispered. "I'd never hurt you. I'd never hurt you."

The knocking came again, more insistent this time. Ben straightened and looked around at the broken TV and shattered mug.

"I'm fine," he croaked. "It's... Everything's fine."

"Sir?" said a male voice, muffled by the door. "Please, open up."

Sighing, Ben got to his feet. He wiped his eyes and his nose on his shirt sleeve, briefly contemplated putting the telly back, then decided not to bother. What were they going to do, call the polis?

He got his warrant card out of his pocket, just in case, and opened the door.

Two skinheads in bomber jackets stood there in the corridor. Ben hesitated for half a second before starting to close the door. But that was all it took.

A fist hit him. A battering-ram. He tasted blood, felt his brain rattle inside his skull as his head snapped back.

And then, the world lurched sideways, and Ben fell straight through the floor, and into a smothering void of absolute black.

CHAPTER FORTY

HAMZA AND THE THREE CID OFFICERS SAT IN A SEMI-circle around Logan, their jaws practically in their laps.

They had seemed sceptical when Logan had first started telling them about Hoon, but as more details had emerged, they'd become increasingly shaken. They believed him now, alright, he could tell by the slack-jaws and the numb expressions.

They'd trusted him. They all had. They hadn't liked him, obviously, nobody *liked* him, but they'd believed in him. They'd put their faith in him, time and again.

And he'd sold them all out, just as often.

When he'd finished filling them in, he asked a female DI to get in touch with the Procurator Fiscal's office. Hoon would do time for this. Assuming he didn't top himself before that, of course.

"You sure you want me to do that, sir? Assistant Chief Constable will be here any minute for the press conference. Might be worth kicking it up the line to her."

"What? Shite." Logan checked his watch, then shot a glance out the window at the brightening city beyond the glass. It was going to be a nice day. Weather-wise, at least. Everything else was still up in the air. "Aye. Bugger it. Let her handle it. Might as well get her working for her money."

Logan waited until everyone had returned to their stations before asking Hamza for an update.

There was still no word from Tyler. No sign of anyone at Bosco's, and no trace of the DC's car. Uniform was keeping an eye out for it, and for any vehicles registered to Maximuke, but there had been no hits so far.

"Anything from the web and social media appeals?"

Hamza gestured to the other officers seated around the Incident Room. "That's pretty much what this is. Following up on a lot of tips, but mostly all junk so far. Nothing that's panned out, anyway."

"What about building sites?" Logan asked. "Bosco's company must've been working on a few projects. The legitimate side of his business, I mean."

"A couple. We checked. Nothing doing," Hamza said.

The door to Logan's office opened, and Sinead emerged. Half her face was a swirl of lines from where she'd been sleeping on her folded arms. Her eyes darted fitfully from Logan to Hamza and back again. "Anything?"

Logan shook his head. "Not yet."

Sinead's expression remained mostly neutral, like she'd been braced for bad news and hoping for good, and the lack of fresh information had landed squarely in the middle.

"We finished going through those words yet?" she asked.

Hamza glanced back at his computer. "I haven't had a chance, I've been—"

"Right, then," Sinead said, heading for the desk she'd been using earlier in the night. "I'll crack on."

Logan almost told her to go home. Almost told her to go and get more rest.

But he knew he'd be wasting his breath. She dealt with things the same way he did. She got on. She kept busy.

"Grab yourself a coffee and a bite to eat first," Logan told her. She started to object, but he was having none of it. "That's a bloody order, Constable."

Sinead relented. "Right, sir," she said, then she went plodding out of the Incident Room.

LOGAN STOOD IN HIS OFFICE, trying to give himself a skoosh of deodorant without removing his shirt. This was proving difficult, and he knew the icy-cold burns he inflicted on himself by blasting the spray from too close range would come back to haunt him throughout the day.

It was a token effort before the arrival of the Assistant Chief Constable, done out of courtesy more than any sort of professional deference. He was, not to put too fine a point on it, honking. The deodorant barely made a dent. What he really needed was a hot shower, a scrubbing brush, two good meals, and twelve hours sleep.

Maybe a haircut.

Then, and only then, he might start to feel human again. But none of it was possible. Not while Maddie and Harris were missing.

And Tyler, too. Where had that daft bastard ended up? 'Drive past.' That's what Logan had said. Don't make contact, don't get involved. Drive past, scope it out, leave. If he'd followed that, there shouldn't have been a problem.

So, where was he?

There was a knock at the door, and Logan hurriedly disposed of the deodorant in his filing cabinet, and tucked himself in.

He'd expected to find the Assistant Chief Constable there,

but instead, Sinead held out a disposable cup and a small paper bag. A pleasing amount of grease was soaking through the bag, turning the paper shiny and transparent.

"Breakfast, sir," she said, offering it out to him. "That's a bloody order."

He accepted both gratefully. "Thank you. How you holding up?"

"Shite. You?"

"Much the same," Logan told her. "Quite the night."

"So I've been hearing," Sinead said.

She stepped forward and hugged him. It came out of nowhere, and he could only stand there, hot cup of coffee in one hand, bag of something deliciously greasy in the other, until she'd finished.

"Right, then," she said, with a slightly sheepish smile. "Back to it."

"Back to it," Logan agreed. He held up the cup and the bag. "Thank you again."

"No problem. Oh!" Sinead said, half-turning then turning back. "Any word on Tyler?"

"He's... around," Logan said. He regretted the lie immediately, but went with it, anyway. "I'm sure he'll check in soon."

"Aye," Sinead said. The lines on her brow deepened momentarily, before fading again. "I'm sure he will."

She left, then, and Logan closed the door. He devoured half of the roll before he made it over to his chair. It was bacon and fried egg. The bacon was a bit too well-done, and the egg was dry and rubbery, but it was up there with the best things he'd ever eaten.

His stomach growled, wanting more. He tried to appease it with a couple of breadcrumbs from the corners of the bag, but by the sounds it made, it was largely unimpressed.

Wiping his hands on his shirt—because he couldn't really

make it any worse at this point—he took out his phone and tried Tyler's number. Unsurprisingly, it went to voicemail.

After that, he called the hospital to check-in on Vanessa. She was recovering well, the nurse told him, although there was talk of some minor surgery on the right leg. She'd offered to transfer the call through to Vanessa herself, but he'd been quick to decline.

She knew he'd be in touch when he had news on Maddie. She might not trust him with much, but she'd trust him on that.

He checked the time before making the next call. It was rapidly approaching nine o'clock. The press conference was in just under forty minutes. The bastards would already be assembling downstairs, no doubt rubbing their hands with glee.

The next call was the hardest. It rang eight or nine times before he heard the voice on the other end offer up a croaky, "Hello?"

"Sorry. Did I wake you?"

"Wake...? What?" Shona gave a sleepy groan down the line. "Shit. Yes. No. What time is it?"

"Just about nine," Logan said. "I, eh, I owe you an apology. We ran out, and I didn't get back to you."

"No, it's fine. It's fine," Shona said, although she wasn't entirely convincing. "How was everything?"

"Not good," Logan said. "Alice—Ben's wife—she was dead by the time we got there."

He heard Shona sitting upright. All the sleepy slurriness left her voice in an instant. "Oh, God Almighty. Oh, Jesus. I'm sorry, Jack. Oh, God. That's... That's... Oh, God. How is he?"

"He's... rough. He's taking it hard."

"Well, of course, he is. I mean... Jesus. What a world," she said. "Give him a hug from me, will you?"

"Eh, aye," Logan replied, thinking of Ben's empty desk sitting out there in the Incident Room. "Aye, I will do. I'm going to arrange for Uniform to come over and take a statement from you this morning, if that's OK?"

"Yeah. Sure. Of course," Shona replied. "I'll have to get into work, obviously, but—"

"Work? I don't think you should be going into work," Logan told her. "Not after what you went through."

"Ben's wife will be coming in," Shona said. "I should be the one to look at her. I owe him that much."

"Ben would understand. Let someone else do it," Logan insisted. "What you went through... You could still be in shock."

"I'm fine, Jack," she said. "I'm dandy."

There was a knock at his door, and Hamza poked his head inside. "She's here," he whispered.

Logan gave him a thumbs up in acknowledgement, then turned his attention back to the call.

"Listen, I have to go. Sorry. Big press conference coming up, and I need to brief the Assistant Chief Constable. I'll get Uniform over there in half an hour, and I'll call you back when I can. OK?"

"Grand," she replied, and he could hear the forced smile in her voice. "And I'm fine. Honestly. Bye for now."

She hung up the call before he could. Logan swept the crumbs from his desk, necked a big glug of his now-lukewarm coffee, then dumped the cup and the bag in the wastepaper basket beneath his desk just as sharp knuckles rapped on his door.

Years ago, Logan had first come to know of Assistant Chief Constable Michaela Haldane by her nickname—'The Impaler.' The name had been given to her due to her elongated features and pale white skin, which gave her a certain vampire-like quality. Hence, 'Vlad the Impaler,' had become the more phonetically pleasing, 'Michaela the Impaler,' before being shortened to just the second and third word for brevity's sake.

Unlike the creatures she resembled, she entered without

being invited and closed the door behind her. She wore the full dress uniform, minus the cap, which she carried tucked under one arm. Her expression suggested she was either sooking on a soor ploom, or wasn't impressed by what she saw.

"You look like a sack of shite, Jack."

Not a soor ploom, then.

"Ma'am," he said, standing. He looked down at himself, then conceded her point with a nod. "Aye. Well, you know how it gets in the trenches. Maybe you remember?"

"I do. Very well. And I never looked like that," she said. Her nostrils flared. "I saw victims that didn't look like that. Quite a mess you've got here."

Logan glanced around the office. He'd seen it worse.

"Not the room. The situation," Haldane said, sighing. "Still, you always did say Petrie was faking. Maybe we should've listened to you."

It was the closest Logan was likely to get to an apology, he knew. May as well take it.

"Aye. Maybe you should," he agreed.

She took a seat, then indicated for him to do the same.

"You'll have to fill me in on where we're at. I'll lead the press conference, you can answer any direct questions I specifically defer to you," she instructed. "That means no jumping in. No adding your tuppence worth unless I tell you to. I lead, you follow. Yes?"

Logan would've been happy not attending the bloody thing at all, so he had no problem with keeping his mouth shut.

"Sounds like a plan."

"Yes. Well. I get the sense 'a plan' is something you're often lacking," Haldane said. She took Logan's notepad from his desk, removed a silver pen from her breast pocket, and clicked the button. "We don't have long, but from the start, please. Tell me what's happened."

And so, he did. Her face remained largely impassive for

most of it, as her hand scrawled and scribbled like it had been possessed.

Logan told her everything, from the badge in his flat onwards, right up to the disappearance of DC Neish, and the death of Alice Forde.

"OK. Well, then," Haldane said, clicking the button on her pen and returning it to her pocket. "I'll have DCI Grant brought in to relieve you."

"Snecky? What the hell for?" Logan demanded.

"Come on, Jack. Your daughter has been taken. You're hardly going to be thinking objectively on this. You're too close. Far too close. DCI Grant will take point, you can offer your insight as and when requested. I'm aware you and Petrie have your little history, and so your guidance might prove useful at points."

"Bollocks," Logan spat.

The Assistant Chief Constable fixed him with a dangerous glare. "I beg your pardon."

"Sorry. Bollocks, *ma'am*," Logan said. "No disrespect to the man, but Snecky couldn't catch VD in an African brothel, let alone Owen Petrie. The man's a total fucking clown. Again, no disrespect meant."

"DCI Grant will lead. You will advise," Haldane reiterated. "You will still accompany me to the press conference, then Detective Superintendent Hoon will supervise until Grant can offload his cases and head north."

"Oh. Aye. I didn't tell you that bit, did I?" Logan said. He sat back in his chair, getting comfortable. He might even enjoy this part.

"Which bit?" Haldane asked, priming her pen again and holding it ready above the paper.

"Before you hand things over to Hoon, there's something you might like to know..."

CHAPTER FORTY-ONE

LOGAN PEEKED THROUGH THE DOOR INTO THE ROOM WHERE the press conference was being held, and immediately felt his hackles rise.

They had swarmed into the place, filling it from front to back with their cameras, and their recording equipment, and their smug-as-fuck wee faces. The ladies and gentlemen of the national press.

Bastards, one and all.

The stage had been set at one end of the room. Four tables had been set out in a long line, with just two chairs behind them. One of the chairs was just off-centre enough that the person sitting there wouldn't have to straddle the legs of tables two and three. That one was the Impaler's, Logan reckoned, judging by the way the second chair was tucked away near the far end of the fourth table.

She'd remained pretty stoic when Logan had told her about Hoon. She'd pointed out to him that he was making a very serious accusation and then, when he'd made it clear he understood, she'd gone to speak to the man himself, although not without instructing Logan to find himself a new shirt and to 'do something' with his 'bloody hair'.

A Uniform had tracked him down a spare shirt. It was a size too small, but he'd just about get away with it if he avoided any sudden large movements.

As for the hair, he settled for dampening it down with water and brushing his fingers through it a few times so it didn't appear to be plastered to his head.

He'd managed another blast of deodorant during the shirt change procedure, so he no longer smelled like some sort of farm animal. He smelled like some sort of farm animal that had been dunked repeatedly in cheap antiperspirant.

He wasn't convinced this was better.

"You ready?" asked Haldane, appearing in the corridor behind him. Her cap was on her head now, and where it had been tucked under her arm there was now a clipboard with her notes.

"You see Hoon?" Logan asked.

"I did. It's being dealt with," she said. "For God's sake, don't bring it up in here. And if any of them have somehow gotten wind of it, leave the talking to me. Yes?"

"Aye. Whatever you think, ma'am."

She gave the curtest of nods. "Yes. Good. So, I'll go on, make my prepared statement, then I'll bring you on for questions. You will wait until I ask you a question directly before answering. You will answer through me, and I will add anything I feel is necessary. Yes?"

"Like I said. Whatever you think."

"Yes. Good. Watch for my signal. It will be this." She made a very clear and obvious beckoning motion with one hand. "Got that?"

Logan was tempted to ask her to show him again, just to be on the safe side, but resisted. "Got it."

"Good. Yes," Haldane said, then she touched her hat to

check the angle, checked her tie in much the same way, and went striding through the doors and up the steps at the side of the stage.

Logan could see and hear the flashes going off already, each *pop* projecting an animated shadow of the Assistant Chief Constable on the *Police Scotland* backdrop at the back of the stage.

"Vultures, the bloody lot of them," he muttered to himself as he watched Haldane take her seat and pour herself a glass of water from the jug in front of her.

She set her notes out on the table, unrushed and uncowed by the sense of urgency radiating off the members of the media. The air was positively humming with anticipation. Logan recognised a few of the print journos. Some bastard from *The Sun*. Some other bastard from *The Daily Record*. Assorted other bastards from various other rags. They were all practically slavering down themselves at the thought of what was to come.

"I want to thank you all for coming out this morning," Haldane began. "I'm going to start by reading a prepared statement, then I'll be joined on stage by Detective Chief Inspector Jack Logan, who has—until now—been leading the investigation I'll be discussing. I'll take a few questions at that point, but I'm sure you all appreciate that we don't have a lot of time."

Logan's attention drifted in and out as she read through her statement. As he'd expected, at any mention of the name 'Owen Petrie,' a murmur of excitement rippled through the audience. This was big news. Front-page stuff. A nice fat bonus, maybe, if he remained at large for a few weeks and killed a couple of kids.

Bastards.

The statement gave the basics, but was light on detail. Petrie had escaped Carstairs. Two members of staff had been killed. He was now in Inverness, and had taken Harris Bell.

While she did go into some detail on Harris, and said she'd be providing additional photographs to those the force had already sent out, she didn't mention his connection to Sinead, or her role in the polis.

She didn't mention Maddie or Alice, either. That was no surprise. Keep the message clear and to the point. 'A very bad man took an innocent young boy.' That's what got attention. That's what had people keeping their eyes open. Muddy the message, and people switched off.

The Assistant Chief Constable was nearing the end of her statement when Logan felt a tap on his shoulder.

"Got a second, sir?" Hamza asked.

Logan glanced back at the stage, then motioned for Hamza to join him a few steps away from the door.

"Aye. What's up?"

"The three-word thing, sir. We've cracked it. Well, one of them. Sinead's working on the other one, but it shouldn't be long now that we've got this one figured out."

Logan's heart missed a beat. "Where is it?"

"Off the A862. Near Bunchrew House."

Unlocking his phone, Logan handed it over. "I got the app. Punch it in."

Hamza took the phone, opened the *what3words* app, and typed in 'idealist.mentions.toast.' The map zoomed in to show a location to the northwest of the city. A ten-minute drive. Probably less.

"Right. Thanks. Go back. Help Sinead with the next one. I'm going to check this out."

Hamza looked past him into the press conference room. "Aren't you supposed to be on stage soon?"

"Supposed to be, aye," Logan confirmed, but in a way that suggested he wouldn't be.

"You shouldn't go alone, sir. You should take back-up."

Logan shook his head. Enough people had been put in danger because of this thing with him and Petrie. Too many.

No more.

"I'll call if I need support. In the meantime, keep it to yourself." He stole a look into the next room. Haldane was saying his name now. She'd be giving the hand signal at any moment. "Oh, and if there's a chance to hide somewhere before the Impaler comes looking for me, you're probably going to want to take it."

THERE WAS a can of Red Bull rolling about in a bag in the passenger footwell. Logan managed to snag it while keeping the car going in a straight line, and guzzled it in a couple of big swigs. The caffeine should take the edge off his tiredness and help keep him sharp.

Or sharper than he currently felt, at least.

The road heading into Inverness was pretty slow-moving at this time of the morning, but traffic flowed freely as he headed across the Telford Street bridge.

Telford Street became Clachnaharry Road, which in turn became the A862. The houses on his left were large and grand. They stood on the rise of a small hill, looking out across the final stretch of the Caledonian Canal at the less affluent Merkinch on the other side.

The journey took just over seven minutes. As he neared the spot marked on the map on his phone, he slowed until the Volvo was crawling along the quiet stretch of road.

To the right of the road was a large, well-tended field. To the left was a barbed wire fence, a lot of jaggy bushes, and about an acre and a half of stinging nettles.

"Aye, figures," Logan muttered, pulling off the road onto a grassy verge and cutting off the engine.

The red dot on his map showed him the spot he was looking for was over the fence, through the jaggies, and deep into the nettles. Nothing was ever bloody easy.

He looked both ways along the road. Nobody watching, as

far as he could tell.

The barbed wire fence wasn't too great an obstacle for a man of his stature and inside-leg measurements. There was a wee worrying moment in the middle when the ground on the other side turned out to be an inch or two lower, but some quick thinking and the judicious application of fingers in just the right places kept the pointed metal barbs from doing any real damage.

The jaggy bushes were more problematic. They stood in a line like a military regiment, the last line of defence between the road and the sea of stinging nettles. Logan had to backtrack a good thirty or forty yards until he found a gap big enough to squeeze through without tearing first his trousers, then the flesh from his legs.

Once through, he skirted close to them until he was back level with his original starting point and turned so the wee blue arrow on his phone that represented him, was facing the wee red dot that represented whatever surprise Petrie had left for him to find.

The nettles were evil bloody things, and he was grateful he was a boots guy and not a shoes guy. A shoes guy would, not to put too fine a point on it, be royally fucked right now. But, as a boots guy, he was able to make his way freely through the field of nettles, sustaining only the occasional sting through his trousers and socks from some of the larger specimens.

After a minute or so spent picking his way around the denser patches, and another few seconds pointing himself in the right direction again, he arrived at the spot marked on the map.

Idealist.mentions.toast

At first, he saw nothing. Nothing more than the same big patch of nettles he'd just waded through, at any rate. He checked the map, looked around like this might somehow help him get his bearings, then bent over and checked the ground in front of him.

He found it a couple of paces to the right, hidden under a

canopy of nettle leaves. It was an Aldi Bag for Life. One of the good ones. Sturdy.

Logan pulled on a pair of gloves, partly for evidence handling purposes, and partly to ward off the bloody nettles.

He prised the top of the bag open. There was a shoebox inside. There was also, he noted, a lot of flies.

The smell hit him a half-second later, almost knocking him onto his arse. Christ. It was ripe. There was something dead in the box. Something on the turn.

Reaching into the bag, he raised one corner of the box, waited to make sure nothing was going to come scrabbling through the gap, then opened it all the way.

"OK," he muttered, peering down into the box. "What the hell is this now?"

"Yes!" Sinead exclaimed. "Got it."

Hamza looked up from his computer just as Sinead held her phone up for him to see. It showed a map of Inverness. A little location marker was positioned out to the east of the city.

"Old Military Road. Behind the airport."

"Nice work," Hamza said. "I'll text it to the DCI."

"Right. Right, yeah," said Sinead.

She sat back in her chair.

Her fingers tapped out an impatient rhythm on the desk.

She sat forward again.

"Or, we could go scope it out."

Hamza stopped tapping at his phone screen. "What, not tell Logan?"

"Oh, no. Tell him. Send it over. I'm just saying, once you've done that... We could go."

Hamza looked unconvinced. "We should probably wait until—"

"Harris could be there," Sinead said, her eyes pleading. "And... I know something's happened with Tyler, and you don't want to tell me. They could both be there."

Hamza beckoned for her to show her phone again. He squinted at the screen, figuring out exactly where the marker was. "That's just a big field, isn't it? Hit the satellite overlay."

"Where's...? Oh."

Sinead tapped a button at the bottom right corner and the map image was overlaid with a bird's eye view of the same area. It showed a large, empty field to the north of Inverness Airport.

A big, wide-open space. Broad daylight. How dangerous could it be?

From out in the corridor, he heard a woman's voice shout.

"Where the bloody hell did Logan get to?"

"Guess the press conference is finished, then," Hamza said. He grabbed his car keys from his desk and gave Sinead the nod. "Right, then," he whispered. "Let's go."

LOGAN HADN'T REACHED into the box itself, and he had no great urge to do so.

Inside, sitting on a stack of plastic bags, was a human hand. It lay on its back, fingers curling upwards like the legs of a dead spider. The wrist was a grisly stump of sinew and bone that suggested it hadn't been removed with any great care or precision, just rather a lot of elbow grease.

It wasn't particularly big, but it had belonged to an adult, judging by the general condition of it. A man, he thought, although he couldn't be certain. Not Maddie's, though. He could say that much.

That had been his first thought when he'd seen it, but it hadn't lasted more than a second or so before he concluded it wasn't hers.

It had probably come from the victim behind the hotel. He hoped so, at least. One handless guy was enough to be dealing with right now.

He replaced the lid on the box and stood up, the constant goading of the nettles starting to get uncomfortable.

This didn't make a lot of sense. A victim who had been mutilated to hide his identity. A clue leading here to his hand. The fingerprints were intact, which meant there was at least a chance of getting an ID, assuming the victim had been known to them.

If that was the case, then Petrie wanted him to know who the body belonged to.

If it wasn't the case, and the fingerprints didn't help identify him, then...

He had no idea. What would be the point?

He called it in and arranged for Uniform to come out and cordon off the scene, and for SOC to come out and take the hand away. Let's see how Geoff bloody Palmer liked the jaggies and the nettles.

It'd be run for prints. If they got a hit, then at least they'd have something else to pursue. Some other way of getting closer to Petrie.

Although, since Petrie had given them the lead himself, just how reliable could it be?

A text came through on his phone. He saw Hamza's name, and tapped to open it.

Found it, it read. And then, there was a link which, once clicked, opened a map on Logan's screen. Near the airport. Opposite end of the city.

He found a stick in the nettles and jammed it into the ground near the box to act as a marker.

That done, he set off back towards his car, his fingers tapping away at the screen in response to the message.

On my way.

CHAPTER FORTY-TWO

HAMZA PULLED ACROSS OLD MILITARY ROAD AND brought his car to a stop on the right-hand side of the road, roughly level with where the icon on the map pointed. Two trucks, which he had been holding up for a while as he'd crawled along scoping the field out, went thundering past, horns blaring, slipstreams shaking the car.

"This looks about right," Sinead said from the passenger seat.

"Aye. Think so," Hamza agreed. "See anything?"

Sinead shook her head. "No. You?"

"No. Just a field."

Another truck passed them in a cloud of diesel fumes. Over on the right, behind the field, an EasyJet plane took to the air.

Sinead watched it. Since moving to the city, she and Harris had made a game of trying to guess where each plane they saw taking off was heading. It had started normal enough—France, America, Australia—but the suggestions had gradually become more ridiculous until they verged into the surreal.

The last one they'd seen, Harris had decided was going to, 'The Nexus of All Things.' When Sinead had asked for clarification as to where that was, he'd said, "Your face," then erupted into wild, uncontrollable laughter that had reduced them both to fits of happy tears for reasons neither of them could explain.

The thought of it proved too painful. She flicked her eyes from the plane to the field, then unbuckled her seatbelt. "Let's scope it out. Did you text the DCI?"

"Aye. Before we left the station. Gave him a map link," Hamza replied. He shot a glance in the rearview mirror and put a hand on Sinead's arm. "Wait. Don't open the door. Truck coming."

Sinead turned in her seat and saw the truck approaching. It would pass in the left-hand lane, Hamza's car blocking two-thirds of the right-hand lane, facing the wrong way.

The truck slowed as it passed, and Sinead was about to open her door when it swerved in in front of them, its brake lights turning solid red.

She shot Hamza a wary look as the truck stopped with a *hiss* of hydraulics.

It was a large box-truck, the kind of thing used for transporting cargo long distances. Supermarkets used them all the time, but this one was unmarked. Hamza's eyes automatically went to the number plate, but it had been obscured by a spray of mud.

"I don't like this," he said, putting the car into gear. Sinead hurriedly clipped her belt back into place and instinctively grabbed for the handle above the door.

Before Hamza could pull away, the truck's back door opened, revealing four men wearing black balaclavas. Two of them held shotguns, and Hamza bellowed at Sinead to, "Get down!" as he floored the accelerator and pulled out onto the other side of the road.

The second truck came out of nowhere. Neither of them saw it, but they felt the impact as it ploughed into them, sending

Hamza's car into a tornado-spin that threw them around like ragdolls.

The inside of the car was filled with dust, and noise, and glass, and airbags. The interior lights came on. The horn blared.

And then, with a *crunch*, the movement came to a sudden, jarring stop.

The car was upside-down, although Hamza didn't realise this at first. It was only when he saw the feet approaching the side window that he was able to grasp it, and even then it took a bit of working out.

His arms ached. His hands positively *screamed*.

There was blood on his airbag. There was more spattered across the thousands of pieces of glass that sat on the inside of the roof like a stack of uncut diamonds. Was that his blood, or...?

Sinead.

He turned to her, the movement sending shockwaves of pain down his spine. She was hanging upside-down, like him. Her face was cut. There was a lot of blood. She wasn't moving.

Hamza tried to say her name, but the words sounded distant and far away.

Something crunched beside him. Footsteps on glass.

His door was opened with a *screech*.

A shotgun appeared.

A face.

A smirk.

There was a bang. A pain. Excruciating.

And then, there was nothing at all.

LOGAN WAS HALFWAY BACK to his car, through the nettles but not yet around the jaggy bushes, when he spotted the van.

He'd been expecting them to start turning up, but not yet, and not any that looked like this. Those would have blue lights on top. This one was white and unmarked. It slowed as it passed, and Logan caught a glimpse of a black bomber jacket sitting behind the wheel, and then it was off again, continuing its journey along the road.

Logan watched it until it rounded the bend and drove out of sight. It was one of Bosco's. Had to be.

He took out his phone, swiped to his contacts. Four rings later, Shona Maguire answered.

"I'm still fine!" she insisted, before he could say a word. "No one from the police has turned up yet, if that's what you're calling for?"

"Actually, it isn't," Logan said. He had his eyes fixed on the spot where the van had disappeared. He'd passed the turn-off for Bunchrew House on the way here. It was maybe forty seconds up the road. Add in fifteen seconds to turn...

"Social call, then?" Shona asked.

"Eh, no. Not quite that, either."

The van reappeared, slowed as it passed in the opposite direction, then continued on again. He pretended not to notice this time, but kept track of it until it was out of sight again.

"I've got a bit of a favour to ask you," he said. "It's a big one, too. I'd say feel free to say no, but... well, you can't. Sorry to put this on you."

"Is it dangerous?" Shona asked, after a momentary pause.

"No. Well... No, it shouldn't be," Logan said.

He heard her take a breath down the phone, composing herself.

"Right, then," she said. "What do I need to do?"

Logan explained as quickly and efficiently as he could, recited the information she needed, then answered her questions as he climbed over the fence and plodded up the marshy incline that led to the road, and the Volvo parked on the verge.

He stressed the importance of it again, wished her good luck, then they said their goodbyes. He had just taken his car keys from his pocket when he heard the van approaching again, the engine giving a guttural grunt of complaint as the driver shoved the pedal to the floor.

Logan stepped in behind the car, as if making room for the van to pass, but then it screeched to a halt beside him, the side door sliding open even as he adjusted his grip on the keys so they stuck out through the gaps between the fingers of his clenched fist.

He saw three men, got the impression of more, all masked up. All moving quickly. Voices shouted in Polish, or Latvian, or whatever it was. Hands grabbed for him. Eyes blazed and mouths sneered through the gaps in the balaclavas.

The first of the grabby bastards howled and spluttered as Logan drove the key to his flat's front door into the fleshy part at the bottom of the man's jaw. It pulled away with a satisfying *schlop* sound, spilling blood onto the tarmac at their feet.

The man stumbled back, gagging and gasping, but Logan was already moving, shifting his weight, throwing another punch.

A cheek was torn open through the woollen mask. A man screamed and swore. Logan didn't understand the language, but he got the gist of it, all the same.

Something hit him on the back of the legs, right across the knees. His legs went from under him. He hit the ground hard.

He saw a shotgun. He saw an iron bar. He didn't know which of them hit him, just that pain exploded across the side of his head, making his eardrum sing and his vision go white.

Jesus Christ. One of these days, someone was going to give him brain damage.

The ground rolled. He reached for it, trying to stabilise himself, but it wasn't there. Nothing was there but empty space.

As he fell sideways, he saw the eyes of the men staring down at him from behind their masks.

He tried to speak, but whatever part of his brain controlled his mouth was clearly still reeling from the impact.

A boot connected with his ribs. Another with his lower back.

He tried to get up, but a foot stamped on him, smashing him down onto the road. He coughed wetly. Something ground against something else in his ribcage.

Hands grabbed at his hair, pulling him backwards, forcing him to scrabble up onto his knees. A bag was pulled down over his head. He swung a punch, but it was a limp and useless thing, and whoever was on the receiving end laughed it off.

He felt movement. Impact. Heard the van door sliding shut.

And then, from nowhere, something connected hard with the side of his face, and he lost his slippery grip on consciousness.

CHAPTER FORTY-THREE

PAIN.

That was his first thought.

Or no, not thought, exactly. It was too early in the process of coming round to form thoughts yet. The subconscious part of his brain was stirring. The conscious part, ironically, was still anything but.

Pain.

That one had been a thought. Not fully-formed, but heading in the right direction.

His legs twitched, the animal part of his brain doing what it could to jolt the rest of it into life.

Instincts propelled Logan upwards before his eyes were even open. More pain—one of the many—tore at his wrist. Metal rattled. He was jerked back to the floor by the chains that shackled him in place.

His eyelids felt sticky, like something wet had dried there, fusing the eyelashes together. He forced them open, then hissed in the blinding glare of a spotlight that stood on a tripod, pointing his way.

He could feel the heat of it on his face. Not burning, but hot enough to be uncomfortable. Even behind his eyelids, he saw a shadow move across the light, passing from left to right.

A voice whispered in his ear.

"Look who's awake."

Logan twisted, ignoring the fire the movement ignited in his ribcage. He swung with a fist, but the chains snapped him back.

For a moment, he saw a figure looming just beyond the edge of his pool of light. He saw a smile. He saw eyes that had been burned into his brain a decade before. Cold. Cruel. Callous.

"Petrie!" he hissed, just that glimpse of the man sending a much-needed jolt of adrenaline buzzing through his system. "Where are they? What have you done with them?"

The reply came from elsewhere in the shadows. That voice, the hoarse whisper of a former sixty-a-day man who'd done his throat irreparable damage.

"If you'd been paying attention, I already told you where the boy is. But the rest? All in good time, Jack. All in good time."

Logan pulled on his chains. They were attached to an old-style radiator. A great big brute of a thing that wasn't going anywhere.

The floor beneath him was a mess of plywood and loose carpet tiles, like the place was in the middle of being ripped up and packed away.

The light was still too dazzling for him to see much of anything beyond the edges of its beam, but he thought he got the impression of shapes behind it. People, he thought. Watching him.

"I swear to God, Petrie—"

"Oh, please, Jack. I don't think God's listening. Do you?" Petrie replied. He was over on the left now, moving just beyond the border where light fell away into darkness. "And I'd rather you called me by my real name."

"Owen?"

"No. You know the one I mean."

"Aye, well you can get that idea right out of your fucking head," Logan spat. "You're no' a supervillain, Owen. You're a sad wee bastard with a big ego. That's it."

In the shadows, Petrie snorted. "Aye, well. Could a sad wee bastard do this?"

There was silence.

Stillness.

Nothing.

"That's your cue to hit the fucking lights," Petrie whispered, his voice even lower than usual and clearly not meant for Logan's ears.

Logan would've laughed at him—made a point of it, just to piss him off—had the lights not come on then, and knocked the bottom right out of his world.

They were there on the floor, kneeling, hands behind their backs, tape across their mouths. He'd lined them up, Ben on the left, then Hamza, then Tyler, then Sinead.

And there, right at the end...

"Maddie!" he gasped.

His daughter. His little girl. Her eyes were two bulging spheres of panic. They were fixed on him, begging, pleading, desperate.

"It's going to be OK. It's going to be OK," he assured her.

Petrie laughed at that. A theatrical, throwing-the-head-back guffaw that rang around the room.

"No, Jack," he said. "It really isn't."

Logan didn't so much as glance at the bastard. Didn't give him the satisfaction. Instead, he looked along the line of kneeling figures on the floor. Sinead and Hamza were in bad shape, and were struggling to hold their heads up. Tyler looked more or less fine, although one of his eyes was all but swollen shut, and the fear on his face... Christ. The fear.

And then, there was Ben. Ben may have been on his knees, but he held himself upright and rigid. While the others all stared at Logan, DI Forde's gaze remained fixed on Petrie. Burned into the murderer's back. He followed the bastard's every step as Petrie approached the spotlight, picked up the cable, and turned the beam off with the click of a switch.

Spots swam before Logan's eyes, big fat blobs of white that slowly cleared to reveal Bosco Maximuke and two of his men leaning against the wall at the back of the room. Bosco gave him a cheery wave as Logan's gaze fell on him. To the Russian's right, Valdis shoved his hands in the pockets of his bomber jacket and looked along the line of hostages.

"Surprise!" Bosco called.

"No' really," Logan spat back. "We've had you two pegged together for a while."

Bosco's smile remained fixed, but his brow furrowed in the middle for a moment. "Bullshit."

It was Logan's turn to frown. Of course they'd known about the two of them. Why wouldn't they have known? They'd made it obvious.

Hadn't they?

"Do you mind?" Petrie asked, stepping between them and derailing Logan's train of thought. "This is my part. We agreed."

Bosco gave a wave of a hand, giving Petrie the floor. He gave a grateful nod, then turned his attention back to Logan.

Petrie was standing right behind Tyler, slap-bang in the middle of the line-up. DC Neish tried to turn to see what he was doing, but Petrie clamped a hand on his head and turned him to face front again. He made no attempt to turn Ben's head, though. Watching Petrie strut around would be causing the DI more pain than if he wasn't watching, and the fucker knew it.

"Well," Petrie said, smiling broadly. It was a little squint, the mouth pulled down at the side where his head was dented. If anything, it just added to his overall effect. "Here we are. Do you have any idea how long I've dreamed about this, Jack? This moment, or one like it? I mean, I had no idea who'd be filling these roles..."

He moved from Ben down to Sinead, bonking them all on the head and saying, "Bing," or, "Bong," like he was playing musical notes.

"But, I knew there'd be someone. You always find someone to reel into your web, don't you, Jack? Someone to corrupt with your influence." He looked along the line. "But my, you've been busy."

"Let them go, Owen."

Petrie's smile fell away. "You will speak when I tell you to speak, Jack." Reaching to the back of his belt, he produced a kitchen knife. It wasn't particularly long, but it was plenty big enough to do serious damage to anyone on the receiving end. He wrapped an arm around Hamza's throat and wrenched him back, his face all twisted up in rage as he pressed the blade of the knife against the DC's cheek. "Or this one loses an eye. Got that?"

Logan didn't dare reply. Not out loud. He nodded his understanding, and Petrie threw Hamza forward onto the floor. His already badly-injured face hit the plywood, and he let out a grunt of pain.

Petrie gestured to the two skinheads flanking Bosco. "Our guest fell. Pick him back up, would you?"

Both men looked to Bosco for confirmation. He gave it with a nod, but Valdis hung back for a second or so before following his fellow bomber-jacket. Together, they hauled Hamza back up onto his knees, then retreated to the back of the room and took their places at Bosco's side.

"See, this is the effect you have, Jack," Petrie said, ruffling Hamza's hair. "This one and the girl there. They came alone. Would you believe that? The two of them, out to the middle of nowhere, following a clue I'd left for them. Alone. I mean... What's up with that?"

He put his hands on his hips and shook his head like a parent who wasn't angry, just *disappointed*.

"Couldn't believe how well it worked out, though. You going one way, them the other. We've been watching those sites for... Well, a while now. I really thought you'd crack it sooner. Some of the lads were starting to get pretty bored waiting for someone to show up." Petrie jabbed a thumb back over his shoulder at Bosco and his men. "They were getting frustrated. Me? I was just excited to see who'd turn up where. And, honestly? It could not have worked out better."

His expression turned back to one of admonishment. "But they came alone. The two of them. Did you tell them to do that, Jack?"

Logan said nothing, just stared at the bastard and subtly felt around the edges of his handcuffs.

"That was a direct question. You can speak," Petrie said. He waved the knife vaguely above Hamza's head. "You *will* speak."

"No," Logan replied. "I did not tell them to do that."

"Aha! So, why do you think they did it? Rhetorical question, don't reply," Petrie said. "I'll tell you. Because they wanted to impress you. Oh, sure. They'll say they had other reasons. Urgency, maybe. Desperation. But you and I both know the truth. They wanted to make DCI Jack Logan proud. They wanted to be more like you."

He caught Sinead by the hair and bent down so his face was next to hers. She whimpered with the pain it brought. "Well, they will be just like you, Jack. At the end. In fact, it'll be difficult for anyone to figure out which bit belongs to who. That's how alike you'll all be."

Petrie planted a kiss on Sinead's cheek—a big, rubbery, cartoonish smacker complete with a *mwah* sound effect—then released his grip on her. Tyler shot her an anxious look, but Petrie spotted it and manhandled his head to the front again.

"This one, too. Broke into Bosco's house, would you believe? I mean... he's got balls, I'll give him that much."

"Not for long," Bosco chipped in from the back of the room. "Fucking show him what happens to sneaky little bitches who get in my business."

Petrie patted Tyler on the shoulder. "He means it, too. He brought pliers specially. I'm not even sure I'll be able to watch, and... well. As you know, I've got a high tolerance for that sort of thing."

He wandered along the line and stopped at Ben. The DI was still glowering up at him, bloody murder in his eyes.

"They all followed your lead, except DI Forde here, who ran away to a hotel after... Well, after his wife tragically passed." He laid a consoling hand on Ben's shoulder, but it was promptly shrugged off. "Ironically, we followed him. Both of you, actually. Right to the hotel's front door using a...?" He clicked his fingers a few times.

"GPS tracker," said Bosco.

"Yes. Thank you." Petrie smiled and shook his head. "Amazing how much technology can change in a decade, eh? Bosco's been keeping tabs on you for months."

Logan could feel all their eyes on him now. His colleagues. His friends. His daughter. They were all looking at him— looking *to* him for some sort of solution. Some sort of way out. This was a nightmare, and they were waiting for him to wake them all up.

He didn't look back at them. He couldn't. Instead, he kept his gaze on Bosco, and continued to fiddle with his handcuffs. Maybe there'd be some sort of weakness there. Something he could exploit.

Maybe, this wouldn't be the end. Maybe it didn't have to be.

But the cuffs were solid. The chain was strong. Even if he could get free, there was no way he could get to Petrie in time.

No way he could fight him, Bosco, and the two skinheads in his current condition.

As he watched Owen Petrie—Mister Whisper—pace back and forth behind the line of kneeling figures, his knife swinging freely in his hand, Logan couldn't shake the feeling that maybe this *would* be the end, after all.

CHAPTER FORTY-FOUR

"Ask me why I'm doing this," Petrie instructed, pointing the knife at Logan.

"Jesus fucking Christ, Owen—"

"Ask me why I'm doing this," Petrie said again, the words slithering out of him, cold and dangerous things.

Logan sighed. "Why are you doing this?"

"Ooh! Good question," Petrie replied. "I mean, you and I both know why I'm doing it, don't we? But, for the benefit of the audience..."

He cleared his throat several times, coughed into his hand, then opened and closed his mouth, drawing his lips back over his teeth like a singer doing warm-up exercises.

Then, when he was finished, he began.

"Detective Inspector Logan, as I knew him—congratulations on the promotion, by the way. Very well deserved. See, he and I had quite the unique relationship dynamic. I tortured and killed children, he tried to stop me."

He held both hands up and chuckled, like he was reciting an amusing anecdote.

"I know, I know. Hardly the great love story of our time, and yet... Jack was *obsessed*. Weren't you? Relentless. I had people on the inside at the time, and they told me that I was just all-consuming for you. I was all you spoke about. It was flattering, if I'm honest. OK, maybe a *touch* creepy, but... you know. Flattering."

Petrie wandered along the line until he reached Maddie. He looked at her apologetically. "I hear your obsession even broke up the family." He rubbed the back of a hand lightly down Maddie's face. She shuddered and whimpered through her tape-gag at his touch. "I'm so very sorry to hear that. I was really rooting for the three of you."

"Get away from her," Logan barked.

"Uh-uh, Jack," Petrie snapped, waving his knife. "Careful, or the Paki loses an eye." Petrie looked back at Bosco and the others. "Can we still say that? 'Paki'? Is that still allowed?"

The Russian shrugged. "Fuck knows. Let's hurry this up."

Petrie turned back to Logan and pulled a face. "Getting impatient, isn't he? Where was I? Oh! Yes. So, to cut a long story short, he found me, eventually. I have to admit, I was impressed. That was proper detective work.

"Anyway, like in all the best stories, there's a chase. He's nippy for a big lad, I'll give him that. I try to hide. He finds me. We're up on top of a car park. I've got nowhere to go. Caught, fair and square." He held his hands out, wrists together. "'Slap the cuffs on, officer. Take me away.' But no. Oh, no. DI Logan had other ideas. He was getting me down off that roof, alright, but he was sending me via the most direct route."

Petrie pointed with a finger and moved it downwards as he whistled through his teeth, the note getting lower and lower, until...

"Bang. Impact. Next thing I know, I'm in hospital, full of tubes, and wires, and Christ knows what else. I'm pissing and shitting into a bag. But I don't really know any of it. Not clearly. I've got an impression of it, that's all," Petrie continued. "What I do remember—the only vivid thing in my head—is the last thing that I said to you, Jack, before you pushed me over."

Logan opened his mouth to respond, but Petrie pointed the knife at Hamza, silencing him. Instead, the detective just shook his head, pleading with his eyes. Not this.

Please, God, no. Not this.

"Anyway, I go under again. Next thing, it's three months down the line. I'm somewhere else. Still all tubes and wires. And everything's... slow. Like black treacle. I try to move my hands. Nothing. Then... I don't know. A minute later? An hour? They move.

"But I'm not worried about it, for some reason. It's just... the way it is. It's a nagging background concern. See, the front of my head is still full of those last words I said. They're written there, in big shiny gold letters, hanging there in the air." Petrie shrugged. "It was probably the drugs, I suppose."

At the back of the room, Valdis looked at his watch, then whispered something to Bosco. The Russian made a swatting motion, like he was batting away a fly. Valdis crossed his arms sullenly and went back to watching the show.

Logan's mind was whirring, searching for a way out. The handcuffs were solid, but maybe there was another weakness he could exploit. Bosco didn't know that Logan was already aware of his team-up with Petrie. Why? They'd signposted it with the shoes on the body.

He must've known they'd clocked one of his vans leaving the scene. Hoon would've passed that little nugget of information on. So why was he surprised?

The more Logan thought about it, the less it made sense. Petrie might have nothing to lose with a stunt like this, but Bosco had spent decades skirting around the law, never revealing too much of his hand, always avoiding prosecution.

This was a risky play for him. This could bring him down for good. So, why put everything he'd worked for on the line?

Did he owe Petrie in some way? Was there some loyalty there that Logan didn't know about?

Or, was it something more obvious?

Before he could think any more about it, Petrie launched back into his monologue. Logan desperately wanted to tell him to shut the fuck up, but it would be Hamza who would pay the price. And, by the looks of him, the DC had already paid more than enough.

"After that, I get flashes. Glimpses of memories," Petrie said. "I'd close my eyes, and months would go by. Years. I'd blink, and there'd be a different face there, looking down at me. Poking at me." He pointed the knife at Logan. "And yours, Jack. Always yours. Popping up. You and me in rooms together. You and your photos. You and your questions. Just the two of us, over and over again."

He resumed pacing and tapped all five people in front of him on the head with the flat of the knife blade.

"See, you tell yourself that you've got people. You've got friends. Family. You tell yourself that you care about them. But deep down, you know the truth. It's me and you, Jack. It's always been me and you. It's pathetic, I know, but I'm the love of your bloody life."

"Holy shit," Bosco spat from the back of the room. "Just do what fuck you are doing so we can get out of here."

Petrie sighed. "You know your problem, Bosco? No flair for the dramatic." He shot Logan a look that bordered on apologetic. "I've known him since he was a lad, fresh off the boat. He worked for me. My building company. I gave him his start, introduced him to some friends of mine. Influential ones.

"We've been keeping in touch these last couple of years, and when he mentioned you. When he expressed his deeply-held feelings for you, well..." He put a finger to his head and turned it, like the spinning of a cog. "Let's just say, a plan started forming. You've cost him a lot of money over the years, he tells me.

Personally, I'm not fussed about money. You know me, Jack. You know me better than anyone. I take my pleasures elsewhere."

He stopped near Ben, gave him a cheerful little wave, then turned his back and started to walk slowly back along the line. He turned the knife over and over in his hands, his lop-sided smile playing across his face.

"Getting back to the point. Those words that were in my head. Shining there. Those words I said to you. The thing that made you push me off that roof. You remember them, don't you? You remember what I said."

Logan didn't reply. He fought the urge to look at Maddie, overpowering as it was.

"Come on, Jack," Petrie urged. "You remember. I know you do. What was it I said I was going to do? You can speak. You can say it."

He couldn't. The words wouldn't come, *refused* to come.

Petrie huffed out a big breath. "Fine. I'll say it, then." He laid a hand on Maddie's head. "I told you that I was going to rape your daughter, and that I was going to make you watch."

Maddie let out an inhuman sound beneath the tape. It was like nothing Logan had ever heard before, and it pierced his heart like an icy spike. She tried to shuffle away, but Petrie twisted his fingers through her hair and held her in place. His eyes were blazing now, his face knotted up into a vicious sneer.

"After that, Jack. After I'm done. Once I'm *spent,* you're going to pick which one of your friends here is going to be the first to die. Refuse, and he rapes her," Petrie said, pointing to Bosco. "Refuse again, and it's your man there's turn." He pointed at Valdis, who shifted uncomfortably and glanced down at the floor. "And so on, and so on. There's a truck full of big strapping Polish lads downstairs. They'll all take their turn on her until you choose. Until you look one of these fine folks here in the eye, and you say, 'That one. That one dies first.'"

"Petrie, don't," Logan pleaded.

"You knew this was coming, Jack. That's what I mean about me being the love of your life." He reached into a back pocket and produced the postcard that had been weighing Logan down since he'd found it. "I gave you an ultimatum. Jump off that roof, or everything that happened next was on you. You didn't jump."

"I'll do it now. I'll jump. I'll do it. Just let them—"

"Oh, stop. Stop. We're way past that now," Petrie said. "Look at you. It's disappointing, I'll be honest. You knew I was coming. You knew how to stop me. But you didn't. And why?"

Petrie walked around the kneeling group and stopped just beyond Logan's reach. He squatted down and smiled, not unkindly.

"Because deep down somewhere, you wanted this. You wanted it to come down to me and you. The two of us, face to face. That was how it was always going to end, Jack. I mean, aye. You probably hoped you'd be the one holding the cards, but you can't have it all ways."

He stood up, ignoring Logan's shouts as he went strolling back over to Maddie.

"Petrie, don't. Don't do this. Don't." His eyes flitted desperately to the back of the room. "Bosco. Bosco, please, this isn't you. This isn't you!"

"What you fucking know about me?" Bosco hissed, launching himself from the wall and charging forwards. "For years, you fucking in my way. You interfere. You throw weight around. You burn my fucking office to ground!"

He barged past Petrie and stopped in front of the kneeling DCI. "Well, fuck that shit! It is over. You'll be gone. Done. No more. Maybe then, I get some fucking business done. Yes? Yes. Maybe then, things go back to normal."

"What are you talking about?" Logan asked.

He didn't know. He seriously didn't know.

"It's no' going back to normal for you now, Bosco. We know. The whole bloody force knows. You and him. Petrie. Your photos were all over the press conference today. Kill me if you like, but they're coming for you, Bosco. It's over."

A look of concern flitted across Bosco's face, then was gone. He snorted and wagged a reproachful finger at Logan. "Good try. Sow seeds of doubt. Clever."

"I'm no' sowing anything, Bosco. It was the shoes. The shoes the dead guy was wearing. They were mine. From my flat."

"Yes. Of course. That was point..." Bosco said. He looked across to the man with the knife for confirmation. It was clear that the plan had been Petrie's, and that Bosco wasn't quite up to speed with some of the finer details.

Shite. Logan had hoped that one would catch the Russian off-guard.

But, if he knew the shoes had been Logan's, and that his van had been seen leaving the scene, why didn't he know the polis had linked them together? What was Logan missing?

Wait.

"The badge," Logan said.

Bosco frowned. "Badge? What badge?"

"We're wasting time here," Petrie said. "This was meant to be my big moment. Can we—?"

Bosco ignored him. "What badge?" he asked again.

"In my bed. Petrie left it. A calling card, letting me know he'd been in the flat," Logan said. "You thought he'd gone in, grabbed the shoes, and left, didn't you? I mean, what were you trying to do? Set me up? Or... Or...?" He shook his head. "Doesn't matter. The point is, Owen couldn't resist leaving a wee calling card. We knew he was in my flat. We knew your boys dumped the body wearing my shoes, which could only have come from my flat. So, two and two together, that's how we knew about you and Petrie, Bosco. That's how the whole fucking world now knows."

Logan saw the change in Bosco's expression. There was a storm coming, but Logan wasn't going to be the one to take the brunt of it. Instead, the Russian turned to Petrie. His voice, when it came, was perfectly calm. Troublingly so.

"What the fuck is he talking about?"

"It's... He's..." Petrie shrugged. "OK. Fine. I thought it'd be funny. Wind him up. You know? The thought of me being there in his house. In his bedroom. I bet that wormed its way in there, didn't it, Jack?" he said, tapping the injured side of his head. "I bet the thought of me in there was eating you up from the—"

"You left fucking *clue*?" Bosco hissed. "What the fuck are you thinking? You say you need into his place, need shoes, you don't tell me why. All part of your stupid game you play with him. Your revenge mission. Fuck it, I help. You say you want us to get rid of your fucking friend you cut to pieces? To mess up his face? To finish him off? Fine. We do. But we are not meant to be connected, you and me. Us? We two? There meant to be no fucking link."

"In my defence," Petrie said. "Your men couldn't tell east from west. He wasn't meant to be left at that Premier Inn. He was meant to be at the one where the wife and daughter were staying. That was the whole point of the exercise. That was meant to freak him out. And there are no cameras there. Nobody would've figured it out."

He indicated Valdis and the other skinhead at the back of the room. Valdis glowered back at him, his arms still folded.

"So, really, if the police have linked us, then that's those idiots' fault, not mine. They messed up, not me. I mean, don't shoot the messenger, but that's the truth of it."

Bosco glared at him for a long time, muttering below his breath in Russian. Finally, with a wave of his hand, he relented.

"Just fucking get it over with. Then I sort out your mess."

Petrie's smile returned, broader than ever. "Make sure he watches," he instructed, pointing the knife at Jack.

There was a *crack* as Petrie hit Maddie with a backhanded slap that sent her spinning to the floor.

"Don't you dare! Don't you fucking dare!" Logan howled, the chain clanking as he heaved on it, slamming it against the underside of the old iron radiator.

Tyler struggled to his feet, but Bosco was at him in two big paces. The Russian drove a headbutt into the DC's nose, dropping him like a stone.

Hamza threw himself at the Russian's legs, driving a shoulder against them. The attack was weak and limp, though, and Bosco felled him with a knee to the side of the head.

Logan heaved against his chains, clanking them against the radiator. Bosco bent and drove a punch into Logan's already burning ribs, then the Russian was behind him, wrapping an arm around his throat, holding his head in place.

"He wants you to watch. So, you watch," Bosco said. "Front row seat. Best view in the house."

Maddie was squealing, screaming beneath the tape, bucking and thrashing as she fought to fend Petrie off. He had her on her back, side-on to her helpless father, her legs pinned beneath him, the knife in his hand.

"During everything that's about to happen, I want you to keep something in mind, my dear," Petrie told her. "Your daddy there knew I was coming. He knew I was coming, and he brought you here, anyway. Keep that in mind for me, will you?"

He turned to Logan, winked, then he hacked at the neck of Maddie's jumper with the knife until it split enough for him to tear it the rest of the way, revealing her bra and the flesh of her stomach.

"*Petrie!*" Logan howled, struggling against Bosco's grip as Petrie pushed his daughter's bra up, exposing her breasts.

"She's a wild one, I'll give her that," Petrie said, grinning back at Logan as Maddie continued to struggle and fight. He beckoned the two skinheads from the back of the room. "Come here. Hold her shoulders and help me get her legs open."

Valdis looked from Petrie to Maddie, then over at Bosco,

even as his colleague trotted over to Petrie's side. There was a brief conversation in Russian between Valdis and his boss. Harsh words spat back and forth, crackling in the air between them, before Valdis relented and, with a sigh, went to lend a hand.

Valdis took the shoulders, pinning them, while the other man helped Petrie with Maddie's legs. She kicked out frantically. Desperately. Hopelessly.

Petrie undid the buttons of her jeans with one big pull, exposing her underwear. Maddie's eyes met her father's, begging him to help her. To save her. To make this stop.

Please. God. Make it stop.

"Now, make sure he watches every second. Cut his fucking eyelids off, if you have to," Petrie said, forcing her jeans and her underwear down to her knees. "I've waited a very, *very* long time for this."

CHAPTER FORTY-FIVE

SHE WAS ALL BUT NAKED NOW. JEANS AND UNDERWEAR down at her ankles, bra pushed up almost to her throat. Petrie was laughing and whooping with excitement as he undid the button on his trousers. The other skinhead—the one Logan didn't know was holding Maddie by the thigh, his fingers digging into her soft flesh. He was sniggering, too, eyes darting hungrily across her naked body.

Valdis had a hand on each shoulder, but he was staring straight ahead, not at Petrie but past him to the wall beyond.

Logan struggled in Bosco's grip, but the Russian's arm was tight across his throat, and the bulk of his weight was too much to fight back against.

"Bosco, Bosco, please," Logan whispered. "Stop this. Please."

"Shut fuck up and watch show," Bosco said, his voice a growl in the detective's ear. He tightened his grip further, cutting off Logan's air supply.

Logan choked, wheezed, tried to swallow, but there was nowhere for anything to go.

And then, with a little hiss of laughter, Bosco eased back a little, and Logan gasped in a series of frantic breaths.

"Turn her over," Petrie commanded. "Make her face her old man. Make him look into her fucking eyes."

Valdis and the other man helped flip the squirming Maddie over. Petrie bent over and punched at her, like he was trying to get a pillow into just the right shape.

Beside him, Sinead heaved herself onto her feet. She threw a kick at him that caught him in the side of his stomach, and then the second skinhead caught her with a right hook that put her down. Her head hit the floor and she lay there, unmoving.

"Maybe she is next, yes?" he suggested, which drew a choking whine of rage from beneath Tyler's tape. The skinhead cackled at him, then went back to holding Maddie.

"You can't trust him, Bosco," Logan whispered. "He's right. I know him. Better than anyone. He set you up with the badge. He wanted us to know you were working together. He wanted you exposed."

"I sort that shit out after you are all dead," Bosco told him.

"Fuck's sake, Bosco. Think about this. Think about what he is," Logan hissed. "You don't know what he's capable of."

Bosco lowered his head, bringing his mouth closer to Logan's ear. "I guess your daughter is about to find out."

This was it, then. His Hail Mary. His only chance. He had to play this just right.

"And what about yours?" he asked.

He heard the hesitation. The tiny grain of doubt in Bosco's response.

"What you fucking talking about?"

"Your daughter, Bosco. He's got her."

"Bullshit."

"He has. He's taken her."

"Olivia is at home with her mother."

"She isn't. She won't be. She's stashed away somewhere. Tied up. Crying her fucking eyes out."

Bosco pulled his grip tighter again. "How the fuck would you know this?"

"Because I know him. I know how he works. How his mind works," Logan told him. "You want to kill him, don't you? For exposing you. You're planning to kill him. And what, you think he didn't anticipate that? You think he didn't want a contingency plan? He's got your daughter. He's got Olivia."

"What are you two whispering about over there?" Petrie asked. He stood above Maddie, one leg either side of hers, his trousers hanging from one ankle. "I want you paying attention, Jack. Not chit-chatting."

"If you think this is bad, wait until you see what he does with her," Logan whispered. "Kids are his thing, Bosco. You have no idea."

"What did he say?" Petrie asked, waving his knife in Logan's direction.

"He says you have my daughter," Bosco replied.

Petrie laughed. "Your daughter? Why would I have your daughter?"

Bosco looked from Petrie to Logan and back again. There was the faintest easing of his grip.

"You tell me," the Russian said.

Valdis stood up, placing himself directly behind Petrie. Bosco's other man continued to hold onto Maddie's leg, his gaze now fixed on her bare arse.

"He's lying, obviously. Jesus, Bosco, you think I'd be that stupid?"

"You were stupid enough to leave fucking badge."

"Why would I have any interest in your fucking daughter?" Petrie demanded. He sounded impatient. Irritated. The bulge that had been forming in his underwear waned. This was really taking the edge off his big moment.

"Because you are sick fuck," Bosco said.

Petrie gave a little shrug. "Aye, well, you've got me there, right enough. But I don't have your daughter. He's filling your head with shite to try to turn you against me. It's pathetic, really. Don't be a bloody idiot."

Bosco released his grip on Logan's neck. "I am idiot?"

"That's not what I'm saying," Petrie replied. "I'm saying—"

"Phone Olivia," Bosco said, tossing his mobile to Valdis.

"Jesus Christ." Petrie sighed. "Fine. Phone her. Maybe then, we can get back to business."

While Valdis phoned, Petrie leaned past Bosco and pointed the knife at Logan.

"Always one last trick up your sleeve, eh, Jack?" he said. "Well done. You've bought your daughter a few more seconds. Whoop-de-fucking-doo."

"She is not answering," Valdis announced.

Bosco's gaze flitted to Petrie. "She always answer. She always have fucking phone in hand. Try again."

For the first time since Bosco had mentioned his daughter, concern creased the lines of Petrie's face. Bosco was squared up to him now. With a clicking noise and a jab of his thumb, the Russian instructed his other man to get to his feet.

The three of them surrounded Petrie, all three of them eyeballing him. In the silence, they all heard the ringing from Valdis's phone.

Eight rings.

Ten.

Twelve.

A click of someone answering. Logan's stomach tightened. His heart stopped.

"The number you are calling is not available to take your call..."

"Bosco, think about—" Petrie began, but the Russian cut him off.

"Call her mother. Put it on speaker."

It took sixteen or seventeen rings for the phone to be answered. The woman on the other end sounded annoyed when she finally answered. Her accent was English. Essex, maybe.

"Bosco. You're a fucking dick," she barked. "She's not meant to be picked up until two. I've got her until then. We were going to have lunch. I bought fucking Lunchables in, and everything."

"What are you talking about?" Bosco asked, his gaze still fixed firmly on Petrie.

"Olivia. What the fuck else would I be talking about? When did you come get her, the middle of the bloody night?"

"She is not there?"

"No! She's not..." The penny dropped. "Wait. She's with you, isn't she?"

Petrie opened his mouth to speak, but Bosco raised a finger to silence him.

"I joke," the Russian said. "She is here. On iPad, as usual."

"Oh, fucking hilarious. Yeah, you got me there, alright. Proper laugh, that—"

On a signal from Bosco, Valdis terminated the call.

"Where is she?" Bosco demanded.

Petrie rolled his eyes theatrically. "Oh, for Christ's sake, Bosco. I don't know. This is him, isn't it? He's done this."

"I'm no' the one with a history of it, Bosco," Logan said. "Where is she, Petrie? What have you done with her?"

Bosco looked from Valdis to the other skinhead, then gestured angrily to the hostages. "Watch them. They fucking move, you kill them."

A meaty hand caught Petrie by the back of the neck and bundled him towards a door at the side of the room. Petrie tripped and stumbled, his trousers trailing behind him.

"Ow. Ow, fuck's sake, Bosco. Don't be so bloody stupid!" Petrie spat, and then he was thrown through the door into what looked like a stairwell beyond, and the room echoed with the sound of Bosco's roar.

"Where is she?!"

Logan heaved on his chains, but the radiator was heavy, and securely fixed to the wall.

"Cut that shit out," the second skinhead warned. He side-eyed Valdis, muttered something in a language Logan didn't understand, then looked down at Maddie.

She had rolled herself onto her back, and was trying desperately to wriggle her jeans and underwear back up.

"Ooh. Look at her go. She look so fucking hot. Yes?"

"Shut the fuck up, Olek," Valdis hissed.

The other man—Olek—sniggered and dropped into a squat beside Maddie. She froze, cowering as he reached a hand out and grabbed one of her breasts.

"Leave her alone!" Logan cried, hauling on the radiator again.

Olek squeezed her breast hard, making her whimper in pain. He raised his eyes to Logan and grinned. "I think she enjoy." He stopped squeezing and traced a hand along the length of her stomach. "I wonder what else she—"

Valdis grabbed him by the back of the jacket and hauled him to his feet. Angry words were exchanged. Harsh. Clipped.

Olek shoved Valdis in the chest, forcing him back a couple of steps. He turned back to Maddie, hunger in his eyes. "Maybe I take a go first. Yes? Give Petrie sloppy seconds."

He reached for the buckle of his belt. Valdis caught him by the shoulder, swung him around, then drove a headbutt into the centre of his face. Olek's nose exploded. He stumbled back, gasping, then went down in a flurry of frantic punches from Valdis.

Valdis followed him to the floor, raining blows on Olek as he spluttered and choked on his blood.

He let up only when the other man's eyes were rolling in his head, and his chances of getting up without medical intervention were close to zero.

Valdis sprang back to his feet then, spent a few seconds staring in horror at the gasping wreckage he'd left on the floor, then turned to face Logan.

"This is... This is not me," Valdis said, indicating Maddie. "I do not rape women. I do not hurt children. This is not me."

"I know, son. I know," Logan said. He shot a glance to the door. He couldn't hear raised voices now. They'd have worked it out. They'd be back any second. "Help us. Get me out of these."

Valdis shook his head. He shrugged off his jacket. "I... I can't. I'm sorry."

"Valdis, please!"

The skinhead draped his jacket over Maddie, covering what he could of her. "I'm sorry," he said again, aiming it at her this time.

He took a Stanley knife from his back pocket and extended the blade. Logan felt a surge of hope, but then he tossed it onto the floor. It landed near Tyler, but with his hands bound behind him, there was almost nothing the DC could do about it.

Without a backwards glance, Valdis turned and ran for the other door at the far end of the room, and went barrelling through it.

"Shit. *Shit!*" Logan cursed. He looked at Maddie, then across the faces of his colleagues. His friends. Hamza was barely with it. Sinead was rousing, but slowly. Tyler and Ben's heads were tick-tocking between him and the door, clearly having come to the same conclusion that he had.

There wasn't much time.

"It's going to be OK. We're all going to be OK," Logan promised.

He pulled on the chains. Gritted his teeth and *heaved*. His muscles burned. Metal groaned. Pain ignited in his broken ribs and he collapsed with a gasp, his head spinning as darkness crept in from the edges of his vision.

He couldn't do it. It was too hard. Too solid.

"I'm sorry," he sobbed, bent over. Broken. "This is all my fault. I'm sorry."

He thought of everything that had happened. Harris. Vanessa. Alice.

God, *Ben*. What he must be feeling. What he must be going through.

He thought of Harris. Alone somewhere. Tortured. Terrified. Was he even still alive?

Would it be better for him if he wasn't?

He thought of Maddie. Of what had happened to her. Of everything that might be about to.

His little girl. He made her feel safe, that's what she'd told him. Despite everything, despite all those failures over all those years, he made her feel safe.

He saw her as a baby, felt her weight in his arms.

As a five-year-old, over his shoulder, giggling.

As an eight-year-old, snuggled against him, falling asleep as he read her a story.

His daughter. His princess. His everything.

Slowly, like Atlas himself rising, Logan placed one foot on the floor, then the other.

He closed his eyes.

He clenched his jaw.

And he pulled with everything he had.

The pain tore through him. Through his ribs and through his wrists. It licked across his skin and buried through his insides, pouring into him, filling him up.

He thought of Harris.

He thought of Alice.

He thought of Maddie.

And he pulled, and he pulled, and he pulled.

CHAPTER FORTY-SIX

LOGAN HELD HIS DAUGHTER WHILE SHE SOBBED AGAINST him. While her body shook. While shame and relief and everything in between came tumbling out in her tears. He'd never felt her so fragile. So afraid.

He still wore the chains, but the radiator was on the floor now, and water was pooling beneath the buckled pipes that bent outwards from the wall.

"Ambulance and back-up on the way," Tyler said, his voice slurred, throat croaky. "ETA five minutes."

Ben was kneeling over Sinead, holding her hand. She'd insisted she was fine, but she hadn't let him go yet, and her grip was tight.

Hamza coughed. There was a rattle to it that Logan didn't like the sound of. The DC was on his feet, but it didn't look like it'd take more than a strong gust of wind to knock him on his arse.

There had been no movement from the door yet. No Bosco. No Petrie.

But, it was only a matter of time.

"I have to go get him," Logan said. Maddie's arms tightened

around him. She shook her head. More than anything, he wanted to stay there, to hold onto her, to keep her safe.

To do his job.

But he had another job, too. And there was still one victim unaccounted for.

"I'll be back. I'll be right back," he whispered.

Reluctantly, she released her grip on him. She was dressed again now, Valdis's jacket zipped up in place of her torn jumper.

"Please, be careful," she urged.

"I will," he told her, then he hissed in pain as he stood up. "Tyler. You fit?"

"I am, boss," Tyler replied. His face was a mess of blood and bruising, but he was up, and he was standing, and that was the best they could hope for right now.

"Ben, you OK here?"

"Just go get them, Jack," Ben said. "We're fine. I've got them."

Logan twisted the chains around his arms, making them short enough to use as a weapon. "Good. Tyler, let's go nail these bastards."

———

THEY FOUND Bosco one flight of stairs down, blood pumping through his fingers where he clutched at his gut. He was leaning on the bannister, a red trail behind him suggesting he'd dragged himself up a dozen or so steps before stopping for breath.

"Oh... fuck," he spat, when he saw Logan and Tyler hobbling down the stairs towards him. "How the fuck are...? Shit, shit, fuck, shit!"

"Where's Petrie?" Logan snarled.

"Where you fucking think?" Bosco spat. "Piece of shit stab me. Piece of fucking traitor shit."

Logan cursed, then went hurrying down the steps past the bleeding Russian. "Tyler, watch him. I'll get Petrie."

Tyler fixed Bosco with a cold glare. "Got him, boss. You go."

The DC and the gangster held eye contact as they listened to Logan go clumping and clanking down the rest of the steps.

"What the fuck you waiting for, *policeman?*" Bosco spat through his blubbery lips. "Do your job. Call me fucking ambulance."

Tyler drove a punch into the spot Bosco was clutching, drawing a yelp of pain.

"Where's Harris?" he demanded.

"Ow, fuck!"

He hit him again. Harder. His face twisted into a mask of fury. "Where is he? Where's Harris?!"

"Fuck you!" Bosco snapped.

Suddenly, Tyler's hands were on his throat, forcing him backwards until he hit the wooden railing at the top of the bannister.

Another punch slammed into his stab-wound. The hand still on his throat forced him further back, until he was leaning over the stairwell, six or seven storeys above the ground.

"Where is he?" Tyler hissed. "What did you do with him?"

"Fuck. Jesus. I don't know! OK? I don't fucking know!"

Tyler yanked Bosco's hand away from the wound and jabbed his fingers into it, drawing a guttural roar of pain from deep in the Russian's throat.

"I'm going to ask you again, and then I'm going to throw you over this fucking drop," Tyler warned. His face was next to Bosco's. The look in his eyes said he was telling the truth. "Where. Is. Harris?"

"I swear. I swear, I don't know. He wouldn't tell me where he was, even if I wanted to fucking know. I never saw the boy. Not once. Not once!"

"You're lying!"

Bosco's eyes went to the drop, and the ground far, far below.

"No! No, it is truth! Why the fuck would I protect Petrie now? After this? After he took my Olivia?" He shook his head. Or as much as the hand on his throat would allow, at least. "No. I do not know. I do not know. I swear! I swear!"

Tyler's lips drew back over his teeth. He pushed, and Bosco scrabbled for the railing, his bloodied hands slipping as his fingers failed to grip the wood.

"Tyler."

DC Neish turned at the sound of his name. DI Forde stood there at the top of the stairs, a rectangle of red across his mouth marking where the tape had been. He looked old. Tired.

But he was standing. And that was the best they could hope for.

"Don't, son," he urged.

"But... but everything he's done," Tyler spat. "Everyone he's hurt. Why shouldn't I? Logan did it. Why shouldn't I?"

The reply came from down the stairs.

"Because you're a better copper than I am, son."

Tyler looked in the direction of the voice just as Logan rounded the corner of the next flight down.

"Petrie?" Ben asked.

Logan shook his head in response, not taking his eyes off Tyler. "Gone."

"He was just going to watch it all," Tyler said. Bosco was teetering on the bannister, his eyes almost popping out of their sockets. "He was going to watch what Petrie did. He was going to kill us."

"Aye, he's an arsehole. You'll get no arguments there," Logan said. "But you're not, son. Well, I mean... Aye, sometimes. Often, actually." He looked up at Ben. "Where was I going with that again?"

Tyler looked momentarily confused, then caught the grim

smile on Logan's face. "Funny, boss," he said, very much not laughing.

"You're no' a killer, Tyler," Logan continued. "I don't say it enough, but you're a good officer. You've got a bright future ahead of you. Don't blow that on this waste of space. Do your job. Bring him in. He'll no' wriggle his way out of this one."

Tyler's grip tightened on Bosco's throat. His muscles tensed. He looked first at Logan, then up at Ben standing above him.

He'd hurt so many people.

He'd been about to kill them.

He'd threatened Tyler's *mum*.

The DC's muscles tensed. His eyes blazed with barely-contained fury.

"Bosco Maximuke," he said, spitting the words out in disgust. "You're under arrest."

"OK, OK, yes. Yes. But my daughter. Please. Olivia. Save Olivia."

Logan clicked his tongue against the back of his teeth. "Aye," he said. "About that..."

OLIVIA SAT on the couch in Shona's living room. For once, she had no headphones on, and while her eyes were fixed on a screen, it was Shona's TV, and not an iPad.

She perched there transfixed, hand fishing around in an almost-empty bowl that had, until recently, been full of popcorn.

"OK, this is an oldie," announced a young man on the TV. He had a guitar strapped to his chest and was looking out across a sea of teenage faces. "Well, it's an oldie where I come from..."

Shona appeared from the kitchen, a can in her hand. "More Coke?"

"Please," Olivia said as, on screen, Marty McFly launched

into the opening bars of *Johnny B. Goode*. She took the can, cracked it open, and slurped. "For a kidnapper, you're pretty nice."

Shona shifted uncomfortably. "Please stop calling me that. Like I said, I'm a... friend. Of your mum's. I'm just—"

"Yeah, yeah," Olivia said, shooing her out of the way of the TV.

"Enjoying the film?" Shona asked, taking her seat beside the girl.

Olivia nodded in reply. "Yeah. For something so old, it's pretty solid."

"Well, if you think this one's good," Shona said, picking up another Blu-ray box from the coffee table. Her phone rang, flashing up Logan's name. She sighed with relief and reached for it, before tossing the box into Olivia's lap. "Just wait until you see the sequels."

CHAPTER FORTY-SEVEN

LOGAN SAT IN HIS OFFICE, SWALLOWING A COUPLE OF Ibuprofen and hoping they worked some sort of miracle.

He'd refused the hospital, but had insisted the others were taken in and checked. They'd been taken in a convoy, a police escort topping and tailing the procession of ambulances.

Shona was taking Olivia home. Persuading the girl to come with her had been surprisingly easy, she said. Olivia had come along without asking too many questions and hadn't seemed remotely worried. She'd seemed oddly excited about it, in fact, like it was nice to get the attention.

They'd watched *Ghostbusters* and *Back to the Future* back to back, then Shona had driven her home, laden with DVDs and Blu-rays. Olivia had said she would call next week.

Shona wasn't quite sure how to feel about that.

After Logan had finished the call, he'd cadged a lift back to base with one of the CID boys. There, he'd taken a short but thorough bollocking from the Assistant Chief Constable who, to his dismay, was still knocking about, and then he'd briefed her on everything that had happened and retired to his office to process the morning's events.

It had taken him just a few minutes to conclude that he couldn't process them right now, and possibly never would.

What Petrie had almost done...

He shook his head, forcing the image away. The bastard was still out there. He still had Harris.

But where?

I already told you where the boy is.

What had he meant by that? What had they missed?

He got up, went to the door, and addressed the various officers sitting at the desks in the Incident Room. "The boy. Harris. Any update?"

There was some reluctant murmuring. No. No update. No word. No sign.

Logan closed the door and returned to his seat.

If you'd been paying attention...

When? To what?

He sat back in his chair, rocking it from side to side. Even that movement was enough to make his ribs grind together. For now, he welcomed the pain. It was keeping him awake. Keeping him sharp.

Not sharp enough, it seemed. He had no idea what Petrie had supposedly told him. He had no idea where Harris was.

He grabbed a pen and flipped open his notebook. Maybe if we went back to the start... Or, no. Would it be better to work backwards from the end?

Or...

He sat forward.

Both.

He was on his feet again in an instant, throwing open the door almost as quickly.

"The hand. In the field. Did we get prints back yet?"

A uniformed sergeant turned in her chair. "Aye, sir. It's in your inbox. It came through about half—"

Logan was back at his computer before she'd finished the

sentence. He saw the mail there, waiting for him. Double-clicked. Scrolled until he found the name.

He staggered back from the desk.

Oh, Christ.

Of course.

Bud Vance.

The scrote from the flat downstairs.

LOGAN HEARD Petrie's slow clap as the door flew open on the third kick.

"I'm sure you used to be able to do that in a oner, once upon a time," he called from through in the living room.

The smell in the flat was choking. Emptied bladder. Emptied bowels. The coppery tang of blood in the air.

He saw the girl, Tanya, propped up in a chair in one of the bedrooms, her throat cut, her eyes wide-open and staring at nothing.

Another victim. Another life lost.

"Bad timing on her part," Petrie said, and Logan turned to see him standing in the living room, Harris held in front of him like a shield. "Had to be done, though. If it's any consolation, I took very little pleasure in it."

Harris was gagged, just like the others had been back in the abandoned office building. He didn't look scared. Not really. There was almost no emotion on his face at all, like his brain was shutting everything down, blocking everything out.

Petrie had the knife to his throat. Bosco's blood still clung to the blade.

"Thought it might come down to this in the end," Petrie said. "This was the contingency plan, in case you slipped by us. That's why I gave you a hand." He chuckled at that, almost fondly. "I couldn't trust you to find the place yourself, even though... Keep your friends close, but your enemies closer, eh, Jack? Don't get much closer to home than this. If it's any consolation, he said some pretty horrible things about you. Bud, I mean. The way he spoke, you'd think the two of you were arch enemies!"

Petrie snorted out a staccato laugh, but it died away quickly and his face darkened. "And, well, for obvious reasons, I couldn't have that."

"Let the boy go, Owen. It's over."

"Oh, you're absolutely right, Jack," Petrie said. "It is over. This is the end. And, might I say, thank you for remaining as reliable as ever."

"What's that supposed to mean?" Logan asked.

Petrie gestured to the hallway behind the DCI. "Well, where's the clomp of running feet? Where are the Uniforms, or the negotiators? If I look out that window, will I see a big circus of flashing lights and polis?"

Logan didn't respond, and Petrie let out a triumphant little laugh.

"Aye. Thought so. You couldn't resist, could you? You and me, Jack. That's what it always comes down to, doesn't it? You and me. Just the two of us."

"If it's just the two of us you want, Owen, then let the boy go," Logan said.

He took a step closer, but Petrie moved back, tightening his grip on Harris.

"Ah-ah. Not so fast there, Jack," he hissed. "See, I need the boy. For this. For the end. I knew I wasn't going to get away anywhere. Not in the long run. I knew someone would spot me sooner or later, and I'd be brought in. But I wasn't having that. I wasn't having some fucking nobody catch me trying to sneak out of the country with a fake passport and a false moustache. Fuck that, quite frankly. That's now the finale either of us wanted. We wanted this. All this. Me and you, together at the end."

"You're a fucking headcase, Owen. Has anyone ever told you that?" Logan asked. He took another step. Petrie backed further away.

"I will cut his face off, Jack. Stay where you are," Petrie hissed.

"Alright. Alright. Easy, Owen. Easy," Logan urged.

"This was all for you. For *us*. For the dance we've danced all these years. For the game we've played."

"It's not a game, Owen."

"That's what Bosco kept saying, when I was setting things up. He was an idiot. You? I expected better of. Of course, it's a game! It's always been a game! And here's how the game ends," Petrie said, in that rasping whisper of his. "You watched my son die. And, while it's not the same as your daughter—I'd rather have fucked her in front of you and listened to you both screaming for me to stop—I know you care about this boy. That's why you came here. To plead for his life. Or to throw your weight around and try to scare me into letting him go."

Logan began to reply, but Petrie wasn't done talking.

"That's why you *think* you're here, Jack. But it's not. You're here because I want you here. Because I *brought* you here. You're here so you can watch him die, like you watched my son, die."

"He wasn't your son, Petrie," Logan said. "He was a wee boy you tortured and brainwashed."

Petrie shrugged. "Aye, well, is that not what all parents do to us, in the end? Maybe I just took it a bit further than most."

"I'll give you this. You were right about something, Owen," Logan said. He shuffled forwards, just a few centimetres. Petrie noticed and shifted back, maintaining the distance between them.

"What was that, then?" he asked.

"It was an obsession. Me and you. I can see that now. I wanted to be the one to stop you. To bring you in. To make you pay for what you'd done." Logan blew out his cheeks. "And, Christ, it cost me everything. Or... nearly."

Another shuffle. Another step back.

"See, when you had me chained to that radiator today. When you were going to... hurt my daughter. When I looked into the faces of my friends. Well, let's just say I re-evaluated a few things. Considered my priorities. And I realised something very important. Would you like to know what it was?"

"Indulge me," Petrie said. "I'm all ears."

"I realised that you're just no' worth the bother, Owen," Logan said with a disinterested shrug. "The game's not over because you say it is, it's over because, well, I can't be arsed playing. It's no' about you and me anymore. I've realised that. I don't have to be the one to take you down. Hell, I don't even want to be."

"What the fuck's that supposed to mean?" Petrie demanded.

"I didn't come here to plead for the boy's life, Owen. I knew you'd never let him go. So, my job wasn't to come barging in here to try to rescue Harris," Logan said. He took another step. Petrie retreated further, his knuckles going white as he gripped the knife harder. "My job was just to get you to stand near the window."

Petrie had just started to frown when one of the panes of glass behind him shattered. His hand went limp. The knife slipped from his fingers.

Logan caught Harris before the boy could fall, and pulled him in close so he didn't see the body slumping to the floor behind him, or the hole where its right eye had been.

"You're OK, son. You're OK," Logan told him. Through the window, on the rooftop of the building across the road, sunlight reflected off a lens. "You're safe now. We've got you."

CHAPTER FORTY-EIGHT

IT RAINED. OF COURSE, IT DID. IT WAS ONLY FITTING.

Alice Forde was laid to rest in a small, private ceremony, attended only by family and close friends. It was nice, as funerals went. Wee bit too much about Jesus in it for Logan's taste, but Alice had always been a believer, and it was what she would have wanted.

Ben said a few words. Nothing much, just a minute or so about their time together, how he was going to miss her. The usual.

Logan had sat up the back on an empty pew, standing and sitting whenever the Minister told them to. He didn't join in with the singing, though. He may not have seen eye to eye with Alice on a lot of things, but even she didn't deserve that.

And then, they were all at the graveside.

And then, Ben was shaking all the offered hands, accepting all the hugs, reminding them about the do at the community centre. Tea and sandwiches. Plenty to go around.

And then, it was just him and Logan, and a hole in the ground.

They stood at opposite ends of it, both looking down at the coffin, with his smattering of dirt on top.

"Thanks for coming," Ben said.

"Of course."

"Just wanted to make sure the bugger was really dead, didn't you?" Ben asked. He tried a smile. It didn't sit comfortably.

"Aye. Something like that," Logan said. "I really am sorry, Ben."

Ben nodded, but didn't meet Logan's eye. "You and me both, son," he said, then he sniffed and wiped his eyes on the back of his hand. "You spoken to the others?"

"On the mend," Logan said. "Keen to get back to it."

"More bloody fool them."

Logan gave a grunt of agreement. "You can say that again. They're a good team, though. They'll do you proud."

Ben looked up, a questioning look on his face.

"I'm done, Ben. I've had enough. I told the Impaler."

"When?"

Logan shrugged. The rain pattered off the shoulders of his overcoat. "Now. I wanted to wait until after..."

His eyes flitted to the grave between them.

"I've done enough damage. It's time I moved on."

"Back to Glasgow?"

Logan shook his head. "No. Somewhere new, I think. Just for a while."

"Thought you'd want to be closer to Maddie."

"Aye, well. Eventually, maybe. She's..." He looked up at the sky, blinked in the rain, then sighed. "She's back to blaming me. And quite bloody right, too. That postcard. I should never have brought them up here, knowing what it said."

"They'd have been in just as much danger elsewhere, Jack," Ben said.

"Aye. Maybe," he said. "But best not to be around her or Vanessa right now. Give them space. They need it."

Ben swallowed. "Right. Aye." He turned and looked in the direction the other mourners had gone. They were clustering under brollies, as they made their way back down the hill towards their waiting cars.

"There's sandwiches made," he said.

Logan followed his gaze. The corners of his mouth turned up a fraction. It wasn't a smile. Not really.

"Another time, maybe," he said. He pulled his collar up against the rain. "Tell the rest of them I said cheerio, will you?"

Ben nodded. "Take care, Jack."

"Aye, you too, Benjamin," Logan said. He shoved his hands deep into his coat pockets. "You, too."

ANOTHER GRAVESIDE. Another time. Logan propped the flowers in the little holder by the headstone, spent a few seconds trying to get them to stay together, then gave up and just let them splay apart.

They were a bit past their best, curling up at the edges, but they were the best the local shop had to offer, and he wasn't exactly spoiled for choice up here.

"I wish you'd been there, Detective Sergeant," he said, addressing the headstone directly. "You'd have kept us on track. Stopped it getting as far as it did."

There was a chill wind blowing in off the water. Logan shivered in it and stamped his feet on the frosty grass.

"Still, we got them," he told her. "Everyone responsible. We got them. I just... I wanted you to know."

He rubbed his hands together and blew on them, then looked across the graveyard. He was the only one in it, every other bugger having more sense than to come out in this cold.

"Don't suppose you know when the next ferry is, do you, Caitlyn?" he asked. When he got no reply from the headstone, he shook his head reproachfully. "Some bloody help you are."

He said his goodbyes then, rejoined the path, and headed for the gate. The roads were surprisingly busy, despite the time of year. Or maybe because of it. He had no real grasp of how Orkney's tourist seasons worked. Summer would be hoaching, he'd imagine, but maybe there was some draw to the place in the winter, too.

"No' the bloody weather, that's for sure," he muttered to himself as he crossed the road and headed for a hotel with a pub attached at the front.

A log fire welcomed him as he entered. The smell of lager and spirits swirled through the place, giving a faint blue edge to the flames in the hearth.

It was a smell that would've proved too enticing at one time. Challenging, at others. Now, he barely noticed it.

There were ten or eleven other patrons in the place, some drinking alone, but most in groups of two or three. A couple of them glanced his way as he entered, but they mostly paid him no heed.

An old man in a shirt and tie stood on the other side of the bar, leaning on it for support. He smiled as Logan approached, but it was an effort for him.

"You alright, there? What can I get for you?"

"Uh, hi. I was actually just looking for the ferry times heading back. Forgot to take a note."

"I've a winter timetable here. Hold on," the barman said.

He bent to look under the bar, and Logan caught his own reflection in the mirror that ran along the back wall. His beard was coming in. Not on purpose, he just hadn't bothered shaving in a while. He could do with a haircut, too.

"It's down here somewhere," the old man muttered.

Logan looked along the bar a little and saw the hand-written notice stuck to the mirror.

Staff wanted. Accommodation provided.

"No, can't see it, sorry," the barman said. He straightened with some difficulty. "I think I can remember, though..."

"Actually," said Logan. "It's fine."

He looked around the bar, with its fire, and its bare stone walls.

He looked through the window, to where the shore of the island gave way to the shimmering North Sea.

He turned back to the barman. To the sign. To a new beginning.

"I've just had a better idea."

EPILOGUE
TEN MONTHS LATER

THERE WAS NOTHING IN THE LOCAL PAPER. NOTHING OF interest, anyway. There had been a roof leak at the supermarket. The ferry prices were going up. The food bank had too many beans and not enough baby milk.

That sort of thing.

It had been a quiet day. Most days were at this time of year, after the summer rush, but before the winter season had started to kick in. It was the third time that week he'd read the paper. It somehow got no more or less interesting, regardless of how often he read it.

His record was nine times. That had been a fortnight ago. At the rate he was going, this week he was on track to break double figures.

The fire was getting low. He took a wander over, poked at it until the arse was about to fall out of it, and laid on a couple more logs.

There were a couple of dirty glasses on a table. He thought about leaving them for a bit, giving himself something to do later, but decided to treat himself by grabbing them now.

He returned to the other side of the bar, plunged one glass

in the sink to wash it, but left the other sitting at the side. No point overindulging. There were still plenty of hours left in the day to fill.

He'd just returned to the newspaper when the door opened. The story was about the revised bin schedule, and he'd read it twice already, and yet something about it was so hypnotically fascinating that he didn't look up until he'd reached the end of the second paragraph.

"Alright, boss?"

Logan gawped across the bar. That hair. That grin.

"Jesus Christ."

"No' quite," Tyler said. "Although, you... With the beard and the hair. That the look you going for, boss?"

"Just Jack's fine, son. I'm no' your boss now," Logan told him. He looked Tyler up and down, like he couldn't quite believe what he was seeing. "What brings you out here?"

"Thought we'd take a wee jaunt over," Tyler said. Behind him, the door opened, and Sinead came in, laughing with Harris.

Logan's heart soared at the sight of them. Fit. Well. Happy.

Not that he let on, of course. That wouldn't do at all.

"Alright, sir?" Sinead said.

"Hi, Jack!" Harris said.

"See? He gets it," Logan said, pointing to the boy. "Alright, son? Look at the bloody height you're getting."

"I'm the second tallest in my class," Harris told him.

Logan glanced surreptitiously around, then leaned in closer. "Let me know who the tallest is, and I'll have him taken care of."

Harris laughed, although it was a little uncertain, like he wasn't sure if Logan was being serious or not.

"What can I get you all?" he asked. "On the house."

There was a knocking from the other side of the mirror at Logan's back. He rolled his eyes and tutted. "On me, then. No' on the house."

Tyler eyed the selection of drinks on offer warily. "Is... Is this not a struggle? All the... You know, with...? Temptation, and that?"

Logan looked around at the pumps and the optics, as if only now seeing them for the very first time.

"Well, I hadn't actually thought much about it until now," he replied. "So, thanks a lot."

He sorted them out with drinks, then joined them at the big table in the corner. They talked about everything and nothing. About Bosco's conviction. About how Ben was doing. About Snecky's not-so-triumphant return to MIT North.

"Hamza made Detective Sergeant," Tyler said.

"Aye? Good for him."

"Yeah, it was going to be one of the two of us," Tyler said. "But since Sinead's now officially out of uniform and on the team, we didn't want me outranking her."

"Plus, Hamza's better," Sinead added.

Logan snorted into his Coke.

"Aye," Tyler agreed. "Plus, he's better."

"How's Plainclothes treating you?" Logan asked Sinead. Harris had a bag of crisps sitting open on the table in front of him. Logan struck like a viper and nicked one for himself.

"Hey!"

"Shut up, I paid for them," Logan said, nudging the boy with an elbow.

Harris grinned, but angled himself so the crisp packet was out of Logan's immediate reach.

"It's good, sir, yeah. Different," Sinead said. "Lot to learn."

"Aye, well, if this Muppet can do it..." Logan said, shooting Tyler a look. "And like I told him, it's just Jack. I'm no' polis, anymore."

A look passed between both detective constables. Tyler tilted his head a fraction in Logan's direction, but a flick of Sinead's eyes bounced it right back at him.

"What do you want to say?" Logan asked. "Spit it out, I'm no' getting any younger."

"It's just... Well, Snecky. He's... He's made it clear he's keen to relocate. There's a CID job in Aberdeen. We think we can get him to go for it."

"Nice one. Sooner you can get shot of that useless bastard, the better," Logan said.

"Aye. Except... Everything's still in a bit of upheaval," Tyler continued. "Now that Hoon's gone. The new Detective Superintendent is settling in, but she's not quite got the lay of the land yet. She wants a safe pair of hands, and she reckons Snecky's reliable. Aye, no' good, obviously, but reliable."

He fired another sideways look in Sinead's direction, and she took over.

"And, well, DI Forde suggested that maybe we might be able to get a replacement for him. For Snecky, I mean."

"A safe pair of hands," Tyler said.

"The safest," Sinead added.

"Oh aye? And who...?" Logan sat up. "Wait. Fuck off. No."

"Come on, boss, it'd be—"

Logan crossed his arms across his barrel-like chest. "Not a fucking chance. No way. I'm done. I'm out."

"Ben checked with the Impaler. She'd be up for it," Tyler said. "Now that all the Petrie stuff has died down, she'd be up for you coming back."

"Well, good for her," Logan said. "But no. Lovely offer, and it's great to see you both, but no."

"But there's a case, sir," Sinead said. She reached down the side of her chair and lifted a briefcase onto her knees.

"She carries a briefcase now," Tyler said with a smirk.

"Not always," Sinead replied, slapping him on the arm. She opened the clasp on the bag and produced a cardboard folder. "We're really struggling on it. We could do with your input."

"It's a belter, boss," Tyler said. "Murder. Blackmail. Infidelity..."

"A guy with a Hitler moustache," Sinead added.

"Guy with a Hitler moustache," Tyler confirmed. "Seriously, it's got the lot."

Sinead slid the folder into the middle of the table, angled in Logan's direction. It sat there between them, unopened, its contents a mystery.

And he always did love a good mystery.

But he had a job here. A life.

Or, not a life, exactly.

An existence. It wasn't bad.

And there was still that second glass to clean.

He looked at the bar, and the newspaper sitting on it.

He looked out the window, and saw the graveyard that lay between him and the shore beyond.

He saw the well-tended grave of Detective Sergeant Caitlyn McQuarrie.

"Ah, bugger it. Wait here," he said, pushing his chair back from the table. "I'll get my coat."

ABOUT THE AUTHOR

JD Kirk is the author of the million-selling DCI Jack Logan Scottish crime fiction series, set in and around the Highlands.

He also doesn't exist, and is in fact the pen name of award-winning former children's author and comic book writer, Barry Hutchison. Didn't see that coming, did you?

Both JD and Barry live in Fort William, where they share a house, wife, children, and two pets. This is JD's 13th novel. Barry, unfortunately, has long since lost count.

JOIN THE JD KIRK VIP CLUB

Want access to a **photo gallery** of Highland locations from the DCI Logan series, **exclusive short stories**, discounts, and all my latest news? Visit the link below to join my **FREE** VIP Club.

link.jdkirk.com/vipclub

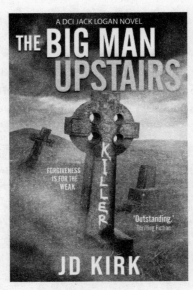